The Fields

The Fields

ERIN YOUNG

FLATIRON
BOOKS
NEW YORK

THE FIELDS. Copyright © 2022 by Erin Young. All rights reserved. Printed in the United States of America. For information, address Flatiron Books, 120 Broadway, New York, NY 10271.

www.flatironbooks.com

Designed by Gabriel Guma

The Library of Congress has cataloged the hardcover edition as follows:

Names: Young, Erin.
Title: The fields / Erin Young.
Description: First edition. | New York : Flatiron Books, 2022.
Identifiers: LCCN 2021034513 | ISBN 9781250799395 (hardcover) |
    ISBN 9781250853363 (international, sold outside the U.S., subject to rights
    availability) | ISBN 9781250799401 (ebook)
Subjects: LCGFT: Thrillers (Fiction) | Detective and mystery fiction.
Classification: LCC PS3625.O97 F54 2022 | DDC 813/.6—dc23
LC record available at https://lccn.loc.gov/2021034513

ISBN 978-1-250-79941-8 (trade paperback)

Our books may be purchased in bulk for promotional, educational, or business use. Please contact your local bookseller or the Macmillan Corporate and Premium Sales Department at 1-800-221-7945, extension 5442, or by email at MacmillanSpecialMarkets@macmillan.com.

First Flatiron Books Paperback Edition: 2023

10 9 8 7 6 5 4 3 2 1

The Fields

1

She ran without thinking, without direction, desperation driving her deep into the fields. The endless rows of corn were an oppressive labyrinth, ripe heads bowing above her, snagging her hair. Blades whipped her palms as she thrashed through the towering stalks, not looking back.

She stumbled on rutted ground, dry soil crumbling beneath her feet. Her sneaker, shucked half off her heel, slipped from her foot. She let it go, the earth spiking through her sock. Blood thrummed in her ears. The night was clotted with clouds, the darkness pressing. She could feel the pollen erupting around her, gritting her eyes. Her mother's voice singsonged in her mind. *Don't forget your meds, sweetheart!* A sob burst between her breaths.

Her lungs were burning. The thrumming in her ears was louder. Something out there. Coming closer. She felt a fresh stab of terror as light smeared the shadows, the knotted canopy shimmering green above her. She threw herself down, curling around the brace roots, eyes squeezed shut. The drone circled overhead, whining like a dentist's drill. Her eyelids were rinsed with a pallid glow.

Slowly it passed, strobing the fields. Was that a shout she heard beneath its fading hum? Low growl of an engine in the distance? She curled herself tighter into stillness, at one with the roots and the soil. A mouse hiding from a hawk.

As her breaths slowed, the pain—kept at bay by adrenaline—came on. There were points of it across her body: the back of her skull, struck so hard her vision had exploded with light, two fingers of her left hand where she'd fallen, bending back with a nauseating snap, her thigh where the flimsy cotton of her clothes had been ripped open. But worst of all was her neck, where the pain was concentrating in a burning pool.

She went to touch her throat, but flinched when her fingers slid into something slick and pulpy. Her T-shirt was soaked. She had thought it was sweat, the night air so close she could barely breathe. But she could smell the blood now. Warm metal. Iron and rust. Sparks of memory: a tumble from her bike, knees split open on blistering asphalt, her uncle's slaughterhouse in Fayette, squeals of half-stunned hogs and arcing blades, red beads on her palm welling at the razor's sting, hot press of another hand to hers.

Her whole body was shaking, teeth chattering. She knew she should get up, but her limbs were leaden. Her breath quickened. The darkness swayed in front of her, a murmur of wind to shiver the corn. There was laughter in her mind. The fields, waist-high with spring crops, rippled before her as she ran. He was behind her, coming up fast. The delicious shock of his arms catching around her waist, her laugh ending in a shriek as she was lifted into the air. His lips on hers; salt-sweat and corn dust. Desire striking a bell inside her.

James.

Her thoughts snagged on him. Shaking confetti from his hair on their wedding day. Straightening his tie in the mirror on his way to work, blowing her a kiss from the front door that she would catch in her hand and pitch back to him. Nights in the beautiful home they had made together, buzz of cicadas through the windows, his brow a knot of concentration, screen glare reflected in his glasses, equations gliding up the lenses. The creak of their bed as he crept in, murmuring an apology as she shifted awake.

"Where have you been?"

"Working."

"What time is it?"

"Time for sleep."

Her neck throbbed. The wetness was spreading. She felt a strange fluttering deep inside and realized it was her own heart, fast and faint like tiny wings, beating against her chest.

She saw herself in the kitchen mirror, hours earlier—eyes red, blond hair wayward—as she snatched up the keys and left the house. The drive: AC drying her eyes, the calm-voiced directions of the GPS. Out from manicured neighborhoods along the blaze of the strip mall, Wendy's and a funeral parlor, Bob's Lube and the dentist, a woman grinning on the billboard outside, bugs swarming her neon smile. Past the Kum & Go gas station, over the railroad tracks, skirting the oil-black slick of the river, streetlights fading behind. A water tower rising ahead, standing sentinel over the vast dark of the cornfields. She had driven this route before, her mind on him, but fear had always made her turn back before she reached that flag on the edge of the screen, not knowing what she might find. Moths tilting at the windshield. Distant taillights bleeding red streaks through the darkness.

The fluttering in her chest was fainter. Soil puffed up with each gasp of breath to speckle her dry lips. She had never felt so thirsty. James, leaning in close on their wedding day, champagne fizzing in his glass. *Oh God. James?* Her thoughts were ebbing, memories fading like a freight train rumbling across the prairie night, wind in its wake.

So thirsty. So tired.

Time for sleep.

2

R iley Fisher glanced at the screen again. The GPS still wanted her to turn right, the arrow flashing insistently. Twenty-three minutes since dispatch had called. She drummed her fingers on the wheel, willing the lights to change. The usual flow of morning traffic— pickups and eighteen-wheelers—thundered past on the highway.

"I can walk from here."

Glancing in the rearview mirror, Riley saw Madison had looked up from her phone. "It's fine, sweetheart."

Her niece held her gaze for a moment, then returned to whatever it was she'd been engrossed in since Riley had rushed her from the house, grabbing the girl's backpack and hustling her into the car. The screen's glow highlighted the sharpness of Maddie's cheeks.

The blast of a horn behind told her the lights had changed. Riley turned left. She was driving down Lafayette, passing the department— the opposite direction to where she should be headed—when she saw Logan Wood in the parking lot, sunlight winking off his badge.

Spotting her, he jogged to the sidewalk, hand raised. As she stopped, Logan opened the door and ducked his head in. He was wearing avia-tors. A black T-shirt beneath his khaki shirt was embossed with the department's letters in white across the neck: BHCSO. Black Hawk County Sheriff's Office. "You headed to the scene? I just got the call, but Carter isn't off shift yet and we're short on cruisers."

"Get in."

Logan slid in, repositioning the Mobile Data Terminal so his broad frame would fit in the Dodge Charger's low-slung seat. He spotted the girl in the back. "Oh. Hey, Maddie."

"Hi," she said, not looking up.

Logan looked at Riley, his tanned brow creasing.

"Ethan," she murmured in answer, maneuvering her way into the traffic. "I've just got to drop her home."

Six blocks later, Riley pulled up outside the house on the shabby fringes of one of the poorer neighborhoods in Waterloo. The street was potholed, weeds growing between the cracks. The houses hunched close together, flags limp in the airless morning. Rusted grills and sagging lawn chairs protruded from grass grown wild. Outside her sister-in-law's house a hulking red tow truck was parked on the curb. On the door, MASON LEE'S AUTO REPAIRS was underlined with a wrench.

Maddie climbed out, phone still gripped in her hand. There was a white skull on the case, hollow eye sockets staring between her fingers. Riley didn't know when it had changed from the sparkled pink one she'd bought for her niece's fourteenth birthday.

"I'll see you soon," she called through the window.

Maddie turned to go, tossing her dark hair and swinging her backpack onto her shoulder.

"Hey! I love you."

The girl glanced back. A smile softened her face, briefly. "Love you too." Then she was gone, disappearing behind the tow truck's red bulk.

Riley waited until the screen door closed, then pulled away.

"About as chatty as Jake and Callie first thing in the morning," Logan observed.

Riley didn't answer. She'd met Logan's niece and nephew a couple of times and had found them bright and garrulous. A surprise, given what they'd been through. Maddie had been more like that: quicker with smiles and affection, a year or so ago. The frayed friendship bracelet on her wrist the girl had spent hours braiding for her, all her favorite colors—peacock blues and ocean greens—was testament to that. *It's her age,*

Aunt Rose had said. But Riley wasn't so sure that was the problem. Her gaze went to the rearview, the tow truck still visible as she turned the corner, then put her foot on the gas.

Moments later they were crossing the Cedar River, which gleamed like a sheet of steel, winding its way through miles of farmland and prairie to join the Iowa River that flowed into the mighty Mississippi. Fumes from factories on the riverbanks smeared the sky. The Cedar soon disappeared behind them but maintained its presence in the creeks that fingered their way through the dense woods of the state park. All the waterways here were joined like green veins.

Logan tilted the screen of the MDT, enough for him to read the details listed alongside the GPS map. The destination flag was planted in the middle of nowhere. "A farmer called it in?"

"Just under an hour ago."

"Who's on scene?"

"Schmidt and Nolan. Cole took the call."

Riley tried to keep her tone neutral, but she saw Logan look sideways at her and knew he'd caught the bite in it.

She turned off the highway before they reached Cedar Falls, where she'd started her journey, and finally she was on track, heading north into the county on empty back roads. Cornfields stretched away, signs naming the types and provenance of the corn staked along the roadside. Most bore the name Agri-Co—one of the largest corporations in America, responsible for much of the country's seed development and a major supplier of agrochemicals. There weren't many farms in the Corn Belt that didn't use their products, either sowed in the soil or sprayed on it.

Logan slapped at his neck. "Goddamn bugs." He studied his hand, then fished a bottle of sanitizer from a pouch on his utility belt, next to his gun. He squeezed a blob into his palm and rubbed his hands together, filling the car with a chemical whiff. "Bugs, shit, and corn." He slid his disinfected palm toward the blade-straight road, lancing ahead beyond the windshield, clouded with dust. "On and fucking on."

It was almost a year since Logan joined the department, moving with his folks from Flint. His father, niece, and nephew had been badly affected by the crisis there—when lead seeped into Flint's water supply after city officials changed the system in an attempt to save money, then tried to cover up the devastating consequences. His mother had determined that a new start in the great green-gold of the Iowa prairie would be good for them all. But Logan seemed to be finding it hard to adjust, not least because he'd been a detective back in Flint, and the transfer had seen him demoted to a deputy in Patrol, and a rookie at that.

"Might as well start calling it home," Riley told him, looking out over the fields of soy and maize unfurling before them in gentle waves. Here and there, red barns rose from the rippling green like the prows of graceful ships, the blades of Aermotor windmills rising like masts above them. Farther off, silver towers of wind turbines and grain silos marked some of the larger farms in the county, the air gauzy with dust. Closer was a water tower, its potbellied bowl teetering on spindly steel legs. The sky was a blaze of blue, just a few wisps of white cloud. A cottontail day, her mom would have called it.

"So damn flat," murmured Logan. "Like God went and stomped on it."

"Missing the purple mountain majesties of Michigan?"

"We had hills. Hills like you've never seen, flatlander."

"It's Sergeant Flatlander to you, hill-boy." Riley checked herself as she said it. They'd bantered like this through the six months he'd been assigned as her partner, back when she'd still been a deputy in Patrol—Logan mocking all things Iowan, usually the performance of the Hawkeyes, her ribbing him about his obsession with the gym, his regime of vitamins, and his need for cleanliness.

But things were different now.

Logan was grinning, though, teeth white against his fake tan. *Radiation bronze,* she'd joked once, regretting the words even as they were leaving her mouth. He hadn't laughed at that one, his family still suffering the aftereffects of the lead-poisoned water—his father almost dying from Legionnaires' disease, his niece and nephew struggling with learning difficulties and behavioral problems.

Ahead, someone had nailed a sign to a utility pole. Riley caught a flash of red, white, and blue painted letters.

VOTE LOCAL! VOTE COOK!!

That morning the news stations had been chattering about State Senator Jess Cook's lead against Governor Bill Hamilton in the latest gubernatorial polls. Cook, a farmer's daughter and staunch advocate for environmental protection and sustainable agriculture, seemed to be riding well on small but forceful waves of protest that had dogged Hamilton's campaign. Only yesterday, the governor's car had been egged by demonstrators in Des Moines, protesting his ties to Big Ag firms, whose backing had helped keep him in power for three terms, but whose practices had forced families out of business and damaged whole ecosystems.

Riley had caught the coverage as she'd been getting ready, pausing as she towel dried her hair to watch Hamilton striding up the steps of the capitol with a brisk wave for the cameras. He was looking older these days, hair stippled gray at the sides, but still with that confident walk and self-assured smile. It was years since she'd seen the governor in person, on the day of her parents' funeral.

A billboard loomed up, decorated with a logo—three yellow ears of corn against a red rising sun. The lettering became clear as they approached.

ZEPHYR FARMS.
KNOWIN' WHAT'S BLOWIN' IN THE WIND.

The GPS indicated a right turn just after it.

"So it's Zephyr's land she was found on?" Logan was frowning at the billboard.

"You know them?"

"Me and Carol took the kids to an event they ran last Halloween. Haunted farm thing—creepy hayrides, pick your own pumpkin. Zephyr's a cooperative."

"Right." Riley nodded.

Cooperatives were how some smaller Iowa farms had been able to survive the relentless advances of Big Ag. By dominating the market in hybrid seeds, fertilizer, and pesticides—the holy trinity of crop production—through aggressive trademarking, swallowing up the competition, and tactical lobbying at the highest levels of government, giants like Agri-Co had come to control much of the nation's agricultural wealth. A necessary evil, some called them. Progress, said more. But to those whose forefathers had farmed this land since the days of the first families from New York, Philadelphia, and Virginia, who'd settled here after the Black Hawk War when the Ioway had been driven west, these corporations were vultures, polluters, and thieves.

"I'm surprised you haven't heard of them, Sarge. They won some commendation from the mayor last year. It was in *The Courier.*" Logan grinned at her. "But then Zephyr is all about organic produce. Farm to table. You know, *real* food. Not that chemical swill you eat."

Riley saw the dirt track at the last second, obscured by a fringe of maize. She turned sharply, wheels skidding in grit, seat belt tightening against her chest, Logan grabbing for the door handle. The car forged a path between the green rows, bouncing over rutted soil, each shock jolting through Riley's hands, tight on the wheel. Overhanging stalks bent back from the grille, ears of corn bumping off the roof. A bird darted across the windshield.

"Did you meet the owner of Zephyr when you came?" Riley checked the MDT for the name. "John Brown?"

Before Logan could answer, the radio crackled. Someone was calling dispatch.

"I called half an hour ago. Where the hell are they?"

That voice, all force and arrogance, was unmistakable. Jackson Cole.

Riley brought the car to a halt in front of a group of vehicles block-
ing the narrow dirt channel between two high walls of maize. A John
Deere tractor loomed like a green giant over a cruiser and another black
Dodge Charger, older and more battered than hers—Cam Schmidt's.
As the dust settled, Riley opened the door. The heat closed around her
like a fist.

3

The men were just beyond the vehicles, dwarfed by the corn. There was Deputy Cameron Schmidt, awkwardly tall and too old now to wear those extra inches well—so old, in fact, that no one in the department knew whether it was his stooping shoulders or his twenty plus years as a detective that had earned him the nickname *Hunch*.

Cam Schmidt was speaking to a man Riley didn't recognize—late sixties and spindle-limbed, with a brown face that was as wrinkled as a raisin. The farmer, she guessed. He was carrying a shotgun broken over one arm. At Schmidt's side was Jackson Cole. The deputy's arms were folded, creasing the khaki shirt across his back.

Cole was the first to turn at Riley's approach. "Thought you'd got lost, Sarge."

His smirk showed the crooked front tooth she'd once found charming, back when they started together in the department as rookies. A humble blemish in this otherwise perfect Iowa man, linebacker broad with a thatch of corn-blond hair and denim-blue eyes. She'd discovered, in the years since, the tooth wasn't his only flaw.

It was six months since her promotion, but Cole hadn't let her forget how pissed he was about it. Barely a day went by without some comment or look—nothing she could ever discipline him for, just enough to let her know she'd never win his respect.

Cole's eyes narrowed as Logan appeared from behind the tractor. He was clearly wondering what the deputy was doing arriving with her. Good. Let him wonder.

"Sarge." Schmidt gestured to the man beside him. "This is John Brown. He made the call."

Riley extended her hand. "Sergeant Riley Fisher, head of Investigations, Field Services Division." She caught the tic that jumped at the corner of Cole's mouth and felt a little surge of satisfaction.

"An honor, ma'am." Brown's drawl was low and long. Pure Iowa.

Riley was surprised by the earnestness in his tone and the strength of his hand gripping hers. She could feel the calluses roughing his palm. He wore an old Hawkeyes T-shirt faded from too many wears and washes. There was writing carved into the stock of his gun. GOD BLESS AMERICA.

"I knew your grandfather, ma'am. Sheriff Joe Fisher was a friend to us, even after he left the department. Worked with the mayor and the city council. Made sure we kept our lands, even though them sons of bitches tried every trick to take them. Haven't seen him for years. How's he doing?"

Riley released Brown's hand, her mind filling with an image of her grandfather staring from the worn depths of the armchair in the old folks' home, drool stringing from his puckered mouth. Last week's visit had been brutal. "He's fine, thank you. Tried every trick? Do you mean Agri-Co?" She'd heard this complaint before about the agricultural giant. Brown nodded. His lips pursed and Riley thought he might spit. "How much of this land is yours, sir?"

"Well, between us here at Zephyr Farms we have fifteen hundred acres." There was a clear note of pride in his tone. "From the banks of the Cedar to the county line."

"That's pretty sizeable, isn't it?"

"The Browns are in a cooperative with the Garrett, Davis, and Wilson farms, Sarge," Schmidt said.

Brown nodded. "We grow vegetables and soy, but most of our crop is dent corn."

"Dent corn?" asked Logan.

Brown smiled, his eyes creasing. "Not from around here are you, son? Most of what you see in Iowa is dent—gets its name because the kernels are all indented by harvest time."

"It's mostly used for livestock feed," Riley added for Logan's benefit. "And ethanol production."

"That's true, ma'am. But here at Zephyr we only use ours for cornmeal. Real good flavor when it's dry milled."

"My sister got a bag when we were here at Halloween," Logan said. "My mom swore she's never made better corn bread."

Brown's smile made Jackson Cole scowl.

"It's a new variety. We've been working on it for over three years. It's up for the Iowa Food Prize." Brown scanned their faces, expecting a reaction. "It's a big deal. The winner will be announced at the state fair in August. Near ninety thousand farms in Iowa and most of them'll be there. If we win that prize, Zephyr will sure be front and center of the map. Knock on wood, we'll be set for life. Let Agri-Co try and come for us then." His zeal faltered, his eyes darting to the corn. "But if word gets out that . . . "

"It was you who found the body?" Riley asked.

"Yup, ma'am. Had the eagle out this morning."

"Eagle?"

"That's what we call our crop drone. She helps us check things are growing as they should. I saw some stalks in the north of this field were damaged." He gestured. "Took her in for a closer look and . . ." He trailed off, his gaze sliding back to the dense web of corn.

Riley shifted her position, drawing his attention, keeping him focused while checking his face for any sign of a lie. "We'll need to see the drone footage."

"All arranged, Sarge," Schmidt interjected. "Mr. Brown says he was driving home three nights ago when he saw another drone—not his—over his fields."

"I'd been out at our grain silos with Ed Wilson," Brown explained. "We saw its lights from the road. I knew our bird wasn't up—she was in my truck. We thought it might be one of the sellouts." He tilted his head east, then west.

"Sellouts?"

"There're a lot of them around here now—farms who've signed up with Agri-Co." Brown's voice strengthened. "Men here used to understand everything about what they were growing. Been sharing seeds since settler times. As my daddy would say, go to your neighbor's field with many pockets. But then Agri-Co got to trademarking everything, taking away our God-given right to save seeds and share our knowledge. Now, most folk don't even know what they're putting in the ground. Just get their seeds delivered from Agri-Co's labs, sign their NDAs, and accept their share when the reaping's done. Those farms are nothing more than *wombs*. Where Agri-Co gets to test their crops and gain the data for themselves. Data worth billions. Heck, I understand their need. I wouldn't be here now if we hadn't formed Zephyr. You sink or swim on getting big or selling out. But our neighbors have *helped* make Agri-Co the monopoly it is today. Too powerful to challenge. Too big to fail. Corn breeding and genetic engineering—you name it, they're in it. Just a handful of firms now control America's food supply. They set prices for consumers and wages in the industry."

Riley noticed Logan nodding at Brown's words. She'd heard Senator Cook on the radio, railing against these same issues that were driving family farms into the ground.

"They're protected by levels of insurance and government subsidies us little folk can only dream of," continued Brown. "And they get to go to all these poor, struggling farmers who're not so proud anymore that they won't offer up their own soil for another man's seed, if it'll see them through another harvest."

"And you think this drone might have belonged to one of these farms?" Riley cut in before Brown could continue his diatribe.

"Well, I'm pretty sure it was one of Agri-Co's bootlickers that sabotaged Frank Garret four years back, before he joined us. Five acres of soy, ready for harvest, sprayed with the wrong herbicide. An accident, they said. Killed the whole crop." Brown's gaze returned to Riley. "This drone I saw was moving low over my fields. Flew off when me and Ed tried to follow it in my truck. I'd have taken it out if I could." He jogged the shotgun on his arm.

Riley ignored, for the moment, Brown's willingness to break a federal law. "You didn't come out here when you saw the footage? Have a look yourself?"

"No need." Brown's nose wrinkled. "I knew what I was seeing. I called it in right away, just came to meet your men here."

Riley met Schmidt's eye. With luck they had a clean scene. As clean as could be in this heat at least. "And Mr. Wilson will attest that you were with him? The night you saw this drone?"

John Brown started to nod, then realized the implication of Riley's question. "Oh, certainly, ma'am," he said quickly. "And my sons were with me at the farm later that evening. Wives and grandkids, too. We've been working all hours. Getting ready for the state fair."

"We'll need a list of your colleagues and employees in the cooperative. Anyone with access to your lands."

Brown thrust a hand through his thinning hair. He looked pained, but nodded. "Anything you need." He hesitated. "How quiet can we keep this, ma'am? Will it be made public it's Zephyr's land she's been found on? I mean, God knows I'm sorry for her. But with our corn up for the award—?" He wedged his thumbs in the pockets of his faded jeans. "Woman had no business out here, far as I can see." Brown shook his head. "No business at all."

"We'll do what we can," said Riley, her calm tone not revealing what she knew to be true.

The Courier would have this within hours. But even before that, locals would spread it like pollen, the news jumping from farm to store, auto repair shop to bar, leaving its traces everywhere, in grave tones and shaking heads, another Bud ordered *out of respect*. Kids would come, take selfies with crime scene tape. Post them on Instagram.

Riley turned to Schmidt. "Nolan's with the body? OK, I'll take a look. You called the ME?"

"Just about to, Sarge."

Riley nodded to Cole and Logan. "Set up a cordon and start the log. I don't want anyone else entering these fields until we've worked the scene."

After pulling on a pair of protective overshoes, she pushed her way into the corn, following Schmidt's directions. The detective's last words played in her mind.

She ain't pretty, Sarge.

The corn reared around her, knitted close, the silks like russet hair hanging limp from the ears. Her grandfather's voice sang out of the past. *Knee-high by Fourth of July.* The old sayings no longer worked. These crops were well over her head and it was only late June.

There was some shade from the sun's nuclear glare, but the heat was suffocating, trapped inside the green thicket. It had been a humid start to the season, following a wild wet spring, tornadoes skipping about the state, eight deadly touchdowns since April.

It wasn't long before she smelled it—the rot-sweet stink of death. A few yards later, she heard the bleep of a camera. Flies buzzed her face. Ahead, she picked out Bob Nolan's bulk. The crime scene investigator was crouched among the roots. His green polo shirt with the yellow letters *CSI* had ridden up, while his cargo pants had slid down, exposing an unfortunate amount of pale skin, fuzz, and crack. The blue gloves at the ends of his freckled arms made him look clown-like.

Nolan rose at her approach, fending off the encroaching stalks. Gripping his camera in one hand, he hitched up his pants. His equipment case was open on the ground. He wore overshoes and a face mask from around which his auburn beard tufted. "There's a spare mask in there, Sarge." He nodded to the case. "She's ripe."

Riley had seen many bodies over her twelve-year career in Black Hawk County. RTA victims hacked from twisted metal. Overdoses and suicides. Victims of summer tragedies pulled from lakes and winter misfortunes dug from frozen fields. Farmers drowned in their own grain bins. But it was still a punch to the gut as she looked over Nolan's shoulder to see what the cocoon of roots contained.

The woman was lying on her side, face obscured by her hair that streaked blond across her cheeks, matted with dried blood. Her legs were bunched up, arms flopped in the soil close to her head, as though she were curled asleep. One sneaker was missing, a foot protruding, white ankle sock grimed with dirt. Her clothes—cotton pants and T-shirt—

were ripped in places, revealing gray-green mottled skin. She was swollen with decay and rent with dark wounds, the blood black and congealed, the flesh pulped raw. Her insides squirmed with maggots.

Riley grimaced as she reached for a mask, trying not to breathe through her nose or mouth. The stench—a toxic perfume of pungent methane and acrid ammonia—was trying to enter her any way it could. Her whole being felt assaulted by it.

"She's been out here a few days at least. And in this temperature . . . ?" Nolan shook his head.

"Do you have a rough time of death?"

"At this point, I'd say it's going to be three or four days ago. The maggots are still in the early stages and much of the tissue is intact."

"So around the same time as this drone the farmer says he saw?"

"Could be. Webb will hopefully be able to give us a more exact time after she's done the autopsy. Has Hunch called her?"

"He's doing it now. First impressions on cause?" Riley looked past Nolan at the body. Those wounds? The woman looked as though she'd been torn at by something.

A fly landed on Nolan's mask and twitched across it. "It's too soon to say for sure. These scratches on her arms—" He moved with care, his protected feet soft on the soil. Despite his size he was always remarkably delicate at crime scenes. "They look like defensive wounds. Two of her fingers appear broken, torn nails too, and there's a pretty big welt on the back of her skull. I think this is probably our culprit, though." Nolan pointed a blue finger toward a jagged, maggoty wound in the woman's neck, partially obscured by her hair. "Blood loss would have been substantial."

"Weapon?"

Nolan's sweat-greased brow furrowed. "I don't know. It's an odd wound, for sure. The skin's too ripped up for a knife, I'd say, unless maybe a serrated one?" He paused. "Whatever it was, this was a vicious attack. Tore right through the muscle in places."

Riley felt a tightening in her gut like a knot being pulled taut. Her eyes strayed to the woman's hands, clutched in front of her face. She could see the pink glimmer of polish on one chipped nail, the soil black beneath. She imagined those hands splayed in the dirt, digging in against the pain. Something on top of her. Ripping at her.

Stay still, or I'll hurt you.

"Sarge?"

Riley realized Nolan had been speaking. "Sorry?"

"I said I've done most of my midrange shots. Going to move her hair now. Get a look at her face. See if we can start on identification."

She nodded, watching as Nolan parted the woman's hair, gentle as if she were a lover. Riley took in the woman's gray-hued face. High forehead and snub nose, a small mouth and soft jaw. The features shifted in her mind, redefining themselves into a woman alive. Alive and much younger. Shock pulsed through Riley. "My God."

"What is it?" Nolan asked. "Sarge?"

"Chloe," murmured Riley.

Girlish laughter, a head bent close to hers, blond hair tickling her arm. A whisper in her ear. Warm breath, sickly with cotton candy.

He's looking at you, Ri!

Riley's hand curled into a fist, fingers digging into her palm, which was veined with a tiny white scar. The same scar she knew would be there, under all the blood and grime, on the dead woman's palm. "Chloe Clark," she repeated, not taking her eyes off the body. "We were—" She faltered on the word, then let it out. "Friends."

4

They arrived through the course of the day, dust from the cars pluming over the dirt track. Sheriff Reed, two deputies from the K-9 unit, and more from Patrol called to help search the fields, or stopping by to rubberneck and talk with colleagues, mopping their brows in the stewed heat of the afternoon. Yellow lines of crime scene tape were strung up to garland the fields. Thunderheads mushroomed in the west.

Twilight brought the bugs, followed by reporters from *The Courier* and a local news crew, hovering at the edges of the tape, cajoling the officers they knew for information. Things like this didn't happen in Black Hawk County, where stores still closed on Sundays and strangers were noticed.

The missing sneaker was found some distance from the body, then a partial set of tire prints on a narrow track that ran along the north line of the field, eventually joining the road. The whole state was crisscrossed with such tracks: nameless arteries connecting countless isolated farms to the world.

Bob Nolan's camera continued to click in the bruised evening light, each flash exposing a new aspect of the body. Every livid wound. Every inch of spoiling flesh. Soil samples were taken, maggots collected. The day shift changed over, deputies leaving, Logan Wood and Jackson Cole among them, others arriving, checking in with Riley before being entered in the scene log.

It was late when she finally left Zephyr's fields, driving the few miles

to Cedar Falls, the lights of the town drawing her in from the cornfields'
deep dark. Crossing the railroad tracks, she turned down the road toward her house, on the edge of a creek among the shadowy fringes of
the state park. The porch light was on, a dull star glimmering between
the sycamore trees. Our Victorian dame, her grandfather had called the
house; her pale blue turret perched high as a bonnet above the porch
that wrapped around her like a white petticoat.

Riley pulled up in the yard next to her grandfather's pickup—an
ancient, full-throated Dodge half-eaten by rust. It was parked outside
the old storage shed, which stood a short distance from the house,
where the overgrown lawn sloped down to the creek. The rotten structure was piled with the odds and ends of generations of the Fisher
family. Strata of things stored, junked, or forgotten: broken furniture,
collars from dead dogs, and Fourth of July bunting tangled in Christmas lights, mildewed tents, and hunting gear.

As she killed the engine, Riley caught music coming through the open
windows of the house. Ethan was home.

She sat there for a moment, feeling the day dragging at her. The smell
of the body—*Chloe's body*—lingered. It would be days, she knew, before
it left her. Willing herself to move, she slid out of the car. The night
seethed with the live-wire hum of cicadas. Scrounger was barking at the
screen door. There was a halo of moths around the porch light, shadows
fluttering over the sun-bleached cushions of the porch swing. Crushed
beer cans lay scattered beside an overflowing ashtray.

Riley nudged Scrounger back as she entered. The dog was an ex K-9
from Bremer, destined for lethal retirement. After reading his story in
the paper, she'd found herself driving across the county line to the shelter where he'd ended up after a long, distinguished career. Sad eyes behind the cage bars, whiskered face pressing hopefully against her hand.

"What's up with you?" she asked as Scrounger panted at her side
through the kitchen into the central hallway—heart of the house—
off which were the seldom-used family dining room, the living room,
and a bedroom. The music was louder here, coming from the bedroom,
where light spilled beneath the door. Something country—guitars and

melancholy. Crouching by the safe under the stairs, Riley unholstered her Glock 19 and typed in the code. Stowing the gun, she kicked off her soil-dusted boots and retraced her steps to the kitchen, shadowed by Scrounger.

As she flicked on the light, she saw the dog's water and food bowls were empty, no sign of them having been refilled since the morning. She clenched down the anger that rose, hot and sudden. She didn't have the strength for it tonight.

After feeding Scrounger, she stared uselessly into the half-empty fridge before grabbing a couple of cheese slices and a beer. She flipped open the can and downed the beer, its cold fizz stinging her parched throat, then peeled the cellophane from the cheese and stood at the counter, tearing corners off the plastic-tasting sheets.

She'd taken another can and was heading for the stairs when Ethan emerged from his room. They stood facing one another, several yards of worm-eaten floorboards and a threadbare rug between them. She could have moved on with a perfunctory hello—nothing said about that morning or Scrounger—but for the cloud of sickly smoke that billowed out with her brother.

"God damn it, Ethan!" The words flew from her mouth with a force that surprised them both. "How many times?"

"Give me a break, Ri. It's my house as much as yours."

She hated when he called her that—what her friends once called her. Far too familiar for anyone, let alone him, to use now. "Yeah, and it's my job that keeps it ours. A job I'd lose if that crap was found here."

Ethan shook his head, moved past her into the kitchen. Stubble shadowed his face. His eyes were red-rimmed, his T-shirt grubby. Forty years old—five years older than her—and it was like living with an adolescent. "You can grow your own in California, for fuck's sake."

She wasn't about to get dragged into another pointless debate on drug laws across different states: Ethan bitching about Iowa's draconian regulations and being behind the rest of America. "It's not just about the law." Riley followed him into the kitchen. "What if Maddie found it?"

"You think she's not seen pot before?" He turned on her. "Her mother and that piece of shit smoke it in front of her! *Bitch*," he hissed through his teeth, yanking open the fridge.

Riley wasn't sure whether the invective was meant for her brother's ex-wife, Sadie, or for her. "I had to drive her home this morning. Again. I was late to a scene."

He fished out a beer, kicked the fridge shut. "I was working late. Like you used to."

Riley stared at him. She almost laughed. In what world could her brother think a graveyard patrol shift and pulling drinks in a dive bar for his good-for-nothing friends were the same? She had followed him intending to have a go about the dog, too, but the will now left her. The fight was gone. Just the futility of an eternal argument and the smell of a dead woman on her clothes remained. "Fuck you, Ethan."

Upstairs, the heat of the shower stung her skin. The water swirling into the drain was gray with dirt from the fields. Riley closed her eyes, letting it wash over her, her mind flickering with images. The body in the roots. The shock of recognition. Sheriff Reed's frown deepening as she told him she had known the deceased. His questions. When had she last seen Chloe Clark? Who were her family? Where did she live?

Riley had been able to give him little. It was twenty years since she'd been friends with Chloe and Mia and the rest of their gang from school. When she left Cedar Falls High—that summer—there had barely been a day when she didn't think of them, or wonder if they thought of her. But time had dimmed the memories, which only returned when she'd run into one of them unexpectedly over the years. If the town had been smaller, she might not have come back, but with thirty-seven thousand inhabitants in Cedar Falls and almost double that in Waterloo—sixth most populous city in Iowa—such encounters were blessedly infrequent.

God, why did it have to be her?

After showering, she pulled on a T-shirt from her university days, GO PANTHERS stamped across the chest. She sat on the bed, the stitched joins of the patchwork quilt, made by her grandmother, prickling her bare legs. Her wet hair was ruffled by the ceiling fan's revolutions. The room, with its yellow walls that the morning sun turned to butter, had witnessed the lives of four generations of her family. It was the room her grandfather had been born in and where her great-grandfather, George Fisher, had kissed his wife and son farewell before leaving with the Thirty-fourth, bound for Italy and the Winter Line. It was where they mourned him when he didn't return, one of the many who never made it home from Europe, the blue star on the flag outside the house changed to gold for the fallen. It was the room her father had been brought home to, three years before Eisenhower deployed the first troops to Vietnam.

Later, it had become her parents' when her father moved the family from Des Moines to care for his dying mother. He had continued to work through the week in the city, making the two-hour drive home at weekends. Riley, aged eleven, had slept in here with her mother those first few months, both of them unnerved by the depth of this new darkness; the clamor of the bugs and the naked power of the storms, the unknown things that moved in the creek, unsettling the waters.

Leaning against the headboard, Riley scanned the messages on her phone and tried to focus on the report from Schmidt, organizing her thoughts for the morning briefing Sheriff Reed had summoned her to. But soon her eyes were drifting to the photographs that decorated the vanity. Joe Fisher in his sheriff's uniform. Her mother and father at their wedding—Michael Fisher, the eminent lawyer, straight-backed and proud, Jenny Fisher, the legal secretary, smiling up at him. She and Ethan perched on a John Deere tractor, pulling faces at the camera. Aunt Rose and her partner, Lori, in the hospital with baby Benjamin. Maddie, two summers ago, braided hair and dimpled grin.

These were the only ones she kept on display, all the others shut away in albums in the den. But this house was one big album—every corner breathing with memory. The porch where she'd sat with Chloe and Mia, aged twelve, swelling with pride at the smile her mom flashed her as she brought out cookies for the new friends she'd made. The bed in her old room down the hall—now Maddie's—where the three of them had scrunched in sleeping bags, sharing sweets and hushed laughter while snow pattered at the window. The green gloom of a late summer's evening on the edge of the creek, katydids clicking in the grass as the razor stung her skin. The blood smeared across each of their palms.

Never tell.

Pushing herself off the bed, Riley crossed to the closet, floorboards creaking. Flicking on the light, she reached for the top shelf, pushing aside a tennis racket and ice skates. Behind was a saggy cardboard box, its weight surprising her as she lifted it down. Setting it on the floor, she sat cross-legged before it. Her hands rifled through its innards, pulling out trinkets and mementoes. Game tickets for the Iowa Cubs, cards for birthdays glittering her fingers. Spent shells from days shooting with her grandfather, a hunting trophy and a T-shirt from Arnold's Park. *I survived the roller coaster!* A copy of the order of service from her parents' funeral.

The yearbooks from Cedar Falls High were at the bottom. She discarded sophomore and junior years, took up the freshman one. Opening it, she scanned the pictures, memories sparked with every shot of the bleachers, the bad hair and acne-pocked faces, the homecomings and productions. She came upon them suddenly. Chloe, Mia, and herself, all on the same page. Fourteen, on the cusp of fifteen. Best friends since junior high. She felt a stab of something. Regret? Longing? She should have gotten back in touch with them.

Too late now.

As Riley lifted the book to get a closer look, something fell out into her lap. It was a photograph, trapped between the pages all these years like a spider—long dead—but still with the power to shock.

There she was at the Iowa State Fair with Mia and Chloe, arms hanging around each other's shoulders. Daisy Dukes cut so high you could see the pockets hanging down. Legs tanned and lean, crop tops and lip gloss. Girls playing women. Her breath caught as she saw the gold star necklace. A gift from her grandfather on her fourteenth birthday.

For my little deputy.

Her mom had whispered that her granddaddy had paid good money out of his pension for it, and she was to keep it safe. Behind her, in the photograph, the blue sky was deepening, and the fairground rides were studded with pinpricks of light. The photograph was torn. One side ripped away.

The missing image was a ghost in her mind, rushing toward her from out of the past. Smell of corn dogs and cotton candy. Harsh rattle of rides. Blare of music and spinning lights. A hand threading through hers. Fingers tightening.

5

The next morning, on her way in, Riley stopped at the Sweet-Tooth bakery on Main Street for pastries and coffee. There was a copy of *The Courier* on the counter, news of the murder splashed across the front page, headline shouting over a shot of cornfields under a brooding sky. The "Young Woman Found Dead" wasn't named. Deputies from Patrol had gone last night to inform Chloe's parents and her husband. They were still with them, according to a text from Schmidt.

The drive from Cedar Falls to Waterloo was ten minutes on the highway, but since she was halfway down Main, Riley took the route through the suburbs, along the umbilical cord of gas stations, motels, and fast-food outlets that connected the two cities.

The change was always abrupt. From the tree-shaded avenues, quaint shops, and taproom bars of Cedar Falls to the abandoned warehouses and decaying neighborhoods of Waterloo. If not for the University of Northern Iowa—where she'd majored in criminology—with its annual influx of students and money, Riley guessed Cedar Falls would have slumped into the same depression as Waterloo. There had been some brave attempts at regeneration in recent years—microbreweries sprouting on weed-covered lots, kayaks for hire on the Cedar River, and an annual Pride festival fulminated against by local churches. But they were fighting a strong downward pull.

Waterloo had once been a thriving industrial city, founded in 1845, built on corn, meat, and patriotism, connected to Chicago and Omaha by the old Illinois Railroad, and by the flow of the Cedar to the Mississippi. But the agricultural downturn of the eighties had caused a recession that changed the landscape. After that, only the biggest companies had been able—encouraged by successive governments—to survive and thrive. Many places in America were two-job towns, but in Waterloo it wasn't unusual to work three. Even some of the deputies in the department took shifts with Fire and Rescue or as rangers for the state park to make ends meet.

Riley thought back to John Brown's complaints against Agri-Co. *Too powerful to challenge. Too big to fail.* It was true that the bigger these companies became the more they were able to pull into their orbit—land and research grants, government subsidies and political support. But those weren't the only things these giants sucked up. Across the country, whole communities were being left as ghost towns as local firms and families, unable to compete, were forced to close down. The lifeblood of rural America was being drained, leaving husks of cities, where poverty and crime rushed in to fill the void. It was a legacy all too visible in the boarded-up factories and processing plants that loomed like broken tombs around the city, haunted by vagrants and hookers, and cruised nightly by the squad cars of Waterloo PD.

Jess Cook had claimed she would put the power back in the hands of small business, investing in communities rather than companies. Perhaps she should vote for the senator? It was just habit, really, that had seen her cast her ballots for Bill Hamilton in the past. She didn't owe the governor any loyalty. It was years ago that her father had worked for the man in Des Moines.

Turning down East Sixth, she pulled into the parking lot of the department. The brown-brick brute of a building with its pillbox windows was attached to the county jail and surrounded by the offices of bail bondsmen and attorneys. Together, the sheriff's office and jail were served by one hundred sworn officers and forty civilians covering Black Hawk County. Riley parked the Dodge beside the row of cruisers and the Harley Road Kings of Motorcycle Patrol. A few of the cars' engines were idling, keeping the interiors Arctic cold. Last night's storm clouds had only threatened, and the humidity remained unbearably high.

Greeting the desk sergeant, she passed through security with a mental salute to her grandfather, whose picture had pride of place on the wall of heroes. Carrying the pastries, she entered the fluorescent-dazzled corridors of Field Services Division. The place smelled of cleaning chemicals and coffee.

The bullpen was more frenetic than usual, phones trilling, deputies calling to one another. On one desk a copy of *USA Today* was open on a page detailing a cyberattack on a petrochemical company in Polk County. Riley had caught a bit of the story on the radio. Eco-terrorists had been blamed. It was the second time the group—who called themselves Mission Earth and were thought to be Iowa-based—had made national news. The picture beside the headline showed the group's slogan spray painted on a wall. AS THE SEAS RISE, SO SHALL WE. The FBI was investigating.

Logan was at his desk, engrossed in something on his computer. His dark hair was slick, no doubt fresh from the gym showers. Above him, taped to the wall near the dartboard, which still had a torn scrap of a picture of Hillary Clinton stuck to it, was a poster of missing teen, Gracie Foster. The sixteen-year-old, who'd disappeared without a trace from her home in Waterloo ten days ago, had been the department's biggest case. Until yesterday.

Sergeant Hal Edwards, head of Patrol, thickset and in his late fifties, with a bushy moustache last fashionable in the eighties, was in the doorway talking to Jackson Cole. They looked round as she passed. Edwards nodded, but didn't break his conversation. Cole locked eyes with her for a beat before turning his attention back to his sergeant. Riley guessed they'd all now heard she'd known the dead woman. The memories that had surfaced with Chloe's body and kept her awake long into the night scratched at her mind.

Focus on the job. Just another case.

The next room along, much smaller than Patrol, belonged to Investigations. Through the internal windows, Riley saw Cam Schmidt on the phone. His suit jacket was crumpled over the back of his chair. On his desk were foam cups, manila files, and a grease-stained takeout box from Wok and Roll. Framed photographs showed his children and grandchildren. Another was of him and his wife, Sue, pink-cheeked and grinning beside their bikes. Riley had seen the maps on Schmidt's desk, charting the cycle routes he and Sue planned to take on their next trip, red lines spidering north across the border into Canada. Wild prairie and mountains, lakes and pines. *There's nothing like it, Riley. Like you're really in the world. Part of it.*

There were four other desks in the room, including hers and the one used by Bob Nolan, who spent most of his time between crime scenes, the lab, and the evidence room. The others were empty. The department had lost two detectives in the past six months since Riley had been made sergeant—Carl Kramer to a bowel cancer diagnosis and Eric Hansen to early retirement. Hansen had talked some bullshit about wanting to spend more time with his grandkids, but she knew it wasn't family duty that prompted his departure. Both he and Schmidt had vied for the position of sergeant, along with half a dozen deputies from Patrol, including Jackson Cole. Schmidt had taken her promotion on the chin—one of the first to buy her a beer. Others hadn't been quite so ready to be ruled by a woman, especially not a younger woman who might just have won it on her granddaddy's reputation.

They would need to fill at least one of the posts, but with the department's budget up for renewal and concerns over further cuts to their already stretched services, Sheriff Reed wanted to wait. For now, he'd assigned a rookie, Amy Fox, to help out with the day-to-day casework, answering phones, and filing paperwork. Schmidt and Nolan seemed quite content to have the bright twenty-two-year-old hurrying around the place, quick with smiles and coffee.

"Morning," Riley mouthed to Schmidt, proffering the box of pastries.

"That's great, Doctor Webb," Schmidt said down the phone, fingering out a Danish with a grateful nod.

Good. He was talking to the ME already. Hopefully he'd have news on when Chloe's autopsy report could be expected.

Throwing her jacket over her chair, Riley took the rest of the pastries and left Hunch to it.

Down the hall, past the chaplain's room, she arrived at the sheriff's office. At her knock, a gruff voice called her in.

Sheriff Robert Reed was behind his desk, a stack of files beside him and a copy of *The Courier* open in front of him. On the wall were commendations from local organizations and charities, and a cross-stitch by his wife that spelled out the department's motto: EXCELLENCE IN LAW ENFORCEMENT, a few flowers embroidered around it for good measure. Reed's face was the color of rare steak from the afternoon spent in the fields. His cropped white hair was so thin she could see his scalp, livid red.

"Sergeant." He eyed the pink box she set before him with a raised eyebrow. "Sweetening me up?"

Riley smiled, but said nothing. She didn't want to show her hand quite so soon.

"You've seen this?" Reed tapped the paper.

"Yes, sir."

"I've had the county attorney on the line already. Less than two months from the state fair and with the gubernatorial coming up? You know how vital this next budget is to the department. I want this case handled quickly. Efficiently." Reed reached for his coffee, fingers curling over the words on the mug: GOLD STAR FOR THE WORLD'S BEST SHERIFF. He claimed he'd been presented it by kids from one of the local elementary schools, but around the bullpen he was the prime suspect.

"I understand, sir."

"I didn't want to discuss it yesterday, in front of the others. But I want to be certain your history with the deceased won't cloud your investigation in any way."

"No, sir. I barely knew her." The lie came easily, Riley determined to avoid more personal questions. There was no need for Reed to know any more about her past than he had to.

After a moment, Reed smoothed his green tie over his khaki shirt, decorated on the sleeve with four gold chevrons. "All right. Given the seriousness of this case, I'm prepared to grant temporary assignment for one deputy from Patrol to Investigations."

This was what Riley had been banking on. And why she'd brought the pastries. "I want Logan Wood, sir."

"I expected as much," Reed responded, eyeing the pink box with pursed lips. "Is that wise? Wood's been here five minutes."

"He was a detective in Flint, sir. He'll be an asset."

"That may be so. But there are those in the squad who'd sell their mothers for such an assignment, even a temporary one."

She knew Reed meant Jackson Cole. Knew, too, that Logan might catch some flak. But she wasn't about to let Cole's stung pride get in the way of this case—*her* case. "Wood can handle himself, sir."

"Very well. I'll notify Sergeant Edwards. But I'll keep this under review."

"Thank you, sir."

"Fisher?" Reed said as she turned to leave. "The whole community will be watching us on this. You understand?"

"Yes, sir." She held his gaze and, after a pause, he nodded.

As Riley closed the door behind her, she knew the question Reed hadn't spoken. She'd seen the same doubt in the eyes of others since her promotion as Black Hawk County's first female sergeant.

6

"**G**ood news or bad?" Schmidt asked as Riley returned to Investigations. He didn't wait for her preference. "Kristen Webb hopes to have an initial autopsy report this morning." He held up his hand at Riley's surprise. "Here's the bad. The backlog at the state lab has increased. Webb says it'll be months before we get DNA."

Riley cursed. So much for Reed's insistence of a quick turnaround. They had no suspects as yet. No witnesses either. Reed's last words lingered in her mind. That unspoken question of whether she was up to this. Ever since her promotion—the discontent of Jackson Cole and others still souring the place—she'd half-feared Reed was just waiting for her to fail so he could turn around and say he'd met some diversity quota, but it hadn't worked out.

"Morning, Sergeant." Amy Fox entered, a laptop and a file squeezed under one arm and a tray of drinks balanced in her hand. "Deputy Schmidt."

"You're an angel, my dear." Schmidt beamed as Fox set a coffee on his desk.

Riley took one. Her first three hadn't been enough to compensate for her lack of sleep, her thoughts circling Chloe long into the night. Chloe laughing, arm linking through hers as they met on the corner for the walk to school. Chloe lying in the cornfield, torn up and lifeless. No. Reed was wrong. She was the best person here to take this case. "Has Nolan sent through photographs?"

"Yes, Sarge." Fox put the laptop on Hansen's old desk. "And we've got the drone footage from the farmer at Zephyr, John Brown. Do you want to see?"

"Get the scene pictures up first." Riley told them about Logan joining the team.

"We'll sure be ticking a heck of a lot of boxes." Schmidt's eyes wrinkled. "Two women, an old fart, and a darn vegan!"

Riley sipped her coffee as Amy Fox got to work, carefully moving a poster of Gracie Foster along the corkboard. Gracie was smiling in the picture, but her eyes were sad. Riley had interviewed the girl's mother in their falling-down house, the woman clutching a glass of liquor in one hand, the other nervously working a cigarette to and from her cracked lips. Poverty, alcoholism, drugs, and a string of no-good men. Riley had promised to do everything she could to find her daughter, but that hadn't stopped her suspecting that Gracie—whose school reports had marked as a truant—might be halfway across the country by now. *Possible runaway* had gone on the file, even as the missing posters were going up around the city.

In her mind, Riley saw a truck juddering to a stop in the dust of an empty highway. A man grinning down. *Hop up, sweetheart.* A giddy feeling as she pulled the door closed, and the truck rumbled forward, eating the miles. Image of a girl's face, pale and pinched, in the side mirror. Not Gracie Foster's, but her own.

She concentrated on Nolan's report as Fox pinned the prints to the board.

The CSI had sent through only a handful of the hundreds he'd taken at the scene, but they were more than enough, when puzzled together, to re-create an image of Chloe's decomposing body curled among the corn. There were also photographs of the partial tire print on the dirt road to the north of the field, a cast of which had been taken, and Chloe's sneaker, found some distance from her body.

Fox was almost done creating her gruesome collage when Logan Wood appeared in the doorway.

"Sarge?"

"Edwards filled you in?"

"He did." Logan looked like he wanted to add something, but his broad smile said enough.

"Welcome to Investigations, Deputy. You can take Kramer's desk. I'll make sure you get new credentials."

Logan crossed to Kramer's desk. He looked suspiciously at it, as if it might be in some way contagious, then sat, taking a pad and pen from his top pocket.

"OK." Riley leaned against her desk, cradling her coffee. "Schmidt, take us through what we have so far on the deceased."

Schmidt picked up a file and licked a finger to flick through the pages. "Our deceased is Chloe Miller, thirty-five. Formerly Chloe Clark. Wife of James Miller, thirty-eight." Schmidt glanced up after he'd read out their address. "So, they're from one of Cedar Falls' more affluent neighborhoods. Miller works for GFT—Green Fields Technology. It's based out near Elk Run Heights. Website says they specialize in corn breeding. Chloe volunteered twice a week at a thrift store until about two years ago. It appears she hasn't worked since. Based on her husband's job and the part of town they're from, I'm guessing she didn't have to."

"How long have they been married?" Logan interjected.

"Coming up on ten years," Schmidt answered, scanning the page. "Would have been their anniversary in September." The room was quiet. He went on after a pause. "Neither of them is in the system. No arrests. No warrants. No traffic tickets even. They were both born in the area. Have families here still. James Miller's eldest sister, Margaret, is a nurse at Waterloo City Hospital. James and his sisters went to school in Waterloo. Chloe attended Holmes Junior High and Cedar Falls High." Schmidt's eyes went to Riley.

Riley tensed under his gaze. Did Hunch know something more than just the fact she and Chloe had been at school together? He had worked here under her grandfather. Surely Joe Fisher wouldn't have said anything to him? But what about Jackson Cole? Could the same be said for him? What might any of them now be whispering about her in the locker room? If Reed knew about her past—about California—she had no doubt she'd be stripped of her badge. A badge that had brought her back to life. A job that *was* her life.

She shifted, hiding her unease behind a sip of coffee.

Schmidt continued. "Looks like James Miller is one smart cookie. Got himself a scholarship to Cornell CALS."

"Cals?" asked Fox.

"College of Agriculture and Life Sciences," Schmidt told her.

Riley centered her mind. If James Miller had made it all the way to a top university in New York, what had brought him back to this dying town? Family? The job at GFT? Chloe? She had no recollection of his name from their school days, but with seventeen elementary, six junior, and three high schools in Cedar Falls and Waterloo, that wasn't surprising.

"That's all we have, Sarge."

Riley crossed to the board of photographs. Chloe's face was above her, caked with dust and blood. She thought of Chloe's soft voice, her smile, half hidden by her hand. She steeled herself. "So, we have a young woman found dead, miles out of town. No sense yet of why she was there, or anyone she might have been with. We're due the autopsy report from Kristen Webb later, but from Nolan's initial assessment this was almost certainly murder. Chloe Miller had multiple injuries, including defensive wounds. And these." Riley pointed to the maggot-infested lacerations visible through the rips in Chloe's clothes and the pulped flesh of her neck. "Nolan isn't sure what made them. Hopefully Webb will be able to tell us more, along with cause and time of death. Nolan's first thoughts, based on decomp, are that she died approximately four nights ago, which means it could be around the time the farmer, John Brown, saw the unidentified drone over Zephyr's fields. Was this drone piloted by someone she was with? Or someone looking for her? Hunting her?" Riley tapped her finger on the picture of the lone sneaker. "She was clearly keen to get away from something."

"What about the tire prints?" Logan asked, eyes on the photograph where a rutted line swerved toward the edge of the field.

"Nolan's having them analyzed. John Brown said the track joins the highway about a mile down, but that it's rarely used by anyone from

Zephyr. It's possible Chloe could have been in a vehicle and run from it. Or someone could have been chasing her."

"I'd say the former," said Schmidt. "How else did she get out there? It's a long way from her home. Nothing but farms, fields, and highway. Pitch-black at night. Not the sort of place you go for a stroll. Not a woman like her."

"Let's hold off judgments on her character for now," Riley warned. "Show me the footage, Fox."

The young deputy complied, opening the laptop and positioning it so they could all see. A box appeared, showing a patch of grass at ground level. Fox tapped the touchpad, and the video came to life. Riley watched as the drone's camera captured its takeoff, soaring up over the cornfields. The image remained nice and steady, telling her John Brown was used to controlling it. She saw why he called it his eagle, with its perfect bird's-eye view.

"Me and Sue been thinking of getting one of these," murmured Schmidt. "For our next trip."

After a time, the drone swung sideways, sinking lower. Riley saw what John Brown had spotted: broken stalks of corn near the north of the field. Yards later there were more, forming a faint, jagged line through the field. The drone moved in closer. Suddenly, Chloe's body appeared, visible among the damaged stalks. The picture jerked—John Brown's hands relaying his shock. Riley made a mental note. She wasn't clearing anyone yet, but that spoke to his innocence. The drone circled back, hovered tentatively over the body, then wheeled upward and away, returning to its master—a tiny figure in the distance beside a pickup truck. The footage cut off before it reached him.

"It certainly seemed to give Brown a start," Logan said, voicing Riley's thought. "Although I suppose it's possible he could have known she was there and sent the drone up to cover himself? Manufactured shock?"

"Why leave the body there?" Schmidt said. "If Brown had anything to do with her death, why not try to dispose of her? Why call us?"

Logan shrugged affably. "Just keeping all options open."

Riley nodded. "That brings me to assignments. Schmidt, I want you

and Fox to take Zephyr Farms. I want all those involved in the cooperative interviewed. The four families, their employees, contractors,
farmhands. Everyone. Make sure Ed Wilson's story corroborates John
Brown's. See if Wilson can recall any more details about the drone they
saw. Which direction it flew off in? And check for possible sightings of a
vehicle out there that night. Deputy Wood and I will take James Miller
and Chloe's parents for starters." She scanned them, Reed's insistence
she handle this case quickly and efficiently lodged in her mind. "I don't
need to remind you what percentage of murders go unsolved in this
country. Let's buck the trend with this one, OK?"

"You got it, Sarge."

"Thank you for this opportunity," Logan said, walking beside her
down the corridor. "I won't let you down."

Before Riley could answer, she was brought up short by Jackson Cole,
stepping out in front of them.

"A word, Sergeant?"

"Not now, Deputy."

"I hear congratulations are in order?" Cole said, switching his blue
eyes to Logan. His voice was light, but that gaze was glacial. "Guess you're
the new flavor of the month?"

Riley walked toward him, forcing him to move aside. "You should
get back to your desk, Cole. Since I've taken one of Patrol's best, there
might be more chance for you to shine." She didn't look back to see Cole's
reaction, but her heart was thudding as she pushed out through the department's doors into the glare of the morning.

"What's with you and him?" Logan asked, keeping up with her stride
as she crossed the lot to the Dodge. "I know I've asked before, but—
hey—if I'm getting in the middle of something . . . ?"

"You're not," she said sharply, meeting his gaze over the car's hood.

Logan held up a hand. "Sure, boss. No worries."

Sliding into the car, Riley yanked down the seat belt and snapped it
in. For a moment, she could almost taste the memory at the back of her
throat—acid sting of Fireball shots, cigarette smoke, and Cole's cheap
cologne. She twisted a dial on the dashboard, turning the AC on full.

7

The house of James and Chloe Miller was set back from the tree-lined street. A path through a neat lawn, bordered by orange calla lilies and blue daisies, led to steps that rose to the wrap-around porch. It was the same period and style as the Fisher house, but Riley noted the differences in the bright hues of paint, the weather-proofed wood, clean gutters and windows, the modern deck furniture with cushions that matched. According to the county records, James Miller had bought it six years ago. Green Fields Technology clearly paid well.

There was a cruiser parked on the curb. Pulling up behind it, Riley killed the engine. The street was quiet, just a few kids farther down, wheeling on bikes. As she got out of the car, a curtain twitched in the house next door. She saw a round-faced man in glasses peer out.

Riley took her jacket from the backseat and shrugged it on over her shirt. It was black and well-fitting, the jacket for a joyless skirt-suit she'd last worn at the oral exam for the promotion and, before that, her parents' funeral. It was too hot for the day, but appropriately somber for the setting. Plus, it covered the Glock. She didn't want Miller rattled. Not yet.

Riley headed up the path toward the porch, where wind chimes silvered the air. Before she reached the steps the door opened, and Chad Becker emerged.

Becker was of the same mold as Jackson Cole. Guys who came to the job like they were going to war: steel-capped boots, shades, and buzz cuts. The kind who hadn't paid much attention in de-escalation sessions at the academy, who preferred the gun range and riot prep.

Becker's khaki shirt was creased, and he was pale from lack of sleep. The death duty had taken him well into the next shift. No doubt he'd be glad of the overtime though.

He met them on the path, frowning at Logan. "Sarge," he greeted, a question in his tone.

"How's Miller?" Riley asked.

Her briskness pulled Becker's attention from Logan. "In shock." He glanced back at the door. "He's alone, but his mother and sisters are due to arrive shortly."

"No father?"

Becker shrugged, not knowing.

Riley looked at the house with a nod. She wanted Miller alone. Alone and vulnerable. In her experience most murdered women died at the hands of husbands or boyfriends. The scene and the nature of the crime didn't fit with anything she'd seen before, but that didn't make James Miller any less of a suspect, especially since Chloe had been missing for three nights before she was found, without any report from him.

Her cell rang from her pocket. Pulling it out, Riley saw Kristen Webb's name on the screen. She accepted the call, turning away from Becker and Logan.

"Doctor Webb."

"Sergeant Fisher. I have my first assessment for you."

Riley always appreciated Webb's no-nonsense, straight-to-business style, but she wanted the ME to know she was grateful for the speed of this one. "Twelve hours. That's got to be a record?"

"Don't thank me just yet. Deputy Schmidt told you about the backlog at the lab?"

"He did."

"Well, I've got more."

"More?"

"Let's get the basics done first."

"Fire away."

"OK. Bob Nolan's assessment of the body in situ is pretty much where I'm at. I put time of death at somewhere between seven and midnight on the evening of June twenty-first. I can't be more specific, I'm afraid. The speed of decomposition due to the humidity makes accuracy impossible. I can tell you, based on livor mortis, that she died in the place where she was found. Of course, that may not be where the attack itself took place."

"No," agreed Riley. "At the moment, I believe she was most likely running, or hiding from her attacker."

"Manner of death—homicide. I'm in no doubt. She sustained multiple wounds. Fractures of the small, ring, and middle phalanges on the left hand. Blunt-force trauma to the base of the skull. Deep lacerations to the right thigh, right arm, and neck. Carotid and femoral are intact, but there was significant soft-tissue damage."

Riley listened while Webb listed the wounds, most of which she'd seen for herself in the field, crouched among the corn with the flies. She'd heard many autopsy reports, but this time it was impossible to separate herself from the horror. She felt each of the injuries—little flinches in her own body—as she imagined Chloe experiencing them. Her terror. Her pain.

"Some of these could be consistent with a fall. I found four shards of glass embedded in her left palm. I'll send them for testing. Other wounds are most definitely defensive. At some point she held up her arms to protect herself. The skin of both forearms was raked enough to make her bleed. I've taken samples from the lacerations and nail scrapings. But, as I said, it's going to be some time before we get any results on DNA. I should have toxicology and microbiology by the end of the week."

"Cause of death?"

"Hemorrhagic shock. Blood loss—mainly, although not solely, through the wound in her neck. It wouldn't have been rapid. She could have survived up to an hour with these injuries, possibly less taking into account the heat, her exertions, and if she was on any medication that would speed up exsanguination. I've requested her medical reports."

Riley glanced over her shoulder at Becker and Logan, who were talking, eyes on Miller's house. She braced herself to ask the question. "Any sign of sexual assault?"

"UV screen showed only blood. No trace of semen. No sign of genital trauma either. And, of course, she was fully clothed. However, her garments were torn, and I would say the damage most likely occurred during the attack."

"So, an intention to rape can't be ruled out?"

"I can only tell you what her body tells me, Sergeant." Webb paused. "But here's where she's keeping her secrets. Mechanism of death. The lacerations in her neck, right thigh, and right arm were the major cause of the blood loss. In some places her flesh was ripped away. But I cannot say, with any certainty, what made these wounds. In truth, I've not seen anything quite like them."

Riley caught the hesitation in her tone. "Any guesses?"

Webb let out a contemplative breath. "As I said, there is significant tissue damage, and maggot activity has further obscured any . . ."

"Doctor."

"All right. If pressed, I would say they look like bites."

"Bites?" Riley had heard of mountain lions and bears straying down from South Dakota and Minnesota, and wolves weren't that uncommon when the winters were harsh. She'd spotted one once when hunting with her grandfather, melting into the woods, too fast for her to track. But such animals were usually found in the wild places, along Iowa's northern and western fringes.

"A dog?" offered Webb. "I can't be sure. There's an old friend of mine, Bruce Bain. Forensic odontologist. One of the best. He's down in Florida at the moment, giving evidence at trial—child abuse case, nasty business—but I know Bruce will help if he can."

Riley caught a rare softness in Webb's tone that suggested Bruce Bain might be more than just a friend. Some of her male colleagues had idly speculated Webb was gay, an assumption based on nothing more than the fact the woman was in her early fifties and had never married or had children. No doubt some of them would suspect that about her in fifteen years. Maybe they already did. "Could these bites—*possible* bites," she corrected herself before Webb did. "Could they have been made post-mortem? Something in the fields? A dog, like you said? Or a coyote?"

"I'm afraid not. Whatever caused these injuries, they were made while she was still alive. I agree with Bob Nolan's assessment. It was a vicious attack." Another voice sounded in the background. "I'll be there in a moment," Webb called. "I'm sorry, Sergeant, I've got to go. Another vagrant's been found in that derelict church off Dry Run Creek. Second this month. Cold gets them in the winter. Dehydration in the summer." She sighed. "And we call this a first world country?"

Finishing up the call, Riley returned to the men. After she'd sent Becker on his way, she and Logan headed up to the house. Riley gave him the short version of Webb's report before they reached the door.

"Bites?" Logan said. "What the hell from?"

"A dog, perhaps. Webb knows someone—a specialist. She hopes he'll be able to give us more." Riley pressed the doorbell, which chimed inside the house. There were panes of colored glass down the side of the door.

"Mosquitoes?"

Riley stared at him. "They're not from mosquitoes."

"I mean you," Logan said with a short laugh. "They've been getting you? Little suckers are eating my nephew alive."

Riley realized she'd been touching her neck. Her hand had strayed there, without her notice, while they were talking. She dropped it quickly. "Yeah," she said, turning away to hide the pink scar, which made a perfect oval on her skin.

Beyond the door, footsteps approached. A figure appeared in the glass.

8

James Miller was gray with grief. It had crawled into his face, hollowing it out from the inside. His jaw, shadowed with stubble, was tight. His skin was dry, dehydrated from not enough sleep and too many tears.

"Mr. Miller." Riley showed him her badge. "I'm Sergeant Riley Fisher, Investigations, Black Hawk County Sheriff's Office." She waited, but he showed no sign of recognition at her name. She guessed Chloe hadn't spoken about her to him. That was good. But it smarted. She put away the badge. "Deputy Becker told you I was coming?"

"Yes." Miller's voice was flat. "Come in."

Riley moved past him into the hallway, wiping her feet on the welcome mat. "We're very sorry for your loss, Mr. Miller. I know you must be exhausted. But we need to ask you a few questions to help us with our investigation into your wife's death. You understand?"

James nodded. Shutting the door, he motioned them down the hall.

Riley noted the artworks on the walls—splashes of acid color in hasty swirls of paint, like crime scenes on canvas. Nothing like what decorated her own house: neat cross-stitches of prayers and the Grant Wood prints loved by her mother; *American Gothic,* all pitchforks and cornfields. Riley couldn't remember Chloe being interested in art.

"Our interior designer," James said, as if reading her thoughts. "She picked them for us."

An interior designer? Chloe's fortunes had certainly changed. Riley remembered playdates and sleepovers in the Clark household: lumpy foam mats on the bedroom floor for her and Mia to sleep on; Chloe's pink-cheeked mom in washed-out sundresses; a rusty swing in the back-yard; her dad, a mailman, whistling as he set off on his dawn round, flicking away a Lucky Strike, smoked down to his yellowed fingers.

At the end of the hall she glimpsed a sunny kitchen, doors leading out onto a deck and a leafy garden beyond. James Miller gestured them into a living room. The curtains were partially drawn, throwing the room into soft twilight. There was a hearth with a glass fire built in. A couch spanned the back wall with two matching armchairs on either side and a coffee table in front, magazines neatly arrayed.

It was all very tidy, very nice—and as soulless as a show home. Like a place where no one really lived; not all squashed together on a lumpy couch on game nights, TV dinners and popcorn crumbs, animals pad-ding in and out, calls of kids. Kids? Riley wondered why James and Chloe hadn't had any. Fertility problems, or some other issue? At least there was no child sitting here now, gripping a favorite toy for comfort while being told their world had fallen apart. Riley had been twenty-three when she got that call. It had still been a shattering blow.

"Please." James motioned to the couch.

There were two mugs on the coffee table. One was full, a scum of milk on the surface. The other was empty and off its coaster. It had left a ring on the glass. Becker, Riley guessed.

"Can I get you a drink?" James asked, following her eyes.

"Why doesn't Deputy Wood make us both one?" she said, smiling.

Logan paused, halfway to sitting down. He straightened. "No prob-lem."

James looked unsettled. "I . . ."

"I'll be fine, Mr. Miller," Logan told him. "Coffee, is it?"

Riley caught Logan's eye and knew he understood. This was an oppor-tunity for him to have a look around the place while she eased Miller in.

James sat on the edge of one of the armchairs, shoulders hunched, elbows on his knees, fingers laced.

Riley took her notebook from her jacket pocket. "Deputy Becker said your mother and sisters are coming over?"

"Mom was hysterical. Couldn't even talk. She had to put Margaret on."

"Margaret? Your sister?"

James watched as she wrote. "Yes."

"She's a nurse, right? At Waterloo City?"

James nodded. He sat back, an arrow of sunlight striking the side of his face through the curtain.

Riley noted, beyond the pallor, he was an attractive man: strong cheekbones and jaw. His black hair had the first streaks of gray at the temples. "Mr. Miller, do you know why your wife might have been out there? In Zephyr's fields?"

James shook his head. There was a clatter from the kitchen. His eyes darted to the door.

Riley leaned forward to catch his attention. "Do you or your wife know anyone at Zephyr Farms? Someone who works there perhaps?"

He looked back at her. "No."

Riley changed tack. "You must have been worried? When Chloe didn't come home?"

James's shoulders dropped, and he put his head in his hands.

"Mr. Miller," she said gently, "I really want to find who did this." Those words were always true, but she felt them more keenly than she had before. "Please, help me understand what might have happened to Chloe."

James met her gaze. "I thought she was having an affair, OK?" His voice turned hard, defiant. "I . . . I thought she'd left me."

Riley kept her gaze on him. She guessed he'd not told Becker any of this. What man would want to tell another that his wife was messing around behind his back? That he wasn't enough for her? "Do you know who she might have been with? A name?"

"I didn't know anything for sure. I suspected."

"When did you first start to suspect?"

His shoulders lifted, then fell. "Months ago. I don't know." James started when Logan entered, as if he'd forgotten the deputy was there.

Logan was gripping three mugs. He set one in front of James and handed one to Riley.

"Can I have a drop more cream?" Riley said.

"Sure, boss," Logan said, catching the hint.

"Did you ever confront her? Mr. Miller?"

James glanced at her as Logan left. "No. I guess I was afraid to. I didn't *want* to know."

"Why?"

"I was working too much. I know it was bothering her."

"Your work at Green Fields Technology?"

James nodded, but said nothing.

"What do you do there?"

"I specialize in improving corn productivity, adapting it to challenging environments." James caught the slight shake of her head. "I engineer crops that can withstand drought and diseases."

"I see. When did you start at GFT?"

"When I finished my degree."

"So it was the job that brought you back to Iowa, after university?"

James let out a breath. "Look, what the hell does any of this matter? Where I work? Christ! I'm just saying I was working too hard, and it bothered my wife!"

"You argued about it?" Riley asked him carefully, watching his face, his body language. He was a lean man, but tall and wiry. Chloe was short and slight. He would easily have the strength to overpower her. Pin her down. Hurt her. She thought of those terrible wounds. Possible bite marks, Webb had said. *Made while she was still alive. A vicious attack.*

James met her gaze. "Not big fights. Just bickering, OK?"

"Of course."

"But if she was seeing someone, then it was my fault, wasn't it?" James's voice changed. "My fault for spending too much time at work. Ignoring her. My fault this happened to her." He curled his hands into fists, thumped his knees. "Oh God. *Chloe.*"

Riley could hear the anguish strangling his voice. That was a hard sound to fake. "Mr. Miller, what happened to your wife isn't your fault. I promise we will do everything in our power to bring the person who is responsible to justice." She waited, letting him compose himself. "You say you thought she might have left you? Did she take anything with her?"

"Just her car. And her purse, I think."

A car? Why hadn't Becker managed to get this out of him at least? Could it have been the vehicle that made the prints on the dirt road? Had someone stolen it after attacking Chloe? *Shit,* they could have put out a statewide APB by now. Riley pushed down her frustration. She would get the details in a moment. "You didn't try to call her? Didn't report her missing?"

"I called a thousand times! Her cell kept going to voice mail."

"Did you try to track the phone? Did your wife have an app, perhaps?"

"Nothing worked."

If someone had taken it, Riley guessed they would have removed the SIM by now, but Special Services might still be able to work their magic. "If you can give us the number and your wife's service provider . . . ?"

James didn't seem to be listening. "I called her family, friends. Everyone I could think of. I got in my car that night, drove all over town. Nothing. I thought . . ." He sucked in a breath. "I thought maybe she would get it out of her system. Come home when she was ready. I never thought she was . . ." His voice went hoarse again. "Out *there.*"

Riley heard a car pull up outside.

James twisted to look through the curtain. "My family."

"Mr. Miller, we'll need the details of your wife's car and a description of her purse and what was in it. Will you get those for me? We can let your family in." Riley rose with him. "Also, we're going to need any diaries, calendars, or address books kept by your wife, as well as access to her devices—computer—anything that could help give us an indication of who she might have been meeting."

James faltered, looking overwhelmed. Outside, car doors clunked shut.

"Let's start with the vehicle documents and her phone details, Mr. Miller. And, if possible, contact information for your wife's friends and family. I can send a deputy to collect the rest later."

He left the room, and she heard the creak of stairs. Logan appeared in the doorway with her coffee.

"Family's here," Riley told him, taking the cup and setting it on the table. The doorbell chimed. "Stall them for a moment."

Alone, she scanned the pristine living room. At one end was a chest of drawers. On it was a lamp and candles in hurricane lanterns, the wicks as yet unlit. There were also several photographs. One was of James and Chloe on their wedding day. They made a portrait-pretty couple: him dark and tall, her slim and fair. Another was of an older couple Riley recognized as Chloe's parents, grayer and more wrinkled than she remembered. Chloe had been their only child. Riley felt a rush of sorrow imagining what her death would do to them. She remembered them as warm, tender people. They didn't deserve this. She reached out and touched Chloe's picture. That bright smile held the echo of a young girl's laughter. The laughter turned to screaming in her mind.

A third picture had a grainy quality, the colors starting to fade. It showed a woman and a man on the steps of a ramshackle farmhouse. Three skinny children were arrayed in front of them—a lanky dark-haired boy in faded jeans and two girls in ill-fitting dresses. In the background was a red barn with a damaged roof. An ancient Aermotor windmill with rusted blades towered above it.

There were women's voices out in the hall.

"Here."

Riley jumped at the voice directly behind her. She hadn't heard James enter. He was holding a plastic wallet with documents inside. On top was a small ring-bound book with flowers on it. She pointed to the lanky boy in the grainy photograph. "Is this you?"

James nodded, his eyes not leaving hers. "Chloe's phone number is at the front." He held out the book and the wallet, but didn't let go when Riley took hold of them. "Do you plan to contact our friends? Tell them what I've told you? About the affair, I mean?" Gone was the grief-stricken man. James Miller was now all business.

One of the women's voices rose over Logan's steady tones. "Where is he? I want to see my son!"

"If your wife was meeting someone that night, Mr. Miller, we need to know who it was."

James's gaze was pulled to the door as the voice climbed in pitch. "Because Chloe wouldn't have told them about it."

"The affair?"

"She was a very private person, Sergeant."

That much was true. At least, it had been when they were kids. Chloe had been the shy one. Tentative and watchful, eager to please and cautious to offend. They were qualities that had endeared her to Riley, a tonic to Mia's brashness. But later—after that night—that tentativeness had become infuriating. She had an image of Chloe watching her nervously. Something about to tiptoe from her tongue. Words forming, but never uttered.

"She wouldn't have told them anything," James repeated. With that, he relinquished his grip on the documents and strode from the room.

Out in the hallway, Riley found him comforting an older woman, who was crying uncontrollably. Two younger women were clustered around them, also weeping. Riley recognized all three from the photograph outside the farmhouse, although they appeared very different now—smart clothes and good shoes, salon-styled hair. Logan was pushed awkwardly up against the wall beside the sobbing group.

As Riley moved toward them, James's mother looked up. Despite the quality of the woman's clothes, she could glimpse the vestiges of the poverty she'd seen in that photograph. It was knitted in the woman's skin and bones: years of poor nutrition and struggle.

"You find the monster who did this!"

"Mom," hushed the elder of the two women, eyes on Riley.

Riley met James's gaze. "I'll be in touch, Mr. Miller."

In the Dodge, AC blasting, Riley contacted dispatch to put out an APB on Chloe's missing car, then called Bob Nolan with the vehicle details for when the tire-print analysis came back. After that she got patched through to Hal Edwards, asking if he could spare a deputy to pick up the rest of the items she wanted from the Miller house, and to make sure Patrol knew to keep a close eye on the man himself. She didn't want him leaving town anytime soon. Logan, meanwhile, got in touch with Special Services to pass on Chloe's cell number in the hope they could track it.

Riley looked back at the house while she waited for Logan. That shift in Miller's demeanor?

She wouldn't have told them anything.

Not a threat. But a promise? Something to steer her away from asking their friends and family more personal questions? Pride? Shame? Or something else? "Anything interesting in the kitchen?" she asked when Logan finished the call.

"Looks like he hasn't cleaned for a few days. Plates in the sink. Trash overflowing. Other than that, the place is spotless." Logan sounded impressed.

"Did you hear?"

"About the affair?" Logan nodded. "He only suspected, though. He had no proof?"

"Either way, it gives him motive. Doesn't matter if Chloe wasn't actually playing the field. If he thought she was . . . ?" Riley's eyes returned to the house. What had she glimpsed under the surface of James Miller, beneath all that scattered grief? Something clenched and angry? Something desperate? "OK, let's assume, for now, that there could be a potential lover out there. Maybe someone who wanted her to leave her husband and got angry when she wouldn't?"

She imagined Chloe in her car with another man—a shadow beside her—parking in the dark like teenagers. Cornfields in the headlights, bugs swirling in the beams. Hands on one another. Mouths hungry. Then, an argument. A fight? Chloe scrabbling out of her car. Wounded? Leaving her purse and cell behind. Running into the cornfields. So scared she'd kept on running, even when her shoe was snatched away.

But what about the drone?

"What are you thinking, Sarge?" Logan listened as Riley shared her thoughts. "Yeah, I've been wondering if the drone could be unconnected."

"Oh?"

"Maybe just someone out checking crops?"

"At night?"

Logan shrugged. "Or maybe they were out to sabotage Zephyr's corn, like John Brown suspected? Spray it or something?"

"That sounded like paranoia."

"Don't be so quick to dismiss his fears, Sarge. I know what companies are capable of when there's profit to be made."

Riley met his eyes. "OK."

"Besides, Brown said their corn is up for that award at the state fair. The Iowa Food Prize? I looked it up after we spoke to him. It is a big deal. Past winners have gone on to become powerful voices in the agricultural sector. Could make Zephyr Farms unwelcome competition down the line. Brown said Agri-Co was after his land, didn't he? Before the four families created the cooperative."

Riley remembered how much she'd enjoyed working through a case with Logan back when they were partners in Patrol. She liked the way he thought—methodical and detailed. She was pleased she'd gone to bat for him with Reed. "Then there are the shards of glass Webb found in Chloe's palm. Those wounds." An image of Chloe's body crowded into her mind. "And her clothes . . . ?"

"What about them?"

"Not exactly what you'd wear to meet a lover. Old sneakers, T-shirt. No makeup."

Logan looked thoughtful. "Unless they'd been at it for a while?" He shrugged, gave a half-smile. "I don't know, Sarge. When *do* women stop dressing to impress?"

Riley didn't answer.

A black dress pulled up, hem skimming the thighs. Heels to make the legs look longer. Lips glossed red. Hair, warm from the dryer, shaken over a shoulder in a wave of tawny gold. Step back and stare into the mirror. Not with her own eyes, but the eyes of all those men she'd gone looking for. She knew what they wanted to see.

"What are the first names in the address book?"

Logan flipped through. "Hmm, looks like her doctor. Then, OK, Clark. These are her parents, I'm guessing. This one could be a friend?" He showed Riley the listing, written in Chloe's neat handwriting.

Mia Collins.

9

Mia lived on Iowa Street, on a corner overlooking a McDonald's Drive Thru and Red Bubba's Car Wash and Lube. A spur of old railroad track snaked through the neighborhood, winding alongside the lawns of houses. Riley had played dare along it as a kid, jostling to see who'd stay on the tracks the longest as the horn keened a warning, and the train came rumbling through.

She got out of the Dodge alone. She'd dropped Logan off at Chloe's parents, telling him they would need to work efficiently given the number of interviews they had to conduct. This was true, but it wasn't why she'd wanted to be on her own for this one. Chloe was dead—she would keep her secrets. But Mia was a door into a past that Riley didn't want to walk through with anyone from her present.

The house was a modest one-story with a built-in garage. Toys littered the yard. Whomever her former friend had married to turn her from Mia Adams into Mrs. Collins, he wasn't in James Miller's league. A man next door was watering his lawn. There was a board staked in the grass, plastered with the face of Governor Bill Hamilton.

VOTE FOR YOUR FUTURE!

The man watched as she walked up the path to Mia's front door.

Bracing herself, Riley rang the bell. Her heart was pounding.

The door opened and there was Mia, barefoot and sweaty, a blotchy toddler couched in one arm, sucking on a pacifier. "Riley? Oh my

God . . ." Mia took in the held-up badge without any show of surprise. "Was it her? The woman they found? Was it Chloe?"

Riley's brow furrowed. The news hadn't mentioned Chloe's name yet.

Mia answered before she could ask. "James called. Four nights ago. Woke the kids up. Dan was mad."

Dan. Her husband?

"He was frantic. Saying Chloe had gone missing."

So, Miller's story checked out. But the question as to why he'd insisted Chloe wouldn't have spoken of an affair to anyone still bugged Riley. Surely he would want them to pursue every angle in the hunt for his wife's murderer, especially if a lover was involved? Unless, of course, he was the one who'd killed her.

"I was supposed to meet Chloe yesterday for a drink at Soprano's," Mia added.

Riley knew Soprano's—the Italian on Main, with waiters in bow ties who sang opera as they served. Her father used to take her mom on their anniversary, when they first moved to Cedar Falls.

"I called her, left messages. She never got back. I went anyway, hoping she'd come. I thought maybe she'd had a falling-out with James. That she'd want to talk to me about it. But she never showed." Mia pressed her palm to her chest. "Oh God."

Hearing the hiss of the hose from next door coming closer, Riley put away her badge. "Can I come in?"

Mia led the way down a dim hallway, kicking toys out of her path. They passed a messy living room where a TV was blaring. Two boys were on the couch. They didn't look around.

Mia continued into a kitchen. There was a playpen in one corner, close to a washing machine that was grumbling around. She deposited the toddler in the pen, where he spat out the pacifier and began to wail. "Hey, AJ!" She yanked open the fridge and pulled a Popsicle from the icebox. "Look!" Unwrapping it, Mia deposited the Popsicle in the child's outstretched fist. Her frayed denim skirt rode up as she bent over, showing thighs stuccoed with cellulite and a lurid wink of thong.

Riley looked away.

"Have a seat. Coffee? Something stronger? Jesus, I'm shaking." Mia held out her hand to show the tremors.

"I'm fine, thank you." Riley perched on one of the stools at the counter, sticky with gobbets of cereal. She spoke calmly, professionally, as she would with any interviewee, but inside she was boiling with emotions.

Mia had changed. Her hair, honey gold in childhood, had been bleached many times and was now ash blond. Her face was flushed, sweat patches under the arms of her T-shirt. Long gone was that teenage figure, her breasts and belly stretched by babies. But despite the transformation, Riley could still see the schoolgirl she'd known in the stubborn jut of her chin and those deep-set eyes, green as a summer creek.

Eyes so glazed with drink that night they'd barely registered her: hunched in the corner of Mia's parents' trailer, smeared in blood and earth. Chloe staring at her, shocked sober. Mia stumbling out of the trailer to vomit. Aftershock and corn dogs.

Mia filled two mugs with water and shut them in the microwave. "Is it her, Riley?"

"We need formal identification from her family. But, yes. It's Chloe."

Mia leaned forward, elbows on the counter. She let out a breath. Her head hung down, strands of hair falling across her eyes. She stayed like that until the microwave pinged, then rose and turned away. Her cheeks were wet. She spooned coffee and creamer into the mugs. "Oh," she murmured. "You didn't want one."

"I'll take it. Thanks."

Mia dug the heels of her palms into her eyes. "What happened? *The Courier* said the woman was murdered?" She shook her head. "How? Who?"

"At the moment we're trying to ascertain her movements that evening. Anyone Chloe might have met. Places she might have gone." Riley lifted her coffee. The creamer hadn't fully dissolved. White lumps floated on the surface. "When did you last speak to her?"

"A couple of weeks ago. Just a text. About meeting up."

"Did you meet regularly?"

"Ever since school."

That stung. The closest relationships of Riley's adult life had been with her colleagues in the sheriff's office. Of course, that was the nature of the job—bonds formed in the long dark of graveyard shifts and forged in the face of danger were unsurprisingly strong. But that wasn't the reason she had so little beyond the confines of her career.

What if things had been different? What if Mia hadn't stolen the alcohol from her parents' trailer that night? What if she hadn't taken the bottle when it was passed to her? If she'd woken the next morning in the trailer's bunks with her two best friends, still a bright and carefree kid? What might her life look like now? Like Mia's, perhaps? Toys and diapers. Or Chloe's? Handsome husband and immaculate home. Prom night and weddings, kids and family dinners, drinks with friends over the weekends, arguments about work. None of it perfect. But all of it normal. Looking at the lives her friends had gone on to live, Riley felt like another species.

"I mean, it was difficult sometimes, with the kids and all. But we tried to keep up when we could." Mia locked eyes with her, then looked away.

Was that a flush of guilt in her face? "Do you know James Miller well?"

"Me and Dan went out a few times with Chloe and James when they were first married, but Dan's on the road quite a bit with his work—haulage," she added. "And James has never been a social butterfly. It's always hard for her to pry him away from his job. I mean, God knows it's tough with Dan being away so much, but at least when he's here he's *here*, you know?"

"James worked a lot?"

Mia let out a humorless laugh. "Yeah. He *worked* a lot."

"What do you mean?"

"Oh, I don't know. I don't want to speak out of turn. They're a very private couple."

"If it's something that could help, I need to know."

Mia exhaled. "Chloe thought James might be having an affair."

Riley sat forward. Each thought it of the other? "What made her think that?"

"He was coming home late, more and more. She said he got calls at odd hours that he'd leave the room for."

"Did she ever confront him?"

"He told her he was volunteering."

"Volunteering?"

"Some soup kitchen over on West Fourth Street."

"You think he was lying?"

Mia sucked at her bottom lip. It was a habit Riley recalled from school. "I don't know. Maybe not." She shrugged tightly. "To be honest, it's the kind of thing he's into. Soup kitchens, food banks, races for charity. James has some vision about being the next Henry A. Wallace. Feeding the world."

The name rang a faint bell. "Wallace?"

"You know, that corn seed guy? We had to write a paper on him in science class." Mia flourished a hand through the air. "*Iowa's greatest son,* Pig-Face Petersen called him. Became vice president under FDR."

Memories flickered. Chalk dust on blackboards. Pictures of corn plants and their parts. *Brace roots. Leaf blade. Silks.* Petersen's droning voice. A photograph of Henry A. Wallace—the world's first hybrid seed developer, born in Orient, Iowa. Riley thought of Miller's job at GFT, engineering crops. "Do you know the name of this soup kitchen James said he was volunteering at?"

"It's in a church. I think it's the one near the swimming pool on Campbell? West Fourth, as I said."

Riley looked up from her notebook as she asked the next question, wanting to see Mia's reaction. "Might Chloe have started seeing someone else herself?"

"God no!"

"You sound very sure."

"Chloe would have told me. I would have known." Mia shook her head vehemently when Riley told her about Miller's suspicions. "No. She was madly in love with James, even with his faults. She wouldn't have cheated on him." Her brow creased. "I can't believe he would think that."

Riley continued with the questions, asking about Chloe's friends and family, any signs that she was experiencing other difficulties, any new people in her life, any place she might have been going that evening. But other than remaining adamant that if anyone in the marriage was having an affair it was James not Chloe, Mia wasn't able to offer any information that might help answer why their friend had been found dead in that cornfield.

The toddler finished his Popsicle and started crying. Mia hefted him up. "Stop it," she said, trying to push the pacifier into his blue-stained mouth. "AJ!"

"He's a cutie."

"Cute as a tarantula," sighed Mia, struggling as he wrestled in her arms.

"Why do you think Chloe and James didn't have kids?"

"They tried in the early days. A couple of years back Chloe was talking about doing IVF, but James wasn't interested." Mia set the boy on the floor, where he crawled to a toy tractor and began banging it on the linoleum. "Like I said, he's always going on about feeding the world and saving the planet. That sort of crap. Do you know what he said to Chloe once? Told her having kids was one of the worst things you could do for the environment. She was cut up about it for days."

Riley thought of Logan's sermons on plastic. She'd once seen him go through a trash can in the bullpen and separate out the waste while Jackson Cole and the others watched in scornful amusement. The following week they'd not been laughing when Sheriff Reed announced a new recycling drive, inspired by Logan, with a fine for any officer who ignored it.

"God, this is all so crazy. How can it be real?" Mia let out a breath, then shook her head. "Hey, look, I'm sorry about your parents."

"What?"

"I read about the car accident in the paper. I thought about coming to the funeral. But . . ." Mia tugged a strand of hair behind her ear. "I didn't know if you'd want me there. It had been so long."

Riley's cell pinged in her pocket. "Excuse me." She took it out gratefully and scanned the text. It was from Logan.

Name leaked. Media circus here. Done when you are.

"Damn."

"What is it?"

Riley looked up. "I've got to go." She took a card from her wallet, placed it on the counter. "If you think of anything else—anything at all—that's my cell."

Mia walked her to the front door. "Are you still living at the old house?"

"Yes."

"We talked about you over the years, Ri. Me and Chloe." Mia faltered, cut off by the wail of a train horn. She hugged her arms around herself and shivered despite the heat. "We talked about—that night. Maybe we could get a drink sometime? You and me? There are things I need to say."

For a moment, Riley hung there on the step.

That night belonged to the three of them. At first, she'd felt the pain was almost shared: each of them passing around the razor in silence, hands clasping over her secret. But, in the end, it was that connection that had forced her away from them. Chloe eyeing her, always on the verge of bringing it up. Mia pressing on blithely as if nothing had happened. *Did you see Mike in math class? He's so into you, Ri!* When she realized that although her friends knew they could never really *know*, it had been the loneliest feeling in the world. It made running away that much easier.

"That's ancient history, Mia. Remember, you've got my number."

As Riley walked to her car, Mia watching her go, the train appeared, rumbling slowly over the street crossings, sparks spitting from the rails. Its dark hulk inched past houses, between white picket fences where children played on lawns.

10

Governor Bill Hamilton kept the smile on his face as the cameras continued to flash, capturing his handshake with the head of the delegation, which had arrived that morning from China. Above him, the gilded domes of the capitol smoldered in the evening sun. Across the Des Moines River, the floodlights of Principal Park illuminated the field for the Friday night game. Iowa Cubs versus the Omaha Storm Chasers.

Hamilton's grin faded as he caught the chants from the police blockade down the street. He could see the protestors behind the cordon, shouting and waving placards.

IOWA FOR FARMS, NOT FIRMS!
CORN IS OUR THING. DON'T SEND IT TO BEIJING!

Everywhere he went on this campaign the sons of bitches followed—these climate-crisis cultists with their death masks and slogans. Gage Walker, head of his security, had ordered his team to take pictures, believing some could be connected to Mission Earth, the eco-terrorist group that had launched attacks on several chemical companies in the state—companies Hamilton had supported.

"Governor!" A voice called from the gathered crowd of journalists arranged in front of him. "What do you think of Senator Cook's comments earlier today? That you're cozying up to China because of your failures here at home?"

Before Hamilton could answer, his aide Blake Preston stepped in. "OK, that's all we've got time for, folks!"

Hamilton fixed his smile back on and waved for a final volley of photographs before heading up the steps of the capitol, leaving Blake to address the reporters with details of the delegation's planned state-wide tour—from the industrial towns of Muscatine and Davenport on the Mississippi, through Cedar Rapids to Sioux City on the Missouri. Three other aides ushered the delegates, all black-tie dignified, into the building, away from the chants of the protestors. There were seventeen in the party: officials from the provinces of Shandong and Hebei, chief executives of several Chinese agricultural companies, potential investors, assistants, and translators.

Inside, Hamilton led the way up the wide granite staircase to the first floor, where tables, set for the evening's gala dinner, had been arranged beneath the capitol's dome that soared cathedral high above them. The dome's faraway ceiling was spanned by the banner of the Grand Army of the Republic from the Civil War. On the floor above, visible within the vaulted rotunda, gold statues stood burnished in the honeyed glow of antique lights. Lines from Lincoln's Gettysburg Address circled the walls below a mural that depicted the cultivation of the Midwest by the pioneers.

The delegates made impressed noises at the grandeur of the interior while nodding approvingly at the red flag of the People's Republic of China, raised beside the flags of America and Iowa. Waiters hovered among the guests already gathered there in tuxedos and gowns, sipping champagne. Music from a string quartet drifted over the hum of voices and laughter.

Hamilton moved through the crowd, introducing delegates to his supporters, sharing jokes with donors. His wrist and jaw ached from a day of grip-and-grins. By November he'd be exhausted, running on coffee fumes and polling data.

Most of the guests at tonight's dinner were local businessmen and women: heads of biotech companies and agricultural CEOs. There were some farmers, too—those friendly to his message that progress was not to be feared, but embraced. He needed their voices of support right now, with new tariffs from China slapped on soybeans in retaliation for the president's tough stance on foreign imports. The market was down nearly twenty percent, and small farms, already squeezed to the margins, were feeling the pinch and looking for someone to blame.

God willing, the sight of him side by side with the Chinese would help convince them that he was their best chance of mitigating any further levies—that he would protect the symbiotic relationship between Iowa and the Republic. China, lacking the research and the arable land on which to grow enough crops to support the livestock their burgeoning middle classes fed upon, was ravenous for American corn. Iowa was desperate for the billions of dollars Chinese firms poured into the economy. Like it or not, each was dependent upon the other.

He paused to pose for a selfie with a group of women from a kids' charity.

"Governor." One of his aides slipped in to introduce the owner of a new hotel being built on the river.

Hamilton nodded through the hotelier's fulsome greeting, but his thoughts had shifted to that reporter's comment. He'd known Jess Cook would try to spin this Chinese tour against him. He expected his rival would make reference to recent cases of Chinese nationals accused of stealing seeds out of Iowa's soil, hoping to unlock the priceless genetic codes that would enable them to better grow their own crops and end their costly dependence on American corn. The FBI was delivering leaflets to farmers across the state, telling them to watch their fields. It wasn't exactly yellow peril stuff, but it sure didn't look good.

Cozying up to China?

"Heck, Governor!" winced the hotelier, whose hand he'd been shaking. "That's some grip you've got!"

Hamilton forced an apologetic chuckle. He was turning to introduce the man to one of the Chinese investors when Blake Preston moved in.

"There's a call for you, sir," murmured the aide. "Urgent. I have it on hold in your office."

Excusing himself, Hamilton made his way through the throng. The murmur of music and voices faded behind him, replaced by the sound of his shoes clacking on the marble floor. Approaching his office, he passed the glass case that housed dozens of porcelain dolls representing the wives of all the governors of Iowa, his own wife among them: big-eyed and blank-faced, in a replica of her inaugural gown.

The grand suite of rooms was lined with walnut and oak paneling, decorated with oil paintings and chandeliers. The phone on his secretary's desk was flashing red.

Hamilton lifted the receiver. "This is the governor speaking." He recognized the voice on the other end immediately, although he'd not heard the speaker this agitated before. "I said I would call you." Hamilton fell silent, his face changing as he listened. "When did this happen? Wait. Stop. I want you to tell me everything."

11

The evening was sullen, heavy with heat. The sky threatened rain. Riley waited outside the Hickory Hut. Insects swarmed the joint's light, a sizzle of wings whenever one got too close. There was a sign in the window. IN GOD WE TRUST. FOR EVERYONE ELSE IT'S CASH. Down the street, vagrants shuffled up to a food truck that was doling out soup and cornbread. There were more of them these days. Where the streets used to be a place for veterans and addicts, it wasn't unusual now to find whole families out here.

"Sergeant Fisher?"

Riley started. Her heart sank when she saw Sean Taylor from *The Courier*.

Reporters had been clustered around the department all afternoon, ever since word of the dead woman's identity had broken. There had been a photograph of Chloe on the news, taken on her wedding day, flowers in her hair, a shy smile for the camera. Sheriff Reed had been furious when he'd discovered some rookie in Waterloo PD had been the leak, showing off his inside knowledge with a waitress in a local diner where a reporter had also been eating.

"I'm off duty, Sean."

"Off the record, too?" Taylor grinned, cocking his head. His skin was waxy, green in the neon sign flickering above them.

"I've got nothing for you."

"Well, I might have something for you. If you're interested?"

"Oh?"

"Come on, Sergeant. You know how this works." When she didn't bite, Taylor stepped closer. "I know Hunch was interviewing people at Zephyr Farms this afternoon."

"So?"

"So, you might want to tell him to look at the Garret family."

"Why?"

Taylor shrugged. "Just a hint. I know you've got a lot of people to get through out there."

"That's it?"

"Until you scratch my back."

A waitress stepped out from the Hickory Hut, holding a bulging plastic bag. "Here's your order, hon."

Riley took it and walked to her car.

Taylor followed. "Just a little tip, Fisher. Come on!"

As she reached the Dodge, she turned to him. "You want a tip, Sean? Don't sneak up on cops."

Riley turned on the radio as she eased into the highway traffic. Sports announcements and rapid-fire ads for painkillers and antidepressants, news of a Chinese delegation arriving at a dinner with Governor Bill Hamilton in Des Moines, and an energetic commercial for the Iowa State Fair.

"Ride the big slide and take a journey through Ye Olde Mill!"

She imagined the fair rides being assembled, kegs of Bud rolled into the bars, sound checks on the music stages, hay bales stacked in the barns where animals would be showcased and sold. In a few weeks, lines of trailers would clog the interstate, heading in through the gates of the four-hundred-and-fifty-acre fairgrounds—farming families hauling animals and produce, agricultural companies set to sell tractors and equipment, bands getting ready to play the arena.

"See the butter cow! Share a corn dog or win a purple ribbon!"

Early August, the campgrounds would start to fill. Nearly eighty-five percent of the state would travel there for the ten-day fair, which had been going since 1854. Permanent camping spots were so sought after they were passed down through families.

"Come! Make a thousand memories!"

Riley's hands tightened on the wheel. Who needed a thousand? One was enough to last a lifetime.

She flicked the radio off as a truck thundered alongside her, headlights burning. The smell of ribs permeated the car. Her stomach grumbled. She hadn't managed to get lunch, heading from Mia's to pick up Logan at Chloe's parents', dodging news vans and out-thrust microphones. Mr. and Mrs. Clark, overwhelmed with grief, had been able to give Logan little. Similarly, the old women who ran the thrift store where Chloe had volunteered had offered up only tears and shock, and so they'd returned to the department, where one of Hal Edwards's deputies had brought in Chloe's computer and the documents James Miller had handed over. After being summoned by Reed, fuming at the leak of Chloe's identity, Riley caught up with Cam Schmidt and Amy Fox.

They'd managed to interview most of the Brown family, with the exception of John Brown's two eldest sons, who'd left for Des Moines to begin preparations for the state fair. Schmidt had arranged to see them on their return. Everyone had been helpful, candid. All had been shocked by the discovery of the dead woman, but Schmidt reported there had been some worry, however politely concealed, that this terrible thing could harm Zephyr's reputation and their chance at the prestigious award for their new corn seed.

Riley, telling them Kristen Webb's thought that some of Chloe's wounds could be bites, had asked if there were any dogs at the Brown farmhouse. Fox had seen two docile Labrador retrievers sprawled in the kitchen. Not likely candidates for a savage attack. The Wilson, Garret, and Davis families were next on the interview schedule.

Taking the exit to Cedar Falls, Riley thought about what Sean Taylor had implied. Something dubious about the Garret family? Most likely it was nothing of consequence, just a bit of chum thrown out to tempt her, but she would let Schmidt know. If there was nothing obvious, she could always force the information from Taylor. Iowa had no shield law to protect him from revealing his sources, and although she had rarely tested that, the seriousness of this case, and Reed's impatience to see it solved, warranted full cooperation.

As she drove the quiet backstreets, Riley's mind wandered to her meeting with Mia. She'd shared with her team Mia's conviction that it was James, not Chloe, who had been stepping out in the relationship. More confusion in an already uncertain case. They would need to speak to Miller's friends and work colleagues, and that soup kitchen he'd claimed to have been volunteering at. See if they could get any deeper insight into the man.

We talked about you over the years, Ri. Me and Chloe. We talked about that night.

Riley threaded the wheel through her hands, turning down the track to her house as the first drops of rain spattered the windshield. The yard outside the old storage shed was partly blocked by a red tow truck. She heard the shouts before she reached it.

Lit up, white as ghosts in the truck's headlights, were two figures. One was Ethan. The other was Sadie, his ex-wife. They were facing each other on the lawn. Ethan's face was pale, taut with rage. Sadie's was hectic with hate. They were yelling.

Parking, Riley got out of the car. She saw Mason Lee in the truck's front seat, watching the fight. A red ember smoldered between his fingers. He stubbed it out when he spotted her, and Riley guessed it wasn't a cigarette. The rain pelted her as she crossed the grass toward her brother. Scrounger was up on his paws in the window of the lounge, barking frantically.

"You're a waste of space!" Sadie, six years younger than Ethan and almost half his height and size, was on her toes, screaming up into his face. Her fury was no less intimidating for her slightness of build. Her black bangs dripped rain into her electric blue eyes, narrowed to catlike slits. "Why d'you think I left you?"

"I left you, bitch!"

They didn't notice Riley until she was right up between them. "What the hell's going on?"

"She wants me to take Madison. Again." Ethan glanced at Riley, then turned on Sadie. "I've got to work! How else am I gonna pay your damn child support?"

"*Work?* All you do is sit on your ass."

Ethan jerked his head toward the truck. "Like that loser?"

"Mason's got a job!" Sadie screeched. "He provides!"

"Yeah, provides your fucking pot."

"I'll stay at Tanisha's!"

At the high-pitched voice, Riley saw Madison come flying down the steps of the porch. She hadn't seen that the girl was watching from the shadows.

Maddie didn't even flinch as the rain struck her. "I don't want to be here anyway!"

Scrounger appeared at the screen door, barking over her.

"Christ, Ethan, get her inside." Riley leveled her brother with a glare as he opened his mouth. He clenched his jaw shut, then crossed to his daughter, ushering her up the steps, out of the downpour. Riley turned back to see Sadie stalking toward the truck. She went after her. "Sadie! Come inside. We can straighten this out."

Sadie whirled on her. Her T-shirt was soaked through. She wasn't wearing a bra. "I don't ask for much. One lousy weekend! That's all."

Riley fought the urge to hurl the words back into Sadie's hate-filled face. If Ethan had been a damaged man before he met Sadie, he was a wreck of one now. She'd tried her best to steer him from the volatile girl in the early days of their relationship, when it was obvious they were a terrible match. Flint and tinder, Aunt Rose had warned. But then Sadie got pregnant and that was that. A shotgun wedding, then a move into a cramped apartment above an adult movie store in downtown Waterloo. The marriage that followed had been hard on everyone around them, but none more so than the little girl who'd grown up between them.

"At least give Maddie a hug before you go."

"You're off duty, right?" Sadie yanked open the truck's door and hopped into the seat. "Then stop trying to solve everyone's fucking problems."

Riley was blinded as the headlights blazed full-beam. Mason Lee reversed down the track. She watched the truck veer around and speed off, in half a mind to call in the plate, set State Patrol on them. But she was more concerned about her niece right now.

As she crossed to the house, the rain stopped as suddenly as it had come. Before she reached the porch, Riley heard something down near the creek. A soft rustle of grass. She peered into the darkness but saw nothing. Maybe a woodchuck? If it was another skunk, she'd have to get a trap. The last one sprayed Scrounger in the eyes, and the peroxide she'd had to use to scrub the stench off him had bleached a white stripe across his head.

Ethan was leaning on the kitchen counter, a beer gripped in his fist. His wet hair was plastered to his scalp.

"Where's Maddie?" Riley stroked Scrounger's ear as he came up and nudged her with his nose. He licked her hand.

A door upstairs slammed in answer.

Leaving her brother, Riley stowed her gun in the safe, then headed up. She grabbed two towels on the way to her old room. She knocked, then entered.

Madison was lying on the narrow bed that had once been hers, with its arched wooden headboard that used to make Riley think of a headstone. After her grandmother died, she'd lain there some nights, stretched out stiff, eyes closed, wondering what it would be like to be inside a coffin. The bedside lamp was on, throwing light across the posters on the walls.

"I brought you a towel."

Maddie, who was facing the wall, curled even tighter. "Go away," she mumbled into her pillow. Her boots were still on.

Riley remembered how intrusive it felt when an adult came and sat on your bed, poking at you to talk. Instead, she set one towel on the foot of the bed, then sat on the floor, the other towel around her shoulders. "You know they say those things to try to hurt one another? Because they're angry at each other. Not at you. I know that doesn't make it easier. But I want you to know, Maddie, you're always welcome here."

"Maybe I'll run away."

"No!" Riley said that harder than she'd meant to.

"Why not?" Maddie sat up, glaring at her through the dark strands of hair stuck to her cheeks. "You did!"

Riley felt shock pulse through her. "What?"

"My dad told me. He said you ran away to California. That you vanished from some lake house you all stayed at in Okoboji. Just walked out. He said you were missing for *months.*"

The memories came in a flood. The lake that summer morning, silver as mercury, flat as glass. Arnold's Amusement Park across the water, quiet and still, the reflection of the roller coaster twisting across the surface. Everything so hushed. Everything except her mind.

The shades were drawn in the house behind her—vacation home of one of her father's wealthy clients, which he'd lent to them after her father got him off serving time. Deck littered with crushed snacks and dead sparklers from a party her parents had thrown the night before.

She'd had a choice that morning. Slip into the lake and let those waters curl coldly over her. Or walk out, down the road, past the imposing homes and boats on trailers, past the junk of happy families, all the way to the state highway that ran west. All the way to wildness and free-falling, oblivion and forgetting, beside a great crashing ocean thousands of miles away. Sunrise on another town. Another life. She hadn't meant to return.

Riley felt sick, not so much at the memory, but at the thought that Ethan might have told Maddie more. The reason for her running. That secret was radioactive—it had destroyed her family. She'd learned, years ago, not to let it spill out, infect anyone else.

Maddie seemed to sense that she'd said something serious, as she came and sat beside her aunt, eyes big and anxious. "Is it true?"

Riley swallowed back the dryness in her throat. If she was asking that, maybe Ethan hadn't said much more? "Yes. But it wasn't good. I came back." She thought of Gracie Foster. Would the missing girl eventually wash up as some other department's statistic, wrecked on the hard shores of drugs, desperation, and male violence? It was a shore she herself had come to know well in California. "Promise me you won't, Maddie?"

The girl nodded after a pause. "Why did you come back?"

"Grandpa Joe found me." Riley closed her eyes and leaned her head against the closet doors. It had been a long day. James Miller. The autopsy report. Mia. She couldn't think about Grandpa Joe—about that time—right now.

"This one's going to break."

"What?"

Maddie was looking at the friendship bracelet on Riley's wrist. She reached out, touched it gently. "I'll make you a new one if you like?"

"I'd like that very much," Riley told her, fighting a swell of emotion. "Oh, crap."

"What's wrong?"

Riley felt a tired laugh bubble up inside her. She let it out. "I left the ribs in the car."

"Ribs?"

"Do you want to share? We could crack a root beer?"

"Just us two?"

"Heck yeah. I'm not sharing Hickory Hut ribs with everyone!"

12

He stood alone in his kitchen, trembling. The room was shadowed, shutters closed over the windows, mere cracks of light slipping in. Flies circled, twitching across dishes furred with mold and piled high in the sink, making busy on pans crusted with dried remains. There was trash everywhere—discarded jars and cans of food, dirty clothes, unread copies of *The Courier,* the last edition from days earlier with a photograph of missing teen Gracie Foster.

His gaze skittered over the girl's face. She stared up at him from the page, big-eyed. His mind flared with memory—a battle cry lifting from the football field, cheerleaders flashing lean legs through a whirl of pom-poms. He closed his eyes, remembering the smell of sweat and cut grass and something else—something meaty and delicious.

Touchdown! A whistle blown. Roar rising from the bleachers. Halftime, and he was following that tantalizing smell, a greedy pit opening in his stomach. The hot dogs were being carried out of the school cafeteria by women in hairnets, great pans of them, all slippery and pink. There were trays of pizza, too, but he'd always been a dog man, even though he knew what crap went into the things. God, *that smell.* Game nights and fairgrounds, Fourth of July and backyard grills. A thousand juicy memories. He could almost taste it now. The briny sweetness of the meat, the doughy texture of the bun gumming up his mouth, the tang of mustard.

He fought to hold on to the memory, but already it was curdling in his mind. The hot dog turned to acid in his throat. The cheers faded until the only sound he could hear was the agitated hum of flies in the kitchen's stale air. Another memory now. Darkness and screaming. Hands scratching desperately at his face.

He flinched as his cell vibrated on the counter. He stared dumbly at the screen. A message hovered there.

I'm coming.

As he gazed at the words, his guts seized. Fear and anticipation warred within him. He stabbed clumsily at the phone until another message appeared above it.

I know where she is.

The screen told him he'd written the words just hours earlier. There was his name above them. But he had no memory of typing them. Had he written it in guilt? Intending to confess? Or had he wanted something else? His stomach clenched, and he doubled over, dropping the phone.

For weeks, the hunger had gnawed at him, keeping him awake, pacing through the days that had blurred into endless twilight since he'd closed the shutters over the world, no longer able to bear the bright burn of sunlight. He'd tried to eat. The packets and takeout cartons littered all around were evidence of that. But food he'd once enjoyed turned to dust in his mouth. Nothing seemed to give his body nourishment. Nothing tasted the same. Nothing satisfied. Except . . .

No.

Outside, in the yard, his dog was barking. He jumped at the sound of a car approaching up the rutted road. He staggered to the window and squinted through a gap in the shutters, his eyes aching. In the muted daylight, he saw his arms were covered with scabs. His skin looked like the scales of some creature. His head throbbed with pressure. It felt as though it might burst like rotten fruit and all these sick thoughts would come oozing out of him like maggots.

His dog was barking louder. The car was closer, tires on grit. His stomach growled, deep and low. He could hear his own heart, fast as the throb of drums on the school football field. He could smell the meat again. Sweet and tempting.

She was coming.

13

Riley was woken by her cell. It pierced the foggy depths of her sleep, pulling her into the day. A red dawn was bleeding around the edges of the curtains. The cell's screen told her the time and the caller.

05:18

Cameron Schmidt

"Cam?" she said groggily, struggling to sit as she pressed the phone to her ear.

"We've got another, Sarge."

"What?"

"Another body."

Riley was up and out of the house in thirty minutes, pulling her hair into a knot as she crossed to the car. Work boots, cargo pants, and T-shirt today—too muggy for anything else and, from the details Schmidt had given her, too messy. By the time she was on the highway, the rising sun had lost its gilded promise behind a bank of clouds. The sky was tinged with an ominous green sheen. Twister weather.

Waterloo was lifeless in the stagnant air. Smoke seeped from factory chimneys and the Cedar flowed sluggish and brown. Although the roads were clogged with trucks and trailers, there were few people about, just a few vagrants shambling along broken sidewalks and cleaners and hospital workers trudging to or from shifts.

She followed the directions on the GPS, taking the road toward Hudson, alongside the Black Hawk Creek, which snaked from the river. It wasn't long before she saw the old meatpacking plant on the outskirts of the city, just a block or so outside Waterloo PD's jurisdiction. Its twin smokestacks were dark fingers against the pallid sky, old bricks the color of rust. The bottom windows were boarded over, the ones higher up mostly shattered. A chain-link fence surrounded the site, bristling with barbed wire. Signs hanging from it read COBALT SECURITY, with a CCTV warning below. The main gate was open. Three cars were parked in the scrubby lot beyond. Cam Schmidt's battered Dodge, the K-9 unit vehicle, and a car with the same logo as the signs on the fence.

As Riley was parking, Deputy Peter Hoffman emerged from the building with his K-9, a German shepherd called Bear. Stuffing a pair of shoe protectors and gloves into her utility belt beside her Glock, Riley crossed to meet him, skirting piles of glass and debris that had crumbled from the building over the decades since it had fallen into ruin.

"Sergeant." Hoffman greeted her, flicking a finger from his forehead in a salute. He was one of the old guard who'd served under her grandfather. Like Riley, and anyone who'd been in the department more than a few years, Hoffman had worked various assignments—jail duty, even a stint in Motorcycle Patrol. But none suited him more than the K-9 unit. He loved his dogs like they were family.

Bear strained forward to sniff her, ears pricked. For a gut-tightening moment, Riley wondered if the animal could smell her brother's cannabis on her clothes. But, at a tug on his leash, the dog sat obediently.

"Me and Bear were on our way home when we heard the call from dispatch," Hoffman told her. "Thought we'd offer assistance."

"Who found the body?"

"Security guard. Only a few months into the job, poor kid." Hoffman nodded into the murk of the door he'd emerged from. "Not sure he'll be returning." His nose puckered. "Seen some stuff in my time. But nothing quite like that. We're heading off shift, unless you want us?" He ruffled the dog's head.

"No, go on home." Riley had already called Logan and Nolan on her way over. Half the department would be here in the next hour.

"She's at the north end, Sarge. Past the tanks. Back of the slaughter hall."

After pulling on the overshoes and gloves, Riley ducked out of the sullen morning into the plant's dank gloom. Following a short passage, stepping over heaps of rubbish, she found herself in a cavernous hall. Metal steps ascended to gantries that crisscrossed in between pillars and snaking pipes, conveyor belts and wheels. It all looked like some complex ride at the state fair, only made of metal and rust, fractured glass and hooks. She imagined the steers and hogs shuddering around, the iron spike of blood, steam from spilling guts. Parts of the gantries had collapsed. In places, the floor yawned into darkness. There was a smell of mildew and oxidized steel.

As Riley picked her way through, following the crackle of radio static deeper in, she heard flurries of wings in the vaulted shadows. Water drip-dripped from somewhere. Here and there, among the ruins, were signs of more recent occupation: graffiti sprayed across cracked tiles, empty paint canisters on the ground with cigarette butts and smashed beer bottles, oil drums blackened by fire, a mildewed sleeping bag and a condom hanging from a nail like a greasy cocoon. Bullet holes pocked the walls, spent shells littering the floor. This was going to be an evidence nightmare. She'd have to call Hal Edwards, get some deputies over to help.

Up ahead she caught the flare of a flashlight. There was a distinctive smell now, seeping toward her beneath the mustiness of the abandoned plant. Putrid. Repellent. *Dear God. What a place to die.*

Past a row of huge, cylindrical tanks, she came upon a young man hunched at the bottom of some metal steps. His head jerked up, eyes bright in the gloom. Not far from him was a splatter of fresh-looking vomit. Riley showed him her badge. He struggled to his feet, holding on to the railing. He looked barely twenty, chubby and cherub-cheeked. Probably still lived with his parents. A baton hung from his belt, and he wore a navy uniform with COBALT SECURITY on the breast. She introduced herself, pocketing her ID. "What's your name, sir?"

"Caden Harris, ma'am," he said, his voice hoarse.

"You found the body?"

He nodded. His eyes went to the vomit and his head drooped.

"What time was that, Mr. Harris?"

"An hour ago? I called right after. Then I called my boss. He's on his way," he added, peering anxiously over her shoulder.

Riley's attention moved beyond him as the flashlight's beam lanced toward her. She held up a hand as Schmidt saw her. He was over by a series of dark openings. "Are you here every day, Mr. Harris?"

"No, ma'am. We do a sweep once a month. I was here four weeks ago, and there was nothing. No one. I covered the whole site."

"Do you get a lot of trespassers?"

"Kids, mostly. And a few hobos, though not as bad as at some of our other properties. This one's a bit far out of town."

Riley nodded. The homeless tended to stick together, close to the food trucks and soup kitchens. Safety in numbers.

"But it looks like someone's been camped here for a bit."

"How do they get in? The place looks pretty secure to me."

"Round the back there are holes in the fences. We fix them, but then the junkers come and cut through."

"Junkers?"

"Looking for scrap, ma'am. Steel and such."

"OK, if you can wait here, Mr. Harris. We'll need a formal statement. And copies of the security footage."

"Begging your pardon, ma'am, but there isn't any."

"It says CCTV on the signs?"

Caden Harris looked embarrassed. "My boss says it's a good deterrent. Good as the real thing, nearly." He shrugged uncomfortably. "Cuts, you know?"

Yes. She knew.

As Riley picked her way toward Schmidt, the smell deepened. A vile miasma of decaying fruit, putrefying meat, and rotten eggs. The toxic perfume of death. The air was busy with flies.

Schmidt swung his flashlight toward the floor, lighting her path. She saw several footprints, some whole, others partial, marking the dust. They would have to take the guard's shoes for comparison. She stepped carefully around them.

"What have we got?"

"A Goddamn mess," Schmidt responded grimly, gesturing to the openings.

Approaching, Riley realized they opened into large cubicles with tiled walls. A series of pipes, intersected by sprinklers, spanned the ceilings. There were gutters and drains in the floors. Showers for washing the carcasses. It reminded her of pictures of the gas chambers in Auschwitz. The place was grimed with decades of dirt. In one of the openings was a backpack, curled on its side like a dead bug, along with a few items of clothing caked with filth and a sleeping bag, stuffing tufting out.

Beyond, someone had draped a tarp across the space, strung from two hooks, making a sort of den. The tiles were streaked black. Blood, she thought, looking at the sprays and spatters of it. One large smear disappeared beyond the tarp. The blowfly activity was worse here. The air hummed. Wasps and beetles wheeled clumsily in and out of the frenzied swarm, harbingers of the later stages of decay. Stepping up to the tarp, hand pressed over her mouth and nose, Riley looked over the top.

She'd known it wasn't a simple suicide or overdose based on Schmidt's initial report. But, still, she wasn't quite prepared for what lay beyond, lit up in the flashlight's beam. The body was partly smothered in a blanket, soaked brown with blood. Most of the corpse's bottom half was covered by the folds, but by the greasy threads of bleached blond hair, the once-pink bra and the one gold hoop earring that was visible, it was a woman. Much more than that Riley couldn't tell due to the advanced state of decomposition.

Her skin was marbled black and red, blistered in places where the flesh was beginning to slip. Her face was swollen, tongue poking between her lips like an engorged worm, eyes distended. Her neck was wrapped with something—a belt, Riley realized. It was so tight the skin had ballooned around it. The abdomen was bloated with gas, so much so she knew there was a risk this body could explode. Bob Nolan would have his work cut out for him today. The whole corpse had the grotesque appearance of movement, due to the boiling mass of maggots both in and around it. Riley guessed, by their numbers, there were several generations in there.

"Been here a week or so, I'd say," Schmidt said at her side, moving the flashlight across the scene.

More items scattered the floor near the body: beer cans, what looked like a pill bottle, a shiny crop top crusted with blood, a sandal with a broken strap. A cheap-looking gold purse, some of its innards trailing out, tissues and a lipstick.

"At least," agreed Riley.

"Strangulation by the looks of it. Some of those lacerations could be wounds, but it's hard to tell with the state of the skin." Schmidt waved the flashlight across the walls and floor. "All that blood came from somewhere, though."

The harsh ring of a phone made them both flinch.

"Sorry," murmured Riley, taking out her cell. The screen was lit with a picture of Aunt Rose and her partner, Lori, baby Benjamin snuggled between them. Riley pressed decline, letting it go to voice mail and stuffing it back in her pocket. Her aunt had called yesterday and left a message, Benjamin screaming in the background. Rose had sounded exhausted. Riley had meant to call her back, but she'd been snowed under with the investigation, tracking James Miller's movements the night of Chloe's death.

So far, Miller's statement of the people he called and the places he'd searched when his wife hadn't returned home—Duke's Bar on the edge of town, the Cedar Falls Medical Center, Casey's Gas Station—all checked out, although the five-hour range Kristen Webb had given for Chloe's death couldn't be fully accounted for.

Schmidt, meanwhile, had plowed on through the interviews of the families at Zephyr Farms. Yesterday, after Riley told him about Sean Taylor's comment outside the Hickory Hut, Schmidt had focused on Frank Garret and his family. Frank had a wife, Maryanne, and four grown children—Ryan, Jacob, and Lizbeth, who lived close by and had families of their own, and Hoyt, who still lived at the farm. A search on them all in both the department's files and the NCIC database had yielded nothing more colorful than traffic violations.

James Miller remained their prime suspect, but without DNA, there was no evidence linking him to Chloe's murder. All Riley had was Miller's patchy alibi and his odd behavior during the interview—behavior any attorney could easily explain away as grief. It was nowhere near enough to make an arrest. Today, she'd been intending to visit Miller's employers at GFT and that soup kitchen, hoping to find something that might explain the discrepancy in his and Mia's stories: why James was so certain Chloe had been having an affair and Mia was convinced that the one cheating was him.

But, then, Schmidt's call had come.

Riley looked back at the brutalized body beyond the tarp. First Chloe. Now this woman. The circumstances of both deaths were unusual, to say the least. Could there be a connection? Her eyes went to the belt, wound so tight around the woman's neck it had cut flesh.

She saw it in flashes. Staccato nightmares. Top torn away. Sandal snapping off. Belt tightening. Breath snatched, fingers clawing. Blood spraying. Had she fallen? Tried to crawl away? Desperate to live. The wide smear of blood dragging back beneath the tarp suggested so.

"What are you thinking, Sarge?" Schmidt asked her.

Riley glanced at him. "I'm thinking this is going to be a long day."

14

It was past midday by the time Riley made it out of the plant. She leaned against the Dodge, taking merciful breaths of the humid air. There were more vehicles in the lot now and a deputy stationed at the gate in charge of the scene log.

"Jeez," murmured Logan, peeling off his gloves with a smack of latex. He stared at his slacks.

Riley had been surprised, yesterday, when he'd turned up to his first day out of uniform. She had imagined him wearing something much more casual than the smart suit he'd appeared in. It had lent him an effective gravitas in the interviews they'd conducted, but wasn't the most practical for today's task.

"Does the department pay for dry cleaning?" Logan exhaled, already knowing the answer. "Shit." He crossed to his car, the Ford Crown Victoria that had belonged to Carl Kramer.

Yesterday morning, after he'd received his new credentials, Riley had caught him scrubbing at the wheel and controls with an industrial-sized pack of sanitary wipes. "You know cancer's not catching, right?" she'd asked him, half-smiling.

"Due respect, Sarge," he'd retorted. "But I've yet to meet a cop who ain't a nose-picker or a ball-scratcher."

Riley took a sip from the water Amy Fox had given her. Fox had set their lunch on the hood before heading into the plant with refreshments for the team. The rookie had impressed her today. Fox had seen a few bodies on the job, but this corpse was in a different league. Even

Bob Nolan had been taken aback, shaking his head with a murmured *Goddamn.* Fox had held her nerve—and her breakfast—although Riley had seen her hands shaking while she helped Nolan set up his equipment.

The activity had grown in the hours since, spiraling out around the dead woman, busy as the insects that infested her. Nolan had erected lights to flood the area before setting a camera on a tripod to capture the scene in the round: every spatter of gore, every scrap of evidence that was to be flagged and bagged. Two technicians from the lab were with him, donning overalls, masks, double layers of gloves, and overshoes before stepping beneath the tarp to begin a closer study of the putrefying body, dusting for prints on fallen objects, plucking strands of hair from congealed blood.

Beyond this inner circle, more deputies combed the plant for other items: beer cans and bits of clothing, and the maggots inching their way out of the light.

"We're gonna need more bags," Nolan had declared, surveying the chaos. "State lab will have a cow."

The boss of Cobalt Security had arrived, looking harried. Logan took a statement from him while Riley took one from the traumatized guard. The two had been allowed to leave an hour ago, Caden Harris shuffling out, pale-faced and shoeless. Riley thought Hoffman was right. The kid probably wouldn't return to the job.

After being photographed from every angle, the backpack and purse had been opened and picked through. The backpack was full of men's clothes, threadbare and stinking, and there was another of the pill bottles that had been flagged on the floor near the body, several white tablets still inside. The label was missing any patient or drug information, but Riley noted down the pharmacy it had come from—on the east side of Waterloo, not far from the old folks' home where her grandfather was.

There was also a photograph cracked with handling. It showed a man, a woman, and two boys sitting on a blanket on a stony beach. The woman, chubby and scarlet-skinned, wore a floppy sunhat. The man, auburn haired with a bushy moustache, sat beside her, smiling, hand clasping one of the boy's shoulders.

The purse offered up more. Along with a strip of condoms and a set of keys was a dead cellphone with a cracked screen and a driver's license. It was impossible to accurately match the picture to the bloated, rot-blistered corpse, but by the cut of the bleached blond hair it was possible it was hers. The name on the license was Nicole Ann King. The same middle name as her own, Riley had noted uneasily, holding it between her gloved fingers in the glare of Nolan's lights. The woman was thirty-two years old and lived in Waterloo. A call to dispatch and a check of King's file had brought up a string of charges for consumption in public, possession, and prostitution.

"She's going to come apart when they move her." Logan returned from his car with a fresh pouch of biodegradable wipes. He grimaced. "All those bugs."

Riley shook her head as he offered the wipes. It would be all too easy to succumb to Logan's fastidiousness, especially at a scene like this. "You must have seen a lot of stiffs in Flint?"

Logan glanced up from dabbing at his slacks. "Sure. But there they mostly just shoot each other on the street. Half of them were still warm when we got to them."

Riley took another drink of water. She could taste the death chemicals—ammonia, hydrogen sulfide, indole—coating the back of her throat. Most of the murders she'd dealt with in her own career had involved shootings, or stabbings. Dreadful, of course, but still somehow—human. She'd seen bodies in terrible states, gashed open in car wrecks and ripped apart by farm machinery, but there was something more horrific here. Someone had attacked this woman with animal savagery.

A bead of sweat trickled down Riley's face. She wiped it away with the back of her arm. The sun had failed to burn through the low cloud, and the midday heat was trapped, simmering beneath its cover. "So, what do you think?"

"About our girl?" Logan balled up the wipe. "Well, if she *is* Nicole

King, then judging by her record and what's in her purse, I'd say there's a good chance she was out here for a trick."

"It's a fair way out. If a john met her on the street or in a bar downtown, wouldn't they find somewhere closer?"

"Unless she—or the john—was living out here? We've got men's clothes and what looks like a hobo's den." Logan opened the lunch box Fox had left him, peeling off the fork taped to the inside, careful not to touch the prongs. "Although whoever it was could have only set up camp in the past four weeks. The kid and his boss were adamant no one was here at their last sweep." He inspected the salad, layered with pale lumps of tofu. "I don't think this is organic."

Riley glanced at the foil-wrapped sub Fox had got her. She'd asked for meat, and the label read BBQ BRISKET, red sauce oozing from the edges of the foil. Normally a crime scene wouldn't spoil her appetite, but she wanted to gag just looking at it. It wasn't so much the body, or the state of it. Or even the grimness of this place of death and ruin. There was something else. Something that had crawled inside to gnaw at her.

"Either way," continued Logan, digging the fork into the salad half-heartedly, "whoever owns that backpack and those clothes is a potential suspect."

"Or a witness. We'll start with the pharmacy those pills came from. See whether anyone recognizes the people in that photograph. Then we'll check out King."

"At least King's prints are in the system. Won't want to be doing any next-of-kin IDs on that body. Not even Webb will be able to clean her up enough. Ah, sorry, Sarge." Logan set the salad on the hood and pulled his phone out. He held it up and Riley saw his nephew's name on the screen. "D'you mind? Jake had a baseball game this morning."

"Go ahead." Riley smiled. When the Wood family first arrived, Jake had been a sickly, challenging child—one of nearly thirty thousand kids affected by the water crisis in Flint, the lead poisoning having devastating effects on their health and behavior. The boy seemed to have turned a corner in the last few months.

"Jake, my man!" Logan called into the phone, turning away. "How'd it go?"

Remembering the missed call from her aunt, Riley took out her cell. There was a voice mail.

"Riley, I've seen the news. Your old friend? I'm so sorry. Listen, I know you must be rushed off your feet, but I've had a call from the home. Joe's been asking for you. I thought you might be able to swing by? I'm tied up today. Lori's not sleeping, even with those new pills she's on." A muffled howl in the background. *"Oh, Jeez, Ben's off again. Call me, OK? Love you."*

Riley felt something loosen inside her. It had been months since her grandfather had even recognized her, let alone asked for her. She would go and see him as soon as she was done here.

She finished the water, looking up at the plant, blood-black against the sky. What paths had Nicole King walked in life to bring her here? Where was the fork in her road? The divergence that had led her to this place of slaughter? Prostitution was a common-enough story, even in Black Hawk County. You wouldn't find them lounging beneath the flicker of neon like in dark corners of New York or splayed on the post-cards shoved into your hand on the Las Vegas Strip. But if you knew the right places you could spot them. Lone figures on the roadside and at truck stops in the shadows of smokestacks and silos, dash of rain on wet roads—appearing briefly in the flare of headlights. In the end it was always the same story, no matter the twists and turns. There was always abuse or neglect, desperation or addiction. Which had come first for Nicole King?

It dawned on Riley what the gnawing inside her was. It wasn't revulsion or pity. It was recognition. A knowing, deep down, that if she hadn't had a family determined to find her, this could have been her. She thought of Gracie Foster, out there somewhere—a lost girl in a violent world. Thought of Chloe in the suffocating dark of those cornfields.

15

She'd been off school for a month and, already, Madison Fisher was bored. It was the same every year. The first few weeks were heady with possibilities; meeting her girlfriends at the mall to steal lipsticks from the drugstore, sharing cheese curds at Big Daddy's, giggling over boys on Instagram. But then the excitement ebbed, and the monotony set in. No, Maddie thought—it wasn't the same every year. This year it was worse. Mason Lee was living in her house.

The man had bulldozed into her life, taking up what little space there was with his greasy tools and his junk, ordering her around like he thought he was her father, rolling joints for her mom when she was too drunk, laughing as he moved the flame, making her sway to reach it. His friends were just as bad. Pot-smoking, ass-grabbing losers.

"Fuck my tits, it's hot!" Amelia sat up from the hood of the rusted Chevy she'd been lying on, knees knocking listlessly together as she idled through her phone.

Tanisha, sitting beside Maddie on the dusty ground, rolled her eyes. Amelia, whose mom was a born-again Christian, swore every chance she got outside her home.

Amelia rose up and stretched, her cutoff T-shirt rising high up her midriff. She'd knotted her plaid shirt around her waist, its hem touching the tops of her scuffed cowboy boots. Her blond hair was a frizzy halo in the humidity. She'd begged Tanisha to braid it for her, but she'd refused.

A year or so ago, Tanisha, whose Blackness in a class mostly full of whites had been the curse of her childhood, had started to become an object of curiosity, envy even. The acid shades of eye shadow and lipstick made cool by YouTubers, clown-like on most of the girls they knew, looked good on her. Her hair, source of so many jokes, had been braided by one of her aunts into intricate cornrows highlighted by silver beads. It was now part of her pride, and she didn't want all the wannabes in her grade to take it from her.

Beyond Amelia the junkyard stretched away, cars and trucks piled on one another. Some were nearly new, towed here after accidents, fenders dented, windows smashed, doors caved in. Others were rusted skeletons, plates trailing in the weeds, tires like deflated balloons. Maddie thought it looked like a scene from one of the zombie movies her father liked. She came here alone sometimes, scooting through the backstreets on her old bike, out along the creek, the shade whining with mosquitoes, red-tailed hawks wheeling over the trees. She would bring the pad and pencils Riley had bought her and sketch the cars—put monsters in the shadows, grinning faces peeking through broken glass, eyes in the side mirrors. She thought if moviemakers knew about this place, they'd film here for sure. Although no one really knew about Black Hawk County. Until the body was found.

The three of them had watched the news last night at Tanisha's while the newscaster talked excitedly through the latest details of the murder, his reporter broadcasting live outside the sheriff's office.

Tanisha's mom had brought them food, her brow pinched as she followed the story. "I don't want you going off alone. Any of you. Tanisha, girl, you hear what I said?"

"Yes, Mom."

"I mean it." Tanisha's mom had made sure they were heeding her before squeezing Maddie's shoulder as she set down a plate of ribs, the edges crisped dark.

Maddie loved spending time at Tanisha's. There was always food on the table. Real food. Not like her own dinners, which came with a ping of the microwave and a pop of cellophane, steam scorching her fingers. Sometimes, if her mom and Mason had been smoking, filling the cramped den with that heavy smell, she just ate corn chips or popcorn.

Tanisha had waited until her mom disappeared into the kitchen. "Your aunt's working on that, isn't she?"

"What happened to her?" Amelia had hissed, scooting her chair in closer. "The dead woman? Was she, you know . . . ?"

"What?"

"Raped?" Amelia had mouthed. "My brother reckons she was strangled with her own panties."

"Yeah, but your brother's a freak," Tanisha said.

Amelia shrugged in agreement.

Maddie knew no more than the others—only what the news had told them. Riley would never discuss details of a case with her. But she'd wanted to give them something. "I don't know. But whoever killed her hasn't been caught. He's still out there somewhere."

The three of them had stared at one another, silent and shivery, until Tanisha's mom had reappeared and chided them for not eating while it was hot.

Amelia tapped her foot on the hood of the Chevy. "I'm shit bored. Let's go to the mall."

"I'm out of cash," Maddie told her.

"Me too," said Tanisha, not looking up from her cell.

Amelia swung her legs over the rusted grille and jumped down. "I wasn't thinking of *buying* anything." Grinning, she slipped a hand suggestively into the front pocket of her shorts. "Five-finger discount!"

They all looked round at the crunch of tires. A cherry red pickup rolled toward them, jacked-up wheels jolting through the potholes, spraying muddy water. Maddie and Tanisha rose, dusting off their shorts.

A blond head popped out of the passenger seat, tanned face split in a wide grin. "Hey, girls."

Tanisha groaned. It was Amelia's brother, Jason, aka *The Douche,* as they'd called him ever since he'd followed Maddie into the bathroom during a sleepover at Amelia's last year and tried to make her go while he was watching. Maddie had managed to shove his grinning ass out of the door before ramming the bolt home, but her heart had still been thumping when she'd returned to Amelia's bedroom.

As the truck pulled up, Maddie saw there were three others with Jason. She recognized the driver—The Douche's fat friend, Connor, whose dad owned one of the bars downtown and who sometimes got liquor for them. The other two she didn't know. One was stocky and square-jawed, with a military-severe haircut and arms slabbed with muscle. The other was slim and tanned with wavy brown hair and blue eyes. His plaid shirt bulged at his heart with a carton of cigarettes.

"How'd you guys know we were here?" Tanisha wanted to know, eyes on Amelia, who trotted over, jumping the puddles.

"I said I was bored," Amelia answered, waving her cell. "Did you bring us something?" she asked her brother.

In answer, he bent into the footwell and lifted up a bottle of Fireball. He pulled it out of reach as she lunged for it. "Easy! This one's for sharing. Why don't you hop in with your friends?"

As Jason's eyes drifted to her, Maddie felt herself wanting to inch back, but she stood her ground, emboldened by the feel of Tanisha's arm looping through hers.

"We won't bite," he said, still grinning.

"Don't be a dick," said the one with the cigarettes, leaning forward to shove the back of Jason's head. He looked out at them. "We're going out to the Bible camp." He had a lazy southern drawl.

Not from here, thought Maddie.

"Out there?" Tanisha shook her head, glancing at Maddie and Amelia. "My mom would freak."

"Then don't tell her!" retorted Amelia, slinging a booted foot onto the thick tread of the back wheel and hauling herself into the truck's cargo bed. She rolled her eyes when they didn't move. "What else we gonna do?"

Maddie glanced at the junkyard, rusted steel shimmering in the heat. She knew of the old Bible camp, miles out of town, its cabins abandoned to nature. Older kids talked about it. But she'd never been there. Maybe it would be another place to take her sketchbook? It would sure be cooler in the woods. And there were still many hours left of the day. Hours she did not want to spend at home. Even The Douche was better company than Mason Lee. She glanced at Tanisha and tilted her head toward the truck.

Tanisha hung back, then relented at Maddie's little tug on her arm. "Shit, OK," she said as Amelia whooped in glee, helping to pull them both up into the truck.

"Well, all right then." Jason grinned, unscrewing the cap of the bottle and taking a swig of Fireball as Connor twisted a dial on the radio and music thumped from the speakers.

Maddie watched the piles of twisted metal disappear behind them in the green shadows, gripping the truck's sides as it jolted toward the highway. Through the dust-smeared window at the back of the truck, she saw cigarette guy turn and smile.

16

The next morning, Riley gathered her team in Investigations. All of them were weary, having worked late into the evening processing the scene at the meatpacking plant. By the time they'd finished, visiting hours at the old folks' home had ended, and there had been no time for Riley to get to her grandfather. She vowed to go to him this evening.

She'd struggled to sleep more than a few hours, the two cases churning in her mind: Chloe's savaged body mixing with the mutilated corpse of Nicole King. If they were connected, what sort of killer might they be dealing with? *A monster,* she thought, watching Amy Fox tape up the scene photographs Nolan had sent over from the plant.

The department was humming with word that another woman had been found dead, and Riley doubted it would be long before the press got wind of it. Chloe's murder had been sensational enough, dominating the headlines and pushing aside the latest news on Governor Hamilton and Senator Cook's tightening race. Reed had ordered her to keep a lid on things, but the pressure was building.

"OK. Let's go over where we are. Schmidt?"

"We're through the Brown family interviews. All except his elder sons. They're due back from Des Moines"—Schmidt paused to flip through his notebook—"tomorrow. Still looking into the Garret family, but, as you know, nothing has rung any alarm bells. Despite what that jerk, Sean Taylor, hinted."

Riley smiled slightly.

"Ed Wilson corroborated John Brown's version of events the night of Chloe Miller's death. But we've had no other reports of the drone."

Riley nodded. "I spoke to Special Services this morning. They've not been able to get anything from Chloe's cell. So that's likely a dead end. They're still going through her computer, but they've seen nothing—files or emails—that indicate she was having an affair. Or, for that matter, any sign she suspected her husband of having one. I checked in with State Patrol last night. No reports of her missing car. We've tracked some of James Miller's movements the night of his wife's death—spotted his car on CCTV, confirmed with the people he says he called. There are gaps, but five hours will be hard to account for if he was out alone looking for her. If he did suspect her of cheating, it certainly gives him motive, however, and I do feel there's something he's holding back. I want us to stay on his case."

"Anything specific, Sarge?" Logan asked.

"Miller thinks his wife was having an affair but is adamant none of her friends or family will corroborate this? Then we have Mia Collins pointing the finger of infidelity at him, suggesting he might have told Chloe he was volunteering at this soup kitchen to cover it?" Riley thought of James in the interview: that change in him when he'd found her looking at his photographs. *She wouldn't have told them anything.* She shook her head. "I don't know, it's just—"

"A hunch?" Schmidt finished with a crinkling of his eyes.

"Exactly." Riley felt her cell buzz in her pocket. She let it go to voice mail. "Schmidt, I want you to concentrate on the Miller case. Finish the interviews at Zephyr Farms, then head over to GFT. Speak to James Miller's boss there, his co-workers. Let's dig down into what kind of man he is. What his colleagues think of him. Logan and I will start work on Nicole King."

"Do you think they could be linked?" Schmidt ventured. "Miller and King?"

"We need to keep an open mind, for sure. Logan, I want us to take the photograph we found at the scene to the pharmacy those pills came from." Riley paused as the phone on her desk began to ring.

Fox leaned over and answered it. "Investigations."

"Let's see if we can identify who that backpack belongs to and—"

"Sarge." Fox held out the receiver, cupping the speaker with one hand. "It's Doctor Webb."

Riley took the phone, surprised. The medical examiner had only taken possession of Nicole King a few hours ago. "Fisher speaking."

"Sergeant, I've found something of interest on Nicole King." Kristen Webb sounded unusually rattled.

"You've done the autopsy?" Riley realized her colleagues were watching her. She turned away to listen.

"I've just started the external exam. I'm afraid this body will take me most of the morning. But I wanted to tell you what I've found so far. The deceased was strangled, that much is obvious, although I won't be able to give cause of death until I've inspected the other wounds on her, which," Webb sighed down the line, "are multiple."

Riley saw Nicole's ruined body, maggots squirming out of the flashlight, burrowing deeper into all those black holes.

"Some appear to have been caused by a sharp instrument with a tapered blade. I would say a knife of some kind. I should have specifics for you later. But she wasn't just stabbed, Sergeant. She was *hacked* at. Around the thighs in particular. There's a substantial amount of flesh missing that I don't believe is from maggot activity."

Riley thought of the wounds on Chloe's body—lacerations to the thigh and arm.

"Some of the damage appears to have been made postmortem," Webb continued. "Although, again, I won't be able to confirm anything until I've completed the autopsy. But I found something embedded in her thigh, deep in the damaged tissue. At first I thought it might be a chip of bone, but it's a fragment of tooth. Human tooth. Given how it was lodged in the tissue, I would say it most likely broke off in the wound."

"Bites?" Riley felt the scar on her neck prickle, as though her blood, not just her mind, was rushing to it. "Are you saying there's a connection? That those bite marks on Chloe were made by a person, not an animal? That the same person could have killed King?"

"I don't know," answered Webb. "And even when I've finished here, I doubt I'll be able to say that with any certainty. Not without DNA. Decomposition on both cadavers is too great for proper comparison of the marks themselves. Except, perhaps, by a specialist. I'll contact Bruce again. Tell him it's urgent. The good news is a tooth is a wonderful vehicle for DNA. The bad news is—"

"The state lab will take months to process it," Riley finished. "OK. Thank you. Call me as soon as you're done?"

"Of course."

As the line went dead, Riley took a breath, then turned back to her team. They listened in silence as she relayed what the ME had told her.

"Jesus," murmured Logan.

Amy Fox was staring at the scene photographs, her brow tight. Schmidt was rubbing his head.

"All right," said Riley. "Let's say, for a moment, that the same person did kill Chloe Miller and Nicole King."

"Killed and *bit* them," added Logan, his tone revealing some of the horror he felt.

Schmidt cut in. "Some of their injuries might be the same, Sarge, and certainly the scenes are similar in the sense of isolation. But our victims are worlds apart. Prostitute and addict—and wife of a wealthy bioengineer?"

"Nicole King would have been an easy target," Riley responded. "Someone a killer could have drawn to the plant in exchange for money, or drugs perhaps. Chloe Miller? Maybe she was pure chance? Opportunity? Maybe her husband was right? Maybe she *was* going to meet a lover? Somewhere out in the fields or on the roadside? Privacy. Secrecy. Our killer sees her out there waiting. Alone. Vulnerable." *Hands holding her down. Dirt in her mouth.* Riley forced out the images as they flashed in her mind. "The killer attacks and Chloe flees into the corn. He uses a drone to hunt for her, but is scared off when he spots John Brown's vehicle? He disposes of her car and cell phone. There are enough creeks and lakes around here."

"And the lover?" asked Schmidt.

"Someone else entirely. Someone whose date simply never shows up."

"He'd have seen her on the news by now."

"Would you come forward?" Riley questioned. "Admit you were having an affair with a married woman? A woman you were due to meet the night she was murdered?"

Logan grimaced in agreement. "We'll probably never find him."

"It might not matter if he had nothing to do with the attack. Saw nothing."

"The drone, though?" Logan went on. "I mean, some crazy asshole who lures a hooker to an abandoned factory, strangles and mutilates her, then jumps a well-to-do woman in the middle of nowhere and bites her to bits doesn't strike me as the sort that owns a nice piece of tech. That den—those belongings we found—they belong to some bum, Sarge. Bums don't own drones."

"Whoever was sleeping at the plant isn't necessarily the killer. A lot of people have been through that place. I want our vagrant for a witness though, if nothing else."

Logan exhaled. "So, what are we saying? That the killer could be a planner in the case of King *and* an opportunist in the case of Miller? Crazed, yes, but not crazy enough that he can't cover his tracks, vanish a car, maybe even use sophisticated technology? Someone with knowledge of the local area? Wait—I understand him not hiding Miller's body if she got away from him. But King? Why leave her there for someone to find? Why not dispose of her?"

"He's leaving a message?"

"For who?"

"The world? Us?" Riley shook her head. "Not all killers dispose of their victims. Some want them to be found."

"You're not using the word?" Logan looked her in the eye.

She knew what he meant. "We're not at three yet."

"Three?" asked Fox, looking between them.

"Let's get to the pharmacy, try and identify whose pills and belongings we found with King." Riley paused as Logan stood. "Schmidt, you'll go past James Miller's on the way to Zephyr?"

"I will."

"Pay him a visit, would you?"

Schmidt frowned. "We don't have time of death on King, Sarge. If it's his alibi you're after?"

"I know. But let's just make sure Miller has all his teeth."

The old detective's eyes widened. "Christ."

As she picked up her car keys, Riley's gaze caught on the poster of Gracie Foster, the teenager smiling sadly at her. For the first time, she hoped she was right—that the missing girl really was halfway across the country.

"Three, Sarge?" Fox pressed.

"Department guidelines state that it's three or more victims before we say serial killer."

17

"Ladies and gentlemen, please have your bags ready for inspection."

The group shuffled forward at the tour guide's instructions.

"No need to take off shoes or belts."

Faint amusement rippled through the small crowd as they jostled to deposit handbags and fanny packs on the table where a security guard was searching them.

Thorne waited her turn, allowing the crowd to move her with its tide. She smiled graciously when a fat man with a camera strung around his neck bumped against her, but all the while she watched the guard. Although his manner was friendly, he was giving each item a thorough check.

The carriage house—with its heavy drapes and thick carpets—was stuffy, the press of people making her sweat. She glanced at the door, which the guide had closed to the outside world. She could easily leave. But her feet carried her forward. If not now, then when?

Thorne placed her backpack on the table. The guard smiled, but she saw his eyebrows rise as he took in her short crop of hair dyed bubblegum pink. She cursed inwardly. Alex had told her—*Don't stand out, don't be memorable*—but she'd ignored his advice.

The guard chuckled. "You young'uns. My granddaughter has been every color of the rainbow." He pulled her hoodie from the bag, then a notepad and pencil case. "Couldn't pay her to come on a tour like this, mind."

She'd known her age, too, might single her out. Had an answer ready. "I'm studying history at Iowa State."

"Good for you, miss. Hey, Walter, watch out. We've got a history major here. The young lady might be after your job."

The tour guide broke off his conversation with some of the others to smile over at her.

The guard took out her reusable coffee cup. "Saving the planet too, eh?"

She couldn't even answer as he went to pop the lid. Jesus, fuck. Was he planning a cavity search? She hadn't expected this level of inspection. She was halfway to snatching the cup and running, but then a skinny man wearing an I Heart New York baseball cap fumbled with his bag, sending pens and keys skittering across the table.

"I'm sorry!"

"No problem, sir. Here, let me help." The guard put the unopened cup back into Thorne's bag and slid it toward her.

Thorne stuffed in the notebook and hoodie and slung the bag over her shoulder as the guard bent to help the man, who was still apologizing.

Moments later, the tour guide was ushering the group through a door, out into the dazzling morning. Thorne breathed in the grass-sweet air, the breeze drying the sweat on her forehead. Manicured lawns stretched away, bordered by trees. Ahead stood the mansion: three stories high, a ninety-foot tower soaring over the pitched roof. Built of brown brick and decorated with white eaves, it looked like a gingerbread house, rising in elaborate tiers. The guide led the group through the front doors into a magnificent vestibule, which smelled of polish.

"Ladies and gentlemen, welcome to the official residence of the governors of Iowa."

Thorne's eyes darted, spotting the security cameras as the group was shuffled from one stately chamber to another—a music room dominated by a Steinway grand, a drawing room where a maid was vacuuming, a dining room where state dinners were held. Cameras flashed across cabinets full of glassware and china as the guide explained the history of each room.

"As you can see, it is a fine example of Second Empire architecture." The guide led them back into the vestibule, where the staircase curled upward. "Although it was built in 1866, the mansion was considered extremely comfortable for its time. It had gas lighting, hot running water, and an elevator. There is an elevator in use today, which serves the private quarters of the governor and his family from their own entrance in the basement, where the kitchens are located, along with the office for the State Police, who protect the family."

"Will we be able to see the governor's quarters?" asked the man in the baseball cap, who'd dropped his bag at the desk.

"Only the first and second floors are open to the tour. But you will be able to see his public office, along with the chambers of some of his staff."

Up the stairs, past a stained-glass window, they reached a wide passageway that stretched in two directions, doors leading off. A young man hurried out of one, clutching some files.

"It is, of course, rather busy at present, what with a certain election coming up. Don't forget to vote!" the guide added, with a wink to the chuckling crowd.

The group was corralled around a door two down from the one the young man had emerged from, peering over each other's heads to get a look at the half-dozen people working inside the governor's office, busy at phones and computers.

Thorne stayed at the back. The young man with the files had disappeared and the passage was empty. She moved up to the guide. "Is there a restroom I can use?"

The guide hesitated. "Can you wait until we're back in the carriage house, miss?"

She pressed her lips together, shook her head. "Girl problems."

He went red. "Oh. Right. You can use the staff restroom." He pointed. "Fourth door on the left. We'll wait here for you."

As Thorne headed off, she felt him watching her go, but then the man in the baseball cap stepped in.

"Does the governor work in here?"

Thorne heard the guide reply as she hastened down the corridor.

"No, Governor Hamilton's day-to-day work is mostly conducted from his office in the capitol building. He also has a study in his private quarters upstairs."

Thorne reached the open door the young man had exited. She risked a look inside. Perfect. It was a smaller office, probably for clerks or secretaries. There were three desks with computers and phones on. Behind her, the young man was still talking to the guide, whose back was turned. She slipped in.

She dismissed the three terminals immediately—too exposed. There were cupboards built into the wall behind two of the desks. She knelt down, letting her backpack slide from her shoulder, to check one. There was nothing of use to her inside and the cupboard door creaked loudly as she closed it. She paused to listen for any sound of approach, sweat prickling under her arms. She could hear the guide droning on; the distant ring of phones.

She came to another cupboard, leads trailing to it from the desktop and printer. She looked inside and grinned at the green lights of the router—flashing like a landing strip.

Reaching into her bag, she pulled out the coffee cup and opened the lid. Inside was a Pineapple Nano. She withdrew the hacking device carefully and leaned into the cupboard, easing it into the router's free socket. *Easy as pie,* as her grandmother would have said.

She had closed the cupboard, stuffed her cup back in her bag and was almost at the door, when the young man returned, clutching more files. He blinked at her in surprise.

"I'm sorry," she gulped. "I was looking for the restroom."

"Two doors down," replied the man, frowning. "On your left. *Goddamn tourists,*" she heard him mutter as she stepped out into the passage.

An hour later and they were back in the carriage house, the tour ended. Thorne slipped away.

She was halfway down the street when she heard someone coming up behind her. She turned as a man fell into step beside her.

"Did you get it done?"

"Of course."

"Shit, girl! Alex would be proud."

Thorne smiled. "Quick thinking with the bag, Leo."

Leo grinned as he removed his I Heart New York baseball cap and ran a hand through his black hair. He shrugged off his plaid shirt, revealing skinny arms. The words tattooed along his forearm were as blue as his veins. They were so small they were almost unreadable, but she knew what they said. The same words were etched up her spine. Alex—her mentor—holding her hand as they were drilled into her skin.

As the seas rise, so shall we.

18

The rest of Riley's day was a bust. When she and Logan arrived at the pharmacy—with the pills and the photograph from the backpack at the plant—they found it closed for the afternoon. Instead, they turned their attention to Nicole King.

According to records, Nicole's father had vanished soon after her birth and her mother had died four years ago, the family home swallowed up by medical bills. The only kin she had left was an older sister working in finance in Bangkok and currently unreachable.

Nicole had been living in a room in a dilapidated shared house down near the river, overlooking San Souci Island. There was a Confederate flag hanging outside. Riley and Logan sat in the kitchen at a table covered in cigarette ends and empty pizza boxes, interviewing, as best they could over the barking of dogs chained in the yard, a motley crew of roommates that came and went through the afternoon, in various states of dress and inebriation.

Nicole had last been seen by any of them twelve days ago. Apparently, it wasn't unusual for her to go missing for weeks if she shacked up with one of her boyfriends, a search of whose names in the department's files brought up a pick n' mix of misdemeanors and felonies. They would all need to be questioned.

An inspection of her cramped room at the back of the house, where ivy had sneaked up the window to block out the light and husks of flies littered the sill, yielded more evidence of a life in decay: empty liquor bottles and half-eaten candy bars, tawdry scraps of clothing. The only memento of any hope was a photograph in a heart-shaped frame of a much younger Nicole with someone who looked so like her Riley guessed she had to be the sister, the two of them grinning, cheek to cheek.

It was a relief when Kristen Webb called with the autopsy report, allowing Riley to step out into the afternoon drizzle, leaving Logan to pick through the room. That relief was short-lived, Nicole King's last hours alive making for grim listening. She'd died approximately ten days ago, in the place where she was found. Stabbed, multiple times.

"It was a large, tapered blade," Webb confirmed. "I would say a standard kitchen knife you could buy at any homeware store. The inconsistent pattern and depth of the wounds indicate a frantic attack. It would have certainly incapacitated her. She was then strangled with the belt."

"Cause of death?" Riley asked.

"Decomposition complicates matters, but the physical evidence of the belt, hemorrhaging of the soft tissue of her neck, and fractures of the laryngeal skeleton give me good reason to believe that manual strangulation was the mechanism of death and, thus, asphyxiation the cause."

"Those wounds on her thighs? Where you found the tooth?"

"Well, yes. As I first thought those were made postmortem. Here's the thing, Sergeant: those injuries occurred *after* rigor mortis had passed. Meaning, whoever killed her was with her body for at least two to three days after death. The body is too degenerated to tell if she suffered any sexual assault, either ante or postmortem. I will, of course, send what I can for further testing. Bruce can't get away, but he'll take a look at the photographs and autopsy report."

After that, the day drawing on, Riley dropped Logan at the department, telling him to map their route tomorrow—from the pharmacy to the city's homeless shelters and the soup kitchen James Miller claimed to have been volunteering at.

Driving across town, running two red lights, she called her counterparts at Waterloo's and Cedar Falls's police departments, with whom she'd been coordinating the search for Gracie Foster—the missing girl nudged to the front of her mind with the deaths of Chloe and Nicole.

But there had been no sightings and no new calls to the hotline on the posters.

The clouds were starting to break, sunlight turning the puddles on the deserted lot to quicksilver as she crossed to the old folks' home. The weathered sign outside told her WRINKLES ONLY GO WHERE SMILES HAVE BEEN.

A TV in the reception area was replaying footage from the morning news: Governor Bill Hamilton inspecting a factory with the Chinese delegation, wearing a hard hat and Hi-Vis jacket, surrounded by a bustle of press and security. Hamilton was making a speech about the importance of the long-standing relationship between Iowa and China, hailing a new era of cooperation and opportunity.

As the camera zoomed in on him, Riley thought of the last time she'd seen the governor in person, twelve years ago, at her parents' funeral. Hamilton had been standing in the pew behind her, head bowed. It was just weeks after he'd been elected for his first term. His hand on her shoulder at the graveside, breath fogging the air as he told her he couldn't have done it without her father. His hotshot lawyer.

The news camera switched to show a group of environmental protestors outside the factory gates. There was a sea of placards hoisted over their heads.

AGRI-CO? AGRI-NO!
BIG AG—BIG TROUBLE!

As the governor's motorcade sped past, the protestors held up their hands, painted bloodred.

"You don't have long," remarked the receptionist, tapping her watch at Riley.

Two orderlies were waiting at the elevator with a woman in a wheelchair, so Riley took the stairs up to the fifth floor, where the corridors smelled of disinfectant and boiled meat. In several rooms the TV volume was turned up so high the canned laughter of game shows sounded like eruptions in a stadium. She came to her grandfather's door and was about to enter when her cell vibrated. It was a voice mail from Sheriff Reed.

"Fisher, I want you in my office. First thing."

He didn't sound pleased.

The room was small, its walls flushed in the day's dying light. It was dominated by a hospital bed. A prairie rose stood on the windowsill, in a pot of misshapen clay Maddie had made in fifth grade. There were prints on the walls, Iowa landscapes, which Riley had brought from home, along with one of her grandmother's quilts. There used to be family photographs, but she had taken them away when they'd begun to confuse him.

Joe Fisher was sitting in the worn armchair, wearing striped pajamas and a robe. He only had one slipper on. The other was on the floor in front of him. His bare foot was pale, toes curling under themselves. It was hard to believe this shrunken man with the vacant stare had once been the gold-starred heart of Black Hawk County, back when a sheriff knew the names of most people on his patch, the histories of families going back to settler times, which troubled young men to watch out for, which farms were selling red diesel. He was rarely seen behind a desk, but out there tipping his hat to ladies on Main Street, laughing with the waitresses at the Maid-Rite over a loose-meat sandwich, talking to farmers out in the boonies, almost as knowledgeable about the land, the weather, and its ways as they were long before Agri-Co had risen to dominance. To go from all that purpose, all that respect, to nothing. Home—while the balloons from the retirement party were deflating—to a rambling old house of memories, his wife dead and buried the year before.

At first he'd been OK, hunting and fishing, coming with them on vacations to Lake Okoboji, keeping up with old colleagues down at the diner. There had been enough family drama in those years to keep him occupied, keep him needed. But then he'd lost his son and his daughter-in-law to ice and a dark November road, and a speeding truck that never slowed. After the car wreck, things had begun to change. First, he started losing keys, forgetting names or words. Then, he started vanishing.

Riley, then a deputy, would come home from a graveyard shift and find him pulling up in his rusted pickup, dressed in his pajamas, no idea of where he'd been. There were falls and visits to the emergency room, a fire in the kitchen when he'd left the stove on. And once he'd wandered, lost and naked, into Maddie's room. Unable to trust Ethan, whose marriage was in its long, torturous collapse, she'd relied on Rose to help care for him, but then Lori miscarried again. It had been one of the most painful decisions of her life, but in the end, Riley had been forced to send her grandfather here, to a room without memories, where what remained of his own drifted away. A tide that would never come back in. That was seven years ago.

"Hi, Grandpa." Riley gently slid his fallen slipper back on. "You won't get far in one shoe, will you?" After smoothing down his hair and kissing his cheek, she pulled the chair out from the table by the bed and sat, taking his gnarled hand in hers. His skin was paper crumpled over his bones. "Rose said you were asking after me?" Riley searched his face, but she could see he was gone, sinking back into the fog. Her throat tightened. Was that the last time he would ask for her? "She sends her love. Lori too. And Maddie, of course . . ."

She trailed off, unable to maintain the charade. She didn't want to talk about the meaningless or mundane. She wanted to talk to him about this case—about the memories that had been dragging her down into the murk of the past since she'd seen Chloe's body curled among those cornstalks. The uneasy sense of recognition she'd felt with Nicole King's death had only been sharpened by the woman's life. That dingy room where King had washed up with her sad flotsam and jetsam was grimly familiar to Riley. It was a rundown apartment, nearly two thousand miles away, where her grandfather had finally found her, nineteen years ago. The man in the chair couldn't even remember his own name, but to her the memory was clear as glass.

She remembered the smell on the bedcovers: patchouli and cannabis; clothes strewn across the dirty carpet, the tie-dyed sheet hanging in place of a curtain, warm, salt-tanged air drifting through the window, the sound of waves rushing and receding. She remembered the door opening and one of the girls from down the hall entering with a murmured apology, a figure emerging behind her.

She remembered the disbelief at seeing her grandfather standing there; the rush of love that dissolved in scalding shame as he took in her shabby clothes, the piercings, the dyed hair—the things she had attempted to make herself someone new, the things she had done to try to forget who she was. But Joe Fisher had seen right through it all to the child she had been—before that night at the state fair. The night the gold star necklace he'd bought with his good money had been torn from her as she'd struggled in the dirt. The night she had lost that gift and so much more.

She had cried in his arms while outside the ocean broke against the shore and gulls screamed over the heads of the muscle boys and tarot readers on Venice Beach.

But that man—the one who saved her, brought her home, got her straight and persuaded her into a criminology degree, then the law enforcement academy—was gone. He couldn't help her now. No more than she could help him.

As the door opened and an orderly told her visiting hours were over, Riley stood. Bending, she kissed her grandfather's brow, then left, the harsh discharge of game-show laughter following her down the hallway.

19

What the hell was Hunch doing checking Miller's teeth?"
Riley swore inwardly. Schmidt had texted yesterday to say
he'd done as she had asked. But who had told Sheriff Reed? Her mind
jumped instinctively to Jackson Cole, but although she knew the son of
a bitch would leap at any chance to undermine her, she doubted any of
her team would have spoken to him about this. "I'm sorry, sir. Schmidt
was following my orders."

Reed's eye twitched his displeasure. "Well?"

"I sent you the latest autopsy report from Kristen Webb? She believes
there could be a connection between Chloe Miller and Nicole King. The
bite marks? The broken tooth found in King's body?"

"And?"

"I had cause to consider James Miller as a potential suspect in his wife's
murder. I had to check if he could also be a suspect in King's, given the
possible connection. Without DNA this was the quickest way."

Reed sat forward. "I'll give you a connection, Fisher. James Miller
is an acquaintance of Mayor Angela Roberts. She called me last night,
wanting to know why the grieving husband of this poor murdered
woman was being hounded by my officers at this difficult time."

Shit.

"I agree it wasn't the most subtle course of action. But Miller's alibi is
patchy, and his story doesn't add up. Sir, would you not report your wife
missing after three nights? Even if you thought she was having an affair?"

Reed turned beet red up to his ears. "Neither of those things are enough to build a solid case, and you know it. Suspicion is all well and good, Sergeant. But we must rely on facts. And the fact I want you to rely upon today, and going forward in this investigation, is that James Miller is an affluent and well-respected man in our community. I want you to start treading more carefully. There's a difference between being thorough and being a Goddamn pain in the ass."

"Yes, sir."

Reed grunted and opened one of the files in front of him. "And did he?"

"Sir?"

"Have all his teeth?"

Schmidt said Miller had a perfect set of veneers. "Yes."

Reed picked up a pen. "I said before if I thought your association with Miller's wife was affecting your ability to do your job in any way, I would take action." He let the threat hang there.

"It won't, sir."

As she left Reed's office, Riley hoped she'd sounded firmer than she felt. She'd not been able to get Chloe out of her mind and, now, Nicole King had joined her in the darkness. The horror of both women's last moments alive had crawled under her skin. She felt connected to them in ways she couldn't articulate. Perhaps it was true—she would have been able to separate herself more if her old friend wasn't one of the victims. Chloe was tied to her past like an anchor, and all that tangled mess she'd left down there beneath the years had been coming up at every turn of the investigation. Maybe Reed was right to question her suitability to lead this case.

No, she told herself. She had been right to check out James Miller, if only to discount him. Just because the man was wealthy and well-connected didn't mean he wasn't capable of terrible things. If her past had taught her anything it was that real-life monsters weren't like those in fairy tales—humps and warts and masks to warn you. Sometimes, they were successful and powerful. Sometimes, handsome and well-mannered. The kind of nice young man you brought home to meet your family.

Logan was alone in Investigations, Schmidt having left to speak to Miller's colleagues at GFT, Amy Fox due to interview John Brown's sons at Zephyr Farms. There had been news that morning from Bob Nolan. The analysis from the partial tire imprint on the dirt track by the cornfield had come back. It was a Goodyear, designed for ice and rough terrain, a popular brand that would fit a van or pickup truck, but half the Midwest owned one of those. The tire was also fairly new, a disadvantage in that it hadn't had time to develop any distinguishing features that might narrow the search.

When Riley rapped on the window, Logan jumped up and grabbed his jacket.

"How was Reed?" he asked as they headed downstairs.

"His usual sunny self."

"Hey, I meant to ask—what are you doing for Fourth of July?"

Riley was caught off guard by the question. She hadn't even thought about the holiday. It was less than a week away.

"We're having a party," Logan continued, walking beside her out into the parking lot. "That is, if you have no plans?"

She felt herself blushing. When was the last time her family had celebrated any holiday together? She was pretty sure Logan had guessed as much. God, was she really such an object of pity? "I . . . ? Well, sure."

"Bring Maddie, too, and anyone else," he added over the roof of the Dodge. "Mom and Carol will make enough food for the whole state."

Ten minutes later, they were at the pharmacy in Waterloo.

The pharmacist stared at the crumpled photograph of the man, woman, and two boys on the beach, sealed in the evidence bag. "No, ma'am. I don't know them."

Riley held out another bag with the two pill bottles they'd found at the meatpacking plant—one in the backpack with the photograph, the other near King's body. One had a few white tablets left inside. "What about these drugs? They came from here, yes?"

The pharmacist peered at them. "Well, ma'am, the label sure says so."

"Can you tell me what they are?"

He held the bottle up to the light, reading the letter and numbers embossed on the pills. "Fenozen. It's a phenobarbital."

"What would that be prescribed for, sir?"

The bell on the door of the pharmacy chimed as someone entered. "It's a barbiturate." The pharmacist glanced over Riley's shoulder at the line of people starting to form. "It's sometimes given as an anticonvulsant, but mostly I see it prescribed as a sedative hypnotic, usually for people who suffer with anxiety or sleep disorders. Drug addicts are sometimes put on it when they're in recovery. Helps them through the worst of the withdrawal." He turned and went to the counter behind him. He moved his hand along the top shelf, plucked down a white box. "Fenozen is fairly new on the market. Slightly less addictive than other brands, apparently."

As Riley took the box from him, she heard an elderly woman behind her sigh pointedly. "Is there somewhere we can talk more privately, sir?"

The pharmacist shook his head, the fluorescent lights winking off his glasses. "It's only Jeanie in today," he said, nodding to a young woman stacking shelves. "And she can't work the counter."

"OK, then perhaps you can tell me, sir, is it normal for a label to be left blank, without drug or patient information?"

"No, ma'am."

"So how would these be out there? In someone's possession?"

A sheen of sweat had broken out on his forehead. His eyes darted to the people waiting.

"Sir?" pressed Logan, tapping a finger on the countertop to catch his attention.

The pharmacist leaned in, so close Riley could smell the Altoids on his breath. "Listen, I had some problems with staff a while back. I found drugs were going missing." His voice was low. "Fentanyl. Viagra. Prozac." He nodded to the box in her hands. "But mostly Fenozen."

Riley nodded. "The kind of drugs you can sell on the street?"

"Yes, ma'am. We never found out who it was. I had three women working for me at the time, but none confessed. I had to fire them." His voice rose, as if he was speaking to the rest of the people waiting in line. "I've been run off my feet ever since."

"Did you report the thefts, sir?" He flushed and Riley knew the answer. "OK, we'll need the names and addresses of the three employees you fired."

"I'll have to look out back."

"We can wait."

As the pharmacist disappeared through a side door, keeping it wedged open with one foot while he rifled through a filing cabinet, the line of people waiting coughed and shuffled.

Riley read the label on the box of Fenozen. The list of possible side effects was long. *Nausea, shortness of breath, skin rashes, mood swings, suicidal thoughts.* They sounded as bad as the problems they were prescribed for. Setting it on the counter, she scanned the rows of boxes on the shelves. Drugs to keep you awake and put you to sleep. Drugs to make you hard and make you happy. Make you forget. She thought of her mom's dazed, chemical smile in those last years.

She'd been on the pills when Riley returned home from California with her grandfather. No matter how relieved her mom had been to see her, no matter how pleased she was to watch her finish her senior year, or how proud she was that Riley made it into the University of Northern Iowa, graduating with honors before being accepted into the Iowa Law Enforcement Academy, she never came off those drugs. Riley had read a magazine article that claimed in the past year America had seen more of its own dead from fentanyl, heroin, and prescription opioids than were lost in the whole of the Vietnam War.

The pharmacist reappeared and placed a folded piece of paper on the counter. Logan picked it up.

"Hello, Mrs. Smith," they heard him trill as they headed for the door. "Your prescription is ready."

Outside, Riley slid her shades on. The clouds had dissolved overnight, leaving a pristine sky. The heat was rising. By midday, the tar on the roads would soften and suck at their feet. She headed to the Dodge. "OK, we've got the food bank on Dubuque, right? Then the soup kitchen."

"Sarge." Logan had halted and was looking at the piece of paper the pharmacist had given them. "What's Gracie Foster's mom called?"

"Sarah Foster. Why?"

Logan walked to her, holding out the paper. Riley stared at the second name down, scribbled in the pharmacist's unsteady hand.

H ey, Fox! They let you out on your own?"

Amy Fox glanced up as she crossed the lot to see Chad Becker and another deputy heading toward her.

"Not riding along with Hunch today?" called Becker. "Bet he's gutted."

"Yeah," laughed the other. "The old fart's totally Schmitten!"

The two men laughed harder as she flipped them the bird. Becker broke into the song they'd been singing since she arrived at the department.

"Foxy Lady."

He was still singing as they disappeared inside the department.

"Dicks," murmured Fox, opening the squad car door.

A shadow moved up behind her. "Real originals, aren't they?"

She turned quickly to see Sean Taylor from *The Courier*.

The reporter had one hand up, shielding his eyes from the sun. "Heading out to Zephyr Farms again? Hey, wait," Taylor urged as she went to get into the car. "I've got some info for Sergeant Fisher."

"The Garret family, I know. They've got no records, Mr. Taylor, so unless you—"

"There isn't a record. Not for this. Look, I admit, I was fishing when I spoke to your boss before. I do have information on the Garret family. But it was a stretch. Just because a woman was found dead on their land doesn't mean anyone there did it, right? But I've got a source at the medical examiner's office who told me this morning there's another body. A hooker found dead at the old meatpacking plant? Strangled with a belt?"

Fox cursed beneath her breath and made a mental note to call Riley when she was on the road. "OK," she said carefully.

"Well, I might not have been that far off the mark as it turns out." Taylor ran a hand through his receding hair.

Fox thought he looked genuinely concerned. "Tell me."

"I need something in return." Taylor held up his hand as she shook her head. "You've got your boss to impress, and I've got mine. We can help each other here. This body at the plant? Something's got everyone down at the ME's office real jumpy. I heard there's a connection between the two bodies. Something weird. Look, I know most of it, don't I? I'll get the rest by this evening, or you can give me what I need now, and I'll give you something that could break this case open."

Fox paused, but her mind filled with Becker's mocking laughter. "Bites," she told him. "There were bite marks on both bodies and flesh missing. We found a tooth. Human."

"Jesus," murmured Taylor, but his eyes gleamed like cheap jewels.

"OK. Your turn."

"Hoyt Garret. The youngest son? He had a nickname back in school." Fox shook her head irritably. "A nickname?"

"Yeah. They used to call him Hangman Hoyt."

20

The church on West Fourth Street was filled with the clatter of dishes and a sulfurous smell of boiled eggs and unwashed clothes. Riley made her way through the snaking line of people to join Logan.

"You get through to Sarah Foster?" he asked.

"Went to voice mail. I left a message." Riley cocked her head questioningly. Logan was in the line of shuffling men and women holding trays as they made their way toward the volunteers spooning out food on a row of tables in front of the altar. Christ hung from a gaudy gold cross above them. "You hoping for some breakfast?"

"Apparently, we have to wait in line with everyone else." Logan nodded to the volunteers. "Look at their aprons, Sarge."

Riley peered over the shoulders of those in front of her. She realized the volunteers' aprons were all emblazoned with the same logo: three yellow ears of corn against a red rising sun. It was the logo for Zephyr Farms. She frowned thoughtfully. "Miller said he didn't know anyone at the cooperative."

"Maybe he didn't. It is just a logo."

"You moving, miss?" said a man behind them, his words lisping through the gap left by his missing front teeth. His hair and beard were straggly, his cheeks veined red. He wore an old Christmas sweater that was too big for him, the Santa on the front bobbly with wear.

"You think it's a coincidence?" Logan asked as they inched forward, closing the gap. "Sarah Foster, I mean? She gets fired for possibly stealing drugs. Her daughter goes missing. Then pills from the same pharmacy turn up with Nicole King's body?"

"Foster's a drunk and an addict. If she stole the drugs, she maybe sold them to fund her own habit. Perhaps our missing vagrant bought some from her? That could be the link, if there is one." Riley met his gaze. "But I am getting more worried about Gracie."

Logan nodded.

"You aren't here for food, are you?" asked the elderly woman at the head of the line of volunteers, eyeing Riley and Logan, whose clothes marked them distinctly apart from the tattered congregation.

"No, ma'am." Riley showed her badge.

The woman exhaled and let the ladle she was holding rest against the side of the pot. Inside was a yellow sludge that Riley recognized as cornmeal mush. Her grandmother used to serve it on winter mornings. The cornmeal was made from dried maize kernels ground down into coarse powder. Her grandmother would boil it with water, then bring it to the table smothered in maple syrup.

"We thought you might come," the woman said, nodding to the other servers, some of whom were glancing over. "We've all seen the news." She touched a silver cross that hung around her neck. "God bless that poor woman. What James must be going through?"

Riley took out her notebook. "You know James Miller, Mrs.—?"

"Mrs. Allen. Doris Allen." She watched Riley write her name. "James is a volunteer here. Such a sweet young man."

"Is there somewhere we can talk?"

Doris took up her ladle. "I've got to get this cornmeal out while it's hot, dear."

"Just a few quick questions," Riley pressed. "How long has James been volunteering?"

"He started showing up a few months ago."

"How often does he work here?"

"Usually just once a week. I know he has some fancy job, so he can't come more often. I think he volunteers at other places, too. He's a real charitable soul."

"Do you know where else?"

Doris shook her head.

"Might someone here know? Is he particularly close to anyone?" Riley's gaze went down the line of volunteers. They were all over sixty. None looked likely candidates for an affair.

"We don't get the chance to socialize while doing God's work," said Doris, giving the cornmeal a brisk stir.

"Of course."

Doris paused, setting down the ladle again. "James keeps to himself. We get people like him from time to time—those who've done well in life. Some genuinely want to give something back. Others feel guilty. Some folk think it'll give them a bit of extra credit." She flicked her eyes toward Christ on his cross. "When their day comes." She nodded to the waiting line. "But James always takes the time to talk to our flock here."

The straggle-bearded man in the Christmas sweater huffed.

"We'll be moving along in a minute, sir," Logan told him.

"Are you part of Zephyr Farms, Mrs. Allen?"

Doris glanced down at her apron. "Oh, no, they're our sponsors." Her face brightened. "Been giving us their surplus cornmeal for the past two years, God bless them." Her expression changed. "Is it true? Was it their fields she was found on?"

Riley nodded. "Do you know if James or his wife had any connection to Zephyr? Did he talk about them at all?"

Doris shook her head. "But as I said, dear, none of us know him well."

"Just one last thing, ma'am. Do you recognize anyone in this picture?"

Riley nodded to Logan, who handed over the photograph in the evidence bag.

"It's possible the man there is a drifter," Logan told Doris as she took it. "He might have been staying out at the old meatpacking plant."

Her nose wrinkled. "That place?" Her eyes narrowed at the picture. "I'm sorry, no."

The straggle-bearded man mumbled something.

Riley glanced around. "We're just leaving, sir."

"Nah." The man pointed to the picture as Doris offered it back to Logan. "That's George."

"George?" said Doris. "George Anderson?" She peered closer. "Goodness, yes, I think Roger might be right. He looks a lot different now. Lost a lot of weight. But I think that's George."

"Do you know where we might find him?"

"Down with the war boys," the man lisped at Riley. "By the cement works."

"War boys?"

"Them who served—the Gulf, Afghanistan. They stick together mostly. George was in Iraq, 'gainst that Saddam motherfucker."

"Roger," murmured Doris, glancing apologetically up at Jesus.

The man continued, eyes on Riley. "Anderson did three tours in that hellhole. Came home when he got two fingers blown off."

Riley glanced at the picture. The man's left hand was visible, on one of the boy's shoulders, but his right was hidden by the folds of the blanket. "Do you know how he ended up on the street?"

Roger picked at the Santa on his sweater. His hand was red with scabs, his skin peeling like paper. "Come home expecting some big parade, balloons and trumpets down Main Street. But all you get is nightmares and rage. Wife don't know you no more. Kids are scared. Drink and drugs, then you've lost it all. This fucking country, man." He ignored Doris's wince. "You give your blood, but it ain't enough. It'll suck you dry."

21

Flies droned beneath the light, occasionally descending into a rapid spiraling dance. The kitchen was lit dully by the single bulb, its jaundiced glow washing over the mess of unwashed pans and stained counters, the litter of pill packets and bottles.

He no longer knew what time of day it was. No longer knew much of anything. The smell rising from the frying pan had driven out all other thoughts. The craving was overwhelming, flooding his whole being, intoxicating him. His mouth was juicy with expectation. Fat from the dark sliver of meat sizzled and spat in the pan, prickling his skin. He scratched at his arm, nails nicking more of the scabs, fresh blood beading. Out in the yard, his dog howled.

His stomach cramped, pain needling deep in his guts. He doubled over, fingers grasping for one of the white bottles strewn among the squalor. His hands shook as he flipped the lid. Pills scattered across the counter.

"Fuck." The curse came out slurred, his tongue swollen.

Leaving the meat sizzling in the pan, he pushed one of the pills into his mouth and clawed his way to the sink. It was black with dirt, a foul odor drifting from the drain. He ran the tap and stuck his head under. Copper-tasting water coursed down his throat. He gulped and retched on the pill, then swallowed it down. His vision swam, and he clutched the edges of the sink as the pain gripped him again.

As it subsided, he saw, through watery eyes, that the sink was streaked red. There were crimson marks in the shapes of his fingers all around the edges. He turned his hands over. In the dull light he could see they were coated in blood. He knew it well. Had worked half a lifetime in it.

These big, rough hands had once dumped the carcasses on the boards, stripped back flesh, and hacked apart bone, delved into bags of kidneys still warm from the abattoir. But that was back before they reared animals in cages so cramped they grew up crippled. Back before the drugs were pumped into them to make them bigger, fatter. Before their diseased carcasses were drenched in chlorine and packaged up for the store shelves. Before the local slaughterhouses and family butchers went under, and his job with them.

His eyes flicked to the counter, shadows dancing at the edges of his vision. There, on a thick wooden board, was the slab of flesh he had carved a slice from earlier, the severed edge still seeping blood. He berated himself for leaving it out in this heat. He couldn't afford to let it spoil. Not this meat. The smell drew him back to the pan. The pain in his stomach was gone; just the deep hollow of hunger remained.

22

Yeah, that's George Anderson."

The man sat back, wiping his nose with the back of his hand. He had sores on his knuckles, mottled over a tattoo that disappeared beneath the frayed sleeve of his flannel shirt. The two men he was sitting against the wall with were both nodding at the photograph. The one on the right was clutching a bottle in a paper bag. The one on the left only had one leg. The leg of his pants was tied off with a rubber band. A pair of battered crutches lay in the dirt beside him.

The wall behind them was plastered with graffiti; the pointless vandalism of kids desperate to make their mark. Not many people would see their tags on this dead-end road that led to the cement works. There was a flyover nearby, the rumble of trucks like distant thunder. In its shadow, rubbish drifted. Strung-up tarps undulated in the hot wind that blew grit into Riley's eyes.

She took the photograph back. "When did you last see him, Mr.—?"

"Tom," replied the man who'd spoken, peering up at her, his yellowed eyes full of sunlight. He picked thoughtfully at a scab on his neck, blood beading. "George ain't been around in . . . ?" He looked at the other two.

"Few weeks," said the man with the bottle, taking a swig. "You got any smokes, lady?" He looked between her and Logan.

"I'm sorry, no. We think George might have been sleeping out at the old meatpacking plant, near Black Hawk Creek."

"No one's crazy enough to sleep there."

"Yeah, I heard he was out there," said the man with one leg. He nodded when his comrades looked at him. "Dennis told me. Said George was acting real strange."

"Dennis Packer was that?" Tom chuckled. "He's one to talk. Man's fucking loony tunes."

"George was acting strange how?" Riley asked.

The man with one leg shrugged. "I dunno. Ask Dennis Packer."

"Where can we find him?"

"In the ground," replied the one with the drink. "Died last week."

"Shit," said the man with one leg. "I didn't know that." He grabbed the bottle, raised it, and took a swig. "God bless that crazy fuck!"

Logan passed them a photograph of the backpack they'd found at the scene, men's clothing strewn around it. "Do you recognize these?"

"Yup," answered Tom. "That's George's stuff. What d'you want with him, anyway?"

"We need to speak to him about a woman. A sex worker called Nicole King."

Tom gave a rough bark of laughter. "George? With a hooker? No chance."

"Why do you say that?" Logan asked.

"George was always talking about his wife." Tom nodded to the photograph in Riley's hand. "He kept that picture on him all the time. Used to kiss it and say a prayer before he bedded down. That's his wife, Abby, and his two boys. They went to her family in Kansas City when the house was repo'd. George hoped she would take him back once he got himself clean. He'd never get with some skank."

"He was on drugs?"

Tom shrugged.

"Fenozen?" Riley prompted.

Tom chuckled. "Yeah, he was on the purple hearts. Couldn't get enough of them."

"Purple hearts?"

"It's what we call 'em," answered the man with one leg. "No medals for us—just drugs to help us sleep. Cut through the nightmares. Purple hearts do the job. Or benzos or red birds."

Tom spoke again. "George took what he could to help. He was fucked up after his third tour. He didn't just lose his fingers. Man near lost his mind out there." He shared a look with the other two. The one clutching the drink grunted knowingly.

"Did he ever get prescription drugs from a woman named Sarah Foster?"

"Foster?" interjected the man with one leg. "Say, ain't that the name of the girl what's missing?"

"Gracie Foster," said Riley. "Sarah's her mom. Do you know them?"

"Nope. Just seen the posters all over."

"Strikes me there're a lot of things two cops could be doing today, rather than chewing the fat with us," added Tom. "Missing girl. Missing George."

"Why do you say George is missing?"

Tom gestured to the picture. "George wouldn't have left that. Or his stuff. Man in our situation leaves those things behind, he ain't coming back. I'd check the river if I were you."

"Or the vanishers got him?" mused the man with the drink.

"Vanishers?" Riley asked.

"That's classified," said the man, taking a swig. His eyes swiveled to Tom. "What does it matter to them if a few of us get disappeared? They won't do shit." He looked back at Riley. "Why don't you go do your job, eh? Leave us be?"

Riley reached for her wallet. "It matters to me," she said, meeting the man's hooded eyes. She pulled out two twenty-dollar bills. The three men watched her. "It matters very much." She held the notes out. The man with the drink licked his lips but let Tom take the cash.

"None of us have seen it," said Tom, pushing the money into the pocket of his worn-out jeans. "But folk at the shelters have spoken of it. A white van snatching people off the street."

"I've heard no reports of anything like that."

"Why would you? These are people who have nothing. No one. Who's gonna report them missing?"

"Reckon they're harvesters," said the younger man with one leg.

"I heard about the Chinese disappearing prisoners and stealing their organs to sell to rich people."

Tom shook his head. "Nah, what would they want with old George's parts? I reckon it's some company doing experiments."

"Or the U.S. Army," offered the man with the drink. "After recruits."

"Thankfully, I'm fucked," said the one-legged man, grinning.

Riley met Logan's gaze. She wished she hadn't given up the money so readily. "OK, well, if—"

"We're telling the truth, lady," said Tom, his yellow eyes unblinking. "We don't know who they are, but we know they're out there. Taking people."

"A white van isn't much for us to go on," said Logan. "What about make? Model? Plates?"

"You offering me a job?" Tom laughed humorlessly and shook his head. "Then fuck off and do yours."

Riley and Logan walked back to where they'd parked, leaving the men to their sun-seared slab of wall.

"Vanishers?" said Riley, arching an eyebrow. "That's a new one."

"People snatchers? Organ harvesting?" Logan looked back at the men as he reached the Dodge. "They were playing us like fiddles."

Riley exhaled, feeling foolish for handing over the cash. "Still, I'll see if there're any reports that match up. We need to find Anderson, if he's out there." She paused. "This Dennis Packer they mentioned? Webb said she'd had a few homeless come in recently. I'll check with her, see if any of them have been ID'd." She pulled out her cell.

"You hungry, Sarge?" Logan nodded to the backseat, where he'd deposited a cooler earlier. "I packed enough for two. It'll be better than your usual plastic crap. No ranch dressing for a start."

She put the cell to her ear. "Hey. Iowa was built on ranch."

"You know they use some of the same ingredients in paint?"

"You really take the fun out of things." Riley listened to the phone ring. "OK, I'll share your rabbit food." She slid into the car and turned the AC on while Logan got the cooler. Webb's phone had gone to voice mail, and Riley was about to leave a message when she heard Logan shout. There was a clatter and Logan jumped back. "What the hell?" Riley was out of the car in an instant. "Logan?"

Logan was on the curb, staring down at the scattered contents of the cooler. Among the foil packages and Tupperware boxes of salad and fruit was a slab of raw meat. Riley realized it was the tongue of some animal— hog by the size of it, its liver-colored surface mottled and cracked, black veins and gristle protruding from the severed end. She glanced at Logan, who looked genuinely shocked, thrusting a hand through his hair. Looking back at the tongue, Riley knew who had put it in there. Saw by Logan's hardening expression that he knew, too.

"Cole," she murmured.

23

Thorne looked up from her laptop at the sound of an approaching car. It was an SUV. Female driver, no one else inside. Thorne watched, but the woman didn't even glance in the direction of the old Mustang parked on the side of the road. The streets around the governor's mansion were some of the wealthiest in Des Moines, and she'd worried her rusted American Muscle might receive unwanted attention, but the place was quiet. She could see the mansion through the trees, rising beyond the carriage house. Its grounds were empty. No tours today.

"Bet she's got one kid, max," said Leo, following the SUV in the rearview mirror.

Thorne was back to tapping at the keys. "What?"

"Seven seats? Bet she's only got one kid."

"This isn't exactly a gas sipper," Thorne murmured, adjusting the GorillaPod that was gripping the can to the door handle. The cantenna—the first directional waveguide antenna she'd made under Alex's supervision—was covered in stickers, hiding the Pringles label. She checked the screen again.

"Not the same. You inherited this." Leo shrugged. "You'd never buy a new one."

True. She hadn't even wanted the Mustang, which had lived in the darkness of her grandmother's garage since her father's death. It was the only thing, except for life, he'd given her. She had toyed with selling it, but Alex said it would be worth keeping if it helped the cause. It was the last thing he'd said before he went on the run after Polk County, the FBI closing in.

"We're in!" She smiled in triumph as the cantenna picked up her Pineapple Nano connected to the router in the cupboard and masquerading as part of the mansion's WiFi network—a perfect man in the middle, allowing her to search their systems without breaking any firewalls. Thorne scanned the list of devices—desktops and printers, laptops, even music systems. Several, as hoped, were poorly configured. "Don't leave your doors open, people."

Leo chuckled over her shoulder.

Thorne's grin widened. "Campaign strategy meetings. Personnel files." She scrolled through photographs of staff—job descriptions and references sliding up the screen.

"Hey, go back. There." Leo tapped the screen on a photograph of a square-jawed, unsmiling bald man. "I've seen him at the rallies. Looked like protection. Not State Police, though."

"Gage Walker," said Thorne, reading from the file. "Says here he joined the governor's detail a year ago. Head of Rampart." She glanced at Leo. "Alex mentioned them, I think?"

Leo already had his cell out and was searching. "Yeah. Rampart. Private security company. Former cops, ex-army, and cyber operations specialists. Pride themselves on discretion and efficiency." He raised an eyebrow. "Euphemisms for we'll fuck everyone up and not tell anyone?"

Thorne continued to read Walker's file. Former U.S. Special Forces, tours in Iraq, Afghanistan, South Sudan. HALO and HazMat qualified. What would the governor, already well protected by State Police, want with such a team?

Leo read her mind. "Maybe the son of a bitch is finally getting it? That he's gonna need even more protection if he wins this election? That we're just getting started."

Thorne nodded, but looking at Gage Walker's résumé, Rampart seemed like overkill. She left the personnel files and continued scanning the network for more devices. "Look at this." She pointed to a desktop listed as *Governor 1*. Beneath it was a laptop named *Governor 2*. "All these open ports!"

"What a chump!" Leo laughed, waving his hands in the air. "Hello, hackers! Here I am!"

"OK. Let's . . ." Thorne paused, her fingers poised over the keyboard. Suddenly, she disconnected from the Pineapple and shut the screen.

"Hey!"

She turned to him. "You hire a private security team who specialize in cyber operations, then leave the door wide open for anyone with a Pringles can and a device you can buy on Amazon?"

"But . . ." Leo's face had already fallen. He let the protest trail off.

"It's a honeypot. If I go in, they'll trace me. *Damn it!*" She smacked the dashboard with feeling.

Leo slumped in his seat as Thorne took down the cantenna. "Cook could win? She is ahead now."

"The election is months away. Anything could happen. We have to make *sure* she wins." Thorne turned the key in the ignition. "We go to Plan B."

"Fuck," murmured Leo, closing his eyes.

24

The phone on her desk was ringing as Riley entered Investigations. She set down her coffee and grabbed the handset. "Sergeant Fisher, Invest— Ah, Doctor Webb, thanks for getting back." Riley glanced up as Schmidt entered. The old detective looked eager, eyes on her as he flung his jacket on the back of his chair.

"I heard back from Bruce early this morning," Webb told her, down the line.

"Bruce?"

"The forensic odontologist. He's reviewed the crime scene photographs I sent him from Miller and King focusing on their injuries. The areas of missing flesh, the fragment of tooth. He supports my assessment that the bite marks are most likely human."

Riley's hand drifted toward her neck; the white circle of scar tissue. When she saw Hunch was still looking at her, she reached for her coffee instead. "OK."

"However, Bruce tells me a definitive comparison will be virtually impossible due to the advanced decomposition of King's body. He confirms DNA is our best chance. I've put in a request with the state lab for a fast-track, but I'm not holding out hope."

"Thank you for checking. I appreciate it. But that's not why I called yesterday."

"No?"

"Sorry, I should have been clearer in my message. I had a query on those two vagrants you said had been brought in recently. Found dead in that church off Dry Run Creek?"

"Oh?"

"Has either of them been identified?"

"The first is still a John Doe. But the second—" There was the clatter of a keyboard. "Waterloo PD had him reported as a missing person. A family member identified him two days ago. Dennis Packer. Fifty-two years old. Former veteran."

So, at least one of the war boys' stories matched up. Riley had already checked to see if there had been any reports of a white van disappearing people off the streets, but—unsurprisingly—had had no luck. No one at any of the shelters she and Logan visited yesterday had seen George Anderson in recent weeks, although one volunteer who recognized his picture had commented that he'd grown more reclusive of late. Riley had tracked down a number for his ex-wife, Abby, in Kansas City, but the woman, her voice threaded with pain, hadn't heard from him in over a year.

Webb spoke into the pause. "What's your interest, Sergeant?"

"I'm looking for a possible suspect in the Nicole King murder. A vagrant named George Anderson. We believe he was sleeping out at the plant where King's body was discovered. I have a photo of him, found at the scene. Any chance you could check it against your John Doe?"

"Of course."

Riley pressed the handset to her ear with her shoulder and copied the file of the family photograph into an email.

"It's odd you're calling about Packer," commented Webb.

"How so?"

"Well, his autopsy revealed something rather strange. He—right, here's your mail. Ah. No. He isn't your vagrant."

"You're certain? Anderson has apparently lost weight since the picture was taken."

"That may be so, but I doubt he's changed color. My John Doe is Black."

"Damn. OK. You said there was something weird—with Packer?"

"Yes, his autopsy. Packer died of a niacin deficiency."

"Niacin?"

"Vitamin B3. It's not at all uncommon for people in Packer's situation to have vitamin deficiencies. But in his case, it was so severe it had developed into a disease called pellagra."

"I've not heard of it."

"I'm not surprised. It's extremely rare in the United States these days."

"These days?"

"Pellagra was an American epidemic in the last century. It affected more than three million and killed over one hundred thousand. It was caused, essentially, by poor diet and poverty. After the 1940s, when flour—people's primary food source—became fortified with niacin, pellagra all but disappeared from America and Europe, but it still affects many people in developing countries. It's a pretty horrible disease."

"Sounds like you know a bit about it?"

"To be honest, I had to look it up," said Webb, sounding embarrassed. "The facts are still fresh. It had me quite stumped at first. As I said, it's a horrible condition—causes dermatitis, diarrhea, and dementia. And, if left untreated, death."

"Dementia?" An image popped into Riley's mind—her grandfather standing by the creek in the middle of the night in his pajamas, staring blankly across the dark waters. "Would this disease be noticeable to others? Would people act differently?"

"In the advanced stages? I would say so. The reports talk about increased aggression, emotional disturbances, mental confusion."

Riley thought about her conversation with Tom and the war boys.

Said George was acting real strange.

Dennis Packer . . . ? Man's fucking loony tunes.

She thought of the pills found with Anderson's belongings at the scene of Nicole King's murder, the pills Sarah Foster might have stolen from the pharmacy and sold on the streets. Fenozen.

Purple hearts. No medals for us. Cut through the nightmares.

George Anderson was a veteran. So was Dennis Packer.

"You said poor diet could lead to pellagra? What about certain drugs? Might they cause the deficiency?"

"Potentially. I'd have to do more research. I was planning to—as much for my own curiosity."

Riley glanced around at the sound of conversation to see Logan and Fox entering. They quieted when they saw her on the phone. "Did you do a tox screen on Packer?"

"I did."

"Can you let me know the results when you get them?"

Webb paused. "Well, technically, this was Waterloo's case—"

"I just want to know if Packer was taking a specific drug. A barbiturate called Fenozen."

Webb relented. "All right. Oh, and just to say I'm expecting results on those glass shards I found in Chloe Miller's hand any day now."

"Thanks, Doctor."

Riley put down the phone, her mind working.

Schmidt went to speak, but Logan beat him to it. He'd been subdued yesterday after the hog-tongue incident, but seemed back to his usual self—keen to get going. "Sarge, I got a call back from Nicole King's sister last night. Said she and Nicole were estranged, no contact in years."

"How did she take the news?"

"As if it was inevitable, given her sister's lifestyle. She'll fly from Bangkok next weekend to take care of the funeral arrangements. We can have a more in-depth chat with her then."

"What about King's boyfriends? Anything from them?"

"One was on holiday, with his wife. Another was banged up in county on a drunk and disorderly. Couple more to check out."

"Did you get through to Sarah Foster?"

"I left her a message last night and called again this morning. Nothing yet."

It had only been a day since they'd been calling her, but Riley was surprised Sarah wasn't hanging on the phone, given her daughter was still missing. "Keep trying. We need to find out if she was responsible for the theft of the drugs from the pharmacy. Make sure she knows she's not in trouble—we just want to know if she ever sold to George Anderson. Right, Schmidt—"

Fox stuck up her hand before Schmidt could speak. "Sarge, how did it go at the soup kitchen?"

"James Miller was working there. Seems he was volunteering at a few places, which fits with what Mia Collins told me about him—wanting to feed the world, save the planet. There is a connection to Zephyr Farms, in that they provide the kitchen with surplus cornmeal, but Zephyr gives it to several local charities." Riley flipped open her laptop, on the page she'd been looking at yesterday. "There was a piece in *The Courier*. The mayor gave them a commendation."

Her team leaned in to look at the article, which had a picture of Mayor Angela Roberts holding a plaque out to John Brown, smiling in the foreground with his sons. Frank Garret was there, too, as were the other members of the cooperative, Ted Davis and Ed Wilson.

"It's not much of a connection," Riley finished, closing the laptop. "But I'll be speaking to Miller again. It's possible, through his volunteering, he could have come across George Anderson. The woman we spoke to at the soup kitchen said Miller would talk with their patrons. There could be something there. Did Anderson ever see Chloe in that environment? Target her? I'll check it out." Riley nodded to Schmidt. "OK, Hunch. I can see you're itching to tell me something."

Schmidt straightened. "I was at Green Fields Technology most of the day yesterday, Sarge, interviewing Miller's colleagues. The statements I took were all supportive, commenting on Miller's passion for his job and his hard work. There was no sense of impropriety or any extra-curricular activities that might point to an affair, but I'll keep digging."

Riley nodded. Despite her early feeling that something had seemed off with James Miller during their interview, the picture being painted of the man by those who knew him was pretty damn golden.

Wanted to feed the world. A real charitable soul. Passionate hard worker.

"I've got a few more people to speak to today," Schmidt added. "But I can tell you that Miller's boss has given him a solid alibi for Nicole King's murder. On the day of her death, Miller was working a double shift in GFT's lab."

Riley sucked her lip. If Chloe and Nicole *had* been killed by the same person, it was looking more and more likely James Miller was in the clear. That meant the only suspect she had left was George Anderson—a ghost in the wind. She could almost hear Reed's fingers tapping on his desk.

"I found one other thing out, Sarge," Schmidt continued into her silence. "Green Fields Technology is a subsidiary of a much bigger company." He arched an eyebrow. "Guess which one?"

"Agri-Co," murmured Riley.

"Yes, ma'am."

She picked up her coffee. It had gone cold. "That's not hugely surprising though. Agri-Co is one of the largest corporations in America. It's connected to many agricultural companies and farms in the Midwest, even if just through use of their seeds and pesticides."

"But remember how angry John Brown was?" prompted Schmidt. "You could practically smell his hatred of Agri-Co. He accused them of dirty tricks. Possible sabotage. What if Chloe Miller was murdered—not by her husband, but *because* of him? Because of some association with Agri-Co? Miller is a bioengineer working in crop modification at GFT. Zephyr Farms has this new seed that's up for that big prize at the state fair? Could there be some link?"

Riley thought through the facts. "It's a stretch, Cam. If John Brown killed Chloe in some kind of revenge over a commercial dispute, I can't see him leaving her body in his fields, then reporting it to us. His shock—the drone footage—all seemed genuine. Besides, when people are targeted for business reasons, we're usually looking at kidnappings, shootings, and cover-ups. You saw Chloe's injuries. She was ripped apart. It was savage. Personal."

"Not Brown himself, then, but maybe someone else at Zephyr? Frank Garret was the one Brown said had his fields sprayed by one of Agri-Co's test farms?"

"Sarge, I . . ." Fox faltered as they all turned to her. "Well, I might have something. On the Garrets."

25

Four hours later, Riley was driving the back roads out of the city into the expanse of cornfields, blazing green. Grain elevators and wind turbines winked in the sunlight. Dust clouds followed the slow progress of tractors. Hawks circled on the thermals. She remembered when birds used to follow the plows in the hundreds, wheeling down to snatch up the worms that were unearthed. These days, you hardly ever saw that. Pesticides and synthetic fertilizers might help the corn grow fast and tall, but left no insects for the birds to eat.

Riley glanced at Amy Fox, sitting beside her in silence. "Who do you think left the tip about Hoyt Garret?" In the distance, she could see the water tower near the fields where Chloe was found.

Fox stared ahead. "As I said, Sarge, it was an anonymous caller. I guess lots of people round here know we're looking into Zephyr Farms. Maybe someone from his school? Someone with a grudge?"

"Hmm." Riley thought back through the story they'd just been told by one of Hoyt Garret's former teachers at the junior high school. The story was a decade old, but didn't seem to have dimmed in the mind of the teacher, who had recalled in queasy detail how Hoyt had acquired the unsavory nickname—Hangman Hoyt.

"Turning's just ahead, Sarge," said Fox, motioning to a dirt track.

Riley turned onto the narrow road that lanced between cornfields toward a series of farm buildings.

The Garret family farmhouse was an old, two-story box-frame. It was dwarfed by an enormous red barn, grain bins rising behind it. Farm machines lay dotted near pickup trucks and a horse trailer. Three curly-haired children in their underwear were playing catch through a whir-ring sprinkler, screeching whenever they got sprayed.

"Hey?" called a man, stepping out through the screen door as Riley and Fox climbed out of the Dodge. He was thickset, with curly fair hair threaded with gray. He stared at them warily.

"That's Frank Garret," Fox murmured at Riley's side.

"It's all right, Pop. I got this!" A young man was hastening from the barn. He wore a baseball cap with Zephyr's logo on it, jeans smeared with engine oil, and scuffed work boots. He was only twenty-four, but his beard made him look older. His blue eyes were round, almost fish-like, his lips thick and red. "Deputy," he puffed, nodding to Fox. His eyes went to Riley. "Hoyt Garret, ma'am," he said, tugging off the baseball cap and proffering his hand.

"Mr. Garret," greeted Riley. Hoyt's grip was strong. The teacher's voice came into her mind. *I had to pry him off her.* She managed to keep her tone friendly. "I'm Sergeant Riley Fisher. We spoke on the phone earlier. We just have a few questions."

"Let's go out back," said Hoyt quickly. "The house is crazy. We're packing for the state fair." He jerked around at a shriek from one of the kids.

"Are they yours?" Riley asked as Hoyt led them away from the house and barn.

"Oh, no, ma'am. Them's my sister, Lizbeth's."

"They live here?"

Hoyt nodded. "Since she split from her husband." He cleared his throat. "Lizbeth's, um, out of town." He halted in the shadow of a line of oaks that bordered the property. Flies danced in the shade. Sweat glistened on his forehead. "How can I help?"

"We want to talk about Jessica Wright."

The name caused heat to flare in Hoyt's tanned cheeks. "What about her?"

"You were at school with her?"

"Yeah."

"There was an incident?"

Hoyt hung his head. "I don't like to talk about that."

"I'm sure," said Riley, keeping the calm, sympathetic tone. "It must have been tough for you?"

His head shot up. "It was! I never meant to hurt her. It was a mistake. A misunderstanding."

"Why don't you tell us about it?"

Hoyt clutched the baseball cap. Riley noticed one of his hands had an ugly scar on the side, a deep gash that curved from his little finger around to his wrist. It had been stitched crudely, the edges puckered.

"That looks nasty," she said, nodding to it.

"An accident," Hoyt answered. "Cut myself with a saw. Few months back." He shifted the baseball cap so it covered the wound. "Has something happened? To Jessica?"

"No, Mr. Garret. She's fine. We're just following lines of inquiry around the death of Chloe Miller."

"I told you where I was, the night that woman died in our fields," Hoyt said, fixing on Fox.

"You were with your older brothers?" said Riley, drawing his attention back to her. "Ryan and Jacob?"

"That's right. We were here with my folks until around nine. Then we went to the Thunder Ridge Roadhouse. Had a few beers. Talked about our plans for the fair."

Riley nodded. Fox had checked in with the roadhouse. None of the staff recalled seeing the three brothers, but there was a Hawkeyes game on that night and the place had been packed. "You see, Mr. Garret, there's been another woman found. Out at the meatpacking plant near Black Hawk Creek. She was strangled. With a belt."

A line of sweat trickled down Hoyt's cheek. "Yeah?"

"Why don't you tell us what happened that day at school?"

"Jessica startled me is all. When she came out of the stall."

"In the girls' bathroom," said Fox, her tone sharp.

Riley glanced at her. "Go on, Mr. Garret."

"I was just curious. Like all boys, right? I just wanted to look." His face was as red as the barn. "I went into the stall next to where Jessica was. She saw me and came out, yelling. I got scared. She wouldn't stop shouting. I thought she was gonna hit me!"

"What happened next?"

"There was a sweater on one of the sinks. Maybe it was hers? I don't know. I grabbed it. I just wanted her to stop yelling so I could talk to her." Hoyt was wringing the baseball cap in his hands, eyes averted. "I . . . I put the sweater over her face to stop her shouting. It happened quick."

Riley could see the pulse in his neck throbbing. "One of your teachers said you tried to strangle her with it."

Hoyt flinched. "I don't really remember."

Riley said nothing. The teacher had told her that when he'd finally managed to pry him off the girl, Jessica Wright had been fighting for breath, and Hoyt Garret had an erection.

Hoyt met her gaze. "I know I done wrong that day. But Jessica's parents forgave me. They got the school to let me stay. I promised to pray for her every night, ask God for forgiveness. I kept my word."

"Where were you on June eighteenth, Hoyt?"

"I . . . I don't remember. Why?"

"We believe that's when this woman was killed at the plant." Riley watched as he pulled out his cell.

He scrolled through the calendar. "I was out at the grain silos. There were others from Zephyr there, too," he said, glancing up.

"All day?"

"Until five. I'm not sure what I did after. I think I might have gone for a beer. Yeah," he nodded. "I was at Duke's Bar with John Junior."

"John Brown's son?"

"Yes, ma'am."

"OK. Thank you, Hoyt."

"That's it?"

"For now."

As Riley headed back toward the car, Fox at her side, she heard Hoyt call out behind her.

"Tell Jessica I still pray for her!"

Back in the Dodge, Riley rolled her shoulders, trying to loosen the tightness that had set in.

"Do you think he was telling the truth?" Fox asked.

"It should be easy enough to check his alibi, although the wide range we have for a time of death on King is going to make things challenging." Riley let out a breath as she eased the car over the ruts of the dirt road. "There was something though. He seemed spooked even before we started asking him about Jessica Wright."

"Cops do that to some people," offered Fox.

"Sometimes people with something to hide. Did you see the scar on his hand?"

"I did, but it looked a few months old like he said. Farmers have accidents all the time."

Riley thought of the way Hoyt had moved the cap to cover it. She sighed. Maybe he was just self-conscious. "Well, given his background and the fact Chloe was found on these lands, I want us to keep an eye on him."

Jessica's parents forgave me. Got the school to let me stay.

Her parents? What about Jessica? Did she forgive you, or was she hushed by all the adults? Told not to make a fuss?

Riley's knuckles turned white around the wheel as her mind filled with darkness and earth. His hand across her mouth. The chain of her necklace snapping as she struggled. Ahead was a broad oak, branches splayed against the sky. Her eyes moved beyond it to the distant water tower that rose over the cornfields. The fields where Chloe had died. Chloe—sprawled in the warm grass next to Mia, face flushed with alcohol. Both of them singing that stupid rhyme as he took her hand and led her away.

First comes love! Then comes marriage!

In the darkness, his weight pressing down on her. Ugly words in her ear. Mouth hot on her neck, teeth sinking. The clink of a belt buckle. For just a moment—a split second—Riley wanted to wrench the steering wheel between her hands, send the car rushing headlong into the trunk of the oak. *Stop!*

"Sarge?"

Riley realized Fox was looking worriedly at her. Had she said that out loud?

Her cell rang through the car's hands-free system, making her flinch. It was Sheriff Reed. She pressed the screen to accept it, letting out a breath. "Sir?"

"Have you seen *The Courier*? Goddamn rag has it splashed all over the front page! That son of a bitch, Sean Taylor!" There was a rustle of paper. "Cannibal Killer Terrorizes Town! We'll have national news here at this rate. *International!*"

"Sir, I'm on my way back from the Garret farm. I'll come straight to you."

"I won't have our county becoming a magnet for hacks and freaks! Bundy? Dahmer? Those abominations just attract more ghouls! I want to get ahead of this. Go on TV. Show we're determined to catch the killer."

"That's a great idea, sir. We could use it to appeal for information. We need to find George Anderson as a priority."

"Yes, well." Reed's tone lost some of its edge. "In the meantime, I'm giving you more bodies. I've just spoken to Hal Edwards, squared it with him."

"Thank you, sir, but I—"

"It's just temporary. Not a promotion. They'll be on overtime. I'm giving you Jackson Cole and Chad Becker."

"Sir, I—"

"I'll see you back here, Fisher."

The line went dead.

Fuck!

Riley slammed the wheel with her palm. "How the hell did Taylor get that?" She looked at Fox when the woman didn't respond.

The young rookie was staring down at her hands, her face scarlet.

26

"**W**hat did you say?"

"I ripped Fox a new one." Riley exhaled. "But, to be honest, Taylor would probably have gotten it anyway. Seems he has a source at the ME's office." She combed a hand through her hair. "God, I'm sorry. I shouldn't be talking about this. I just . . ."

"Why don't I fetch us something stronger?" said her aunt.

Rose Fisher was just over five feet tall and stocky—a tough little nugget of a woman, with short dark hair salted white. She had to stand on her toes to reach the higher cabinets. She edged down a bottle of bourbon with her fingers.

Riley noticed a large bag of cornmeal among the sacks of rice and sugar. She recognized the red label, with the three yellow ears of corn. "Zephyr."

"Sorry, hon?"

"Zephyr Farms. You use their stuff?"

"Not me—Lori. She's been baking like crazy." Rose plucked two glasses off the draining board and set them on the table. "It helps relax her when she can't sleep. Look." She opened a cupboard, pulling out Tupperware boxes. "Cornbread. Cupcakes. We're a darn bakery! Please, take some, would you?" Rose patted her stomach. "I can't eat any more."

Riley watched her aunt pour four fingers of bourbon into each glass.

Rose slid one across the table, past their cold coffees and a carton of baby formula. "At least your sheriff has given you some extra hands. I know you've been working all hours."

Riley said nothing, thinking of Jackson Cole's triumphant smile as he and Chad Becker sauntered into Investigations for the briefing that morning. Cole and Logan had locked eyes, but she guessed there wouldn't be any more hog's tongues turning up now that Cole was in the room he'd always wanted to be in. She would make damn sure the move wasn't permanent, however.

It wasn't just her personal feelings toward him. Cole was one of those officers who used their position to their own advantage: showing his badge for free coffees at the diner, letting his pals off speeding tickets. Little things, nothing really report-worthy. But she remembered her grandfather's words on cops who thought they were not simply enforcing the law, but above it. *That sort of rot gets into a force and before you know it the whole damn department is corrupt.*

Rose leaned across the table, placed a hand on her arm. "I've been worried about you with this case. Your old friend? How are you doing? Really?"

Riley thought of the steering wheel in her clenched hands—the sudden, overwhelming desire to twist it toward that tree and slam herself into oblivion. She hadn't felt like that in a long time. It had shaken her. Part of her wanted to confide in Rose, but when had digging up those bones ever helped? She had an image of her father sitting across from her, hands clenched, face white. *Riley, what happened? You have to tell me. What did he do to you?*

"I'm OK."

Rose sighed. "I keep thinking about it. That poor girl."

Riley glanced round, hearing footsteps. She was glad of the interruption as Lori entered.

Lori Bell looked small and thin. Despite the warmth, she was wearing a thick flannel robe over her nightgown. In her late forties, she was nearly a decade younger than Rose, but she appeared older since the birth of their son. Shadows framed her eyes, and her black hair hung limp around her shoulders. "Oh, hi, Riley. Just got Ben down," she said, putting a hand on Rose's shoulder and brushing her forehead with her dry lips.

"Why don't you join us, sweetheart?" Rose moved to get up.

"No, that's all right. I'm going to take a nap." Lori filled a glass of water at the sink. She paused to take a muffin from one of the Tupperware boxes Rose had left out, then drifted back toward the stairs, smiling a dazed goodbye.

Rose waited until a door closed softly above them. "She's looking better? Don't you think?"

Riley nodded, but if anything she thought Lori looked worse. "How's she doing on the new meds?"

"We're taking it day by day. We'll get there."

Rose sounded confident, but Riley saw the pain in her aunt's eyes. The path to motherhood had been a long road for both of them. They had tried for years, spending all their savings on hormone treatments and donors, Lori miscarrying four times. Rose had wanted to give up, but Lori was desperate. The only pregnancy that had ever taken in her was the one kicked out of her by her violent ex-husband. She had run from him a long time ago, changing her name, her life. But until she met Rose, she'd never dared hope to bring another child into her world.

Lori was in her third trimester when the epilepsy came on, her first grand mal seizure sending her into early labor. A deep, postpartum depression had followed Benjamin's birth, which had seen her lose her beloved job as a teacher at the local elementary school. Rose had said it was hard to know now what was making her worse—the depression or the medication.

Riley heard the creak of a floorboard above. "Is she still sleeping in the nursery?"

Rose nodded. "Doesn't want to leave his side. I understand, but—" She exhaled. "It doesn't do much for romance. I sometimes wonder what we were thinking. At our age?" She smiled. "Then I look at Ben."

Riley squeezed her aunt's hand.

Rose swirled the liquor in the glass. "How's Maddie?"

"She's OK. Out with her friends most days."

"I've been worried about her. That boyfriend of Sadie's? He seems pretty unsavory, no?"

"I checked Mason Lee out when they got together. He doesn't have any records. He's a jerk, yes. But I think adding more fuel to that fire won't do Maddie any good."

"You could talk to Ethan? See if he can step up to the plate more?"

"There's no talking to him. You know that."

"You know what I regret most in life? That your father and I weren't on better terms when he died. I don't want that for you and Ethan."

Riley finished the drink and stood. "I'd better go. I have an early start tomorrow."

"Ethan was young, Riley. He was taken in by him as much as the rest of us. Maybe it's time to forgive. Forget."

"Say goodbye to Lori for me."

Riley headed out into the night air. A breeze had picked up, fluttering the Fourth of July bunting strung up on houses in preparation for the holiday. She halted at the Dodge, swamped by a foul rush of emotions. She splayed her palm on the car's hood, waited until they passed. The wind in the trees sounded like waves on a shore.

27

Sirens wailed in the distance. There had been a shooting in Waterloo. Fourth of July always brought out the crazies, but it was still Jackson Cole's favorite holiday. Every year, without fail, he would go to his parents', get lavished in praise and home-cooked food, then head around to his old pal, Billy's. Flags and sparklers, Bud and hot dogs, watching the fireworks while Billy's hot wife paraded around in those tight stars-and-stripes shorts. But not this year. Fisher had seen to that.

Cole looked at his watch. His mom would be serving up warm apple pie right about now.

"He's back." Chad Becker nodded to the liquor store.

Hoyt Garret had emerged, carrying a six-pack and a bag of chips. They watched him cross the street to his pickup. He opened the door, tossed the stuff on the seat, then headed down the street on foot.

Cole let him get a short distance, then put the unmarked car in gear and followed, crawling to the next set of lights. Hoyt slipped down a side street, approaching a saloon bar, where a crowd of revelers was draped in flags and patriotic hats. The bar was a real dive. The kind of place where they only played eighties rock and the first patrons of the day were often also the last.

Hoyt disappeared around the back. Cole turned the car down the potholed street. A firework exploded over the rooftops, a premature flash in the late afternoon sky. At the back of the bar was a lot, full of Dumpsters and stacks of empty beer crates. A faded mural advertising Coke adorned the building's brick façade. Hoyt was at a fire door. It was ajar, and he was talking to someone inside. Cole turned the car into the fore-court of a gas station opposite and killed the engine. The fire door shut, but Hoyt lingered, kicking at the ground, hands stuffed in his pockets.

"What does Fisher expect him to do?" mused Becker, eyes on Garret. "Strangle some girl in the middle of the street for us to see?"

"Fuck knows."

It was the second night in a row that they'd followed Hoyt Garret on Riley's orders, from Zephyr Farms' grain silos to Duke's Bar, then home to the family farm where he lived with his parents. Cole suspected Fisher had contrived the stakeout to keep him out of the way. He'd been waiting for a chance at assignment to Investigations—better pay, more shots at glory—for years. His hopes had risen with every opening: smiling inside as he'd clapped Carl Kramer on the shoulder, told him not to worry, he'd be back after chemo. It had been a body blow when Riley got the promotion. Clearly, she'd been given the post because she was a woman—political correctness gone nuts—but that hadn't eased the sting any. Then, when she'd picked Logan Wood for her team? An outsider? A fucking *vegan*?

But, at last, Reed had seen sense. If Riley thought she could get rid of him now . . .

"So, come on." Becker was looking at him, mouth curled in a grin. "Is it true?"

"Is what true?"

"The rumors? You and Fisher. Did you—y'know?" Becker's smile widened as he curled his thumb and forefinger into a tight circle that he eased his other finger slowly through.

Cole smiled, but said nothing.

"Wow," murmured Becker, a note of awe in his tone. "What was she like? 'Cuz she seems kinda frigid. But sometimes they're the wild ones, right?"

Cole leaned forward as the fire door opened. The man who emerged to greet Hoyt Garret was tall, with dark hair. He was wearing a sun-bleached Nirvana T-shirt untucked from his jeans. Cole craned his neck, unable to see the man's face. The two spoke for a moment, Hoyt looking furtively around. Something was exchanged between them, hands passing back and forth, then they parted ways, Hoyt leaving the lot.

The man headed back inside. He turned to pull the door shut and, for a moment, his stubble-shadowed face was lit by the red glow issuing from the depths of the bar.

"Well, well," Jackson Cole murmured, feeling that perhaps tonight might be worth missing his mom's apple pie after all.

The door of the dive bar closed, and Ethan Fisher disappeared inside.

28

It was early evening and fireworks lit the sky like a war.

Scrounger was agitated, pausing to flop down beside Riley where she sat at the dining room table, then jumping up and barking at another volley of bangs. Riley was finding it hard to concentrate. The room was growing darker, flashes painting the walls.

She had been in here all afternoon, taking advantage of the relative quiet of home, away from the department—always busy on a holiday—to look over the reports from her team, the autopsy findings and scene photographs. They were spread out in a macabre jigsaw across the table, fluttering under the ceiling fan. A bloody puzzle of ruined flesh.

She'd only taken a break to make Maddie some lunch, having to toast the bagels, just enough peanut butter and jelly left in the cupboard to mask their staleness. Her niece had gone hours earlier, climbing silently into the back of Mason Lee's truck, Sadie in the passenger seat, flicking her cigarette butt onto the dry grass, eyes on Riley. Maddie was going to Tanisha's tonight. At least she would get some decent food. Ethan was working at the bar and would be there until the early hours.

Riley took up her beer. It had gone warm, leaving a watermark on the surface of the table. She rubbed at it with her thumb, hearing her mom tut. Back when they were still a family, they'd eaten in here every night, the head of the table taken up by her grandfather, the other end occupied by her father at weekends. God knows when they'd last used it. The lace curtains over the windows were yellowed by sun, the glasses in the cabinet dust-filmed.

As she drank, Riley's eyes strayed to today's copy of *The Courier,* Independence Day celebrations glossed over in favor of a photograph of Sheriff Reed outside the department, erect and unsmiling, his gold star badge reflecting the glare of news camera lights. To the right was a grainy photograph of George Anderson—the most recent one his wife had had—and a number to call with any information as to his whereabouts.

Reed, doggedly downplaying Sean Taylor's grisly revelations, had told reporters they merely wanted to eliminate Anderson from their inquiries. But, in the department at least, he was now the prime suspect. It was Anderson's belongings with Nicole King's body. The meatpacking plant was only five or so miles from the cornfields where Chloe was found. And Anderson's vanishing only furthered the likelihood of his guilt.

Riley's eyes lingered on the picture—Anderson sitting in a lawn chair, hands in his lap. His right ended in a stump where two fingers had been. Even with the disability, as a former soldier, he would have had the training and strength to overpower the two women.

Yesterday, she'd talked on the phone with Anderson's commander, now retired, who spoke of him as an exemplary serviceman. He and his unit had been in some of the bloodiest fighting in Fallujah, where nearly one hundred U.S. personnel lost their lives. Four months into his third tour, during a day of heavy street fighting with insurgents in Ramadi, Anderson had been shot. His body armor saved his life, but the medics hadn't been able to salvage his fingers. Anderson was sent home and, later, medically discharged.

Clearly, the experience had damaged him beyond the physical—the downward spiral into alcoholism, the eventual loss of his job as an insurance salesman, the collapse of his marriage, the repossession of his home, the drugs. But while his path to the streets was apparent, there was little in his background, or in the statements from his commander and his wife, that suggested to Riley he was a man capable of the kind of violence that had been done to Chloe Miller and Nicole King.

She wondered again about the drugs they had found—Fenozen—

and the reports from vagrants and volunteers that Anderson had not been himself of late. Had the drugs caused some imbalance in him? Caused him to do these things? For a moment, she hoped this was the case; something to excuse the savagery of the attacks. But looking at the photographs from the crime scenes, she knew that nothing—no excuse, no reason—would negate the horror wrought on these women's bodies. The bite marks, the lacerated skin, the missing flesh.

She went to the kitchen, tipped the dregs of the warm beer down the sink, and took a fresh can from the fridge. On the counter by her laptop, its screen gone dark, was the crumpled copy of *The Courier* from four days ago. "Cannibal Killer Terrorizes Town!" As she picked up the paper, intending to toss it in the trash, she knocked the laptop and the screen came to life on the page she'd spent an unpleasant few hours on earlier—a list of the world's most notorious cannibal killers.

It was comprehensive and lurid, the site's authors reveling in the details, with pictures of the killers and links to audio recordings of some of them nonchalantly discussing their crimes. Riley had heard of many of these monsters, but she'd never been required to delve deeper than the headlines.

There was Dahmer, of course, the poster boy for depravity, who'd lured young men to his house before drugging, dismembering, and, in some cases, eating them. The young man from Florida who'd stabbed a random couple to death in their driveway and was found chewing on the husband's face, growling like a dog. The man who'd advertised on a cannibal chatroom, looking for someone willing to be consumed, and, more shockingly still, had found someone. Finding the complicit victim's penis too tough to eat, he'd fed it to his dog before cutting the body into pieces. He then stored it in a freezer and dined upon it for months. There was the woman who'd killed her abusive husband, deep-fried his hands, and ate his ribs BBQ-style. The Duisburg Man-Eater from Germany, who said he ate his victims to save on food bills and found children the only truly satisfying meal. The Gray Man. The Butcher of Rostov. The Crossbow Cannibal.

In many cases, the perpetrators were suffering from extreme mental

illness: schizophrenia, paranoia, psychosis. Some were victims of severe abuse. Others were pure sociopaths, unable to feel empathy, able to
kill without guilt or mercy, and to engage in the most depraved acts—
infanticide, necrophilia, cannibalism—with curiosity and pleasure. They
were the bogeymen of nightmares. The wolf in disguise who plans to
eat the girl. The witch who fattens the children. The giant who grinds
the bones to make his bread.

Only real. And found the world over.

George Anderson had gone through a mental as well as physical eval-
uation prior to joining the military. His former commander had ad-
mitted it wasn't the most robust of processes, but maintained he would
have known if Anderson was suffering from some extreme personality
disorder. *I knew my men more than my own family, Sergeant,* he'd told
her crisply. *If Anderson was the murdering type, I'd have seen it.*

If she took the commander's assertion as fact, Riley was left with the
possibility that something had happened to Anderson, either in Iraq or
sometime after, that had fundamentally changed him enough to turn
him into the kind of monster that might have chased Chloe into the
corn, savaging her neck, arms, and thighs with his bare teeth. The kind
of beast that had stabbed Nicole King multiple times, then strangled her
with his belt, keeping her dead body for several days, and, according to
Webb's assessment, biting into her decaying flesh so hard his tooth had
broken off.

But the drone? Chloe's missing car?

Riley understood why Reed and some of her colleagues had alighted
so readily on Anderson. It wasn't just the evidence. As a vagrant and
an addict, he already lived on the margins, outside the boundaries of
society. It was easier, more comfortable, to think of a brutal killer as
someone like him—desperate, dejected, and nothing like themselves.
Besides which, their only other suspects, James Miller and Hoyt Garret, had alibis for one or both murders.

Nonetheless, the two men lingered in her mind: the angry, grief-
clenched husband, who hadn't alerted the police when his wife had
gone missing, and the school pervert turned penitent, spooked by their

presence at his farm. Riley planned to pay James Miller a visit after the holiday. She wanted to know if he'd seen George Anderson at the soup kitchen, but she also wanted the chance to scrutinize him again, maybe get more of a sense of Chloe, too. The shock of her old friend's murder had perhaps clouded her eyes that first visit. Reed's warning about treading carefully around James Miller played in her thoughts, but she brushed it aside.

Trust your instincts.

It was one of the first things her grandfather had told her, after she'd graduated.

It's the best tool we have in this job. Lets us smell the smoke long before others have seen the fire.

She had been that person once. Blind to danger.

Her eyes drifted back to the screen. At the top of the page was a picture of Ed Gein—the Plainfield Ghoul. The Wisconsin farmer had begun by robbing graves for skin and bones to fashion into trophies before murdering two women. Inside his farmhouse, police found corsets and masks fashioned from human skin and skulls, along with a belt made of nipples, a shoebox full of vulvas, and his last victim's heart in a frying pan. Gein had had a terrible childhood, his life in spiral even before the atrocities he committed. But he'd been seen as a shy, pleasant man, a friend to his neighbors and a babysitter to their kids.

That was the thing about monsters. Like the wolf in grandma's clothing. Like the witch with her house of gingerbread. If you weren't careful, you wouldn't see them coming.

Riley thought of her own monster, standing in this kitchen, laughing and joking with her mother, the ice in his sweet tea sparking sunlight as he raised it to his lips. His swept-back hair and tanned skin, denim shirt with the sleeves rolled up, the stubble that made him look older than his twenty-one years. She remembered how she felt as those eyes—glacial blue—met hers. The drop in her stomach like the plunge of a rollercoaster. Her schoolbag on her shoulder; inside it the notebook with his name etched on the back page, surrounded by the plumpness of her hand-drawn heart.

Hunter.

She could still conjure his aftershave. *Eternity for Men.* Calvin Klein. It was rare to smell it now, but if she did, she would be thrown right back into that night. Forced to relive it. *Eternity.* Some sick joke.

Riley took her beer out onto the porch. The evening was breathless. She pressed the can against her cheek, condensation running like cold sweat. Some neighbors were having a party, rockets shooting skyward to glitter across the surface of the creek, throwing the sycamore trees into sharp relief.

There had been fireworks that night too. Chloe's arm slipping through hers as they walked from the campgrounds toward the chaos and lights of the midway. Cotton candy sugaring her breath. A whisper in her ear.

He's looking at you, Ri!

She'd turned to see Hunter strolling behind with her brother and another of their college friends, his eyes on her. Mia rushing up, holding a bottle of Aftershock swiped from her parents' trailer.

Something to start the party!

Riley drained the beer, then crushed the can in her fist, relishing the painful spike against her palm. Another flash lit the sky, lighting the roof of the old storage shed. One of the double doors was ajar. She was sure they'd been shut earlier when she waved Maddie off. Maybe Ethan had gone in there for something? She'd been at him to keep them closed, since the skunk that sprayed Scrounger made its home in there. Cursing, she moved toward the steps, then heard her cell ringing inside the house.

Schmidt's voice came down the line. Riley heard the crackle of fireworks and laughter in the background.

"Sarge, I swung by Sarah Foster's."

Riley had rung the numbers they had for Foster over the past few days, getting only the woman's voice mail. "Did you speak to her?"

"It seems she hasn't been there in a while. Her mailbox was full. A neighbor I spoke to hasn't seen her in over a week." There was more laughter, a muffled call. "He thinks she may have gone away." Schmidt's voice faded for a moment. "I'm on the phone, sweetheart!"

"Gone away?" Riley frowned. "With her daughter still missing?"

"I agree, it's weird."

"Hmm. I'll get Fox to go back through Foster's contacts—friends, family, boyfriends—those we interviewed when Gracie was first reported missing. See if any of them has heard from her."

"Fox called earlier, Sarge. She's finished with the interviews at the Wilson and Davis farms—the last two on our list for the Zephyr cooperative. Nothing to report at either. No connections to Chloe Miller. Quite an achievement in two days, no?"

"You can stop singing her praises. I'm not going to fire her for talking to Taylor."

"All right." Schmidt chuckled, then sobered. "One more thing. Chloe Miller's parents have been calling. They want to know when they can have their daughter's body. For burial."

Riley rubbed her forehead. "We're going to have to stall them. At least until we have more test results back." She imagined the couple's torment, unable to grieve their only child, to put her in the ground and let her go. "Is James Miller requesting this, too?"

"Not that I'm aware of."

"Any response to our appeal for information on Anderson?"

"A few of the usual crazies. There are a couple of potentially genuine sightings, but from a month or more ago. We'll follow up after the holiday. Folks are scared though, Sarge. Can't tell you how many people I've had ask me about the case. Taylor's scoop has them shook up. This ain't LA."

A woman's voice called out in the background. "Cam, honey, these dogs won't cook themselves!"

"Sorry, Sarge. I've got to go. Hey, weren't you going to Logan's?"

Riley cursed. She'd forgotten all about the invite.

"Well, happy Fourth, Sarge."

"You too, Cam."

Putting her cell in her pocket, Riley went to close her laptop. Another bang tore through the sky, like a gunshot. She paused, the page still open on the ghoulish website. Could she look her own monster up? Would that send the memories slithering back down into the silt they'd been dragged up from with Chloe's body? Back down in the dark where they belonged, coiled up, not sleeping—*never sleeping*—but not fully awake either.

She had never dared. Never been brave enough to open that door and see his face, years older, staring out at her from some social media site. Some pedestrian life in some small town. Receding hair and thickened waist. Bland. Dull. Nothing like what he'd been, or what she'd conjured him into. Something larger, darker. Something that might feed on her for the rest of her life. Maybe she needed to see him diminished? Or would that somehow be worse—to see him as he really was? Small and inconsequential. A nobody. Would that just make her feel weaker? Knowing he still had such power over her?

What if he was in prison? Dead? Would either put him to rest in her? God, what if he had a wife?

Kids?

She just had his name and the fact he'd been at university with Ethan, some sort of medical degree from what she remembered. Her mom had been impressed by that. They all had.

Such a nice young man.

She could ask her brother. He would probably know more—might even know where Hunter had moved to. But to do so would be to pull the pin on the grenade that had been lying between them all these years.

No. She couldn't.

There were too many people around them that could get caught in that blast. She would just have to solve this case, then put Chloe and her past in the ground.

Closing the laptop, she snatched up her keys.

29

Maddie sat on the steps of the old cabin, looking out over the creek. Trees shrouded the banks, swamp oaks and black willows, knotted branches trailing like hair in the water. The dense undergrowth, busy with the click and hum of katydids and yellow jackets, had kept her cool through the sweltering afternoon, but, now, as evening fell, its shelter took on a more ominous aspect, full of gathering shadows.

The surface of the creek, thick as pea soup, stirred. An otter appeared, then slipped under, ripples spreading. Earlier, she'd spotted a garter snake entwined around the limb of a tree. She didn't want to be out here when other things crept and crawled from the holes where they'd escaped the heat of the day. Wolf spiders and muskrats. Racers and rattlesnakes.

She checked her cell again. The last message from Amelia had been half an hour ago, and she had no signal now. They'd better get here soon. She didn't want to make the ride back to town alone. Besides which, she was starving, having left home without so much as a bite, feeding those stale bagels to Scrounger when Riley wasn't looking. Her mom had promised to drop her at Tanisha's, but then Mason Lee's friends had come, with liquor and smoke, and that promise had fallen through. Slipping out, she'd texted Tanisha and Amelia to say she'd meet them here.

It had taken her a sweaty hour to get here, peddling along the river, through the state park, out on the back roads through the cornfields, trapped under the furious sun, the water tower rising to meet her over the dark knot of woods. She'd left her bike on the roadside. Amelia said she could put it in Jason's truck later. Slipping into the woods, she'd come to the sagging metal fence that surrounded the Bible camp. Ignoring the old signs that warned away trespassers, she'd squeezed through the gap the boys had led them through when they'd first come here a week ago, Brandon pushing it wider so she wouldn't snag her clothes.

Brandon. With his wavy hair and his half-smile, curled at the corner of his mouth where he kept his cigarette. He was eighteen, four years older than she was. He'd moved here from Memphis with his father, an out-of-work mechanic who'd been offered a job by his brother in Waterloo. The thought of seeing Brandon again made Maddie itch with excitement.

Leaving her sketchbook beside her backpack, she wandered through the undergrowth toward the rest of the cabins. They'd explored most of them last time, she, Amelia, and Tanisha clutching at each other as they crept into the dilapidated shelters, screeching at scuttling insects while the boys shared cigarettes and Fireball shots. Later, they'd lit a fire. Even Tanisha had tried the liquor Jason had brought, wincing at its cinnamon sting. Brandon's eyes dancing with flames.

Maddie climbed the steps into one, its broken windows laced with webs. The back wall was covered in graffiti. Poems and profanities. She scanned the words in the deepening twilight.

Rachel gives head like a pro.

Fuck you all.

AJ 4 Lizzie, 4ever

Make America Gay Again!

We are all snakes, feeding upon ourselves.

She had a pencil in the back pocket of her cutoffs from doodling earlier. She was etching her name into the wood when she heard it.

At first, she thought it was an insect. Turning, she expected to see a bee or beetle hovering in the gloom. No. Too loud. A whining, like a dentist's drill. She went to the doorway and scanned the shadows. There—moving above the canopy of trees—a faint red light. It was a drone.

Hidden in the cabin's doorway, Maddie kept her eyes on the light as it blinked through the trees, flying north. It made her uneasy. Who would have something like that out here? There was nothing but the woods and the abandoned cabins and, beyond, cornfields and isolated farms. Maybe those security signs weren't as old as they looked? Maybe trespassers really should keep out?

As the drone continued north, its whine fading beneath the buzz of cicadas, she stepped out of the shelter of the doorway. The woods were darker now. She jumped at a rustle in the bushes. She was at the cabin where she'd left her backpack, bending down to pick up her cell and see if she had a signal, when a hand came out of nowhere and grabbed her.

30

"**T**hanks."" Riley smiled as Carol Wood handed her a Solo Cup full of Coke and ice and spiked with bourbon. It burned her throat as she took a sip.

The party was in full swing at the Wood house, grill smoking, Springsteen blaring through the kitchen windows, a game of cornhole under way.

"Cheers!" Carol's hair, dark like Logan's, bounced around her shoulders as she shook her head, grinning. "My brother damn near took my head off when he saw I'd bought these." She held up the red plastic cup. "*Solo* Cups, Carol? That's what it means! One use!" Her eyes went to where Logan was talking with their father, waving away the smoke from another round of burgers. "God love him."

"He's certainly shaken a few things up in the office."

"I'm sure." Carol's grin faded. "Look, I hate to ask. But these murders? I've been talking to the other moms, and, well, we're pretty freaked out. Should I be worried? I don't want to keep the kids indoors, but I'm scared to let them out." She looked over at her son, wrestling with Logan. Jake yelled as Logan turned him upside down. "I've never been comfortable around guns, but I've been thinking of getting Logan to hook me up."

"I understand. We're doing everything we can to catch the killer." Riley knew the words sounded as hollow as they felt. She wanted to do more—more to keep her town safe, give Chloe's parents closure, and bring Chloe and Nicole's killer to justice. But her prime suspect had vanished, and until DNA results came through, she had little on which to build any kind of case.

"We moved here for a fresh start. Somewhere safe." Carol's gaze remained on Logan. "It really hit him. The crisis in Flint. Him being a cop and all—our protector." She glanced at Riley. "I'm sure you've seen stuff on the news. But it was bad." She nudged a fallen party hat with her foot. "It wasn't just the physical effects—the kids with their learning problems, our father nearly dying of Legionnaires'. Those things were awful. But it was the trust, you know? Realizing those we thought were protecting us were letting us die to protect their own interests." She let out a breath. "Money. In the end, that was all those sons of bitches cared about. Especially since most of the people suffering were Black or poor or both. I guess we were the lucky ones. We could afford to leave."

"I'm sorry."

Carol took a drink and brightened. "Did you see the debate between Governor Hamilton and Senator Cook yesterday?"

"I missed it."

"God, she's a powerhouse! Hamilton was smiling that fake smile, trying to distract from the fact that under his administration this state has seen massive rises in pollution and poverty. But Cook was running rings round him."

"Right," said Riley, feeling a little discomforted by Carol's frankness. Politics had become so tribal, so toxic of late, that she wasn't used to people discussing their thoughts so candidly. But Carol clearly wasn't one to mince her words, and the bourbon seemed to have loosened her lips even further.

"To be honest, I thought she was a bit kooky at first. But hearing her last night?" Carol blew through her teeth. "It's the fact she's really going after the big boys, you know? Agri-Co and the like. Stripping their tax breaks and subsidies. Fining the polluters." She swirled her drink. "Guess I'd forgotten what it's like to have a politician that actually cares about people."

Logan headed over, two hot dogs balanced in one hand, a beer in the other. He looked relaxed in a Spartans T-shirt, shorts, and sliders. He handed Carol a dog. "I think Pop's getting tired. We might want to do the fireworks soon."

Carol took the hot dog and squeezed his arm. With a smile for Riley, she headed over to their parents.

Logan handed Riley the other dog. "Sorry. She can go on when she's had a few."

"Oh, no, she's great." Riley set her drink on the ground between her feet. As she bit into the hot dog, she realized how hungry she was. "God, that's good." She licked ketchup off her finger. "Is this one of your weird meat-free things? Made from dinosaur DNA or something?"

"Nope. Just your good old-fashioned scrapings from the slaughter-house floor. Eyeballs. Testicles. The works."

"Mmm."

"No Maddie?" he asked, watching his niece, Callie, celebrate a corn-hole win with a cartwheel.

"She's at a friend's."

"Well, I'm glad you made it."

"Me too." Riley meant it. Just being out of the house, away from those photographs, she felt lighter.

Logan grinned as his niece scored again. "Go, Callie!"

Riley knew he loved his niece and nephew, but this evening she'd seen just how much he doted on them. It was uplifting to witness, yet at the same time made her long for such connection in her own family. Maybe she and Ethan and Maddie would have been more like this if things had gone differently? It was a vertiginous thought: how life's twists and turns could lead you into a moment that would change it forever. Chance meetings. Bad choices. Snap decisions. And, suddenly, there you were, lost in the dark of a cornfield, or an abandoned factory. Alone and helpless.

She drained her drink. "Do you think you'll have your own? Kids, I mean?"

"Well, that came outta the blue!" Logan grew serious. "Yeah, sure. But the job?" He shrugged. "It's hard to keep a relationship, let alone take it to that next level. How 'bout you?"

She saw a motel room, glass of wine smeared with lipstick on the nightstand, crumpled sheets, and morning bleeding through the curtains; avoiding her eyes in the bathroom mirror, gritted with yesterday's mascara, heart sinking at the creak of the bed. "Probably not anytime soon."

Logan's cell rang. He fished it from his pocket, then frowned at the screen. "That's weird." He held it up. "Schmidt."

Riley patted her pocket, realizing she'd left her cell in the car.

"Hey, Cam, happy—" Logan fell silent, his frown deepening. "What? OK, yes. She's here."

"What is it?"

Logan looked at her. "Jackson Cole just arrested your brother."

Maddie's scream tore through the trees, sending birds clapping into the sky. She batted aside the hand that had grabbed her and whipped round. *"Amelia!"*

Amelia laughed breathlessly. "Shit! I didn't expect you to yell so loud!"

"What the fuck?" Jason strode through the bushes toward them, a six-pack in one hand, firecrackers stringing from the other.

Tanisha came after him, her eyes cat-like in the gloom, bruised with eyeshadow. She was followed by Connor, red-faced and sweaty, arms full of beers. Behind came Brandon.

Maddie flushed as she saw him, not wanting him to think her some silly scared kid. "Nothing," she answered Jason, keeping her gaze on Amelia.

"We were just messing," Amelia told her brother, taking the hint. "It's almost dark! Let's start the fire." She took Tanisha by the arm and glanced meaningfully at Maddie, eyes flicking to Brandon.

Maddie's heart had started to slow, but it sped up again as Brandon approached. She felt horribly self-conscious, acutely aware of the smudge of chain oil on her thigh and her hair, messy from the ride.

"Hi," he said, with that lazy smile. "You found your way back then?"

"Yeah," she said, trying to sound nonchalant as she sat on the cabin stairs. She moved her sketchbook, giving him room to sit. As his bare arm brushed hers, she felt a delicious shock go through her. "Did you guys see a drone on your way in?"

"*Shit!*"

They both looked around at Amelia's yell to see her hopping back from a bush, dropping the twigs she'd picked up for the fire, hands fluffing her hair.

"Jesus," Jason complained, dumping the beers and firecrackers by the pit.

"Fucking spiders!"

"Pussy."

"Fuck you."

Brandon looked back at Maddie. "A drone?" His face was hard in the twilight, chiseled by shadows.

Maddie pointed through the trees. "It went that way, just before you showed up."

Brandon's brow creased. He turned to the others. "Hey, Jason. Maddie saw a drone."

Jason shrugged. "So?"

"So, we might have someone spying on our party."

Jason took a rocket from one of the bags they'd brought and waved it. "Then I'll shoot the motherfucker out of the sky."

Brandon lowered his voice. "The only thing we have to worry about is his aim."

Maddie laughed.

"What's this?" He picked up her sketchbook and flipped it open before she could stop him. "Did you do these?"

"Oh God, don't!" Maddie tried to take it from him.

"They're awesome."

She felt the flush go right up to her ears. "Yeah?"

He met her gaze. "Yeah."

Something fell out of the pad onto his lap. A photograph. Maddie had forgotten she'd slipped it in there after taking it from the dining room table when Riley was making her lunch. "No!" she cried as he turned it over.

Too late.

Brandon's face changed, his eyes widening. "Jesus! What is this?"

She tried to snatch it from him, but he held it out of reach.

"It's nothing. I took it from home. My aunt had it."

"Your aunt the sheriff?"

"Sergeant," Maddie corrected, her throat dry.

"Is this the dead woman they found?" Brandon murmured, eyes fixed on it.

"Here, shit-face," Jason said, coming up to thrust a beer at him. "What's that? Naked selfie with your mom? Holy shit!" he exclaimed, catching sight of it.

Jason's shout summoned the others, coming over to crowd around the photograph, staring in horror and fascination at the picture of Nicole King's rotted corpse, splayed naked on the steel table under the autopsy lights.

31

The lights of the squad cars lit up the barn's interior in blue and red flashes. Riley stood with Matt Kruse from Narcotics, looking down on the cannabis plants at the back of the hayloft. The scent of the leaves was pungent in the stuffy dark.

"Hardly the bust of the century," muttered Kruse. "Five plants? I left a damn good barbecue. What the hell was Cole thinking, calling out the cavalry for this?"

Riley said nothing. She was pretty sure she knew the answer to that. And it had little to do with Hoyt Garret, now down at the sheriff's office in a cell with her brother. Frank Garret was apparently already there, seeking to bail out his son.

Leaving Kruse to photograph and bag the plants, Riley descended the creaking ladder from the hayloft and headed out into the muggy night. Hoyt's mother, Maryanne Garret, was waiting anxiously on the farmhouse porch with three curly-haired children in their pajamas, half-asleep on the porch swing. They were the kids Riley had seen playing when she'd come here to question Hoyt—his sister, Lizbeth's, children.

Lights were on in the farmhouse and figures moved in the windows. Two patrolmen were searching the house with the help of Peter Hoffman and Bear. Riley hadn't heard the K-9 bark since he'd alerted them to the plants, which suggested they'd found all they were going to. Here, at least.

She had no idea if Jackson Cole had ordered a search of her own house, off the back of her brother's arrest for possession. She could hope not, given how few officers were on duty tonight. But she wouldn't know anything for certain until she got to the department.

Leaving the kids on the porch swing, Maryanne Garret approached, her face wan in the cruisers' lights. "What's happening?"

Riley told her what they'd found.

"And you think they're my son's?" The woman looked exhausted, gaunt, and drawn, as if she'd been suffering far longer than tonight.

"Well, as I said, ma'am, two deputies caught him selling marijuana earlier this evening in Waterloo." *To my Goddamn brother.*

"What will happen now? Will Hoyt go to jail?"

"The amount your son sold was minimal. It would usually be classed as a misdemeanor, punishable most likely by a fine since it's his first offense. However, cultivation of the drug with intent to distribute is a felony. Up to seven thousand dollars in fines and five years' imprisonment."

"Oh God." Maryanne Garret staggered.

Riley caught her arm. "Ma'am, let me get you some water."

"No. I don't need water." Maryanne pressed her palm against her chest. "I can't take much more," she breathed, staring out across the blackness of the cornfields. "Lizbeth? Now my son?"

"Lizbeth?"

Maryanne's gaze flicked back to Riley. She shook her head and waved her hand. "My daughter. She's not been well. She's—at the hospital."

"As I said, Mrs. Garret, this is Hoyt's first offense." Riley gritted her teeth, thinking of Jessica Wright. "It will be taken into consideration." She saw the two patrolmen emerge from the farmhouse with Hoffman, Bear close at his side. "Excuse me, ma'am." Riley crossed to meet them. "Anything?"

"Nothing, Sarge," Hoffman replied. "It's clean."

"All right. I'll leave you with Kruse." Riley nodded to the other two deputies. "Make sure Mrs. Garret gets settled."

As she climbed into the Dodge, Riley looked in the rearview mirror to see Maryanne Garret being led into the farmhouse. Hadn't Hoyt said his sister was out of town?

All the way back to Waterloo, speeding along the back roads, the sky over the city exploding with fireworks, Riley's mind raced. She should have been tougher: should have kicked Ethan out of the house for smoking that shit. Should have busted Mason Lee and Sadie— got them sent to rehab, or jail. Filed for custody of Maddie. Riley had known the threat to herself and her job, but she'd always feared what could happen if she acted. What would it do to Maddie to witness her parents sent down for drugs? What would it do to the threads that held together what remained of her family? Frayed as the bracelet her niece had made her. What was left binding them, really, but wisps of guilt and blame, fear and need? One tug and they would break.

What would this mean for Ethan? He'd need a lawyer for starters. She had called an old friend of their father's on the way to the Garret farm, left a message. As a first-time offense for a small amount, her brother would most likely be granted probation over a trial. But he may well lose his job. It wasn't as if what he earned at the bar made much difference to their lives, but once again she would be left with the responsibility of taking care of them both.

Riley felt a flame of rage flickering inside, but it wasn't just Ethan who had lit that fire. She imagined Jackson Cole's glee at catching her brother. She knew he wouldn't have thought about how the arrests might impact the investigation. This wasn't about Hoyt Garret or the murdered women, or Ethan, or drugs. No. This was revenge. For the promotion she'd got over him and for the drunken night she ached to take back.

It remained in flashes, shot through with liquor and the throb of music. She was just two years into the job, a deputy like Cole. They'd gone out to celebrate—everyone in Patrol and Investigations. A man they'd caught for the brutal assault of a schoolgirl had been convicted and sent down. The men had been triumphant, clapping backs and grinning. But

Riley had only been able to think about the lousy sentence the judge had handed down. Ten years—eligible for out in five. The sentence for the girl would be far, far longer. What did justice mean when criminals got parole and victims got life? While the men celebrated, all she'd wanted to do was set a match to the world. And all the Fireball shots and cheers hadn't quenched that rage.

She'd staggered out of the bar at last call, Cole's arm around her shoulders to steer her, the raw air making her head spin, snow heaped on the sides of the road like dirty sheets, streetlights blinking amber, red. She remembered, vaguely, the walk to his apartment, a sparse bachelor pad near the river. Remembered sitting in his kitchen, that rage like acid in her throat; words and tears and cigarette smoke pouring out of her, and the hiss of the beers Cole opened.

She remembered talking about the past, opening herself up to him, desperate for some connection. Someone to help her make sense of it all, soothe her rage. Some real human contact beyond all those faceless men in all those nameless bars she'd fucked to forget. A friend. Back then, Cole was probably the closest she had to one. She couldn't recall much of what she'd said. Had she told him about that night at the state fair? That rip in her life? That tear in her family? Had she told him about running to California? The wild girl she'd become? The drugs she'd taken and the things she'd done to survive? Things that, even now, could get her fired.

What she did remember was the morning after, waking naked in his bed, a solid wall of pain behind her eyes and scalding shame rising in her as she turned to see him lying beside her, flushed with conquest. She'd dressed in silence, shaking her head at his offer of coffee, breakfast, a lift to work.

At the door, she'd been searching for the words with which to ask him not to speak of it to anyone, but Cole must have thought her hesitation something else because he'd leaned in to kiss her. She had flinched back from him, repelled, and watched his pride deflate like a punctured tire. That moment on his doorstep had opened a chasm between them, his bruised ego left perched on one side, her silent shame clinging to the other. It was a gulf that had never been bridged in all the years since. A gulf that had only widened with her promotion.

The city was thrumming with heat, hazy with smoke from bonfires, as Riley parked in the department's lot. She entered through the back, wanting to avoid any encounters with reporters. The place was quiet, most deputies out on patrol, watching for drunk drivers and kids throwing firecrackers. She glanced through the window of the door that led into reception. The night-shift desk sergeant was there, a wedge of cake on a plate beside him. Beyond, Frank Garret paced, his face clenched and pale. She tapped lightly on the window to get the desk sergeant's attention.

He came out to meet her, brushing cake crumbs from his uniform. "Sergeant?"

He looked embarrassed, struggling to meet her eyes. Riley guessed most of those here knew now that Cole had arrested her brother. By morning, everyone else would know, including Sheriff Reed. "Has my brother been booked?"

"Deputy Cole's just finished processing him. He's to be released on his own recognizance, pending arraignment. He'll be brought down shortly."

"Any searches conducted?"

"Only of his person."

Riley hid her relief, her gaze flicking to reception. Frank Garret had gone to sit on one of the plastic chairs that lined the wall, elbows on his knees. "Has Mr. Garret said anything?"

"No. But he got his son a top-drawer attorney. Max Olson. He arrived an hour ago."

"Olson?" Riley was surprised. Max Olson was a partner at one of the city's most prestigious firms. "For a few plants?"

"Took Cole back a bit, I can tell you."

Riley caught the desk sergeant's smile and felt a small rush of gratitude.

There were two deputies in the bullpen. One was Chad Becker, reclining in his chair, feet up on the desk. A cake, iced with the American flag, was by his boots, carved up and oozing jam. They looked around as she passed. Becker took his feet off the desk as she stopped in the doorway.

"Where's Cole?"

"Interview room five." Riley held Becker's gaze until he sat up and cleared his throat. "Sarge."

As she approached the interview room, the door opened and a thin man in a pinstriped suit emerged. She'd not met him personally, but she recognized him. His image was on a billboard outside his offices. Max Olson, attorney-at-law. Hoyt Garret was with him. Olson glanced at her, lips pursing as he strode down the corridor. Hoyt's eyes darted to her, then he hung his head and hastened after the lawyer.

Jackson Cole was in the room, muttering to himself as he snatched up papers from the desk. He didn't notice Riley enter, but startled when she slammed the door. He straightened, closing the file he'd been organizing. His pale blue eyes were guarded, but he smiled that crooked smile of his. "Sergeant."

"What the hell are you doing?" her voice was low, but as his smile wavered, she knew he heard the fury in it.

"My job."

"Your *job* was to follow Hoyt Garret. That was it."

"He broke the law. What was I supposed to do?"

"That's bullshit and you know it. You were following a possible suspect in an active murder investigation. What probable cause did you have to search him for drugs?"

"I watched him sell them."

"Olson will chew that charge up and spit it out. You've compromised us. Hoyt Garret knows, now, that we're following him."

Cole's eyes hardened. "Let's talk about bullshit, shall we? That hobo, George Anderson, murdered those women. Everyone believes that. You just wanted me out of the way. That's all Garret was. A fucking wild-goose chase."

"Without Anderson, without DNA, we know nothing for certain." Riley struggled to keep her voice calm. "Garret gave me cause to suspect he might be hiding something."

"Yeah. A Schedule One narcotic. And who knows what else he might be selling? Coke? Meth?"

"There was nothing else. Just five lousy plants." Riley flattened her palms on the table. "This isn't a game, Cole. This isn't a pig's tongue in someone's lunch. Two women are dead. I won't have you damage this investigation just to try and ruin my reputation."

"Ruin your reputation? I wouldn't dream of it, *Sarge.* You're doing a good enough job of that yourself."

She straightened, let out a clenched laugh. "God, that's all this is about, isn't it? Your fragile ego? I'll bet you wet your shorts when you saw my brother with Garret."

Cole came around the table, clutching the file. "Like I said, I was doing my job. Maybe it's about time you started doing yours. Show us you're more than just a tick in the sheriff's box. More than just a shadow of your granddaddy."

She wanted to punch him then. Bust that crooked tooth right out of his mouth. "I should discipline you, you son of a bitch."

"But you won't, will you?" Cole came right up to her.

He leaned in and, for one awful second, Riley thought he was going to try to kiss her.

"I know you, Fisher," he murmured. "Remember that."

There was a knock at the door, and the desk sergeant entered. Cole stepped back.

"Your brother's in reception, Sergeant Fisher." The sergeant paused, looking between her and Cole. "He's been released."

Ten minutes later, Riley was striding across the parking lot, Ethan at her side. Her brother climbed into the passenger seat, his belongings—a few crumpled dollars, keys, a Zippo—balled on his lap in a plastic bag. As Riley twisted the key in the ignition, her brother went to speak.

"Don't," Riley murmured. "Just don't."

As she drove toward the exit, she saw Frank Garret getting into a pickup truck. Hoyt was already in the passenger seat, head bowed. He glanced in her direction. The young man looked terrified.

32

The three wore bandanas over their faces. Only their eyes were visible, glinting in the gloom as they emerged from the elevator on the mansion's third floor.

"You're on your own from here," said the young man who'd let them up. His white kitchen jacket seemed to glow in the shadows. "You have an hour." He pointed down the corridor. "His office is at the end."

"Where's our exit?" murmured Thorne, tucking a strand of pink hair back under her black beanie.

The man pointed in the other direction. "Bedroom. Fourth door to the right. Window's open. You tell Alex we're square now. OK?"

Thorne nodded as he pushed the button. The elevator doors closed, throwing the corridor into deeper dark.

She headed down the passage, Leo and Dex following her past paintings and family portraits. Their sneakers were soft on the carpet. Thorne watched for cameras, which she'd seen on the lower levels during the tour. Seeing none, she guessed the first family valued privacy over security up here. She reached the door at the end and entered cautiously. A wood-paneled study lay beyond. There was a lamp on low, casting the room in buttery dusk. A chandelier hung from the ceiling, and bookshelves lined the walls. Velvet drapes obscured the tall windows.

Leo went to one of the windows, keeping watch over the driveway. He had been edgy all the way here, had tried talking her out of this for days. But if Hamilton won the election what damage might be done over four more years?

Thorne went straight for the leather-topped desk, where a screen and a keyboard waited. On the desk were photographs, a signed baseball, and a well-thumbed copy of the *Des Moines Register*. The headline was visible in the lamplight: "Double Murder in Cedar Falls. Is Former U.S. Veteran a Cannibal Killer?"

Thorne took her kit pouch from her backpack and slipped the collection key out. Sticking one end into a small, portable hard drive, she inserted the other into the terminal beneath the desk. Her gloved fingers tapped across the keys, firing up the computer, while Dex crossed to a filing cabinet.

Leo looked round. "All OK?" he asked tensely.

"Yep," she murmured, waiting as the computer connected to the key, diverted from its normal setup process. She had preprogrammed the tool to search specifically for text—emails, documents, calendars—to speed up the process. She watched as they popped up, one after another, as the data was copied onto the hard drive. Dex rummaged through the filing cabinet's drawers, photographing documents with his phone, the flash snapping at the shadows.

"Shit!" hissed Leo.

Outside came the purr of an engine.

"It's too early!" Dex joined Leo at the window. "Fuck! It's him!"

Thorne continued watching the documents ping across onto the hard drive.

Leo grabbed her arm. "We're out of time!"

She shook him off. "I'm not leaving without *something*!"

There was a clunk of car doors closing, a teenage girl's laughter. Thorne ignored it all, watching the screen.

Her companions had gone, fleeing down the corridor. There was a soft rumbling noise—the elevator ascending.

"Shit!" She snatched the key from the computer while it was still downloading and stabbed the off button on the terminal. Stowing the key and the hard drive in her bag, she ran into the hallway. Leo and Dex were at the bedroom their accomplice had pointed them to. The elevator pinged. She wasn't going to make it. She ducked into the nearest door as the elevator opened, voices spilling out.

It was a bathroom, marble sink and gold taps briefly illuminated as she pushed the door to and stood in darkness, heart thumping. She hadn't prayed in years, but she did so now.

Beyond the door, came a female voice. "I'm going straight to bed, darling. I'm really not feeling well."

"I'll have Charles make you some chamomile," came a man's reply. "Do you girls want some cocoa?"

"Yes, Daddy!"

Thorne listened to doors closing and the faint throb of pop music. She waited in the dark a few moments more, then peered out. Lights blazed in the passage now, bright as day. The music came muffled through a door opposite. A man's voice drifted down the hall from the study. The door was ajar. Thorne stepped out into the corridor. She started in the direction Leo and Dex had gone when the door opposite opened.

The girl who appeared was grinning. The grin froze on her face as she saw Thorne. Her eyes went wide. She screamed. As a man shouted in alarm, Thorne ran down the passage, leaving the girl screaming behind her.

The bedroom was in shadow, curtains drifting in the wind. Leo and Dex were long gone. As she ran to the window, she could hear cicadas. Beyond, the thick trunk of a tree was illuminated by lights that bordered the driveway, three stories below. She climbed out, pausing on the ledge, head spinning at the drop. Steeling herself, she pitched forward, reaching for the nearest bough. Her hand, slick with sweat, slipped.

She cried out as she lost her grip and fell, crashing onto the branch below, leaves snatched away by her clutching hands. She tumbled down, smacking her head on a branch, bark scraping the skin from her cheek. Two more boughs broke her descent, then she was free-falling, the ground rushing up to meet her. She landed on her back, the breath knocked out of her. As Thorne lay in the grass, there was a shout above her. A man was in the window, looking down. The bandana had slipped from her face in the fall and hung loose around her neck. Governor Bill Hamilton was staring straight at her.

Thorne pushed herself up onto her hands and knees. Then, she was off and running across the manicured lawn. Behind, more shouts sounded. A flashlight lanced across her, skewering her in its beam. She plunged into the trees that bordered the gardens.

33

The smell of sulfur from spent fireworks lingered over the city for the next two days. The skies grew overcast and the temperature climbed. Townsfolk wilted in the sweltering spaces between air-conditioned homes, offices, and cars. Insects swarmed and farmers sent up crop dusters to spray their fields. Chemicals turned the air bitter.

Local news stations and papers replayed the stories of the murdered women, highlighting the fact that the sheriff's office hadn't caught anyone. With every story, fear grew. People talked in bars and barbershops, worrying if their town was safe. Sales were up at gun stores. The photograph of George Anderson remained on the front pages, while the pictures of Chloe and Nicole disappeared into the folds of the story, as if the women had played their roles and were no longer relevant to the drama. At some point, Riley knew they would simply be known as the victims.

At the office, she found herself the subject of gossip with her brother's arrest; sidelong looks and conversations died when she entered a room. She avoided any further confrontation with Cole, addressing him emotionlessly, pushing her anger down inside.

Reed, furious after the arrests of Hoyt Garret and Ethan, had grilled her on the status of the case. She knew he needed her—that it would harm the investigation if she were taken off it now—but there was always her next performance review. Her only slight satisfaction was that Reed hadn't been at all impressed by Cole's actions: Max Olson, attorney-at-law, now breathing down his neck.

Reed had, however, suspended all surveillance of Hoyt Garret.

"For Christ's sake, Fisher," he'd said when Riley sought to defend her decision to watch Garret. "Boys can be creeps. Back before all this Me Too hullabaloo, I imagine half the men in this department behaved badly."

God, if she had a dollar for every man who saw that movement as an attack on his liberty to be a douche bag. . . . "Garret wasn't just a creep, sir. He choked a girl. Got off on it."

"I'll not see what little resources we have squandered chasing petty criminals and Peeping Toms. Not when we have a double murder on our patch."

Riley had accepted his decision, but it hadn't stopped her from asking Amy Fox to do some digging into Lizbeth Garret. It bugged her that Hoyt claimed his sister was out of town, but their mother had said she was at a hospital.

The hotline for information on the whereabouts of George Anderson continued to ring, but with less frequency, the few genuine tips pursued without success. Anderson seemed to have vanished from the world, only his tattered belongings sealed in evidence bags to show he'd ever been there at all.

Sarah Foster, too, was still missing. Schmidt had gone through the woman's contacts—ex-boyfriends, family, and friends—leaving messages for the most part, many people away for the Fourth of July weekend. Riley had put out an APB, but they'd had no reports as yet. Gracie was in her thoughts more and more, the missing teen greeting her with that sad smile from the poster on the office wall, alongside the autopsy and scene photographs. Possible connections drifted in front of Riley: the theft of the drugs from the pharmacy where Sarah worked, the disappearance of her daughter, the pills from the same pharmacy found near Nicole's body. But without more threads to bind them they remained frustratingly disparate.

She'd done some research into Fenozen, but nothing jumped out, the pharmacist in Waterloo reporting no incidents of concern. Online, she came across a recent story of a spate of suicides among teens on a certain brand of acne medicine, a piece on why a drug for Parkinson's might cause compulsive gambling, and articles on antidepressants that had been linked to violent murders. But there was nothing on Fenozen beyond the side-effects listed. She was still waiting for the toxicology screen from Kristen Webb on the vagrant, Dennis Packer, who'd died of the rare niacin deficiency—pellagra—but it looked as though the drug would not be the lead she'd hoped. And so, after the holiday weekend, as Iowa geared up for the countdown to the state fair, Riley decided it was time to return to James Miller.

It had been eleven days since she and Logan had stood on this porch, the doorbell ringing through the house beyond. The wind chimes were still today, no breeze to shiver them. The sky was curdled with clouds. As the door of the adjacent house opened, Riley saw Miller's neighbor—a balding man in glasses—making his way to his mailbox. The man raised a hand.

"How're things with your brother?" Logan asked as they waited. "I heard his arraignment is scheduled for tomorrow."

"It is."

"You got him a good lawyer?"

She nodded. The old friend of their father's she'd called had recommended one in Waterloo who was confident he could get Ethan off with probation and a fine. Her brother had, however, been fired from the bar, his boss worried about catching heat from the sheriff's office. Riley had questioned Ethan over his connection to Hoyt Garret, managing to bite back a comment about his seeming predilection for friendships with sex offenders. But her brother said he was barely an acquaintance, just someone he knew from the bar, which Hoyt and his older brothers, Ryan and Jacob, sometimes patronized. If Ethan went on probation, he would have to submit to random drug tests. If he failed, he would be sent to jail. For the past two days, they'd moved around the house in silence, keeping out of each other's way. The tension was unbearable. The slow build of heat before a storm.

"Maybe Miller's at work." Logan mused as Riley pressed the bell again.

After a few more moments, they heard footsteps. The door opened.

It seemed to take James Miller a second to register who they were, his eyes dazed, hair unkempt, face coarsened by a beard. He had lost weight since they were last here and looked like he hadn't been sleeping.

"Sergeant." The word was pushed out on a heavy sigh.

"Can we come in, Mr. Miller?"

James's eyes narrowed. "Do you have anything new?"

"Just a few more questions, if we may?"

James hesitated. As he looked beyond them, his face drew in. Turning on his heel, he moved down the hall, leaving the door open. Riley looked around to see the neighbor making his way slowly up his garden path, eyes on them.

Inside, James led them into the living room. He sat on the couch while she and Logan took the armchairs. The cushions were rumpled, and there was an empty bottle of vodka on the glass table.

"They're only interested when the cops come." James jerked his head toward the window. "My neighbors." He barked a laugh. "Not one of them has come to see me." His eyes flicked to Riley, his tone low. "When can I have my wife, Sergeant? For burial? I just want this over with."

"We're doing all we can to make that happen, Mr. Miller. I understand how hard this—"

"Don't give me that," James cut across her. "How the hell *could* you understand? I've answered every question. Given you every piece of information I can think of. My family and friends have been interrogated. My colleagues. What more do you want from me?"

Riley took the photograph of George Anderson from the file she had. "Have you seen this man before?"

James's eyes went to the picture, then darted back to her. "Yes. In the papers."

"His name is George Anderson. We want to speak to him in connection with the murder of a woman named Nicole King."

"I know all this." James folded his arms across his chest. "One of your detectives—Schmidt—phoned to tell me there could be some link. With Chloe. Asked me if I knew him. I already told him I didn't."

"Until we get the results from further tests, we can't know for certain that this man had anything to do with your wife's death. But he is someone we want to question." Riley held out the picture. "Can you take a closer look?"

James took it reluctantly.

"Perhaps you saw him when you were volunteering at the soup kitchen?"

James's eyes snapped up, as if he was surprised she knew about this. "Well," he said, after a pause. "If I did, I don't remember him." He tossed the picture on the coffee table and sat back.

"When we first spoke, I asked if you knew why your wife might have been out in Zephyr Farms' fields. Whether you knew anyone there?"

"I don't."

"Zephyr sponsors the soup kitchen. They provide cornmeal. Did you know that?"

"I . . ." James pushed a hand through his hair. "I don't think so. No." When Riley didn't speak, he exhaled and leaned forward. "I helped out at a few places, OK? I've no idea where they got their stuff from. And I've no memory of him." James's eyes went to the photograph and lingered there.

"Could Chloe have met Anderson somewhere?"

"I don't see how. Your colleague said he's a vagrant."

"Did she ever volunteer with you?"

"No."

"She worked at that thrift store. It has links with local homeless charities. Is it possible she could have met him there?"

"She hadn't worked there in ages. And how would I know who she met? Why don't you go and ask the women who run it? You make charity sound like some sort of crime! Jesus, you try to do some good in the world and—?" He didn't finish, just shook his head.

Riley had known this was a long shot. If James knew of any possible link between Anderson and his wife, he would have surely told

Schmidt. The connections—Chloe found in Zephyr's fields and James volunteering at a charity that used their corn—were tenuous at best. Still, she felt disappointed. Another path closed off. She decided to try a different tack—thinking of the question Schmidt had posited in the briefing. "What about the company you work for—Green Fields Technology? It's a subsidiary of Agri-Co, yes?"

James stared at her. "What of it?"

"Agri-Co has come under fire in recent years. They've been accused of forcing small farmers out of business."

James shrugged, but his eyes didn't leave hers. "That's the story of America, isn't it?"

"Some of the cooperative at Zephyr Farms allege to have had trouble with Agri-Co. Crop sabotage, among other claims. Might anyone there hold a grudge against Agri-Co, or against—?"

"I'm sick of this!" James stood suddenly.

Riley was taken aback by the force of his tone. "I'm sorry, Mr. Miller, I appreciate this must be difficult. But I don't want to leave any stone unturned in the search for your wife's killer."

"All these questions? Insinuations?"

"Mr. Miller—"

"You're treating *me* like a suspect when you should be out there looking for the son of a bitch who killed my wife!"

"We are looking, I assure you. What about the affair you believed she was having? Have you had any more thoughts about who she could have been meeting that night?"

"No!" Somewhere, a phone rang, echoing through the house. James flinched. After a pause, he strode to the door. "Excuse me."

As he left the room, Logan raised an eyebrow at Riley. "You might want to handle him with softer gloves, Sarge. I think he's fit to fall off the edge."

Riley said nothing. She had seen grief do different things to different people. She'd seen it make them sad and neurotic and, yes, guilty and angry, too. But James Miller seemed to be exhibiting all of these emotions at once. It made him hard to read. She wanted to push him further, but she thought of Reed's warning. Another call from the mayor might endanger her career. The thought of her and Ethan trapped together in the house, not a job between them, was a distinctly unpleasant one.

Rising, she wandered the lounge. She could hear James out in the hall, speaking too low for her to catch the words. Her eyes alighted on the chest of drawers. The framed photographs she'd seen—the wedding portrait of James and Chloe, the picture of Chloe's parents and the one of James and his family outside the old farmhouse—were gone. She crossed to the chest and eased open the top drawer. The photographs were inside, lying beside an album. Too painful to be on show? Her fingers brushed the album, an old, leather-bound type.

"Sarge?"

Riley glanced around at Logan's warning murmur. "Stall Miller for a moment."

Logan paused, looking as if he was going to say something, then left the room.

The album clearly belonged to Chloe, the first pages filled with photographs of her in diapers, cradled by her mom and dad. Riley heard footsteps heading away down the hall, James now off the phone. She heard him talking to Logan in the kitchen, cupboards being opened. She continued flipping through the pages.

There was Chloe as a toddler, holding a flower, her mom kneeling with her. First ride in a hay cart. First paddle in a pool. Riley found herself smiling. Her nostalgia was followed by a wave of sadness. They had shared much of their childhoods: so many formative moments. If things had been different, they would probably still be friends. She and Chloe and Mia, meeting every month for martinis in Soprano's to bitch about their husbands and share their hopes for their kids. How normal was it to be thirty-five and living with your stoned older brother in a museum of a house with nothing but a death-row dog for company? Her job was important. But it shouldn't be everything. Chloe's death had laid bare the emptiness of her own life.

Riley sucked in a breath, seeing herself now appearing in school photographs. There she was with Mia in a school play, *Little Red Riding*

Hood, both of them dressed as trees. Chloe, with that flaxen, flyaway hair was the lead in a scarlet cloak. Riley thought of the bite marks on Chloe, the tooth found in Nicole.

All the better to eat you with.

Another page and there they were on a fishing trip with Chloe's father, Mia holding up a catfish, she and Chloe squirming away, laughing. Halloween, dressed as witches. Had James never looked through these? Did he really not recognize her? She looked different now, but still . . . ?

The pictures moved on in time. Cheerleader pom-poms and ice skating. The three of them huddled around a cake in the shimmer of birthday candles. A school dance, short skirts and lip gloss. Riley's breath quickened. She knew what was coming, but couldn't stop herself from turning the pages. She and Chloe and Mia at twelve. Thirteen. Fourteen.

And there it was.

Her breath stopped. It was a copy of the photograph she'd found between the pages of her old school yearbook. Only this one was whole. She and Mia and Chloe, fair lights prickling the sky. Behind them, in the place where hers had been torn away, stood two young men. One was Ethan, gangly and grinning, hair flopping in his eyes. The other, who had an arm loose around her brother's shoulders, was Hunter. His gaze wasn't on the camera. It was fixed on her, laughing and unknowing in the foreground.

Riley inched a fingernail toward his face.

The sound of Logan's cell in the kitchen brought her back to the present. On instinct, she peeled back the clear film and ripped the picture from the page. She slipped it into her pocket as the door opened.

"What are you doing?" James demanded, seeing her at the cabinet, the drawer open.

"Your photographs?" Riley said, holding up the one of James and his family, outside the farmhouse. She prayed he couldn't see the tremor in her hand. "You put them away?"

James strode over and snatched it from her.

Riley stepped back at the fury in his face.

James faltered, looking down at the photograph. He seemed to collect himself with a shaky breath. "Too many memories," he murmured, knuckles white around the frame. "My father committed suicide a few months after this was taken."

"I'm sorry," she said, her heart thudding.

"He was a farmer. Hogs and soybeans." James glanced at her. "He struggled all his life to keep our heads above water. But in the end, he went under." James touched the photograph, his finger on the crumbling red barn. "Went into the barn one night. Put his gun in his mouth." He laid the photograph carefully back in the drawer, beside the one of him and Chloe on their wedding day. "God, she was beautiful." Pain cracked his voice. "If I could have—?"

"If you could have—?" Riley prompted.

"Sarge?" Logan entered. He held up his cell.

"Are we done?" James said briskly. "I have to get to work."

Riley cursed inwardly. "Of course. I'll be in touch if we have any new information. I just ask that you do the same."

Outside, Riley sucked in a breath. She felt like a thread strung too taut, ready to snap. The photograph she'd stolen seemed to burn in her pocket. She barely heard Logan as he spoke, heading for the car.

"Sarge? Are you listening?"

"Sorry. Yes. You said that was Schmidt?"

"He's had a call from the sheriff's office in Mercer County."

"Mercer? Illinois?"

Logan nodded. "They pulled a body out of the Mississippi four days ago. A Jane Doe. Looks like she's been in the water for a while."

As she opened the car door, Riley's gaze went to the house. James Miller was in the window, watching them leave. What had he been about to say? If he could have . . . what? "Why is Mercer County calling us?" she murmured, distractedly.

"They've seen our murders on the news. They reckon it could be linked."

34

They crossed the Mississippi at Muscatine, the broad expanse of water gunmetal-gray, flashing past between the bridge struts. Once on the other side, they were in Illinois, turning south to skirt the green fringes of the Mark Twain National Wildlife Refuge. The sun appeared, shards of amber light sparking off waterways and wetlands, home to deer and turtles, beavers and snakes. It was where she'd been found, facedown in a creek, tangled in broken fishing lines.

Keeping the river in their sights, Riley drove down past the levees into a small, riverside town where a deputy from Mercer County Sheriff's Office was waiting to meet her and Logan at the coroner's. The gold badge on the deputy's shirt was matched by one on his green felt hat. He was short and round, with a moustache and a double chin, which the strap of his hat cut through.

"Deputy Ron Saker," he greeted them, sticking out a hand to Logan. "Sergeant—?"

"Sergeant Fisher," Riley answered, closing the door of the Dodge.

"Deputy Wood," said Logan, shaking Saker's hand with a wry grin.

Saker's cheeks bloomed. "Well, er, welcome, ma'am. Mr. Meyer is expecting us."

The ME met them in his office. Jim Meyer was a wire-thin man in his late sixties. He wore a blue plastic apron over his clothes and a pair of old-fashioned spectacles balanced on the long hook of his nose.

"Any ID on the body?" Riley asked as Meyer led the way down a corridor just wide enough for a gurney. Fluorescent lights flickered. AC vents hummed.

"No, ma'am," Saker answered. "We ran her prints, but nothing came up on any of the databases."

"You got prints?" said Riley, looking at Meyer. After the state she'd heard the Jane Doe was in, she was surprised.

"Just. The skin of her hands came off like gloves when we took her out."

"How long do you think she was in there?"

"I'd say around thirteen days. She was dead before she went into the water though. There was algae in her lungs and stomach. If her heart had still been beating, I would have found it in her liver or kidneys. I'm afraid I can't give an accurate time of death. My best guess is she died approximately twenty to twenty-two days ago. So, around the fifteenth to seventeenth of June."

Riley glanced at Logan. Just days before Chloe was attacked.

"Although she's badly decomposed, she is still better preserved than she should be," Meyer continued. "I would guess she was kept somewhere after she died, a few days at least, in cold storage. A freezer perhaps."

"Cause of death?"

"The wounds I've found were all inflicted postmortem. There are no visible antemortem injuries I've been able to pinpoint. No way to tell if there was any sexual assault, although she was naked when she came out of the water."

"Drugs?" Riley speculated.

"I've sent vitreous and bile samples to the lab for screening, but I doubt we'll get much in the way of results. She's been dead too long."

"We found bits of rope around her," Saker chimed in. His shoes squeaked on the floor as he hurried to keep up with Meyer's stride. "And scraps of plastic. We reckon she was wrapped and weighted down. Possibly in a creek, judging by the algae."

"The water's warm right now," added Meyer, pushing open a set of double doors with his arm, allowing Riley to go through first. "Speeds up the process. With the buildup of gas, she most likely broke her bonds. Popped to the surface like a cork."

"Who found her?" asked Logan. "We weren't told in the report."

"Couple of kids," answered Saker. "Went in for a dip and came up on her." He whistled through his teeth. "Their folks'll need to put a few bucks in the therapy jar."

The ME entered an autopsy room, where a steel dissection table stood, scrubbed clean. Riley smelled the familiar odor of death chemicals. Meyer opened a door on the far side, which led into a cooling room. There were three gurneys inside, bodies on each.

Deputy Saker paused at the door. "I'll wait here," he said, looking beyond them into the room. "I don't need to see her again."

Riley, Logan, and Meyer only just fit in the cramped, chilly chamber. Riley pulled on the mask and gloves Meyer handed to her.

"Hope you've got strong stomachs," the ME said, putting on his mask and dragging one of the gurneys closer. The body was in a white bag, unevenly filled in places.

"So, we have a female. Mid-teens." Meyer began unzipping the bag. "Around one hundred and twenty pounds. Five feet seven."

Riley was struck by the smell as soon as the bag was opened—an overwhelmingly dank odor that smelled like putrefied fish. It made her twist her head away. The body that was revealed was barely human. There were bits missing—a foot, part of one leg, her lips, nose, and ears, one eye, much of her skin and hair. What was left was a raw, livid mass of red and blackened tissue, bones protruding. She looked more like a burn victim, Riley thought. She took sips of air through her mouth.

"Much of the damage you see was caused by the water and the things that got at her while she was in it," explained Meyer. "She was a veritable buffet for bugs, fish, and birds." He pointed to her foot, severed near the ankle, the flesh jagged and loose. "That could have been a boat propeller. OK, so these are what surprised me and what got Deputy Saker and the sheriff's office so excited." Meyer pointed to the torso of the corpse, where his neatly stitched Y incision carved through her. "It's hard to see, but part of her breast tissue has been removed."

"Removed?" Riley leaned closer, looking at the blistered flesh. She thought of Ed Gein, making a belt of nipples and a corset of skin in his Wisconsin farmhouse. A suit of girls.

"Yes, with a sharp blade. Very finely done. Very neat." Meyer almost sounded impressed. "And here," he continued. "See these areas on her upper arms? Her thighs? Her flesh was stripped away, again with some sort of blade. One buttock has the same cuts, although they're harder to see due to lividity. It was done with near surgical precision." He looked at Riley. "I would say whoever made them has worked with flesh before."

"A doctor or surgeon?" asked Riley.

"Possibly. Or a mortician? A vet even?"

"And you think this could be linked to our cases?" Logan said.

"That's not for me to say," answered Meyer. "But I can tell you, in all my career, I've never seen anything like this. Someone cut the flesh from this young woman after she was dead. Carefully. Deliberately."

"Did she have anything on her?" Riley asked. "Anything that might help us with an ID?"

"She was naked, as I said. But she was wearing a ring on the middle finger of her right hand. Quite distinctive. It's gone into evidence at the sheriff's office, but I have a photograph on file. Are you done with the body?"

Riley nodded. She watched as Meyer zipped up the body bag and what was left of the young woman disappeared within its white folds. The smell of death was in her throat.

Ron Saker was waiting for them in the autopsy room. "Well?" he said, eagerly. "Do you think there could be a link to your dead girls?"

"Could be," answered Logan noncommittally as Riley followed Meyer to a computer.

"Here," said Meyer, tapping the keys. He stood back, allowing Riley to see the picture displayed on the screen. "As I said, it's quite distinctive."

Riley felt shock prickle her skin as she stared at the ring: a silver skull with two red crystals for eyes. "How far could a body float?" she asked, pulling out her cell and scrolling quickly.

"It's hard to say. Two bodies could go into water at the same time and be found in completely different places. There are many factors that determine it. The size of the victim, what they ate before they died, the depth and temperature of the water, the flow of the current—"

"Could a body get all the way here from Waterloo? Down the Cedar River?"

Meyer looked thoughtful. "I've heard of a man thrown into a river in a motorcycle accident who traveled nearly two hundred miles in three days. So, yes, I suppose it's possible."

"Sarge?" said Logan, frowning.

Riley held up her phone. There, on the screen, was the missing poster they'd used for Gracie Foster. Her right hand was visible in the photograph. On the middle finger was a silver skull with winking red eyes.

The sun was going down over the Mississippi. The broad flow of water reflected the scarlet sky. A piece of driftwood, strung with a scrap of plastic, floated past. Bill Hamilton watched its progress from the backseat of the car as Blake Preston handed him the pages of his speech. They'd just pulled into the grain processing plant's lot. As his aide ran through the names of the plant's owners, Hamilton's gaze remained on the river.

An hour ago, as the motorcade had driven south for tonight's speech, he'd watched a clip of Jess Cook speaking at an organic farm, talking about sustainable growth.

"We need to return to the idealism and ambition of the past," the senator had told her audience. "Men like Henry A. Wallace, who saw this country through the Dust Bowl and the Great Depression. Wallace was a champion of the small farm, creating vital subsidies to alleviate rural poverty. But Nixon gave away those subsidies to powerful corporations. It was Nixon's administration who first told you to get big or get out. Who saw food as a weapon in the fight against Communism, securing deals with China and the Soviets to make them reliant on American corn. But only the giants could compete for those markets. As a state, we have lost our family businesses and the diversity of our crops. Government policy has rendered us reliant on foreign money, at the mercy of a hostile global marketplace. The same policies have kept those powerful corporations dominant, and we've all seen what the destructive forces of Big Ag can do to our communities and our environment. Seen the rich get richer while workers' rights and livelihoods are eroded."

She hadn't been able to continue, the applause drowning her out. Like a preacher, she was sermonizing up there. But they were buying what she was selling. Cook had jumped another point in the polls.

"Sir?"

Hamilton saw Blake staring at him. His aide was looking concerned. Hamilton knew he was becoming unfocused, and his whole team had noticed it. He hadn't been able to tell any of them why: his family and staff ordered by him not to speak of the break-in at the mansion. He'd said he didn't want to reveal he'd been a target—that it could show weakness. In reality, it could show far, *far* worse. The hacking device one of Gage Walker's men had found when they'd swept the mansion was evidence of that. "Yes, Blake? You were saying?"

"Is everything all right, sir?"

"Cook," murmured Hamilton after a pause. "She's going to win, isn't she?"

Blake leaned forward and spoke to the driver. "Give us a moment." He looked back at Hamilton when the driver climbed out. "OK, I didn't want to say anything just yet. But I might have something."

"On Cook?" Hamilton shook his head. "We did all the opposition research. Woman's whiter than bleach."

"A staffer on her team got fired last week. Wasn't pulling his weight. I know the guy. He might talk. I was going to get into it when we're back in the city."

"It's not much, is it?"

"Sir, I promise we're going to—" Blake was cut off by the governor's cell ringing.

As Hamilton took it out and saw Walker's name lit up on the screen, his heart skipped. "I need to take this."

"Of course, sir. I'll stall them until you're ready."

"Walker," said Hamilton, pressing the phone to his ear and watching

Blake head across the factory lot to the waiting crowd. The plant's lights had hummed on, illuminating the bellies of the clouds of white smoke that belched from the chimneys. "What have you got?"

"I think we've found her, sir."

Hamilton closed his eyes in relief. "Do you have her?"

"Not yet. Jones spotted her in a photograph we took at one of Cook's rallies—that group we thought could be part of Mission Earth? We matched it with the security footage. I'll send you the pictures now."

"You think you can track her down?"

"We're on it, sir."

Hamilton let out a breath. "Whatever files she took? Whatever she found . . . ?"

"We'll get it done, sir."

Hamilton didn't need to push. He had hired Gage Walker specifically because of his reputation.

Ending the call, he opened the file Walker had sent over. There were two photographs side by side. One he'd seen already—the grainy image taken from a security camera in the mansion's grounds, enhanced to show the woman's face. The second was a close-up of a crowd, zoomed in on a figure with a crop of pink hair, a banner raised in her fist. It was the same woman. Hamilton tapped the image with his finger, making the screen blink. "Got you."

As he closed the file, his cell screen returned to the page he'd been looking at earlier. It was a piece in the *Des Moines Register* about the murders in Black Hawk County. He remembered something he'd meant to ask Blake before he got distracted by Cook's speech. Stowing his cell, he got out of the car.

Blake was there to greet him. "All good, sir?"

"Very good." Hamilton put on a smile as they headed toward the waiting crowd. Behind, the Mississippi had turned to wine in the last of the light. "Get me a number, would you, Blake? For the Black Hawk County Sheriff's Office."

35

They crowded into the high school gymnasium: store own-ers and farmers, worried fathers and anxious mothers, gung-ho men keen for a hunt. The chairs filled quickly, leaving those that shuffled in behind crammed against climbing bars and ropes.

Mayor Angela Roberts, a straight-talking, keen-eyed woman in her fifties, introduced Sheriff Reed. As Reed stood at the podium, the frenetic hum of voices died away. There was a projector screen lit behind him, the logo for the Black Hawk County Sheriff's Office flickering in the center.

Reed cleared his throat into the microphone, which whined with feedback. "I want to thank you all for coming. As you know, our great community has been blighted by the horrific murders of two young women."

Three women, thought Riley. It was three days since she and Logan had returned from Mercer County, and she hadn't been able to get Gracie Foster's bug-savaged face from her mind. It was hard not to blame herself for thinking the teen had run away, for not searching more, despite the fact Gracie was already dead, days before they'd found Chloe; before they'd known something was horribly wrong in their county.

She watched the crowd from her place onstage. Some craned their necks to watch Reed, frowning as they listened. Others fanned their faces, the rumbling air-conditioning unit struggling to cool the packed space. To Riley's right sat Sergeant Hal Edwards, to her left Mayor Roberts, the county attorney, and the chiefs of Waterloo and Cedar Falls police departments. It was a show of strength, of unity. Since word had spread of the murders of Chloe Miller and Nicole King and, with it, fear and suspicion, they needed to calm the growing unease. *We want vigilance,* Reed had remarked to the mayor earlier. *Not vigilantes.*

There was no sign of James Miller. Riley hadn't really expected him to be here, but he'd been in her mind since the interview. The photograph she'd stolen from Chloe's album was in her locker, greeting her each morning with a jolt of unpleasantness. She had thought about taking it down to Special Services, setting up a trace. But there was enough of her past crawling around her right now as it was. Maybe, when this case was closed.

Maybe.

She thought of Miller's anger at being questioned, his fury when he'd caught her looking at the photographs. That cut-off sentence? *If I could have*—what? It seemed pretty certain he hadn't murdered Chloe or Nicole or Gracie, unless his alibis were fake. But there was something not right there. A piece that didn't belong in the puzzle. In her experience, anger often hid fear. But what might James Miller be scared of?

Riley started into the present as she saw Reed nod to her.

"My deputies, aided by officers from our police departments, are working around the clock to solve these murders. Sergeant Fisher, head of our Investigations team, has a few words to say on the case."

Riley walked to the podium as Reed sat beside the mayor. Her skin prickled at the feel of all these eyes on her. Her mouth was dry, but there was no water on the stand. Clearing her throat, she went to speak.

Before she could, a man shouted from the back of the gymnasium. "Why haven't you arrested anyone?"

Others chipped in, voicing their agreement.

"We've got our kids on curfews," called a woman. "This monster should be locked up. Not them!"

A scattering of applause followed her words. Riley held up a hand for quiet, but others wanted their say.

"Black Hawk's reputation is on the line," interjected a man in a John

Deere T-shirt. "The state fair is just weeks away. I've been speaking with customers and suppliers across the state, but these murders are all people can talk about. They aren't interested in our farms and produce right now. Heck, gossip is fast becoming our biggest export!"

There were many calls of agreement at this.

"I understand your worries," Riley said, raising her voice above the protests. "But if we work together as a community, I am confident we can bring this case to a close." She waited until they'd settled into a reluctant silence. "Many of you will have seen this photograph in the news." She pressed the clicker on the podium, and an image appeared on the projector screen. "We need to speak to this man—George Anderson—as a matter of urgency. We believe he's been living on the streets for some time." Riley motioned to the gymnasium's doors where a desk was set up, Logan and Fox seated behind it. "My deputies have flyers with Anderson's picture and a number to call, should any of you see him. Those of you who own businesses, please take a stack. Put them up in your offices. Hand them out to customers. But, under no circumstances should you approach this man yourself. Call us." Her eyes swept the crowd. "Let us do our job." She pressed the clicker again, and another image appeared. It was a woman with a thin face and badly highlighted hair, eyes too wide and too bright. "We also need to find this woman."

"That's Gracie's mom!" called a teenage girl in the front row. "Sarah Foster!"

"We have another number for you to call," said Riley, raising her voice above the murmurs. "If you have any information on Sarah Foster's whereabouts."

The noise built as more people recognized the name of the missing teenager. Riley wondered what the mood would be like when they learned of Gracie's fate. The girl's flesh carved away. Her naked, mutilated body left to the waters until she was scarcely human. Fished out to be laid on a steel tray in a cold room in another state. And no one yet to claim her.

Dental records had confirmed her identity, but the sheriff's office wouldn't make it public until they'd informed her next of kin. Trouble was, there was still no sign of her mother. Schmidt and Fox were working their way through the list of contacts they had, questioning everyone who knew Sarah Foster. But the growing concern Riley had felt for the woman had begun to turn into a feeling that they might now be looking for yet another body.

It wasn't just the county's citizens who were on edge. The department, too, was uneasy. What had started as two murder cases had shifted into something bigger, the bloody threads of which were now spooling out beyond their borders. They had three dead women—all with flesh missing. They had vanished people, swirling rumors, circling reporters, and an increasingly agitated community. They had no firm leads and, without witnesses or DNA results, no certain suspect.

Serial killer. They had now begun using those words around the office, in quiet tones. It wasn't something any of them had dealt with before. Riley had never felt more acutely aware of her position. Her visibility—*vulnerability*—as lead officer could mean one of two things. Either she would crack this case and make her career. Or it might just crack her.

After answering some of the barrage of questions, Riley stepped down from the podium, allowing Mayor Roberts to bring the assembly to a close with a prayer and a reminder to let the law enforcement agencies do their jobs. The crowd filed from the gymnasium, collecting the flyers handed out by Logan and Fox, grim-faced.

Riley crossed to Reed, who was gathering his notes. "Well, we got the word out there, sir. If Anderson is still in the area, he'll find it hard to keep hidden much longer."

"Mmm," Reed grunted, pushing the papers into a file. After a pause, he straightened. His eyes looked tired. "Fisher, there's been a development. I wanted to talk to you about it earlier, but there wasn't time."

"Sir?"

"I spoke to the Behavioral Analysis Unit yesterday."

"Behavioral—? You mean the FBI?"

"Yes. I put in a request for help."

Riley felt her heart beat faster. "Sir?"

"The BAU is sending us two special agents. They're flying in from Quantico. I need you to prepare the briefing."

Riley stared at him. "You're taking the case away from me?" Her voice cracked, and she was horrified to find herself close to tears. She balled her hands into fists, fighting the surge of emotion.

"I'm not taking it away from you, Fisher," Reed said, not unkindly. "I want you to continue to lead the investigation. But they will help you draw up a profile of the killer."

"Sir, I—"

"Sheriff?"

Reed looked around as the chief of Waterloo PD hailed him. "That's the end of the matter, Fisher. Prepare the briefing."

Riley watched him go, caught in a storm of feelings. She knew this would claw a hole in the department's budget, but if the killer wasn't caught soon, she doubted Reed would get to enjoy another term in office. The tension in their community was evidence of that. Saving face was perhaps more important to him now than saving dollars. But this was *her* case. These women—Chloe, Nicole, Gracie—they were under her skin, occupying her waking thoughts and her dreams. They'd become part of her: their violent deaths and lost lives. The thought of strangers stomping in to trample over this investigation was unbearable. Her own past—dredged up with Chloe's body—had become excruciatingly present. If she wasn't able to solve this case, Riley feared she might never be able to push it all back down inside.

She jumped down from the stage, needing to be out of the crowd. She was heading for the doors when she saw Sean Taylor making a beeline for her. By the eager look on the reporter's face, she was sure it wasn't just the case he would ask her about. Ethan's arraignment had taken place while she was in Mercer County. As predicted, her brother had got off with a one-thousand-dollar fine and six months' probation. But his arrest for possession was now public knowledge, and she had no doubt Taylor would be itching to write about it. *Brother of county's first female sergeant a junkie!* Riley swerved into the milling crowd.

She was almost at the doors when someone grabbed her arm. She turned sharply, surprised to see a petite woman with fluffy blond hair scowling up at her. The woman wore an old-fashioned white sundress with blue frills on the sleeves. A gold cross hung around her throat. Riley recognized her after a moment—it was the mother of Maddie's friend, Amelia.

"I need to speak with you, Ms. Fisher." The woman's voice was flinty, her eyes bright with anger. "I don't want your niece playing with my kids no more."

"Sorry?"

"I found this in Amelia's bedroom." The woman thrust something at her. A photograph.

Taking it, Riley stared in horror at the autopsy picture of Nicole King. "Where did she get this?" Even as she murmured the question, she knew the answer. She'd left those photographs out on the dining room table when Maddie was there.

"The girl is trouble. That mother of hers? And her father—arrested for drugs? The apple don't fall far from the tree." The woman dipped her head toward the photograph. "That's sure clear."

"I'm sorry. I'll talk to her."

"What she needs is church. Put the fear of God in her. But until she's saved, don't bring Maddie 'round no more."

Riley was two blocks away—waiting at the corner of Lafayette, drumming her fingers on the steering wheel, eyes on the photograph of Nicole King's body on the dashboard, thoughts flitting agitatedly between Maddie and Reed's announcement about the BAU—when her cell rang. She recognized the code. Des Moines. Thinking it was her father's old friend, the lawyer who'd recommended the attorney for Ethan, she answered. "Fisher speaking."

A deep male voice came down the line. "Riley, it's Bill. Bill Hamilton."

"Governor?" She was so surprised that she didn't realize the lights had changed until someone beeped her.

"Hello?"

"Hang on, sir." She turned sharply into the department's lot and killed the engine. "I'm here, sir."

Hamilton laughed. "You've known me too long for that. Please, call me Bill." His tone sobered. "Listen, Riley, I've been meaning to get in touch. I'm ashamed at how long it's been. I meant to call and congratulate you when I heard you'd made sergeant. You've no idea how much time campaigning eats. Honestly, my wife and kids hardly recognize me." He chuckled again but sounded strained.

"I understand, si—Bill."

"Anyway, I wanted to see how the case is going. We're all in shock here. A *cannibal* killer? In Black Hawk? It sounds like fiction."

Riley guessed Hamilton would be as worried as Reed about all the press coverage and his own reelection prospects. "I assure you, we're doing all we can to solve it."

"This veteran? George Anderson? You think he's the killer?"

"He's certainly a suspect. But without test results or witnesses we can't be sure. My sheriff has asked the BAU for assistance. They're sending two agents to advise us." She kept her tone light, although the words stung.

There was a pause. "That's good."

She had a sudden thought. "Actually, sir, there might be something you could do for us."

"Oh?"

"We're waiting on DNA from the state lab. I know there's a backlog there, but if there was any chance of speeding things up . . . ? Well, suffice to say it would really help us out."

"I'll see what I can do. What about the husband of the first victim? James Miller? Is he a suspect?"

"I—?"

"I'll level with you, Riley. I met James a few years ago in Des Moines. He attended an agricultural conference with his company. I was very impressed by him. He had some compelling ideas about Iowa's role in world farming. I hear he's been doing interesting work at GFT. He seemed to me to be a highly commendable young man. A real champion for our state. Our future."

Riley didn't know what to say. Hamilton's tone was light, but there was an edge to it. Was he warning her off James Miller? How did he even know Miller was a suspect? "Sir, has James Miller contacted you about this case?"

There was another voice in the background. A young man speaking.

Hamilton's voice faded as if he'd cupped a hand over the phone. He became clear again. "I'm sorry, I have to go. I'll give the state lab a call, see what I can do. Please, keep me informed. And, Riley, your father would be proud."

"Sir, I—"

The line went dead.

36

They crammed into Investigations—Schmidt and Logan, Amy Fox and Bob Nolan, two technicians from the crime lab, and Chad Becker. There was no sign of Jackson Cole. Riley went through her notes, leaving the others to talk among themselves.

Pinned to the boards were the photographs of Chloe Miller and Nicole King. The missing poster of Gracie Foster was still there, but with it now were the autopsy pictures the ME had sent from Mercer County. There was a map showing Black Hawk and the eastern half of Iowa, folded down Illinois along the Mississippi. Red pins marked where the bodies had been found. Zephyr's cornfields, the meatpacking plant, and the creek in the Mark Twain National Wildlife Refuge.

Riley looked up from her files as Sheriff Reed entered with two men. She drew a breath, preparing herself. The first man was of medium height and slim build, in his late forties. He had dark, wavy hair and was clean-shaven with a strong jaw. His black suit was finely tailored and his shoes gleamed like black mirrors. The man who followed was almost his opposite—short and heavyset with thick, sandy hair, curled with sweat at his temples. His cheeks were ruddy, and there were stains under the arms of his plaid shirt, tucked into tan slacks. He had green eyes that darted around the room, not quite settling on anyone.

"Sergeant, this is Special Agent Elijah Klein from the BAU."

The dark-haired man stepped forward at Reed's introduction, offering his hand. His brown eyes were steady. "Pleased to meet you, Sergeant." His accent had the clipped crispness of the East—New York maybe.

"Riley Fisher," she said, shaking his hand. Klein's skin was cool, his grip strong but not overly forceful.

"And Special Agent Steven Gooch," said Reed.

The sandy-haired man dipped his head but didn't offer his hand. His eyes flicked past Riley to the photographs on the back wall. She felt a prickle of protectiveness as he scanned them, taking in all that ruined female flesh with seeming dispassion.

"Agents, I'll leave you in Sergeant Fisher's hands. I'll have my secretary organize a hotel."

"Thank you, Sheriff," said Klein.

Riley waited until Reed had gone, then went around the room introducing the two agents to the rest of her team. Her colleagues nodded, stiff and unsmiling. She knew it was their little show, telling her that she was still their boss. God love them.

Klein shook hands with each of them, repeating their names, calm and courteous. Gooch seemed more interested in the photographs.

The door opened, and Jackson Cole entered.

"And Deputy Cole," Riley finished.

Cole sat on one of the desks, his eyes on her like a challenge.

"Deputy Cole is on temporary assignment," she added, hating herself for being petty but enjoying the flush that crept into his cheeks. She fixed on Klein. "Shall I go straight into the briefing?"

"First, Sergeant, just let me say that we're here to help." Klein smiled. "I know some people feel uneasy when we come in—big bad FBI stepping on your toes, belittling your department, taking the glory of an arrest."

Schmidt chuckled wryly.

"Please, let me assure you, things have changed. Think of us as you would your local medical examiner, except instead of dissecting the bodies of your victims, we'll be dissecting the mind of your killer. Building a profile that can help you catch him. We are here to advise you. Not to overrule you."

Riley noticed a settling in the room at his words, shoulders and expressions softening. It was hard not to relax at Klein's candid tone, his even smile.

As Klein settled into the seat she offered and Gooch leaned against a desk, taking a notebook from the pocket of his shirt, Riley went methodically through the discovery of Chloe Miller's body: the report of the drone from John Brown, Chloe's missing car and the partial imprint from a pickup truck on the dirt road, James Miller's belief that his wife was having an affair, his search for her the night she went missing, and Mia's conviction that it was James who'd been cheating. She went over the testimonies of friends and colleagues, the statements from the four families at Zephyr Farms, and the autopsy report from Webb that revealed the shards of glass in Chloe's palm and the ME's belief that some of the wounds looked like bites, corroborated by Bruce Bain.

While Klein listened, Gooch scribbled in his pad, licking his finger noisily to lift each new page as Riley moved on to Nicole King. She walked them through the scene: the body and injuries, the fragment of tooth Webb found, and the backpack with the family photograph and pills they believed belonged to George Anderson, Iraq veteran turned drug addict and vagrant. She spoke about the possible link with Sarah Foster, who might have stolen drugs from the pharmacy and whose missing daughter had been pulled from the Mississippi. She added that she'd looked into the drug, Fenozen, as a possible factor in the murders, but had found no evidence. Finally, she went through the autopsy on Gracie Foster and Jim Meyer's assertion that someone had cut the flesh from her body.

"They're close," stated Gooch, when she'd finished. He was still writing and didn't look up from his pad. His accent was the nasal drawl of the South. Virginia, or one of the Carolinas.

"Close?"

Gooch underlined something with his pen, then glanced up at Riley. "I've got down that Gracie Foster died first, around the fifteen to seventeenth of June. Nicole King was killed around the eighteenth. Then Chloe Miller was attacked and killed on the twenty-first. They're close."

"It's unusual," Klein explained, "for a serial murderer to kill in such a short space of time. But not unheard of," he added, looking at Gooch. "But no deaths since. At least, none that are known."

"We are worried about Sarah Foster," Riley added. "We're speaking to everyone she knows, but, so far, no one has seen or heard from her."

Klein nodded contemplatively. "It would be helpful to have a list of those contacts."

"Your prime suspect is Anderson?" Gooch asked.

"Yes. We have all departments in the county on lookout for him. There are posters up in every township. If Anderson is still in the area, I am confident we'll find him."

Gooch grunted. "No one else in your sights?"

Riley was irritated by the brusque question. Despite her frustration when Reed told her he'd requested help from the BAU, she'd forced herself to be open to this process. What did it matter how they solved this investigation, so long as they did? But it had been a hard pill to swallow, and her secret fear that Reed didn't trust that she was up to the task had only been heightened by the arrival of the two men. Klein was clearly attempting to mitigate the threat to her authority, but Gooch seemed oblivious to his condescending tone.

"We interviewed James Miller as a potential suspect in Chloe's death," she told him crisply. "The alleged affair gave him motive. However, his alibi is solid for Nicole King. Gracie Foster will be harder to check, given the uncertainty of time of death."

Riley thought of Bill Hamilton's unexpected call: the sense that he was warning her off the pursuit of Miller as a suspect. She hadn't spoken to her team about it yet—didn't want Reed finding out that the governor was now vouching for the man, especially with the BAU here. But rather than quelling her suspicions, Hamilton's call had only raised more questions. Mostly, she wanted to understand why a governor—in the middle of a fraught campaign—would go out of his way to support a suspect in a murder investigation if they were mere acquaintances, however important James Miller's work was.

"You mentioned Hoyt Garret?" Klein prompted. "The one who choked a girl at school?"

"We've struck him off our list," said Riley, avoiding Cole's eyes. "He has alibis for Miller and King." She glanced at Amy Fox, who had been calling around hospitals to check if Lizbeth Garret had been booked in. The discrepancy, although small, was still lodged in her mind.

"No one else?" prompted Gooch.

"No," Riley said tightly. "We're hoping DNA will shed more light."

Klein nodded. "Well, we can certainly help you there. If you arrange for the state lab to send samples to Quantico, we should be able to get results back to you in a week."

The mood of the room shifted, Riley's team looking at one another in surprise. Riley felt it herself—a lift in her spirits. Maybe it wouldn't be so bad having them here. Klein, at any rate.

"Of course," he added, "no matter what the results yield, we still rely on good old-fashioned detective work." Klein looked at Riley. "Sergeant, if we can have copies of your reports? Interview statements, autopsies, scene photographs, and analysis?"

"And I'll want to walk the scenes," Gooch cut in.

"How long does it usually take to work up a profile?" Riley asked Klein.

"We'll just need a few days for the profile. After that, we can work on helping you flush out the UNSUB."

Chad Becker stuck his hand up. "UNSUB?"

"Unknown Subject of an investigation. We do love our acronyms at the bureau."

"How do you flush someone out?" Fox wanted to know.

"There are different ways," answered Klein, "depending on the sort of killer we're dealing with. Some like to insinuate themselves into an investigation. It's a power trip for them. But it can be a good way for us to trap him into revealing himself."

"Yup." Gooch was nodding. "Wouldn't be surprised if you've already spoken to him."

"Have you ever worked a case like this?" Logan interjected. "I mean, the bites? The missing flesh? That sort of thing's got to be pretty rare, no?"

"You'd be surprised," said Klein. "Since I joined the BAU, I've worked on nearly a dozen cases that involved biting, blood drinking, or cannibalism."

"Some real nuts out there," muttered Schmidt.

"Don't underestimate this killer," warned Gooch, slipping his notebook in his pocket. "By the speed with which he's killing, your UNSUB shows me he has a real need he's compelled to satisfy. Whatever started him down this track—whatever stressor triggered him—he has a taste for it now."

37

It was dark by the time Riley got home. She pulled into the yard, dust eddying in the headlights. She was exhausted, her skin gritty from a second day spent walking the murder sites with the two agents in the vicious afternoon heat.

Agent Gooch had explored the crime scenes—strangely innocuous, cleared of police tape and horror—in silence, pausing to write in his notebook, crouch down to view something from another angle, or wander off without warning. Klein was more forthcoming, and Riley wondered if he'd been sent as the acceptable face of the bureau: the smooth bridge between local law enforcement and Gooch's prickly inelegance. He'd talked her through the process of building a profile, which she thought sounded closer to art than science. The BAU, it seemed, relied more on conjecture than hard facts and data, but it was difficult to doubt their effectiveness when hearing examples of the many killers they'd caught. It made Riley think of hunting with her grandfather: his uncanny ability to track quarry, sensing the way the animal would move in the smallest shifts of wind and shadow.

As she climbed from the car, Riley noticed the storage shed's doors were open.

"Damn it, Ethan."

Inside the shed it was musty and dark. There was a box on the floor. She realized, by her mom's handwriting scribbled in marker on the side, that it was a box of their old toys—board games with lost pieces, rag dolls too ragged to send to Goodwill, toy soldiers with missing limbs.

Had Ethan been going through it? She imagined him crouched in the shadows, picking through things from their old life—another life entirely, with laughter and family jokes, their mom and dad giggling over a cremated Thanksgiving turkey after too much wine, their grandfather singing along to Johnny Cash as he drove them to school in his pickup. Sadness welled in her. With their parents dead and their grandfather stripped of anything recognizable, what were she and Ethan but a couple of ghosts lingering in the place where they'd once lived? They should have sold this house and moved on. Started again. How could she have thought either of them could escape the past when they were still mired in it?

She was bending down to close the box when she heard a noise deep within the shed—a soft shushing like a sigh, or a breeze through long grass. She rose, the skin on her neck tingling. As she stared into the darkness, it stopped. She waited, listening intently. Her cell pinged, making her jump.

It was a text message from Kristen Webb.

Can you call me first thing?

Riley gave the ME a try, hoping she might still be in the office, but it went to voice mail. She slipped the cell back into her pocket and stood there listening in the hush. When the whispering sound didn't come again, she put the box back on its shelf. She'd get a proper look in daylight, see what might have made its home in here. Firmly shutting the shed doors, she made her way to the house.

The place was dark, only the porch light to guide her. Earlier, she'd texted Ethan, asking him to pick up food. She hoped he hadn't stopped off at a bar. They had enough problems. When she'd told Ethan about Maddie stealing the autopsy photograph, he and Maddie just ended up yelling at one another. The girl had been grounded, but Riley doubted Sadie or Mason Lee would be effective at enforcing the punishment. With the case filling her waking hours, she'd asked Rose to talk to Maddie, make sure the girl understood what she'd done wrong. Her aunt had been happy to help, but Riley had heard the fatigue in her voice. Lori, it seemed, was no better.

As she trudged up the steps, Scrounger came barking. She pushed open the screen door. Scrounger whined and nosed her hand. She was heading to the safe to stow her gun when she saw it—a white envelope on the kitchen counter, her name written on the front. She wondered briefly if Ethan had left her a note to tell her where he was, but her brother didn't do things like that. When she picked it up, she felt something slide inside. Curious, she tore it open and shook the contents into her hand. First, she saw the glimmer; dull gold in the kitchen's dim light. Then, as it dropped into her palm, she saw it was a gold star necklace with a broken chain.

It might as well have been a bomb rocking her world off its axis. Her breath was snatched. Her legs went weak. She dropped the necklace and the envelope, and lurched out into the thick night air, looking wildly around, her mind reeling. She swiveled on the porch, eyes darting. The darkness was full of threat: the sycamore trees glowering over the house, the creek black as tar, the old shed crouched in the yard, the high whine of cicadas an endless scream. She saw shadows everywhere. Movement flickered in the corner of her vision—a moth made huge by the light. Yanking open the screen door, she ran back into the kitchen, Scrounger barking in alarm. She backed up against the wall, pulling her Glock free. She gripped the gun in both hands, pointing the barrel into the darkness beyond the door swinging on its hinges.

She stayed like that until her arms began to shake and the stock of the gun grew slick with her sweat. Scrounger whined, breaking her concentration. The dog was staring at her, ears and tail down, brown eyes big with worry. Her gaze refocused on the broken necklace that she hadn't seen in twenty-one years—the gift from her grandfather—lying on her kitchen floor, snatched out of time.

The nausea came in a rush. Turning, she ran upstairs. The family bathroom was nearest, and she dived inside, dropping to her knees over the old lime-green toilet, gun on the floor. She retched, eyes watering. When it passed, she sat back against the tub, sweat drying cold on her forehead. She felt weak, her whole body fluttery, like she was made of moths.

The bathroom hadn't changed since she'd moved here with her parents: the oval mirror above the sink, the cracked linoleum. It was the bathroom she had locked herself in that morning when Mia's parents dropped her home early from the state fair, speaking to her mom in low tones outside—*We're not sure what happened.*

It was the bathroom where she'd peeled her clothes off with shaking hands, eyes on the bruises that mottled her body. Not the same body she had left with just days earlier: bundling into the car with Mia and Chloe, singing pop songs from the radio all the way to Des Moines. The trailers in their long white lines pulling into the fairgrounds, the miles of tents, smoke rising, the smell of diesel and a sky blue with promise and the dazzle of fair lights.

Then Hunter. The college friend of her brother she'd had a crush on. The handsome young man her parents were so fond of. His eyes. His smile. The alcohol burning her throat. The giggles turning to dizziness. Hunter's hand threading through hers. Chloe blowing her a drunken kiss, singing that rhyme with Mia as he led her away. Staggering into the woods, away from the crowds and lights, head spinning like a Tilt-A-Whirl. The distant rattle and roar of rides.

The bruises in the bathroom mirror had been livid, each telling the story of her pain. The hard ground where she'd fallen as he pushed her down, a tree root knotted in her back, rough soil scraping her bare arms. Smell of pine needles and earth. Things in her hair. Her necklace ripped from her throat as she struggled. The skin of her wrists clouded purple, red marks on her stomach and thighs.

The awful bite on her neck, his teeth marks indented as a feverish oval from which blood seeped into the Band-Aid she'd tried to hide it with. Worse, though, were the wounds she couldn't see. The ones that hurt in the deepest places: not just in flesh, but in heart and soul. Torn open. Like the skin of her palm, weeks later, carved with a razor down by the creek, blood welling at the oath she'd made Chloe and Mia make.

Never tell.

It was an oath she had broken first, many months later, the words heaved from her in sobs, her parents' expressions frozen, Ethan stumbling from the room, his face ashen. The secret once shared—once detonated—had destroyed them. Not in the first blast, but slowly, inexorably. A sickness in the heart of their family. A poison that lived for years, quietly working in each of them.

Riley flinched into the present as the doorbell chimed through the house.

38

The flood of adrenaline was like a bucket of ice water, bringing her fully alert. Grabbing her gun, Riley slipped down the stairs, careful to avoid any windows. Scrounger was barking. The security light by the front door—which only the mailman and strangers used—was on, illuminating the outline of a figure in the swirled glass panels. The person was tall, well-built. Her heart hammered. The chain was on the door. A strong man could snap it with a solid kick, but she could get her gun up in his face well before that. She reached for the handle with her left hand, Glock gripped in her right. Pulling it open, she took aim.

Standing there, his blond hair almost white in the light, was Jackson Cole. Riley pulled the gun away, but not before he'd caught sight of it.

Cole took a surprised step back. "Hey."

Her whole body was trembling. She wasn't sure whether she wanted to weep with relief or punch him. She swallowed thickly. "What are you doing here?"

"I wanted to talk." Cole eyed the chain across the door, the creases in his tanned brow deepening. He looked past her into the house. "What's wrong?"

"Nothing."

"Bullshit. You're shaking. Let me in."

When Cole pushed against the door, she let him in.

"What happened?" As he entered the hallway, Scrounger came bounding to greet him.

Numb, Riley let Cole lead her through to the kitchen. She put her gun on the counter, shakily aware of how close she'd come to using it.

"What's this?" Cole bent to pick up the fallen necklace.

It felt like he'd grabbed a part of her. She snatched it from him. *"Don't!"*

"All right!" He held up his hands, staring in confusion as she backed away, gripping the chain in her fist. "I'm just trying to help."

"I don't need your Goddamn help!"

"Sure. OK. That's why you almost shot me on your doorstep?" Cole hooked his thumbs into the pockets of his jeans. "I know you didn't want me on this case, but Christ."

She stared at him. The laugh burst out of her, sharp and sudden.

Cole laughed, too, after a moment. "Got me pretty shook up there, Sarge." He nodded to the fridge. "You got any beer? Need to calm my nerves."

Sobering, she opened one of the kitchen drawers and dropped the necklace into it. Shutting it inside, she went to the fridge and took out two cans. Her fingers fumbled as she tried to open the tab.

Cole took the can gently, insistently. "Here." He flipped the beers open, handing one to her. "So what's up?"

Riley lifted the beer, then set it down without drinking. "Why are you here, Jackson?"

He sighed. "I thought we could start again, OK? You and me. Smooth things over, now we're working together?"

"That's temporary."

His eyes narrowed. "We both know Sheriff Reed needs new blood in Investigations."

So, he was here to play nice in hope of a promotion? "If I get the budget for a permanent detective, I'll choose Logan."

His face hardened, the old Cole appearing briefly. He struggled to pull it back. "Look, I'm sorry about your brother. You've every reason to be pissed at me. I should have come to you first, I know." When she didn't respond, he continued. "But Wood? He's been here one damn minute. He's not born and bred in Black Hawk. Not the same as us. You and me."

"That's one of the many things I like about him."

"We've had our differences, sure. But we were close once. I don't mean that," Cole added as she looked away. "Back when we were rookies. Remember? You and me on a graveyard? Pancakes at the Maid-Rite at the end of a shift? That drug bust at the Blue Lagoon? Those crazy fucks trying to cross the river in a garbage can? Yeah," he said, chuckling at her half-smile. "You remember."

She met his eyes. For a moment, she felt safe in that familiarity, that history, back when things were less complicated. Back when they'd been—not close, not like she'd become with Logan—but in it together, watching each other's backs, learning the ropes.

Cole came to her, set down his beer, and placed his hand over hers. It was callused from the gun range. "Can't we get back there somehow? A truce?"

She let out a sigh, too tired to argue. "I don't know how to solve it. This case."

Cole put his other hand on her shoulder, squeezed it.

"Everyone's looking to me for answers." Riley's eyes flicked to the drawer where she'd stashed the necklace. Could Hunter have left it for her? She felt the scar on her neck pulse. Thought of Chloe, curled among the roots. Had she felt such a connection to this case because it was connected? *Perhaps.* Might a brutal rapist go on to become a serial killer? *Yes.* "But I'm lost."

Cole's hand slid from her shoulder, down to her back. "It's OK," he murmured, pulling her to him.

She smelled his deodorant, mixed with sweat and gun oil. She could feel the deep thud of his heart. She closed her eyes. She hadn't been held like this in a long time. All at once, she wanted to tell him. Confide in him. Cole knew her past, or at least some of it. "Remember that night? The night I—?" She faltered, then tried again. "When I came 'round to your apartment?"

"Yes." Cole's voice sounded strained. She felt a muscle in his arm twitch. "I remember."

"Do you remember what we talked about?" She drew back to look up at him, watching his expression. "What I told you?"

"I remember you said a lot of things that night, Riley."

Suddenly, Cole was leaning in. His mouth was on hers, lips parting. Riley flinched, shoving him so hard he staggered against the counter.

"What the hell?" he shouted, rubbing his hip.

"What are you doing?"

"You were talking about the night we fucked! I thought you were after a repeat?"

"*No!*"

"Then what, Goddamn?"

"I wanted to talk!"

"Wow." Cole shook his head. "You invite me in after pulling a gun on me? Act all weird, then start talking about the past? Cuddling up to me?"

"No, that wasn't what—"

"What was this? Some new way to screw with me?"

"No, I—"

"You picked Wood just to get at me, didn't you? You picked him even though you knew how much I wanted a shot at this job!" Cole didn't let her answer. "Yeah, OK, you got the promotion and, yeah, I was pissed. But *Wood*?" He pushed himself from the counter and came toward her.

Her fingers reached instinctively behind her, sliding toward her gun.

"We've worked together twelve fucking years, Riley! One drunken night and you've dismissed me ever since. That's the real reason you didn't want me on your team, isn't it? Because you're still pissed at yourself for fucking me!"

"No!" The denial came out too fast. "I picked Logan because he's a good cop. He doesn't let his friends off when they're caught speeding, for starters."

Cole's eyes widened in disbelief. "And I've not been covering for my junkie brother all these years!"

The flush fanned hot across her cheeks.

"Yeah," Cole said, nodding. "And I never forced you that night, Riley. It's not my fault you're ashamed of what you did. For you to keep punishing me all these years? Well, ask yourself who's the bad cop here." His eyes alighted on her hand splayed on the counter, fingers pointing toward her gun. "You gonna shoot me?" He shook his head. "You're fucking crazy." He strode down the hallway.

The slam of the front door echoed through the empty house.

Back in the bathroom, Riley laid her Glock on the vanity and splashed her face from the faucet. As she straightened, she saw herself in the mirror, threads of water trailing down her cheeks, her skin pale despite her tan. Her fingers tightened on the sink as her mind conjured the memory of waking in Cole's bed, the scratch of his cheap sheets on her skin.

Other images flickered—the dealer in Venice Beach, who made her bed smell of patchouli, the strangers in dive bars and motel rooms— each encounter somehow a replay of the first time, like she was trying to find her way out through it. Only there was never a door, just a deeper spiral into self-loathing.

She felt a bubble of rage rise up and burst in her. Rage at Cole and all those grasping, eager men; rage at her brother who brought that monster into her life and who had fallen apart when she needed him most; rage at her father—*a fucking lawyer*—who never gave her a chance at justice and who'd damned God knows how many other girls to a similar fate at Hunter's hands; rage at her mother for choosing the numbing haze of prescription drugs over the hard fact of her daughter's rape.

But, mostly, the rage was at herself. She peeled back her lips and screamed at her reflection. Then she slammed her fist into the mirror, splitting her knuckles open with the force. She left blood trickling down the sides of the sink and a jagged crater in the center of the mirror, fractures spidering outward. Her face in the glass was broken. Outside, the security light blinked off, leaving the house in a pool of darkness.

39

That night, Riley went to bed with her gun beside her. In the dawn, after a fitful hour of sleep, she went downstairs and drank three strong coffees. Her knuckles had stopped bleeding, but she had to bandage her hand to cover the telltale bruising.

Ethan still hadn't come home. She phoned again, but he wasn't picking up. She was beginning to fear something had happened to him—something to do with the appearance of the necklace. She left another message. She also left a voice mail for Sadie, saying not to bring Maddie to the house, then called Rose to tell her the same. When her aunt asked why, she said it was to do with the case, but that did little to allay Rose's concern.

"Riley, honey, what's going on? You don't sound like yourself."

By seven she left the house, watchful and alert as she crossed the yard to the Dodge. The air was still, mist curling like smoke over the creek. The oppressive darkness was gone, everything in its rightful place: birds chirping, bees humming. No sign that anything was wrong. Except everything was. She threw her jacket on the backseat, then put the sealed freezer bag she was carrying on top of it. Inside were the necklace and envelope.

On the way into Waterloo, she called dispatch and told them she'd seen someone lingering around her house—that it was most likely a reporter, but she wanted someone to keep an eye out. If whoever had left the necklace was still in the area, Patrol would hopefully get a look at them.

In the office, she went back through the investigation paperwork while she waited for Klein and Gooch, due to give their profile of the killer. She found it difficult to concentrate, her mind jumping between the argument with Cole, her missing brother, and all the possibilities of that necklace, shot through with brutal flashes of the night of her assault. It was a relief when Amy Fox entered.

Fox handed her a coffee, then set a pastry box on Schmidt's desk. She'd got the detective's favorite donuts. "I've just spoken to Cedar Medical, Sarge. Lizbeth Garret hasn't been checked in there either. I've put in a request with her doctor to access her medical records."

Riley looked over Fox's shoulder at the file she'd compiled on Lizbeth Garret. There were notes on her background and a photograph showing a woman around her own age, with curly blond hair and freckles. "OK. Let's leave it after that. I don't want you chasing your tail over what's most likely nothing. Maybe Hoyt didn't know his sister was at the hospital? Or maybe he was protecting her? Maybe she has a drug addiction or something?"

Half an hour later, Klein and Gooch arrived, then the rest of her team. Jackson Cole was on time today. He didn't look at her as he entered, his face tight. Schmidt, Logan, Nolan, and Becker all arrived looking eager to see what the BAU agents would have to say about their killer, but Logan's enthusiasm turned to concern when he caught sight of her bandaged knuckles.

"You OK, Sarge?" he asked quietly.

"A stupid accident. I tried to make dinner." Her laugh came out hollow.

Logan gave a half-smile. "And there was me thinking you only used the microwave."

Riley noticed Klein watching the exchange. His gaze went to her wounded hand, and she knew he sensed the lie. "We're ready, Agent," she said stiffly.

"Good morning," said Klein, the room settling at his voice. "We've spent the past two days going over your reports. First let me say that the work you've done on this case is both thorough and exemplary." He looked at Riley. "We have, however, come to a slightly different set of conclusions."

"Different how?" demanded Riley. She felt blindsided. Embarrassed in front of her team. Why hadn't Klein called her first? So much for him not stepping on any toes.

"I'm sorry, Sergeant, I had hoped to go over this with you last night," Klein responded. "I couldn't get through."

She remembered the missed calls she'd seen after Cole had gone. She hadn't even checked who they were from, sitting numbly in the kitchen, gun beside her, another beer cooling her bruised hand. "I had a family emergency." She felt heat rise in her cheeks as Cole's eyes flicked to her.

"Well, while there are similarities that present as highly unusual across your three victims—the evidence of biting, the missing flesh indicating either cannibalism or trophy hunting—there are also divergences in the killer's MO. There are explanations for that, as we shall discuss. But without DNA, we can only work off the assumption that the same man killed all three women. On the subject of DNA," added Klein, "I had confirmation from Quantico this morning. They've received the samples from the state lab. They'll work on getting results as soon as possible. Hopefully within the week."

"That's great news," Riley murmured, wondering what the results would show. Might they lead to Hunter? Could he really be back? Might his traces be found on these women, too? She forced away the sickening thought that Chloe—all of them—might have died because she hadn't reported him all those years ago. Because her family had shushed it away. *Am I to blame?*

"So, our main divergence is on your prime suspect. Based on our findings so far, we do not believe George Anderson is the killer."

Riley felt the words like a shot of ice.

Klein held up his hand at the stir this caused among the others. "I'll let Agent Gooch talk you through the profile."

Gooch took out his notebook. "If we assume all three women were killed by the same man, then the first victim, based on autopsy reports, is Gracie Foster."

Fox put her hand up tentatively. "We've been saying *he*. Can we be certain it's a man?"

It was Klein who responded. "Female serial killers are extremely rare. We're still not entirely sure why. Testosterone is one possible factor. In our experience, women tend to internalize their problems. Men tend to explode outwards."

Fox nodded.

"Gracie Foster's mother reported her missing on the fourteenth." Gooch pointed to the poster of Gracie, the skull ring on her finger a sparkling omen. "Time of death estimated to be the fifteenth to the seventeenth, but the ME reckons she didn't go into the water until around the nineteenth. So, she was kept somewhere, possibly alive, for a day or more, then killed, before being put in some sort of cold storage for another few days. The day before he dumped Gracie in the river, our UNSUB kills Nicole King at the plant. He returns to King's body over the next day or two, which is when much of the mutilation and bite marks occurred."

Klein cut in. "That isn't uncommon with serial killers. And if they can't return to the body, they will often return to the murder site, or the grave. We've caught several by staging ceremonies at gravesites with family and friends to lure them out."

Riley thought of James Miller. His hollow laugh, his vodka breath, his scattergun anger. She doubted he'd go along with any such thing.

"Then, on the twenty-first, he attacks Chloe Miller."

"What makes you think Anderson couldn't have done any of this?" Logan asked Gooch. "Especially given his military background? His broken marriage? Loss of job and home. Drug use?"

"I said we do not *believe* Anderson did this," corrected Klein. "Not that he couldn't have done it. If your only victim was Nicole King, then I would agree—Anderson is a solid suspect. But he doesn't fit with the others, not with what we know at this stage at least."

"I believe your UNSUB is a local man," said Gooch, "or one with good knowledge of the area. He's white. Thirty to fifty years old. Strong and fit."

Hunter matched the age and build. Riley took out her cell. Still nothing from Ethan. She saw Klein was looking at her and stuck the phone back in her pocket.

"He drives a vehicle—either a pickup, or perhaps a truck with cold storage. He almost certainly has access to a residence in the area. There will have been mental health issues in his recent past, possibly combined with alcohol or drug misuse. He will have experienced something that triggered him to begin killing. It could have been the loss of a job, a relationship breakdown. These types of men are time bombs."

Fox stuck up her hand again. "What about Anderson's disappearance? Isn't it odd that no one has seen him for weeks? Doesn't that speak to his guilt?"

"I believe Anderson witnessed the killing, or the subsequent mutilation of King," Gooch answered. "He either fled, or was himself killed by the UNSUB."

"So what do we do?" Schmidt wanted to know. "We have the whole town looking for someone you say isn't our man."

"Gracie Foster," responded Gooch. "She's how you'll find him."

"Gracie was the first," Klein said. "But, more than that, she was important to him in some way. There was no clear sign of strangulation, no obvious savagery or violent mutilation with her. He cut the flesh from her body after her death with precision and care. He kept her in cold storage so decomposition was slowed. He didn't leave her body out in the open to spoil like he did with King. He weighted her down in water. Gracie Foster was someone your killer needed to hide. Either because of a connection to him, or because he regretted the kill—quite possibly both. But the act of that first kill destabilized him. King and Miller's murders were brutal, fueled by rage and compulsion—an overwhelming urge to destroy and to consume. Their bodies reflect a changed state of mind. He is more violent now."

"And the bites?" Logan ventured. "Why does he do that?"

"Often there can be an element of sexual gratification. But, in my experience, it is much more about a need for power. For control."

Riley flinched at the memory of Hunter's teeth sinking in.

"These men have often experienced a lack of that in their lives," Klein continued. "An abusive parent, problems with sexual performance, failure in their careers. It drives them to create that control for themselves. To assume power over another human being's life—and death."

"It almost sounds like you're excusing them." Logan said.

"No," Klein answered. "We're trying to understand them, so we can get better at catching them. Better still, learn to stop them before they start."

"What about Gracie's mom?" asked Fox. "Sarah? Do you think something's happened to her?"

"I'm afraid that seems highly likely," replied Klein. "Given the circumstances of her and her daughter's disappearances. Again, though, Sarah Foster could be a link by which we find him."

"So how do we do that?" Cole wanted to know.

"We need to go through all the contacts you have for Sarah and Gracie," said Klein. "Look into the backgrounds of everyone connected to them with fresh eyes and our profile in mind."

After telling Schmidt and Logan to begin taping up contact details and backgrounds of everyone connected to the Fosters, Riley excused herself. She felt scattered, unfocused.

Klein caught her on the way out. "Is everything all right, Sergeant?"

Riley glanced at her team, busy with their tasks. "Yes."

"You seem distracted."

She saw the gold star falling out of the envelope into her palm, but held Klein's gaze. "You're not here to profile me, Agent."

"No. But I am here to help."

For a moment, she felt seized by a desire to tell Klein everything—Hunter, her past, her fear her monster could have returned. But she shook the thought away. "I just need a moment."

Five minutes later, Riley was sitting in the locker room's hush. The place smelled of deodorant, boot polish, and stale food. A tap was dripping in one of the showers. The sound was hypnotic, calming her agitated mind. She thought through the profile. Yes, Hunter matched some of it. But if Klein and Gooch were right and the killer was connected to

Gracie and Sarah Foster, the only way Hunter fit was if he knew them, meaning he'd most likely returned to Black Hawk some time ago.

She replayed last night: coming home and finding the shed open, the box on the floor, that whispering in the darkness. The shock of the necklace. Then, Cole.

She gritted her teeth.

Ask yourself who's the bad cop here.

Those words had scalded. Mostly because Cole was right. She had protected Ethan when she should have led by example. That was the whole Fisher family's problem: hiding the truth from the world, from each other. Her brother's addictions, her niece's pain, her mom's slide into that painkiller haze—a path Lori now seemed to be following—her grandfather striving to keep his dementia hidden. Then Hunter—the big shameful secret—that in the end consumed them.

If there was a chance Hunter was back and a chance—however small—he had something to do with the attacks, she needed to speak up. She owed it to her team and to Chloe and Nicole and Gracie. Maybe she could get them the justice she'd never had, even if that meant opening herself up to questions and gossip. Even if it meant risking her career.

Rising, she opened her locker and took out the sealed bag with the envelope and necklace inside. It wouldn't take long for Bob Nolan to dust them for prints. She picked up the photograph she'd stolen from Chloe's album, taken that night at the state fair. She had a name and a face. Nolan could run a trace.

40

The light appeared at the edges of her vision, splintering through. It hurt, and she turned her face away. There was a groan somewhere close by. She tried again, cracking open her eyes.

She could see the blanket she was swaddled in and the metal bars of the bed. A tube dangled in mid-air. She followed it up to a bag of liquid suspended above her like a drooping lung. Beyond were other beds. Some were empty, stripped of bedding. Others were occupied, humps of bodies beneath the blankets. The place was lit by spotlights on tripods, glaring off pale white walls. She squinted as her gaze roved. It was all strangely familiar, but she had no sense of how long she'd been here, or why. Had she had a seizure?

There was another groan. She lifted her head, trying to seek the source. The shape in the bed across from her was stirring, the blanket shifting. She sank weakly onto the pillow. She opened her mouth to call out and was shocked by the papery whisper. She was parched. Her tongue was swollen, a dry slug squirming in her mouth.

Her fingers fumbled for a call button. She'd stayed at a hospital as a teenager, after one of her worst seizures, and remembered the button you could press to bring a smiling nurse with a soda, or a painkiller. Her fingertips skittered over the metal bars, but she couldn't find anything obvious, and her hand was stopped from going farther. She felt a pinch in her arm as she struggled, and the tube snaking up to the bag shifted. They'd put her on an IV.

Feeling panicky, she lifted her head again. This place was not quite right. It seemed weirdly insubstantial. Now that her eyes were more accustomed to the light, she realized the pale white walls were in fact plastic sheeting, enveloping the rows of beds in an ethereal cocoon. She tracked the curve of it, up over her head. It looked like some sort of polythene greenhouse. The kind farmers grew vegetables in. Or one of those medical field tents. Beyond its membrane was a sense of shadowy space. Stranger still was the floor. It looked like cracked concrete.

The person in the nearby bed was moaning louder. The blanket had slipped away, and she could see bare feet callused with corns. There was something wrapped around the patient's ankles. Thick brown cuffs, belted tight, the straps attached to the bars of the bed. Restraints, she realized, in mounting fear. The person was in clear distress, and there was no one to help. Her heart thumped. Where was her family? Her kids? She called out again, but her voice cracked into nothing.

Panicking, she tried to sit. Pain lanced through her head, along with the stinging intrusion of a catheter, twisting deep inside. The blanket shifted, and she tugged her arm free. It only came out a short way. A strip of discolored tape, curling at the edges, bound the drip to her forearm, its prick in her vein. But it was her skin that her gaze was drawn to. Her whole arm was mottled with red scabs. It looked as if she'd been scraped over concrete. Had she been in an accident? Perhaps at the farm? The thought snagged in her mind. There *had* been an accident. Hadn't there?

She tried to bring her arm closer to inspect the weird wounds but couldn't. Her wrist was encircled by a leather cuff attached to the bed. She realized she could feel the same pressure around her other wrist and both ankles. She, too, was restrained. What was this place? An asylum? Had a seizure left her with brain damage? Waves of nausea rose up in her. For a moment, she thought she might vomit, but her stomach felt hollow. She had no idea of when she'd last eaten. At the thought of food, her insides clenched. Something clawed at her mind. She shrank from it, not wanting to let it in.

The plastic walls rippled. Her eyes darted to the end of the white tunnel. Something was out there—two thin shapes coming closer. She lay still, heart pounding. There was the whine of a zipper and the plastic sheeting was drawn aside. Two figures ducked in.

"You have to talk to him." It was a woman who spoke. Her voice was weary, and there was a note of hopelessness in her tone. "How long are you going to let this go on?"

The squeak of a door opening. A rustle of packaging.

She risked a look. The figures were standing by a couple of fridges, wires snaking across the concrete floor. There was a cart with metal instruments laid out. The figures were wearing scrubs and face masks.

The larger of the two—a man by his build—was pulling on latex gloves. "I've told you—he's not interested." The man didn't look at the woman as he spoke. "He knows all this."

"But this is crazy! It's out of control."

The man turned on the woman, his voice strengthening through his mask. "Don't you think I know that?"

A loud groan made both figures start.

"Shit." The man was staring at the bed where the patient was stirring. His eyes narrowed. "See to him, would you?"

The woman ducked down and removed something from one of the fridges. Her hands shook as she ripped a syringe from a packet. She advanced on the bed warily, brandishing the syringe like a weapon. "He's coming round quicker than he should."

"Up his dose. I don't want that son of a bitch awake. I've got enough to deal with."

While the woman moved in to administer to the patient, the man remained at the cart, pulling things from packets.

Trapped in the bed, she watched, until her gaze was drawn to the place where the two had entered. The zipper hadn't been fully closed, and a breeze was shifting through the plastic sheeting. Beyond, she caught a glimpse of vast space. The tent was inside some sort of massive structure, the sides and roof of which were rusted corrugated metal. Little gaps here and there let in slants of daylight. Where the light fell, she saw what looked like animal pens, broken bars hanging loose. Any last notion that this was a place of care vanished. A shocked cry escaped her lips. There was movement nearby. The woman in the scrubs was staring straight at her.

The woman came forward, still brandishing the syringe. The patient in the nearby bed had stopped groaning.

"*Please!*"

The woman leaned in. "There, now."

As the woman looked down at her, a memory crawled from the corners of her mind. As it started to come clearer, she whimpered in fear. There was sunlight and screaming. And blood. So much blood.

Oh God.

"It's all right, Lizbeth," murmured the woman, reaching up to twist a valve on the IV. "You're going to be all right."

41

Riley entered her grandfather's room with an uncustomary feeling of hope. An orderly she'd passed in the corridor had commented that Joe was unusually talkative today.

"Hello, Grandpa." She kissed his cheek. "How are you?"

He patted her bandaged hand as she sat. "Still on the right side of the dirt, Ann."

Riley's hope faded. She was used to the strangeness of her grandfather talking to her as if she were his dead wife, or someone else. But it felt worse now.

Joe Fisher turned his attention back to the TV, high up on the wall. A news story from earlier was rolling—some ex-staffer claiming Jess Cook had links to the radical eco-terrorist group, Mission Earth. A snap poll had Cook three points down against Hamilton. There she was, ducking into her car, unsmiling, while reporters crowded toward her, mics outstretched.

"I wish you were here, Grandpa."

"I'm always here, love."

Tears stung her eyes. "The necklace you gave me? The one I lost at the state fair? I think maybe Hunter, the man who—" Riley halted, still unable to say those words out loud. "It's possible he's returned. Might have attacked more women." She trailed off, shaking her head.

All day, while her team busied themselves compiling fresh lists of Sarah Foster's contacts to consider alongside the BAU's profile—friends, family, ex-boyfriends—she'd been thinking it through.

After the attack, Hunter had left her alone. He'd not come by the house again. She remembered her mom—before she told her parents what had happened—asking Ethan where his charming friend was. So why would he return after all these years when he'd got what he wanted back then? Why would he reveal himself? Make himself a target? Her mind, swinging wildly between fear and doubt, had knotted her up in such confusion she had no idea how to untangle herself.

"Sheriff Reed has brought in the FBI. I worry I'm not doing my job. That I'm not in control of the investigation anymore. These women, Grandpa? How they died?" Her voice cracked. "You always told me to leave cases at the office. But I can't. They haunt me."

The anchorman was going through the latest poll. Her grandpa's attention was fixed on the TV.

"Maybe Reed was right? Maybe I am too close to this? Perhaps that's why I can't see it?" She sighed and let go of his hand. What was the point? "I have to go, Grandpa. Ethan's not come home since yesterday. I'm worried about him. If Hunter is back . . . ?"

"We should've found that boy." Joe Fisher's words came in a low growl. His eyes narrowed to fierce slits. His hands grasped the worn arms of his chair. "We should've found him, Michael! Shot that son of a bitch!"

Michael. Her father? "Shot him?" she whispered.

"I searched for him, but you told me to forget it. Said I should leave it, for Riley's sake. You said you didn't want her going through a trial—you'd seen too many women broken by that." The old man's voice was strangled with emotion. "Goddamn it, Michael! We should have done *something*!"

Riley's eyes burned.

"You always were a bad judge of character, son. Better for a lawyer than a cop, I guess. Easier to turn a blind eye to wrong." Joe pointed. "Guess that's why you worked for him so long."

Riley followed her grandfather's finger to the TV screen. The footage was of Bill Hamilton waving to the cameras in front of a new hotel being built in Des Moines. He was smiling broadly. "What do you mean?" she murmured, looking back at Joe, whose brow was puckered.

"How many blind eyes did you turn for him, son?"

"Are you talking about Hamilton, Grandpa?" she said, crouching and looking up at him, her hands on his knees. "Did Pop know something about him? Did *you*?"

His gaze shifted, drifting over her shoulder. His face changed, all the rage draining from it, hard furrows softening into wrinkles.

"Grandpa?"

Joe's eyes fluttered back to her. "Best get to school now, sweetheart."

Riley sat back on her heels. She stared at the TV. Hamilton was still there, shaking hands with supporters. She thought of his call coming out of the blue. His interest in the case but, more specifically, in James Miller.

A real champion for our state. Our future.

The edge in his voice. The subtle sense of warning.

She thought of Miller's seething anger and strangled guilt, his not reporting Chloe missing. Talking to the mayor about the case was one thing, but getting the governor to vouch for him? Reed had cautioned her about pressing Miller, despite her suspicions.

An affluent and well-respected man in our community.

What if the problem with this case wasn't that she couldn't see—but that she had always seen?

Monsters could hide in plain sight if they wore the right masks. Ed Gein—the good neighbor—with a house full of horrors.

He's such a nice boy.

Yes, James Miller had a seemingly solid alibi for Nicole King's murder, and they'd found no evidence that he was responsible for Chloe's death. But what if he was involved in some other way? Something that might hold the key to his wife's murder?

Riley rose, her eyes on Bill Hamilton's smooth and smiling face. As the footage cut back to Jess Cook, who glanced at the camera as she slipped into her car, Riley made her decision.

Out in the corridor, it didn't take her long to find the number on the campaign website.

A voice answered in two rings. "Jess Cook for a better Iowa. How may I help you?"

42

Logan, it's me." Riley eased the Dodge to a crawl. The highway traffic was heavy. "Listen, I'm going to Des Moines. Tonight."

"Has something happened?" He was quick with concern.

"I've got a lead I want to pursue." She glanced at an eighteen-wheeler coming up in her rearview. "It's a long shot, but I need to take it."

"I was supposed to be babysitting the kids tonight, but Carol will understand if you need me."

"Thanks, but I told Klein I'm going to be working from home, digging into Sarah Foster's contacts to see if anyone fits the profile. If anyone asks, I need you to corroborate that. And I need you to work on those contacts for me. I'll email my files."

"Can I ask what this lead is, Sarge?"

The traffic started up again, the warm wind coming through the window, tousling her hair. The truck juddered to life behind her. "Not until I know if it goes anywhere."

There was a pause. "Are you really OK?"

She sighed. "I just need to solve this one."

"I get it. But if you need any—"

Her cell bleeped, another call coming through. She didn't recognize the number. "I've got to go."

"When will you be back?"

"Tomorrow evening. I'll speak to you then."

"Safe travels, boss."

"Thanks, Logan." Riley tapped the screen to answer the incoming call. "Fisher speaking."

"Riley? It's me. Mia."

Riley's surprise dissolved as she remembered she'd given Mia her card during the interview. "Hi." There was silence. "Hello?"

"Hey, look, I'm sorry I missed you."

"Missed me?"

"Last night? I came over?" Mia's tone rose in question. "I thought your brother would have told you. I gave him an envelope. Did he not give it to you?"

Riley felt her hands turn to Jell-O on the wheel. She braked sharply, causing the juggernaut behind to swerve to avoid her. The driver leaned on his horn and flipped her the finger as he thundered past. She pulled onto the hard shoulder, her hands shaking.

"Riley?"

Traffic roared past. The air smelled of diesel and dust. "It was you?" She had thought Hunter was back. Had been living with that horror for a night and a day. She had given the necklace and the photograph to Nolan, asked him to start a trace.

"I'm sorry. I guess I should have waited to see you. I just—" Mia paused, the sound of a baby crying in the background. There was the thud of a door, and the crying faded.

"Why did you have it, Mia? How?"

"Chloe. She went the morning after—you know. She went to where you said it happened. She found your necklace under the trees." Mia sighed down the line. "She always planned to give it back to you. She knew how much it meant to you. But I think she was scared of upsetting you."

Chloe's tentativeness. Something always on the tip of her tongue.

"In the end, she asked if I would give it to you. But then you never came back to school after that summer. We didn't see you again for so long, and by then, I guessed you maybe wouldn't want it. But after . . . ? I don't know, it just felt right. Chloe always wanted you to have it."

"And you gave it to Ethan?"

"Yeah, I—"

"I have to go, Mia."

Riley disconnected the call and put her foot down, tires screeching on the tarmac as she barreled along the highway toward Cedar Falls.

Down the drive, swerving to a stop in a storm of dust, she saw her grandfather's pickup. Ethan was back, but she felt no relief. Only rage. A white flame in her mind. The trees around the creek burned in the last of the light.

Ethan was in the kitchen, stabbing a knife into the cellophane of a TV dinner. He glanced up. His face changed at her expression.

Riley ignored Scrounger as he dashed to see her. "Why didn't you tell me Mia came? Why didn't you call me back? I left a thousand messages!" As the dog barked at her raised voice, she grabbed his collar and compelled him out into the hallway, shutting the door.

Ethan threw the knife on the counter. "I needed to think, all right. Needed some time on my own."

"Time on your own? Right, because your time is more important than anyone else's."

"I wasn't expecting to see her. Mia. It just—brought up some stuff."

Riley's mind filled with an image of that box of their old things, open on the floor of the shed. A cold laugh shot from her. "Brought up some stuff? How do you think it made me feel?" She thumped her chest. The pain felt good and right.

"What do you mean?"

"You didn't ask what was in the envelope? Didn't bother to check?"

"No. I—"

"It was my necklace, Ethan! The one Grandpa gave me. The one your best friend tore from my neck while he was raping me!" There it was: she'd pulled the pin.

Ethan's face drained. "Riley—" His voice was hoarse. "I didn't know."

"You never know! Never think! Not about anyone but yourself! Not me. Not Maddie. When did you last go see Grandpa?"

"I can't deal with this."

As he went to go past her, she caught his arm. He smelled of ciga-rettes and beer. She wanted to punch him, batter him with both fists. "You can't deal with this? When have you *ever* dealt with this?"

"Riley—"

"You knew I was drunk that night! You saw Hunter lead me away!" Her voice was high-pitched, turning from shout to cry. Part of her wanted to stop—was horrified by this naked pain. But she couldn't. The words were spewing out of her like hot bile. "Why didn't you stop him? I was *fourteen*!"

Scrounger was barking beyond the door.

"But it was you who fell apart," she seethed. "You always have. Even after Mom and Dad died, you didn't step up. Didn't help us. Help *me*. It's always up to me. The bills. The house. A job. Your daughter!"

"What could I do? I couldn't help you! Couldn't change what hap-pened! How do I begin to try?" He wrestled from her grip, pushed his way toward the door.

Riley followed. "You don't get to do this, Ethan! Not tonight! You don't get to run away like always!"

He whirled on her. "You were the one who ran away!" He stabbed a finger toward her. "Mom, Dad—we all thought you were dead! Christ, Riley, you have no idea. All those fucking months? Dad and Grandpa hardly slept for trying to find you. But Mom couldn't even get out of bed. They barely spoke a word to me." His voice broke. "They blamed me as much as I blamed myself. Blamed me for what *he* did to you!" Ethan's knees buckled, and he slid to the kitchen floor, his head in his hands. A strange noise came from between his fingers.

He was crying. She couldn't remember when he'd last done that. As Riley stared at her forty-year-old brother sobbing into his hands, she thought of her return from California.

By the time she came home, Ethan had already dropped out of col-lege where he'd been studying law, following in the footsteps of their father. While she had fought to rebuild her life with their grandfather's help, finished high school, and started a degree, Ethan had simply faded into the background. His college friends moved on without him into careers and lives, while he stayed at home, spiraling down into drugs and alcohol, dead-end jobs, and a toxic marriage.

She'd always known she wasn't the only victim of Hunter's crime. But in the family's silence, it had been easy to ignore Ethan's pain. Maybe she should be more pleased, more *proud* of the fact that she had been strong enough to forge a life, a career. More understanding that he had not.

She walked to him, reached a hand toward his shoulder, then let it drop to her side. Instead, she sat on the cracked linoleum in front of him. Scrounger had stopped barking but was pawing at the door.

After a while, Ethan raised his head. His eyes were red. "I found that old doll you used to play with, out in the shed. The one Grandma gave you? That Raggedy Ann thing?" He sniffed, smiling sadly. "You played with it until it was dead, Mom said. In the end she took it away. Told you it had diseases or something."

"I remember," Riley murmured.

"And you went right out and brought the filthy old thing back into your room." His smile faded. "I knew something had happened at the fair. Even before you told Mom and Dad. Something bad. When we came back, I remember you packed up all your toys—your Barbies and teddies, and Raggedy Ann. You put them in a box in the shed. I watched you do it from my room. It broke my fucking heart, Riley." Ethan met her gaze. "I can't begin to tell you how sorry I am."

She shook her head, feeling it all loosen and break inside her. Tears fell to splash onto her jeans. Her breath, clenched tight, shuddered out in a whimper.

Ethan crawled across the kitchen floor and drew her to him. "If I knew where Hunter was, I'd kill him for what he did to you," he breathed. "I'd kill that rapist piece of shit with my bare hands."

There was a sound at the screen door.

Riley twisted her head from her brother's grip to see her niece standing there, face pinched pale, mouth open in shock. "Maddie?"

The girl ran down the porch steps. Ethan and Riley followed her out. "Maddie, wait!"

She ignored them, grabbing her bike and jumping on.

"Madison!"

They went after her, but the girl was gone, peddling madly across the grass, out down the drive.

Ethan turned to Riley, pulling the pickup's keys from his pocket. "We'll catch up to her."

She faltered. "I'm supposed to be going to Des Moines tonight. *Shit!* This case."

"It's OK. I've got this. Riley, I've got this," he repeated when she hesitated.

"I'll be back tomorrow." Riley looked down the drive where Maddie had vanished, imagined what her niece must have thought, seeing the two of them collapsed on the kitchen floor, Ethan growling about killing someone. "Let me explain this to her, OK? When I'm home."

He nodded, then yanked open the pickup's door and climbed in.

She called out, "I'll be on my cell, if you need me!"

The engine groaned to life. Riley stepped back as Ethan reversed. She watched him go. The last of the light was bleeding across the creek. She closed her eyes, feeling the tide of emotion draining from her, leaving her scraped bare.

She was heading for the house when she heard that soft whisper again. This time, she saw it—down near the creek—a gold gleam moving through the grass. Her eyes picked out the black chevrons all along the scaled length; the striped whip of a tail, the sinuous body, thick and muscular, winding through the grass. It was a timber rattlesnake—one of the most venomous snakes in the country—and one of the biggest she'd seen. It was heading up from the creek, toward the shed. As she watched, transfixed, it dipped its wide head to the dust and slowly squeezed its massive body beneath the old warped doors.

43

Lizbeth Garret dreamed she was back at the farm, surrounded by the smells and sounds of home: hay steaming with warmth in the barn, grass summer-sweet in the pasture, her father's curt tones calling the kids in from play, the clatter of plates as her brothers set the table. Her mom had made her favorite. Roast chicken, skin crisped to bursting.

Her father did the carving, as always. He would spend a full five minutes preparing the knife, scraping it across the sharpener in fluid movements, honing the edge. The rasp of that blade always made her stomach growl. Her brothers went straight for the wings and legs, but she never minded. Let them have the bruise-colored flesh, that gamey meat threaded with purple veins. She only liked the perfect, pristine breast.

Her father was carving the bird, meat sliding from the knife in slivers. But there was something wrong. She could see blood running from the flesh. Bubbles of it beading and bursting. She tried to tell him, but he wasn't listening. She addressed her mom, calling out a warning, but the burble of voices and the jingle of cutlery drowned her out. She felt panicky, watching the blood drip along the length of the blade, oozing obscenely out of the dead bird. They would all get sick! But none of them were listening. She looked down as her own plate was set in front of her. All that was on it was blood, glutinous as jelly, dark like wine. Her stomach cramped at the sight of it.

Somewhere, she heard screaming. She left the table and stepped out onto the porch. It was late afternoon, light splintering through the trees. It hurt her eyes. Her skin looked weird—all mottled red. The air was rent with another shriek. Her brother was near the barn, collapsed on his knees by the wood pile. There was a saw in the grass beside him.

Hoyt was screaming like an animal and clutching his wrist, blood spurting through his fingers. Their mother flew across the grass toward him, her cries joining his. Their father was inside the house, shouting down the phone for an ambulance. Her kids were in the window, faces shocked against the glass. No one seemed to notice Lizbeth as she walked toward her brother. Her heart was hammering, wild as a drumbeat. She wanted to turn back, but her feet kept walking her forward. The blood was almost black, spilling in lines down Hoyt's arm. She wanted to look away, but her eyes were transfixed by the pulsing wound.

No.

She twisted, trying to escape. Not wanting to continue.

Her brother was still shrieking, her mom holding on to his arm, fingers slicked red. Lizbeth had almost reached them. She could smell the metal tang on the air, like old pennies warm in the hand. It was all going to happen again.

"My God. Is she awake?"

A man's voice filtered through the screaming. The sunlit world around her cracked.

"She's probably just dreaming. I'll up her dose."

"You told me you'd keep her under. That she wouldn't know any of this."

That voice was familiar, but she couldn't place it. Her mind was swimming with confusion.

"I'm trying my best, OK!"

"Your best?" There was a thud and a clatter. "It ain't good enough, Goddamn it!"

Lizbeth's eyes flickered open. Her relief at leaving the dream faded as she saw the rows of beds and the white walls of the plastic cocoon. She was still in that place. Wherever—*whatever*—it was.

There were two figures at the far end. One had his back to her. He wore a faded T-shirt, curly gray-blond hair skimming the neckline. He was looming over another man, who was pushed up against a cart. This man was wearing green scrubs. She had a flutter of memory—a man and a woman dressed like that. Taut voices and tired eyes.

"You swore you'd fix this! I've done everything you've asked. Put my life—*my family*—on the line for you!"

"I just need more time!"

The curly-haired man was shaking his head, not listening. "And now with the cops sniffing around my place? Christ!"

"You've got your son to thank for the cops. You should be thanking *me* for the fucking lawyer I just busted my bank open for!" The man in the scrubs bent to pick up something off the floor. It was a pair of scissors. He straightened, wielding them like a weapon. "You're not the only one who's suffered here!" Emotion cracked through his voice.

The curly-haired man took a step back. After a pause, he shoved a hand through his hair. "What if I take her to a hospital?"

"You really want to take that risk? I told you what he said he'd do if any of this got out. He's in too deep now." A sharp exhalation. "We all are."

"We can't go on like this." The curly-haired man's voice was low. "John's been asking questions. He knows something's wrong."

"You've not told him anything?"

"No. But I don't know how much longer you expect to keep this quiet from the rest of them." The curly-haired man flung a desperate hand toward the beds. "Or from the Goddamn world!"

"What about the pills?" The man in the scrubs put the scissors back on the cart. "You said you had a lead?"

A pause. "One of my sons got the name of someone who's been selling Fenozen. Some deadbeat called Charles Moore."

That voice. *So familiar.* Lizbeth tried to lift her head, but she was too weak. The world was growing dim around her. She was sinking into darkness again. Waves of fatigue washed over her. She was powerless to stop the tide from taking her.

"If we stop them getting to the street, we might be able to slow this down. Buy ourselves some time."

Lizbeth could hear the screaming in her mind. The tide was washing her back to the dream.

Not a dream. A memory.

"Swear you'll help her."

"When the deal is done, she'll get the best care possible. You have my word."

Sunlight and screaming. She was walking toward Hoyt again. The blood was gushing from that wound. She was almost on top of him. Her mother's face was changing. Turning from fear to confusion. Her father was yelling.

That voice.

44

From Black Hawk County to Des Moines, it was a two-hour drive on roads that arrowed endlessly through miles of cornfields, scattered with farms, silos, and one-gas-station towns. Nothing changed but the light: crimson darkening to indigo. Riley knew it didn't change for days in the vastness of the Corn Belt. There was something oppressive in its monotony.

She had never felt so free as when she'd hitchhiked west from Okoboji, seeing the prairies of Nebraska slip into haze behind her and the ramparts of the Rockies rising ahead; through Colorado and Utah to the Pacific, bloodred peaks and deserts giving way to towering sequoias, air tanged with salt and pine, roads winding through golden fog over chasms that tumbled to the ocean.

God, it felt good to be driving. To be leaving the circles she'd been walking in this case, headed in a new direction. She was taking a risk, but with Logan to cover for her there was no reason Reed would find out. If she ended up with something from her meeting with the senator that could help her solve this case, any fallout from her unauthorized trip would be worth it.

With every mile her mind cleared. She felt deep relief, knowing Hunter hadn't returned. She'd left a message for Bob Nolan, telling him to forget the trace. She felt unburdened, too, by the argument with Ethan. The grenade had been pulled, the shock of the blast was over, and now, perhaps, they could begin to sort through what had been thrown up. Her only worry was Maddie, but Ethan called to say the girl had arrived safely at her mom's. She'd refused to see him, but he planned to go around first thing. After Riley warned him about the rattler in the shed, Ethan hung on the line a moment longer as if he wanted to say something else, but then finished up with a quick goodbye.

Des Moines glowed on the skyline long before she reached it. Street-lights were eventually joined by the glare of billboards; Wendy's and Walgreens, motels and fast-food joints. A seedy-looking bar advertised a bike rally on its light board.

RIDE WITH US TO THE BADLANDS.

It had rained here recently, the streets slick. Everywhere, signs shouted about the state fair.

COME! MAKE A THOUSAND MEMORIES!

It was the city she had spent her first years in, but she hadn't been back in a long time—not since the academy at Camp Dodge. For her, the whole city was the scene of Hunter's crime. Ground zero. Des Moines had changed, though. She hardly recognized parts of it. There were new skyscrapers in the financial district, while the brick buildings that spanned the streets of downtown—façades still advertising busi-nesses that had folded decades ago—were home to hip-looking tap-rooms and bustling restaurants. A rainbow flag hung outside a gay club.

Riley checked into a modern business hotel at the bottom of the hill near the capitol. She ordered room service—a limp Caesar salad and two glasses of tepid white wine that she drank while scrolling through her cell. There was a reply from the pest control service she'd left a mes-sage for. A man called Bub promised to call her in the morning about the rattlesnake. There was a message from Logan, saying he'd made a start on the contacts they had for Sarah Foster. No one matched the profile yet, but he was planning on going in early to continue digging. After that, she climbed into the starched sheets and slept surprisingly well.

The next morning, she woke early. Ignoring the four-dollar bottle of mineral water on the nightstand, she drank from the bathroom tap, which tasted of metal. The sky over the city was slate-gray. The meteorologist on the news warned that a storm front building in the southeastern half of the state could generate a supercell by the evening—the kind of storm that spits out tornadoes. The storm had already brought down power lines in the South and they warned of patchy cell-phone coverage through the day. Riley hoped to be heading home before the worst of it.

The diner she'd been told to go to was a ten-minute walk from the hotel, on the hill that sloped up to the capitol, but there were still two hours to wait. She spent them on her laptop in one of the new coffee bars downtown, going back over the investigation, among the frenetic energy of students from Iowa State. Just before ten, she made her way up the hill. State fair signs were plastered all over the street, with pictures of Thrill Ville rides and country music singers at the grandstand, the Big Slide, and the five hundred things you could eat on a stick. Corn dogs and battered Oreos, deep-fried cherry pie and funnel cake. Several boards highlighted the Iowa Food Prize, and she wondered if John Brown and Zephyr Farms still had a chance at winning the prestigious award for their new corn after all the trouble that had begun in their fields.

The gold dome of the capitol gleamed beneath the brooding sky. Riley thought of her father, who'd spent his last years in that building with Bill Hamilton, helping him on his path to the governorship.

How many blind eyes did you turn for him?

The diner was straight out of the fifties, with red leather stools around the counter, rickety booths, and stained menus. This was the Des Moines she knew. There was a glass case filled with slabs of pie. A man flipped patties and over-easy eggs on a sizzling grill while a pasty-faced waitress served a couple of men in denim overalls.

Riley picked one of the booths, as far from the other patrons as possible. The waitress brought coffee. It was proper coffee. Strong enough to start an engine, her grandfather would have said. Her cell rang, vibrating on the Formica. It was Logan. She went to pick it up, but the door opened with a clang of the bell above it and in walked two women. One was in her twenties, dressed in a smart suit and holding a briefcase. The other, older, with cropped sandy hair and large dark glasses, was State Senator Jess Cook.

Riley switched her cell to silent and rose to greet her. "Sergeant Riley Fisher, Black Hawk County Sheriff's Office." She held out her badge. "Thank you for meeting me, ma'am."

"Jess is fine. I'm not governor yet." Cook slid into the booth, her eyes still hidden behind the dark glasses. "This is my assistant."

The young woman sat beside her boss, opposite Riley.

Cook got straight to business. "You said in your message that it was to do with this case in Black Hawk? The murders?"

"In a manner of speaking." Riley fixed her badge on her belt as she sat. She paused as the waitress came over.

"You wanna order?"

Cook answered. "Just coffee." Her tone was clipped and tense— nothing like the friendly, easygoing manner she'd displayed on the campaign trail. She seemed agitated, nervous even.

Riley guessed these allegations about a connection to Mission Earth must be weighing heavily on her so close to the election. "I'm looking into the background of one of our suspects," she told Cook, her voice low. "I believe he could have some association with Governor Hamilton."

Cook stared at her from behind her glasses. "Then why aren't you talking to the governor?"

Riley glanced at the men in overalls, now tucking into plates of fried food. The waitress was chatting to the man at the grill. "I'm not sure I'd get the most comprehensive response."

Cook cocked her head. "You're not saying the governor—? That he could be involved in some way?" The question was light, but there was a tone behind it.

"I don't know anything for certain," Riley said quickly. "But I do want to understand the governor a little more. His associations."

"And who better to ask than his rival?" Cook's tone was dry. "So, it's my opposition research you're after?"

"I know you're busy, ma'am. But any help would be greatly appreciated." Riley glanced out of the window as a car passed. It was a black SUV with tinted windows, driving slowly. "There are lives at stake."

Cook cradled her coffee, but didn't drink. She was silent for a while. Riley wasn't sure she would answer, but then she turned to her assistant. "Give me a minute."

The young woman hesitated, looking between her and Riley, then rose and headed out.

"Not here," said Cook, her attention back on Riley. "Where are you staying?" She nodded when Riley gave her the name of the hotel. "I'll have my assistant leave a message at reception. I'll tell you where and when."

Riley stood when the senator did. She waved her hand as Cook went to pull a wallet from her pocket. "But you think you can help?"

"I think we might be able to help one another, Sergeant Fisher."

Riley sat as Cook slid out of the booth. Through the window, she watched the senator and her assistant climb into a red Toyota hybrid, which pulled away, heading up the hill toward the capitol.

"You want the check?" asked the waitress, eyes on the mugs of coffee still steaming on the table.

"Thanks."

Riley's cell vibrated again, reminding her she had a voice mail. It was from Logan. She listened, fishing in her pocket for cash.

"Hey, Sarge." Logan sounded excited. "We think we could have a match for the . . ." The line crackled, his voice fading. ". . . name's Charles Moore. He's an ex-boyfriend of Sarah Foster's. Patrol spoke to him weeks ago when Gracie first went missing, but he claimed not to have seen her in months. Schmidt left messages for Moore last week, but he was one of those who never got back. According to her sister, Sarah Foster saw him for six months or so. She broke it off after she was fired from the pharmacy. He's white, forty-three, and drives a pickup. He lives out on . . ." The growl of an engine obscured his words. ". . . very isolated. And get this, boss: Moore has been unemployed for a while now, but he worked for years—as a butcher." There was a muffled voice in the background. It sounded like Schmidt. "Listen, Sarge, we're almost there. I'll call you back."

Riley hardly noticed as the waitress came to take the cash. The words of Jim Meyer, the ME in Mercer County, sounded in her mind as he pointed to the cuts on Gracie Foster's body.

I would say whoever made them has worked with flesh before.

45

The Dodge Charger bounced violently along the rutted road. Logan cursed as his cell was almost jolted from his hand. "Jeez, Schmidt, are you aiming for every pothole?"

"Sorry." Schmidt was hunched forward gripping the wheel, squinting through the dust clouds.

The fields were parched, the grass knotted with weeds. It looked like no one had cultivated them in years. An ancient tractor stood in one, rotted with rust. Farm buildings loomed in the distance, at the end of the dirt road.

Logan managed to jab the call button. Pressing the cell to his ear, he gripped the door handle. "Agent Klein? Yes. We're almost there. No, you need to take a *right* off Hawkeye Road. About a mile past the Brewer Stud Ranch. Say again? Agent?" Logan looked at the screen. "Crap. I'm losing signal."

Schmidt shook his head. "They'll be hunting for a turning point for a bit."

"Keep going?" Logan stared at the distant buildings: a box-frame farmhouse, a barn, and a crumbling silo pointing to the overcast sky. "Or wait?"

"If Moore's home, he'll have seen our dust already." Schmidt didn't take his foot off the gas. "Don't want to risk him running."

Logan glanced back at his cell. Nothing from Riley yet. He wished he had pressed her about what the lead in Des Moines was. He thought about the bandage on her hand, curled up just enough for him to see the split skin of her knuckles. No kitchen accident.

Up close, the farm buildings were even more dilapidated, the timbers of the house bleached by sun and rain. The shutters were closed over the windows. It looked like no one had lived here for years. The barn doors yawned into gloom, rusting hulks of machinery visible deeper in. More rundown outbuildings loomed beyond the house, near the silo. There was a pickup truck in the yard, beat-up and caked with dirt, but still far more contemporary than its rambling surroundings.

Logan nodded to it as Schmidt pulled into the yard. "Goodyear tires."

They got out of the car, wary as they crossed to the house. Scraps of rubbish drifted aimlessly, food cartons and plastic tangled in the weeds.

"What's that?" Logan diverted to what looked like a piece of clothing. He halted as he reached it. "Christ!" It was a dead dog. What was left of its fur was crumpled over its maggoty body. A spray of dark matter had dried in the dust beside its head.

"Who the heck would shoot a dog?" Schmidt muttered in disgust. "And just leave it there?"

The air was heavy. There was a reek coming from the house, which grew worse as they neared it.

"Shit," breathed Logan. "What *is* that?"

The door was ajar, leading into rancid darkness.

Logan took out his badge, but kept his free hand near his gun. He rapped on the door with his knuckles. "Mr. Charles Moore? Black Hawk County Sheriff's Office. We need to speak with you."

There was a noise somewhere within. It sounded like the thud of a door. Logan put away his badge and drew his gun, nodding to Schmidt, who followed suit. They entered the house, weapons gripped. The stench was overwhelming. Logan had to fight the urge to put an arm over his nose. He breathed shallowly through his mouth.

The first room was a dining room, dominated by a table. It was filthy. Dirty plates were scattered across it, busy with flies. There were boxes, cartons, and empty pill bottles strewn about the floor, clothes draped over the backs of chairs and teetering piles of magazines. Three doors led off. Two were closed, one was open. Logan and Schmidt headed for the open door, eyes darting.

"Mr. Moore?" Logan tried again. "We're deputies with the Black Hawk County Sheriff's Office. We just want to talk to you."

Through the open door was a kitchen, cast in gloom, the air alive with flies. Logan swallowed back an urge to retch. The stink was indescribable. There was crockery smashed on the floor and pans furry with mold stacked up in the sink, sitting in greasy water that had gone black. There were three heavy-duty wooden chopping boards and several industrial-sized knives on the counter, all stained dark brown. More stains coated the floor. Logan could almost feel the germs slipping into his mouth, crawling inside his skin. As he headed in, boots crunching on broken cups, things scurried into corners. "Rats," he murmured. There were droppings everywhere.

There was another thud somewhere below them, followed by what sounded like a stifled cry.

Logan halted. He nodded toward the floor. "Basement."

There was a door in the corner. They headed to it, wincing at the creaking floorboards. Logan positioned himself against the frame, hands squeezed around the grip of his Glock. He nodded. Schmidt shoved the door open, and Logan pivoted, lowering his gun into the shadowed stairwell. Dust swirled, the only thing that moved in the half-light.

Logan went first, the stairs groaning beneath his boots. At the bottom, his eyes adjusting to this deeper gloom, he made out boxes and crates against the stone walls, shelves bowing with rusting tools strung with webs. He scanned the space, settling on a door at the far end. Light spilled beneath it. As he stepped toward it, there were several crashing sounds. The light beneath the door winked out.

Logan moved quickly across the cellar, Schmidt following. The two of them positioned themselves. Schmidt reached for the handle. As he pushed it open, Logan swung his weapon into the room.

"Freeze!"

The chamber beyond was in darkness. Logan had a sense of shelves rising up. He stared into the shadows, heart pounding. Nothing moved. After a moment, he took one hand from his gun and felt for a light switch. Finding one, he flipped it. The room blazed into brightness.

It was a storm cellar. There were two freezers against one wall, a narrow bed with a filthy mattress, shelves lined with tins and bottled water furred with dust. Steps at the far end of the cellar led up to what he guessed was a trapdoor. There were signs of a disturbance: jars broken on the floor, the bare bulb hanging from the low ceiling still swinging, throwing its light around.

As Logan started toward the steps, he heard Schmidt swear. Following the detective's gaze, Logan saw that the bed's mattress was stained with what looked like blood. A lot of blood. There was a sad jumble of women's clothes scattered on the floor. From the iron frame hung a pair of handcuffs.

"Jesus."

Both men looked up as, somewhere above them, an engine roared to life.

R iley was leaving the diner when her cell rang. As she took it out, thinking it was Logan with news, she saw a black SUV approaching. It looked like the one she'd seen earlier in the meeting with Cook. As it passed, she saw a man in the passenger seat hold up his cell toward her, as if taking a photograph. She frowned after it, but her ringtone drew her attention back.

Seeing Kristen Webb's name on the screen, Riley remembered the ME had texted her yesterday evening. It felt like a lifetime ago. "Doctor, I'm sorry. I got caught up."

"I understand. I just wanted to let you know that I have some results. Those glass shards I found—the ones embedded in Chloe's hand? They're borosilicate. It's a heat-resistant glass. It's commonly found in medical or lab equipment—syringes, test tubes, that sort of thing."

"So not something Chloe would have likely encountered in the fields?"

The line hissed, distorting Webb's voice. "It wouldn't belong there, at least. You also wanted to know if the vagrant, Dennis Packer, was on Fenozen? Well, there were significant traces of the drug in his system. Although not enough to cause death."

"Do you think Fenozen could have led to Packer's condition?" Riley asked, thinking of the dementia Webb had mentioned as a symptom of the disease, pellagra, and Tom, the vagrant, talking about Dennis Packer and George Anderson's disturbed mental states.

"To pellagra? The drug could certainly be a contributing factor, as I said before, but I don't believe Fenozen alone would cause the disease, even in high amounts. I've made a start on my research. The first thing I came across was a rather unorthodox, but intriguing, paper that talked about pellagra possibly having given rise to vampire legends in the late Middle Ages."

"Drinking blood?" asked Riley, quickly. "The bites?"

"I wondered at first. But it's more to do with one of the symptoms of the disease. I mentioned the dermatitis? The skin becomes very sensitive to sunlight. Pellagra sufferers can experience severe blistering and cracking of the dermis, particularly of parts exposed to sun—arms, hands, neck, and face. Packer himself was exhibiting this condition. But even with a poor diet, it's highly unusual that he developed pellagra here in America. As I think I mentioned, the staples of our diet—flour and cereals—have been fortified with niacin for decades. It's also found in red meat, liver, poultry, peanuts, and many vegetables. It would be hard *not* to get niacin in your diet, even if relying on soup kitchens. It's in poorer parts of the world, in populations who rely mostly on a maize-based diet—rural South America, parts of China and Africa—where it's prevalent."

Riley cursed inwardly. More pieces to add to the puzzle. And now Logan and Schmidt had their sights set on a whole new suspect. *And you're one hundred miles away.* Was she wasting time here when her team was closing in on the killer?

"I'm sorry I don't have more, Sergeant," Webb said into her silence.

"No, it's OK. Thank you for your help, Doctor."

L ogan raced up the steps at the far end of the storm cellar and pushed against the trapdoor. It refused to budge, even as he heaved against it. Either someone had locked it from the outside, or they had wedged something on top of it.

There was the rumble of a vehicle passing overhead.

"Come on!" shouted Schmidt. He ran back the way they'd come, out through the door of the storm cellar, hastening for the basement stairs.

Logan followed him up the rickety steps into the kitchen. Halfway across the room, he skidded on a chunk of rotting food, arms swinging wide. He caught his balance with a curse and sprinted on, rushing through the dining room, jumping strewn boxes, knocking over a chair.

Outside came a shriek of tires. Ahead, daylight flooded the open doorway. It lit up Schmidt as he raced out, gun before him. A shout tore from his throat as he vanished into the light. Logan was almost at the door when the gunshots came.

Five deafening cracks. One after the other.

Something smashed into the wall behind him with a splintering of plaster. Logan threw himself to the floor. Another screech of tires. A harsh yell. Then, a flash of white as a vehicle hurtled past.

Logan scrabbled to his feet and threw himself against the doorframe, panting. Gun gripped, he risked a glance outside. The yard was clouded with dust. Stepping out, he saw a white van bouncing madly down the dirt road toward the highway. "Get the car!" he shouted, squinting to try to get a read on the van's plate. "Cam!" Logan twisted around when there was no response. His eyes went to a shape on the ground, which hadn't been there before. *"Oh, Jesus!"*

Schmidt was spread-eagled in the dust. His gun had fallen from his hand. His eyes were blinking at the sky. Two red blooms were growing on his shirt.

Logan raced to him and dropped down, his gaze on the spreading stains. One in the chest. One in the stomach. "I'll get help, OK?" He raced to the Dodge and got on the radio. "Officer down! Need immediate assistance!" He shouted the address at dispatch. "Suspect's in a white Ford cargo van, heading for Hawkeye Road. License plate—Echo, November—" Logan looked around as Cam groaned. His arm flailed as if he was trying to reach for something. "Just get here!" He ran back to Schmidt. "I'm here." He holstered his gun and grabbed the man's hovering hand. "Just stay with me, OK, Cam? Stay with me."

The breeze blew dust into Logan's eyes as he knelt by the old detective. Schmidt coughed, blood flecking his lips. A hawk circled in the gray sky. The radio crackled, voices puncturing the static as dispatch relayed the message and, all over the county, officers began responding.

46

Riley glanced at the GPS to check she was in the right place. The houses here—on the northwestern fringes of the city—all looked the same. The one-story timber dwellings were dwarfed by the white oaks that lined the streets. There were rocking chairs on lawns and wagon wheels propped up as decorations. It looked like a retirement area.

The wind had picked up through the day. The sun was an hour from setting and the storm clouds that had built in monstrous towers through the afternoon were lit up crimson and violet, swollen with menace. The trees seethed.

As Riley got out, her hair was whipped about her face. She kept her gun in its holster and slid her cell into the pocket of her jeans. She'd lost reception a couple of hours ago. Before that, she'd left a message for Logan, asking him what was happening with Charles Moore. Her anxiety had increased with every hour, imagining Moore being arrested and her not there to lead the interrogation; Reed demanding to know where she was.

All along the street, flags danced. In the east, the clouds shimmered with lightning. The windows of the house she'd been told to come to were dark. There were dead flowers in a pot outside. Riley rapped on the door, checking around her. An elderly man carried a plastic chair in from his lawn, eyes on the sullen sky.

After a moment, the door opened. Jess Cook had changed into a loose linen shirt over jeans and boots. Although the senator's attire was relaxed, her face was anything but. She looked over Riley's shoulder, scanning the street. "You weren't followed?"

"No, ma'am."

"You're sure?"

"I'm certain."

Cook ushered her inside. "They don't know about this place. Not yet, at least."

Riley wondered who *they* were. She'd thought the senator's demand for secrecy in their meeting this evening was to do with the press hounding her about her fall in the polls. Now she was beginning to think there might be something more going on. She felt uneasy, wondering what she'd stumbled into.

She followed Cook through the house to a parlor at the back. There were three frayed armchairs and shelves with china animals gathering dust. A lamp was on low and the drapes were drawn. Standing by the window, peering out, was a petite young woman with a shock of pink hair.

"Lily, this is Sergeant Riley Fisher."

The young woman turned. The black hooded sweater she wore swallowed her slight frame. She had an elfin face and intense brown eyes that studied Riley before flicking to the gun at her hip. "This is a bad idea," she said, looking at Cook.

Her tone was curt, but Riley caught the fear in it.

After a look from the senator, however, the young woman perched on one of the chairs, fingers nibbling at the ragged sleeves of her sweater.

"Sergeant, this is Lily."

The young woman glanced sideways at Cook.

"Thorne," the senator corrected. "My half sister."

"Hello, Thorne," said Riley, wondering what the hell this was about.

"My father had an affair late in his marriage," Cook explained. "Very few people knew about it. I didn't find out myself until Lil—Thorne was nearly in her teens. Her mother had some problems. Thorne was brought up here, by our grandmother."

Riley nodded slowly. "OK?"

"She's in trouble, Sergeant. She's been hiding out here while we figure out what to do."

A rumble of thunder shivered through the ornaments on the shelves. The lamp flickered.

Riley shook her head. She had come hoping to learn more about Bill Hamilton and his connection to James Miller, but now Cook seemed to be trying to involve her in some sort of family drama. God knows, she had enough of that of her own. "Senator, I—"

"The allegations against me this past week aren't entirely inaccurate. I'm afraid this isn't the first time my sister's been in trouble." Cook's eyes were on Thorne. "She's been involved with a certain group for several years now."

"Mission Earth?" murmured Riley. "The eco-terrorists?"

"Eco-*warriors*," corrected Thorne, meeting her gaze. "And fighting for your future."

Riley's attention returned to Cook. "The cyberattack in Polk County? The petrochemical company? That was her?"

"Yes."

"Jesus," breathed Riley, looking at the young woman in a whole new light.

"As I said, she's in trouble."

"What she should be *in*, Senator, is prison."

Thorne jerked to her feet. "This is pointless."

"Lily, sit down." Cook leaned forward to address Riley. "Listen, Sergeant, I do not in any way condone what she and her cohorts have done. I had no prior knowledge of any of it. I'm aware that Mission Earth supports my candidacy, but I've never endorsed or supported them. Indeed, these allegations could have serious consequences for my campaign." She looked at Thorne, her expression hardening.

The young woman cast her eyes downward.

"Until very recently," continued Cook, "I had no idea of the true extent of her involvement in this group. But we are where we are. And my sister is now in real danger."

"What do you mean?"

"Eleven days ago, she and two of her group entered the governor's mansion with the help of a contact inside. They downloaded files from his personal computer and—"

"Senator," Riley stood. "Your sister—and quite frankly you, ma'am—need a lawyer. And you need to not be telling me this. Any of it. Without legal advice and representation."

"Hamilton saw her. She was tracked down by his security. We're not sure how. A member of my campaign staff, who I fired, knew about my relationship to Thorne. It's possible he talked to Hamilton. That they used him as a way to get to me. And to her." Cook tossed her head. "I don't know. But two days ago, men from the governor's private security team went to her apartment. When she ran they shot at her. They fired on an unarmed young woman, running away."

"They're mercenaries," murmured Thorne. "Former Special Forces. I've seen the file of their head, Gage Walker. The one who tried to shoot me."

Riley sat. She looked at the young woman, whose defiance had faltered. There was genuine fear in her eyes. "Why did you go to the mansion? What were you after?" She noticed Cook's head dip at this. "You were trying to get dirt on Hamilton? For your sister? For her campaign?"

"Not without reason, or cause," Thorne replied. "There's been talk for years about Hamilton's links with Big Ag. Rumors of corruption. That he's selling out our state for his own financial and political gain."

In her mind, Riley saw her father heading down the porch steps to his car, briefcase in hand.

How many blind eyes did you turn for him?

"In Iowa, the consequences of his policies become clearer each year. Under his governorship, pollution has doubled. Native species are on the verge of extinction." Thorne's voice was raw. "Companies like Agri-Co only care about profit, not the soil and water they infect with their chemicals, or the wildlife they destroy. Cancer rates are rising from pesticides, and, still, their political allies and lobbyists help them sow their poison. Hamilton is at the heart of it. So yes." Thorne looked at Cook. "I wanted to help my sister. Because I believe she is the best hope our state has of reversing this corrosion. These men with their dollars and their deals—they don't *own* this land!" She smacked her fist into her palm. "What right do they have to treat it as they do? To ruin it for us all." She looked away, eyes bright.

Another roll of thunder surged outside. Somewhere in the neighborhood, dogs began barking.

"What was on the files you took?"

"Most of it's the usual stuff," Thorne said after a pause. "Emails, financial records. I had to disconnect quickly, so some of the data was corrupted. But there was one folder. Called Red Lance."

"Red Lance?"

"It's a series of documents and what looks like a contract. It's in Chinese, but it's mostly unreadable because of the data corruption. No translation software has made sense of it."

"How is this evidence of corruption?" asked Riley, looking between them. "The governor has just been entertaining a delegation of Chinese officials. I'm sure he's had a lot of correspondence with China."

It was Cook who answered. "The document that we believe is a contract has the governor's signature on it and a number—a figure to be precise. One hundred million dollars." She watched Riley, letting the number sink in. "Yes, as a state we do a great deal of legitimate business with China. But the fact one of Hamilton's men tried to shoot my sister tells me there's something here that's not normal. Something he's extremely keen to protect."

"Why did you bring me into this, Senator?"

"When you said this morning that it was the governor you were interested in, with your case—?" Cook's gaze went to Thorne. "I thought you might be able to help us. To be honest, I'm not sure who else to turn to."

Riley shook her head. "You must know this is way above my pay grade. If there *is* corruption here—and I'm far from convinced of that. You're talking bureau level. Homeland even." She thought of Agent Klein. The man seemed like a straight shooter, but neither he nor any of her colleagues knew she was here, knew about the call from Hamilton and her suspicions around Miller. "My reason for coming here was to do with a suspect in my case, as I said. Not the governor himself.

It's just that Hamilton knows the man I've been investigating, James Miller, who—"

"James Miller?" Thorne looked between Riley and Cook. "He's in the Red Lance file."

"What?" Riley sat forward.

"That name is on the documents."

Riley looked at Cook. "Senator, James is the husband of Chloe Miller. One of the victims in my case."

Cook let out a long breath. "I saw the news about that woman, of course, but I didn't make any connection when I read the file. Miller? The name's pretty common. And the last couple of days have been—" She shook her head. "Well, you said there could be some association between your suspect and the governor? I'd say this proves it, no?"

Riley didn't answer for a moment. "Is there anything in this Red Lance file that offers more information about their association?"

"The documents appear scientific in nature," Cook told her. "Equations and charts."

"We thought it could have something to do with corn," added Thorne.

"I said I wasn't certain," cautioned Cook.

"Bioengineering," murmured Riley, her mind whirling.

She thought of James Miller's job at GFT, a subsidiary of Agri-Co, engineering corn to suit challenging environments. John Brown talking about Zephyr Farms' new seed, up for an award with the power to transform their little cooperative on the American stage. Hamilton's defense of James Miller's work in his warning to her. Chloe dead in the cornfields.

She had a sense of things colliding, waves meeting. But she couldn't understand, yet, the tides that had brought her investigation and these revelations together.

Thorne reached into the pocket of her sweater. She pulled out a small metal stick. "I put it on a USB. Everything I had time to take from Hamilton's computer."

Cook turned to Riley. "If we were to give it to you, Sergeant, what would you do with it? Would you be able to help my sister?"

"I don't know," Riley answered truthfully. She paused as the lamp guttered in a tremble of thunder. "I would need to see what connection it has to my investigation. If any."

"I might be willing to testify," Thorne said tentatively. "If it means Hamilton is removed from office."

"Let's not get too far ahead of ourselves."

Thorne hesitated, then held out the flash drive. She exhaled when Riley took it.

Riley rose, the little stick warm in her hand. A metal sliver of secrets and danger. "I'll contact you. First thing." She followed Cook out of the parlor, leaving Thorne sunk in the chair. Thin and pale, dwarfed in her black sweater, she reminded Riley a little of Maddie.

Cook looked up and down the street as she opened the door. "Please be careful with this, Sergeant. I know my sister has broken the law. But whatever punishment she deserves, it isn't to be shot in the back by thugs."

The door clicked shut behind her. It was almost fully dark, the sky boiling black with storm. Riley's hair flew in the gusts. She pulled out her cell as she approached the car. The screen came to life. She had reception again. She halted, pushing her hair out of her eyes. Missed call after missed call was pinging up.

Ethan. Logan. Kristen Webb. Amy Fox. Sheriff Reed. Several numbers she didn't recognize. Ethan again. Logan again. Aunt Rose. Sadie. Her unease grew with every one. Thunder ripped across the sky.

Before she could listen to any of the messages, the phone started ringing. It was her brother. "Ethan? What's—?"

"Where have you been? I've been trying you for hours!"

She'd never heard him like this—frantic, desperate. "I—"

"Maddie snuck out of her mom's late last night. She never came back. Her friends, Rose—no one's seen her since. Riley, she's gone. Maddie's gone."

47

The rain started as Riley sped north out of the city. Huge drops at first, slow but steady. She flicked the wipers on. Her brother's voice stuttered through the hands-free system, crackling in and out. Lightning flared.

"Ethan—listen—have you checked Maddie's cell? Tried to find her location?"

"Nothing comes up. I've tried everything!"

She thought of James Miller, saying much the same thing about the night he'd gone looking for Chloe. She pushed down the urge to panic. "OK. Maddie might not have the app enabled." She looked at the navigation screen. She was two hours from home, more if the storm persisted. "You're at home? All right, I want you to keep the phone free, in case she calls. I'm going to contact the office, get Special Services to see if they can track her cell. Just hang tight." She finished the call, smacking her palm against the wheel as she was forced to a stop at an intersection. Rain lashed the windshield.

She thought of her niece, framed in the doorway, mouth open in shock, Ethan's words about Hunter hanging in the air. Thought of Maddie in her room, weeks ago, threatening to run away. Thought of Gracie Foster—what was left of her—shrouded in a body bag. She pushed the image away. Maddie had been gone less than twenty-four hours. She refused to panic yet.

Riley's gaze flicked to the USB flash drive, nestled in the cupholder beside her seat, a wink of silver in the dark. Rain pounded the roof as she scrolled through her contacts for Special Services. The world beyond the windshield was growing indistinct, smeared with lights. Trucks passed, spewing up gouts of water from the road. The trees were starting to bend in the wind. She was about to tap on the number when the car filled with the buzz of her cell. It was Logan. She stabbed the screen to answer as the lights changed. "Logan, I can't talk right now, I'm—"

"Riley."

The use of her name—not sarge or boss—was one warning sign. His tone was another. It gave her the same thrill of fear Ethan's had, except Logan didn't sound frantic. He sounded desolate.

"What is it?" She turned the wipers on full, struggling to see the road. They raced back and forth, squeaking in protest, barely able to keep up with the deluge. There was another intersection coming up. The lights blinked red. "Logan?"

"It's Cam, Riley. He's dead."

"What? What the hell do you mean?" Some part of her realized she sounded angry, like she'd heard many other people sound when she'd given them notice of a death—refusing to believe the words, furious at the person uttering them, unraveling their world. A truck behind blasted its horn as the lights flashed green. She slammed her foot on the gas. "Logan! Talk to me, Goddamn it! What happened?"

"We went to Charles Moore's farm this morning. To question him."

"Yes—I got your message. Sarah Foster's ex?"

"His place . . . Riley, I've never seen anything like it. Someone—we think it must have been Moore—escaped through a storm cellar. He got away in a van. It came out of nowhere. Cam was shot. I tried—" Logan cleared his throat. "They tried to save him. But—"

The road ahead was growing more blurry, despite the wipers' rapid arcs. Riley blinked and realized her eyes were full of tears.

Oh God. Cam?

She forced herself to concentrate. She had to keep it together. "Where's Moore? Do you have him?"

"Not yet. But we will." Logan's voice strengthened. "There's an APB out on the motherfucker."

Riley imagined the uproar. Cops all over Black Hawk would be on this. It had been years since an officer or deputy had been murdered in the line of duty. Besides which, Cameron Schmidt was known and liked across the county. They would be out for blood.

I shouldn't have left.

"There's more, Sarge. We found Sarah Foster. What was left of her. She was cut up. Butchered. Moore had her body stored in a freezer in his cellar."

"Jesus." The streetlights were fading behind her as she headed out of the city. The road was quieter, just a few trucks rumbling in the distance. Rain dashed the windshield, falling in sheets in her beams. To her left, across the land's flat dark, lightning pulsed, illuminating the monstrous belly of the storm.

"We found clothes, too. They match what Gracie Foster was wearing when she disappeared. Nolan and the lab team are going over it all right now. It's going to take some time. It's a slaughterhouse."

Headlights flared in Riley's rearview. She squinted through the torrent.

"Agent Gooch thinks it could explain why Nicole King was killed where she was. The meatpacking plant? It's been closed for years, but maybe, Moore being a butcher, he or his family had some association with the place? We'll know more when the bureau gets us those DNA results. Klein chased the lab at Quantico today."

The headlights blazed behind her, coming up fast.

"There was a pickup truck in his yard. Goodyear tires."

"The tracks near Chloe's body?" murmured Riley, shielding her eyes from the glare. She could barely see the road. *"Goddamn it!"*

"Moore escaped in a white cargo van. Must have been parked somewhere out of sight."

"White van?" Riley slowed so the jerk behind could pass her. "That vagrant—Tom? He talked about a white van. The vanishers?"

"Shit. I'd forgotten that. What did he say? That it had been picking up homeless people? Christ. We could be looking for more bodies out here. I'll tell Nolan." Logan paused. "Riley. This place? How Sarah and Gracie must've died?" His voice quavered. "Moore's a monster."

"I'm on my way back. Logan, Maddie's gone missing."

"What?"

The vehicle behind—a black SUV—came up alongside her at speed, spraying sheets of water. Riley caught a glimpse of two figures through the open window. One, a thick-necked bald man, was shouting at her. She realized he had something in his hand. Shock punched through her. It was a gun.

"Pull over!" The man was yelling.

Impulse made her slam her foot on the accelerator. The Dodge charged forward, overtaking the SUV. *"Fuck!"*

The line crackled. "Sarge? What's wrong?"

Rain was pummeling the windshield, the wipers not fast enough to clear it. The SUV sped up behind, swinging out to try to overtake her, headlights flaring like beacons, blinding her. Riley put her foot to the floor, the car hurtling through the storm. She gripped the wheel, breath racing. She was gaining ground. The headlights were fading behind her. She glanced in the rearview.

"Logan! Listen, I'm being—!"

She saw the downed tree at the last minute—a splay of branches blocking the road. She spun the wheel instinctively, slamming her foot on the brake. The Dodge jerked around at breakneck speed, twisting violently on the wet road. Riley felt the left-side wheels leave the ground.

There was a sudden, awful weightlessness while she was still in a spin. Everything seemed slow and strange. Then, all too suddenly, the world turned over with a crunch and scream of metal and a shattering of glass. The last thing Riley remembered as she was tossed like a rag doll in her seat was the air bag exploding in her face.

48

Things were falling, tinkling to the ground beside Riley's head. Beams of light shimmered in her eyes. There was a sound of dripping water, and she could smell gasoline. When she licked her lips, she tasted blood. A weird white balloon sagged in front of her face. As she reached out to push against it, pain lanced through her shoulder. She twisted her head. Another sharp pain. She saw the wet road, oddly close to her face, beyond a crumpled ridge of metal and thousands of tiny lights. No, not lights—shattered glass sparkling in headlights. The crumpled metal was the roof of her car. She was still in the Dodge, strapped upside down in her seat. The MDT was hanging off its plinth, wires dangling.

She felt a jolt of panic, which made her breathe in hard, then gasp at the pain in her chest, bruised by the belt that had saved her life. There were voices coming closer. A shadow cut across the headlights. Footsteps crunched on glass. She remembered—the SUV trying to overtake her, the bald man with the gun, the tree in her path.

"Is she alive?"

Riley winced as her eyes were flooded with a flashlight. Thunder surged in the distance.

"Yeah. She's moving."

"Search the car."

"*Shit!*"

"What?"

"We've got company."

It dawned on Riley that it wasn't thunder she could hear rolling toward her. It was a truck. There was a hiss of brakes. Away to her left, she saw a pair of boots jump down and splash through the puddles toward her.

"What happened?" A man's panicked voice. "I saw it go over!"

"It's all right. We've got this."

"I called 9–1–1."

"That's great. We'll take it from here."

"I can help."

"Just get the fuck out of here." A distinctive snap.

Riley knew that sound well. It was the sound of a handgun being racked.

"Jesus, man!" The boots backed away. "No problem, OK? I'm leaving." The boots stumbled back toward the truck. There was a slam of a door, the deep shudder of the engine.

Riley tried to yell for help, but the truck swept past, wheels crushing scattered bits of her car. There was a splintering as someone kicked out her shattered back window. She tried to go for her gun, but was wedged in too tight. She turned her head, saw an arm snaking into the backseat. A hand grabbed her purse.

"Check her."

Another hand, this time on her body. Rough fingers moved around her hip, dug forcefully, invasively, into the pocket of her jeans. She struggled, cried out. The hand withdrew.

"Nothing."

There was another sound now, beneath the rain. Sirens.

"She got anything in there?"

Things fell to the road, tossed from the depths of her purse. Tissues. Keys.

"Maybe she doesn't have anything?" Agitation rising in the tone.

"Why else did Cook meet a cop—*this* cop?"

"Let's just take what we've got!"

Another hissed curse, then running footsteps. There was a squeal of tires as the SUV sped away, leaving her hanging in her seat. As Riley shifted, she caught sight of a little sliver of metal among the shards of glass on the crumpled roof. She forced in a painful breath, reached out, and closed her fingers around the flash drive as the sirens wailed toward her.

49

It was almost midnight by the time Riley arrived in Waterloo. Her wounds—minor cuts and bruises—had been tended by paramedics on the side of the road, but the whiplash made jumping down from the tow truck's cab a painful experience. Her neck felt like it had been put in a vise.

Sheriff Reed came out to meet her, jaw clenching as he watched the wrecked Dodge being off-loaded from the truck, glass falling from the broken windows. She had called him en route to give him the news about the car, but he was no less wrathful for being forewarned.

"My office, Sergeant."

The graveyard shift had begun, but the department was frantic—phones ringing, deputies hastening past, lights on in every room. The manhunt for Charles Moore was well under way.

Reed's secretary met them on the stairs. "Sir, there's a call for you. Mayor Roberts."

"I'll call her back."

Riley's apprehension built at Reed's tone.

Reed closed the door of his office behind her, then went around his desk, pausing for a moment, eyes on his wife's cross-stitch of the department's motto. EXCELLENCE IN LAW ENFORCEMENT.

Riley watched him, her mind teeming with worry. She'd had no updates as yet from Ethan, Sadie, or Rose, all out searching for Maddie. She felt sick with grief for Cam, the detective's face haunting her all the way home, and she was desperate to know how the hunt for Moore was going. But she clamped down her questions, well aware of the precariousness of her situation.

Reed didn't sit. "I'm waiting, Sergeant."

"Sir, as I said on the phone, I went to Des Moines pursuing a lead."

"And you crashed on the way home?"

"Yes, sir. There was a tree in the road." This was the explanation she'd given to State Police after the crash. She hadn't wanted to risk telling the truth—not without knowing the implications, recalling the black SUV that had crawled past the diner where she'd met Jess Cook, the man holding up his cell toward her. Had they tailed her? She was sure she'd made it unseen to the senator's hideout, but she'd assumed, then, she was trying to evade reporters, not armed men with a ruthless desire to protect whatever it was Cook and her sister had stumbled into. Thorne's story that she'd been shot at by Hamilton's private security fresh in her mind, she had left the senator a message, warning her the house might not be safe.

"And this lead you neglected to tell me about?"

This was harder to lie about, but she couldn't tell him everything. Not until she knew how far this went. The men pursuing her might not have meant for her to crash, but they'd shown no care or remorse when she was trapped and wounded. If they were in the orbit of the governor, they would be well protected. She didn't know what she'd become involved in, but she knew for sure it was way above anything she, or Sheriff Reed, had ever dealt with. The trail she had followed on James Miller had opened into an abyss. She'd gone from suspecting him to be hiding some clue to Chloe's murder to discovering he was up to his neck in a potential state-level conspiracy. If she wanted to protect her sources and the evidence—the flash drive sitting snug and dangerous in her pocket—she would have to tread very carefully indeed.

"I was following information on James Miller with someone who knows him through his work."

"After I specifically warned you to be more delicate where he was concerned?"

"Sir, Miller is still a suspect as far as my investigation is concerned. Yes, we had more active leads, but I wanted to follow this up."

"So, you were off chasing loose ends?" said Reed, his voice cold. "While your team was busying tracking down the actual killer?"

Was that blame she heard in his voice? Blame for Schmidt? *He's right,* said a voice. *If you'd been here, it might not have gone down like this. Cam might still be alive.* Her thoughts snagged on him. She had a vision of the old detective at his desk, twiddling chopsticks in his Wok and Roll noodles as he peered at his computer. Cam smiling, handing her a beer at her promotion party. Cam with his maps, showing her a new route he and Sue planned to take on their bikes.

Oh God. Sue.

"Sir, I knew Agents Klein and Gooch were on top of the situation here. When I made the decision to leave, my team was going over old ground. Charles Moore was one of a number of ex-boyfriends of Sarah Foster. He was on our contact list, but he'd only been in her life a short time, and they'd broken up months ago. We had no reason to suspect him until yesterday. None of us could have known how quickly things would unfold."

"But that's the nature of this job, Fisher. As you well know."

That wasn't just anger in his voice, she realized. It was disappointment. She'd let him down.

"Sir, I know I should have been here. I wish to God I had been." She braced herself. "But, please, let me lead the hunt for Moore."

"No. I'm coordinating the search from here. All local law enforcement agencies have been advised, and I'll be doing a press conference first thing. Agent Klein is helping us with our strategy." Reed perched his fingers on his desk. "We'll get Moore's face plastered everywhere. By tomorrow afternoon, the son of a bitch won't be able to move a muscle without being spotted. Waterloo PD is aiding us at the farm. They've sent their CSIs to help Nolan. I'm told it's one hell of a scene."

"Nolan's out at Moore's farm?"

Reed nodded. "With most of your team."

"I can go now. Take a cruiser."

"Fisher, I—"

"I'm fit to work, sir. It's just a mild whiplash."

"I'm putting you on leave."

The shock made her step back. She shook her head, wincing at the spasm in her neck. "Sir, I know I should have told you I was going to Des Moines. But the car was an accident, and no one could have known what would happen at the farm."

"I talked to some of your team earlier, Riley."

"Oh?" she said hoarsely.

"Jackson Cole told me he came to your house the other night. He said you were extremely agitated."

"Sir, Cole is still pissed that I was promoted over—"

"He said you pulled a gun on him."

That son of a bitch.

Reed sighed. He looked exhausted. "I warned you from the start of this investigation that if your connection to Chloe Miller compromised you in any way, I would take you off the case. I fear events of the past few days have proven that."

"Sir, I—" She couldn't finish.

"I will take over. Agents Klein and Gooch will assist me. We can re-evaluate this in a few days." He straightened. "Your badge and gun, Sergeant."

Riley's bruised hand, the bandage filthy with mud from the road, shook as she took off her gold star badge and set it down on his desk. She laid the Glock beside it.

"Go home and get some rest, Riley."

There was no more arguing to be done.

Dazed, she made her way down the stairs. She was passing Investigations when she caught sight of Amy Fox. The deputy was by the photocopier as it hummed and flashed. Her gaze was on Schmidt's desk. Riley halted, her own eyes drawn to it. The desk, with its scattered files, two coffee cups, and a donut box, seemed to take up more space than it actually did, as if all the gravity of the room were being drawn to it. Fox glanced up and they locked eyes.

Riley went in. "Hey."

"Sarge." Fox turned away, but not before Riley saw her eyes were puffy from crying. After a moment, the young woman sniffed and straightened her shirt.

Riley crossed to the photocopier, which was spitting out sheets. She picked one up. It was a wanted poster. Charles Moore's name was at the top and a number was at the bottom.

ARMED AND DANGEROUS. DO NOT APPROACH.

She stared at that square jaw and unsmiling mouth, thinning hair over storm-gray eyes. Their very own cannibal killer. She wondered if he would end up on the website she'd trawled through. Another beast, in human form, for the curious and fascinated to pore over.

Fox was back to staring at the desk, eyes on the photograph of Schmidt and Sue. "He was so kind."

"He was." Riley put her hand on her shoulder. "We'll catch Moore. He'll pay."

Fox turned to look at her. "It's not enough."

"I know. But it's all we've got."

"I heard you were in an accident." Fox scanned Riley's face, as if seeing the cuts and bruises for the first time. "Are you OK?"

No, Riley wanted to say. *My niece is missing, I've been given information people seem willing to kill for, and I've been suspended.* She spotted the car keys on Fox's desk. A thought formed in her frazzled mind. "Are you on anything right now?"

"I was waiting until the posters were done. Sheriff Reed told me to get some sleep." Fox's gaze drifted back to Schmidt's desk. "But I don't think I could."

"Is Logan at the scene?" When Fox nodded, Riley picked up the keys and held them out. "Want to give me a lift?"

On the way to Moore's farm, Riley patched through to Special Services for an update. She'd already called them on the way back from Des Moines, asking them to trace Maddie's cell.

"Hang on, Sarge," said the operator. "Yes. We have a location."

Riley's heart leaped. "Where?"

"OK, it's from last night. Ten minutes past midnight."

As he read out the address, Riley's hope sank. "That's her house. You've had nothing since?"

"I'm sorry, no. That means she's either lost power or removed her SIM. I could put in a request with the service provider, but you know how that usually goes."

"Nothing?" asked Fox, when she ended the call.

Riley sat back in the seat with a small shake of her head. Her neck and shoulder were throbbing, but she didn't want to take any painkillers. The pain, at least, was keeping her alert. The sky was smothered with cloud, no stars tonight. There were distant shimmers, far away, as the supercell moved west. The meteorologist said the storm would hit Sioux City by dawn. There were reports of funnel clouds spotted across the southern half of the state.

"I'm sure Maddie will be OK," said Fox, but her voice was tight.

Nothing was OK tonight.

The rambling buildings of the Moore farm were lit up like Christmas by floodlights as Fox drove up the potholed road. Two deputies from Motorcycle Patrol were at the gate. One held up a flashlight. The other marked their names in the scene logbook. Riley wondered how long it would be before the likes of Sean Taylor arrived, trying to get a good shot or some gruesome details. The creepy old farm would be perfect for their front pages. Another Ed Gein, right on their doorstep.

As Fox pulled up near some squad cars, Riley took a pair of protective gloves and boots from the dash. "Thanks, Fox. Try to get some sleep, OK. They're going to need you tomorrow."

"When will you be back, Sarge?"

Riley hesitated. She had told Fox she'd been put on leave because of the accident. Maybe her team would all be told differently tomorrow. Either way, she didn't have an answer right now.

Outside the farm, dozens of figures moved in the glare of lights, some picking through things on the ground, others putting items in evidence bags. Most of them were rendered anonymous by their white overalls and masks, but she spotted Jackson Cole and Chad Becker over by the barn. She felt a flicker of fury at the sight of Cole, but wanting to avoid any more confrontations, she made her way quickly toward the farmhouse.

Cameras flashed in the yard, lighting up lurid patches of blood. Cam's blood, she knew, by the gloves and syringes left by the paramedics who'd worked on him. She caught sight of Bob Nolan by a pickup truck, overseeing a lab technician dusting the handle and door for prints. Another was photographing the tires. Had Chloe ended up in that truck? Had she escaped Moore and run from him, wounded, into the fields?

She found Logan inside the farmhouse with one of Nolan's technicians, bagging items in the kitchen. The stink was eye-watering. The bright lights made it worse, every smeared and encrusted surface exposed. Flies droned and roaches crawled in shadowed corners. There were chopping boards and butchers' knives on the kitchen worktops, rusty with dried blood. Animal or human would be a question only tests would answer. Riley wasn't looking forward to the results.

The technician saw her first. "Welcome to hell, Sarge."

Logan straightened, clutching an evidence bag. His overalls and boots were filthy and there was a black smudge on his mask. His eyes were hollow. Riley imagined him with Cam, out here alone, waiting for assistance. She should have been with them.

"That's quite some accident," Logan said, staring at her face.

Riley scanned the room. "What have we got?"

Logan held up the evidence bag. There was a white box inside. "A whole lot of drugs." He moved aside to show her a table where more bags were piled, filled with pills and packets. He handed her the one he was holding.

Riley took it. "Fenozen," she murmured, reading the label.

"Loads of it."

"From the pharmacy?"

Logan nodded. "Seems Sarah Foster was stealing it for Moore to sell on the streets. Guess he needed the cash after being laid off. It looks like he was on the stuff himself, too. All fits with the profile. Gooch and Klein said there would be drug abuse. Foster's sister said she dumped

Moore a few months back. Maybe that was the trigger—the stressor or whatever—that set him off? Maybe the combination of losing his girl-friend and his access to drugs?"

"Is she still here? Sarah?"

"Yeah. Nolan wanted to get the tires of the cargo van Moore escaped in analyzed first, so we can try to track it. I got a partial plate, but—" He shook his head.

"It's OK."

"As soon as Nolan's done outside, he'll work on getting her out. Webb is standing by."

"Show me."

Logan led her through the chaos to a door. Riley followed him down the stairs beyond. A bare bulb hung from the ceiling, casting the base-ment in dull yellow light.

"Have you found a drone anywhere?"

"You're thinking of the one John Brown saw the night Chloe died?" Logan shook his head. "Not yet. But—well—you can see what a mess the place is." He led her into a storm cellar.

"My God," murmured Riley, staring at the narrow bed against one wall. There were handcuffs on the frame and the mattress was stained with blood. Clothes were strewn across the concrete floor.

"We think Moore kept Gracie in here, too. Those are the clothes she went missing in. We found Sarah's cell phone upstairs. One of the tech team was able to unlock it. There was a text from Moore, nineteen days ago. He left Sarah a message implying he knew something about Gra-cie. That she was to come to the farm. Her car's in the barn."

Riley thought of Sarah being forced down here by Moore. Her hope for word of her daughter dissolving into terror. Had she seen Gracie's clothes? Had she known she had lost her daughter? Known what was coming for her? The horror of it gnawed at Riley's mind. Sarah scream-ing, pulling at the chains. Moore's footsteps on the stairs. Judging by the blood, he had attacked one or both women while they were still alive. She gritted her teeth, forced the images away.

Logan pointed to the back of the cellar, where steps led up to a trapdoor. "Moore escaped up there." He motioned to an old freezer against the bare brick wall. "Sarah's in there."

Riley went to it. She braced herself, then opened the lid.

There, among plastic-wrapped cuts of brown steaks and goose-fleshed chickens, were chunks of human flesh. An arm, neatly severed at the elbow, the cut tissue frosted with red ice crystals. A slender hand, nails still glinting with polish. A heart, liver-colored, enveloped in a wrinkled skin of cellophane. The most shocking thing, however, was the severed head of Sarah Foster: blue lips, eyes iced over, strands of frozen hair like brittle blond twigs. It was cradled among the many pieces of her; a disjointed jigsaw of human parts.

"Nolan said we should keep the lid closed," Logan said quietly.

Riley closed the lid, but the image remained imprinted in her mind. She doubted it would ever leave her.

"There could be other remains in there. Possibly elsewhere on the property, too, especially if we think those vagrants were right—the white van snatching people off the streets. Waterloo PD is bringing us one of their cadaver dogs."

Riley was silent for a moment. She felt like she was standing in the eye of a storm. Down here everything was still, hushed as a grave, but up there in the world things seethed. Down here was quiet horror. But, somewhere up there, Maddie was missing. Somewhere, Charles Moore was on the run. And, somewhere, were the men who'd chased her off the road.

"Logan, I need your help."

50

Dawn had rinsed the eastern sky blue by the time Riley finished talking. The house was quiet—Scrounger at Rose and Lori's, Ethan out searching for Maddie. She looked at Logan, who'd sat at the kitchen counter for the last hour, letting her speak without interruption. "What do you think?"

"That I need something stronger than coffee." He sat back. "So you think the men who came after you on the road are part of Governor Hamilton's private security?"

"I believe so."

"And you think they were after the flash drive Senator Cook's sister gave you?"

"They certainly thought I had something important. Important enough to pull a gun on me and on a trucker who tried to help."

"What's in these files? You said something about a contract?"

Riley dug into her pocket and placed the USB stick on the counter. "I haven't had chance to look."

"Your laptop still working?"

She slid from the stool to rifle through her overnight bag, rescued from the trunk of the Dodge. The laptop had made it unscathed through the accident, cushioned by clothes in the bag. She put it on the counter, grimacing at the discomfort the movement caused. She'd glimpsed herself in the mirror earlier, been startled by the bruises blooming black across her chest.

Logan leaned in as she lifted the lid and inserted the USB. She could smell the sweat on him. His usually pristine nails were ragged, his hands black with dirt and dried blood. Their faces glowing in the screen light, they watched the file window fill up with folders and documents. Riley scanned them as they blinked to life. Campaign material, financial statements.

"Jesus," murmured Logan. "These are his personal files, Sarge. The governor's personal files." He let it hang there so they both felt the weight of the words.

"There," she said as a folder popped up. "Red Lance." She clicked on it and two documents appeared. She opened one. It was page after page of spreadsheets made up of some sort of equations—lists of letters and numbers in tables. The only thing understandable was the email address the document had been sent from. It was the personal account of James Miller.

"Something to do with Miller's job at GFT?" Logan offered, frowning at the pages. "You said that when Hamilton called you he praised Miller for his work there?"

Riley nodded. "Cook thought it could have something to do with corn." She skimmed the equations. "But we'll need a degree from Cornell ourselves to understand any of this."

"If it is to do with Miller's work, why go to such extremes to keep it secret? I mean, I know agricultural technology is highly valued. But to shoot at a teenager and run a cop off the road . . . ?"

"Depends what's at stake, I guess?" Riley clicked on another document. It was the contract the senator had spoken of. Hamilton's name was at the bottom, under his signature. There was the figure Cook had mentioned. Riley pointed to it. "One hundred million dollars is a pretty big stake."

The rest of the pages was in Chinese, cut through with a random jumble of symbols, numbers, and letters.

"What's all that?"

"Thorne said some of the files got corrupted."

Riley opened another folder. This one contained a tranche of downloaded messages to and from Hamilton's private email, going back eight months. She scrolled through them. Most seemed to be from family and friends: invites to parties, credit card bills, well-wishes for the campaign. Then, back in March, one from James Miller.

Red Lance remains unstable. We cannot move to the next phase until things are under control. Not until I understand what this means. We need to delay.

There was a reply from Hamilton, equally short.

It has to be ready by the date we agreed. Deal must go ahead, on schedule. I'll wire more funds, but it must be delivered. On time.

Riley continued to flick through the messages, her eyes glazing as the emails rolled hypnotically up the screen.

"There," said Logan, pointing.

Another one from Miller.

Something's happened. We need to talk.

"Look at the date," Logan murmured.

"June twenty-fifth." Riley looked at him. "The day after we found Chloe." Her attention was diverted as her cell rang. She grabbed for it, hope lifting on ragged wings as she saw it was her brother. "Have you found her?"

"No." Ethan sounded shattered. "I've been everywhere. All the places she knows. Places we used to go."

Riley told him the bad news from Special Services. She didn't tell her brother she'd been suspended. She hadn't told Logan that yet either. "I'll join you shortly."

There was a long pause. "This feels like karma, Riley. God punishing me for being a shit father. If something happens to her—?"

"Maddie was upset, Ethan. I think this is an act of rebellion. Nothing sinister." *But you know what can happen to a lost girl.* She ignored the voice. "Why don't you come home? Sleep for a couple of hours? I can take over."

"No. Her friends will be awake soon. I want to go to their houses. Look the kids in the eyes. See if any of them are lying." He sounded angry, volatile.

"Ethan, I—"

"I'll speak to you later." The call cut off.

Logan was watching her. "Still no word?" He looked pained. "I'm not sure what I can do to help, but anything you need—anything at all."

Riley felt weariness, bone-deep, dragging at her body. She put her elbows on the counter, propping her aching head up on her hands as she stared at the emails. "I'm too tired to think." She glanced at Logan: his bloodshot eyes, the dirt on his clothes and the blood—Cam's blood— that had dried under his nails. "I'm sorry. I know you are, too."

Logan was back to scrolling through Hamilton's emails.

Riley pulled her bag toward her and fished for the packet of painkillers she kept there. "Can you drive on these?" she muttered, reading the label. Something flashed in her mind. "You said back at the farm that you thought Charles Moore was taking Fenozen? Not just selling it?"

"Yeah. There were lots of open packets in his bathroom, empty ones in the trash."

"So, Moore was on the drug? The vagrant, Dennis Packer, who Webb did the autopsy on—the one who had pellagra—was also on it. George Anderson too, according to Tom and the war boys." She rubbed at her head, willing her brain to work. "Tom said Packer and Anderson weren't themselves—that they were acting strangely."

"But you checked out Fenozen? You said there were no reports of anything other than the usual side effects? Besides, a couple of hobos with drug problems acting weird is one thing. Moore is in a whole other league. The guy's a fucking psycho."

"What about the glass in Chloe's hand? I told you what Webb said? That it might have come from a hospital, or a lab?"

"You saw yourself how many pharmaceuticals were at Moore's place. He could easily have syringes."

Riley shook her head. "I can't imagine Chloe making it out of that place alive and, even if she had, Zephyr's cornfields are on the other side of town, miles from the Moore farm. She couldn't have made it that far, not with her injuries."

"Moore's pickup truck then? He could have grabbed her and tried to drug her? Chloe fights him off, the syringe breaks in her hand? She escapes from the vehicle into the fields?"

"Maybe. I just feel we're missing something." She jabbed her finger at the screen. "Red Lance remains unstable? So, who—or what—is Red Lance?"

Logan leaned in suddenly, looking at the screen. "Look."

"What?" Riley followed his finger to one of the emails.

The subject matter said "Press Release." But it was the name of the sender that had drawn Logan's attention. The email had been sent to Bill Hamilton from one John Brown.

Riley clicked to open it. The screen filled with an image of three yellow ears of corn on a red rising sun.

ZEPHYR FARMS

It was, as the header said, a press release: several pages of facts and figures about the cooperative, showcasing their new hybrid corn seed, highlighting their achievements in the Black Hawk community. She scanned the text. "They're talking about the Iowa Food Prize—making a case for why they should win." She thought of what she'd sensed at Cook's place: the waves in this case all starting to collide.

"They could be lobbying him?" Logan suggested, reading over her shoulder. "Maybe Hamilton has some influence over the award or something?"

She glanced at him. "We've got a lot of connections here. Bill Hamilton and James Miller. Something to do with corn and a deal with China. Zephyr Farms and their seed?" She shook her head, looking back at the screen. "I just don't know how they're connected."

"Let's go and ask Miller, then." Logan looked at his watch. "We've got time. Nolan's got things covered at the farm. Reed wanted us back in before the press conference for a briefing. But that's four hours away."

She straightened. "Ask Miller what, exactly?"

"Well, it's not going to be long, is it, before the news is splashed all over with Charles Moore?"

"Oh God, you're right." Riley wondered if Reed had thought of that in all the chaos.

"We'll go and tell Miller we have a suspect in his wife's murder and that a manhunt is under way. And, while we're there, we'll see what buttons we can press about Bill Hamilton. Then, we'll—" Logan trailed off, watching her shake her head. "What is it?"

"There's one thing I haven't told you."

51

In the dawn, the creek was pale as milk, the surface un-
troubled. Maddie hugged her knees to her chest. She could smell
Brandon's aftershave trapped in her hair, from having lain against him
through the dark, no sound but their breaths and the trilling of night
birds and frogs. He had left an hour ago for a shift at his uncle's auto-
repair shop in Waterloo. He'd offered to return this evening, but Maddie
hadn't decided if she would stay out here another night. She wasn't
really sure what to do.

Her father's ragged voice echoed in her mind.

I'd kill him for what he did to you. I'd kill that rapist piece of shit.

Those words had shaken Maddie to her core. Riley was her rock.
When things were really bad with her mom and Mason Lee and when
she could smell the liquor on her father's breath as he drove her to school,
she knew she had Riley, the woman she looked up to, the cop with a gun
and a badge who turned wrong to right. She'd barely believed it when
her father let slip that Riley had once run away. This new revelation had
stunned her. Seeing her aunt on her knees, weeping in her father's arms,
she realized that Riley might be as broken as all the other grownups in
her life.

She'd come out here wanting to be away from them all. But now she
was growing fearful of the consequences. She was starting to feel guilty,
too, knowing how much Riley, at least, would be worrying about her.
If she came home soon, they would all be relieved. If she waited much

longer that relief might turn to anger, and then when would she get to see Brandon again?

They had lit a fire last night in the blackened circle at the center of the old Bible camp cabins. He had put his jacket around her shoulders. They had talked for hours, sharing the beers and snacks he'd bought from the Kum & Go. He had told her about Memphis, about his alcoholic mother and his luck-lost father. And he'd asked her about herself—things she'd never been asked before, not by her father or mother, not even by Riley—what made her happy and made her sad, what she would be if she could be anyone or anything.

Finally, when she'd been lolling against his shoulder, unable to keep her eyes open, drowsy with beer, he had taken her hand and led her into one of the cabins, scuffed the dead leaves from the floor with his boot, and put down a blanket, which smelled faintly of gasoline. She'd hung by the door, suddenly feeling the weight of her situation—out here alone in the woods with an eighteen-year-old boy she hardly knew. She had wanted him to kiss her all evening, watching his lips move while he talked, his face golden in the firelight. But, all at once, she'd felt afraid.

She needn't have worried. He had put his arm around her, his shirt soft against her cheek, and she had woken that way when his cell had buzzed an alarm.

Maddie yawned and took a sip of pop from the bottle Brandon had left her. As she stowed it in her bag, she caught sight of her phone within the folds. She resisted the urge to put the SIM back in, not ready to burst this bubble. Not yet. She was surprised none of her friends had talked—caved in and told Riley or her father about this place. But, then, they would be admitting that they'd been out here, too, and they were all still in trouble after that stupid photograph.

A flock of birds cast from the trees on the other side of the creek. As they flew over the woods, Maddie heard voices. She stiffened. Surely not Brandon returning? The voices were accompanied by the crack of branches breaking underfoot. Since she'd been coming out here these past few weeks, she hadn't seen anyone else—only that drone, flying north above the treetops.

Maddie grabbed her bag and slipped inside the cabin. She crossed to the webbed window and peered out, cursing as she thought of her bike, left by the perimeter fence. A short distance away, a jetty sloped into the water from the bank, its rotten boards green with moss.

Through the trees, three men appeared. One, older than the others, with curly fair hair, was leading the way, pushing forcefully through the undergrowth. The other two were carrying something wrapped up in what looked like garbage bags. It was long and appeared heavy, the two men struggling. She could hear their breaths.

At the bank, the men set down the thing they were carrying. One bent over, hands on his knees. The other sat on his haunches, eyes on the package. The older man tested the jetty with his boot.

"Fuck!" This came from the man who was hunkered down. His face was stricken. *"Fuck!"*

The older man turned on him. "This ain't the time, Jacob. We've got to keep it together."

"It didn't have to go like that, Pop! Why'd Hoyt shoot him?"

"Your brother was protecting me." The older man lifted his face to the dawn sky. He looked broken. "John was gonna go to the cops. I couldn't talk him out of it."

"We should do something. Call someone."

"Who?"

"You know who."

The third man straightened. "Shut up, Jacob."

"Why not?" demanded the younger man, rising to face him. "He's got the power to get us out of this."

"He's also got the power to throw us to the wolves. You know what he's been threatening."

The man called Jacob shook his head, looked at the older man. "Hoyt's fucked-up, Pop. Been fucked-up since that day with Lizbeth. I could've told you he'd snap."

"We need to keep things moving," said the other man roughly. "We can't keep that monster locked up in the silo. John won't be the only one to come asking questions. Not now that the whole Goddamn state is on the lookout for the van."

The older man pushed his hands through his hair, then nodded. "We'll leave the van out here. Go back to the silos in your truck. When it's dark, we'll take him to Miller, then dump the van."

"Christ," murmured Jacob. "That fucking cop? Now John?"

"The cop was an accident!" snapped the older man. "Son of a bitch came out of nowhere. I had no choice!" He exhaled heavily, then gestured to the long shape wrapped up on the bank. "Just get some rocks, OK? We need to weight him down."

As the two moved into the undergrowth, Maddie saw the older man reach for something at his back. When he tugged it free from his jeans, she saw it was a gun. She wanted to duck down and hide, but she couldn't tear her gaze away. The man looked at the gun for a moment, then drew back his arm and flung it out into the creek.

52

Logan brought the Ford Crown Victoria to a stop a short distance from the Miller house. There was a red tinge to the sky. The sun was rising. Killing the engine, he sat there, thinking through what he might say to get Miller to open up—reveal something about this association with Bill Hamilton. He'd had no sleep, his mind was swamped with fatigue, and now Riley had gone and got herself suspended.

Logan knew there were other things she hadn't told him. Her bandaged hand, that distant look he'd seen in her eyes ever since they'd found Chloe Miller that spoke of something more than just grief for an old friend. He knew there was something else wrapped up in all this. Something that had turned Riley from the controlled, focused, and at times reserved woman he'd first been partnered with into someone new. More vulnerable, more fragmented—yet somehow more real. Maybe, when this was over, he'd tell her he was there if she ever needed to talk.

As he reached for his badge, Logan saw how filthy his hands were. Dirt and blood.

Get Sue, the old detective had breathed in his final moments. *Get Sue.* But there hadn't been time.

It was still early, and the street was quiet. Miller's car wasn't anywhere in sight. A vehicle Logan hadn't seen before was parked outside the house. A black Chevrolet Suburban, dirty from the road. Did Miller have company?

Things had gone further downhill since they'd been here last: the lawn overgrown, the lilies that bordered the path dead or dying. Logan climbed the porch steps and halted as his feet crunched on glass. One of the colored windows by the door was shattered, and the door was ajar. There were sounds within—men's voices, a muffled thud.

Leaving the door, Logan drew his gun and made his way around the side of the house. He knew the layout enough to know he could reach the kitchen without being seen. At the back, the garden was still mostly in shadow. Light spilled through the screen door. Moving around a porch swing and a table, he approached the kitchen window. The blinds were down, but by pressing his face to the frame, he could see a slice of kitchen beyond.

A man was standing at the counter. Not Miller. He was short and stocky, dressed in cargo pants and a black polo shirt. His bald head gleamed. There was a Colt in a holster at his hip. Logan thought of the conversation with Riley and her belief that the men who'd run her off the road were the governor's private security. Everything about this man—the weapon, the way he held himself, his tattoos—said military. He was looking down at an open laptop, his bulk obscuring the screen.

Logan heard noises coming from one of the rooms upstairs—the heavy drag of furniture. A few moments later, a man entered the kitchen from the hallway, carrying a box. He was dressed similarly to the bald man and wore gloves. He, too, was armed. There was no sign of James Miller.

The bald man glanced up as the other dumped the box on the counter. It was full of files that looked as though they'd been hastily shoved inside. "That everything?"

The man with the box nodded. "Jensen's putting the rest in the car. Looks like most of it's out at the lab."

The lab? Miller's place of work at GFT? Logan slipped his cell from his pocket but kept his eyes on the two men.

"We can't leave any trace. Not a fucking scrap."

"We got it all, Walker," insisted the man. "It's clean. What about the cop?"

"Larson called." The bald man closed the laptop. "He and Jones are on their way to her house. Whatever Cook gave her, they'll get it."

The other man was speaking again, but Logan wasn't listening anymore. His heart thumped as he scrolled for Riley's number. There was a footfall behind him. He jerked around to see a figure standing there. Logan's gaze shifted from the man's face to the dark barrel of the gun that was pointing at him.

R iley directed the cabdriver through the residential streets that led to the house of Maddie's friend Tanisha. The sun was rising, but it was early to be knocking on doors. Still, she couldn't stay home and do nothing. Part of her wanted to be with Logan—following the trail that seemed to lead back to James Miller—but she no longer had any authority, and her niece was her priority.

The cabdriver was new to the county and didn't know the area. He'd looked worried when she'd first climbed in. She'd had a shower after Logan left, washing off the blood and road grit, but she still looked like she'd been in a fight. The driver had eyed her bandaged knuckles, the livid marks on her throat from the seatbelt, the cuts on her cheeks. But soon he'd relaxed and become chatty.

"Have you heard about this shooting?" He glanced at her in the rearview. "There was something on the radio about a cop being killed." He shook his head. "These women getting murdered? Me and my wife moved here from Chicago. We wanted a safe place for our kids to grow up. She's due with our first in the fall."

"It is safe, sir," Riley murmured, looking out of the window at the quiet streets spilled with the sun's gold. The streets where she and Chloe and Mia had played. She saw someone cycling along the green fringe of the state park and felt a sharp pang of sorrow as she thought of Cam.

"Sir?" The man chuckled. "Don't think a fare's ever called me that."

"Force of habit. I'm a cop." But her belt felt so light without the weight of her badge and gun. What if this suspension became permanent?

"Jesus. Did you know him? The man who was shot? Were you there? Is that why you're all beat-up?" When she didn't answer, he shook his head. "Sorry. I don't mean to snoop."

"I was in a car accident. The storm."

As the driver diverted his talk to Midwest weather, Riley returned to the thought that had formed in the tow truck on the way back to Black Hawk. She had crashed on the very same road her parents had been wrecked on twelve years ago. Ice and November dark. A speeding truck that never slowed. It was a thought that had shivered through her.

There had never been any reason to think the death of her parents was anything other than an accident, even though the driver of the truck had never been found. The one witness hadn't got a plate—too busy rushing to try to help them. Hit and run. Drunk driver? An illegal immigrant who panicked? It happened. But her father had worked for Bill Hamilton—a man now implicated in a major conspiracy, whose men had shot at a girl and had run her into that crash—and that shiver of thought had stayed with her all the way home.

She was pulled into the present by her cell. She let out an exhalation at the name on the screen. "Maddie! Thank God! Where are you? Are you, OK?"

"I'm at your place." Maddie's voice was small with fear.

"Madison? What's wrong?"

"Riley . . . there are men in the house."

53

"Can you wait here?" Riley asked the cabdriver, directing him to pull up a short distance from the drive that led to her house.

He looked pained. "I'll miss the morning rush. Can catch six or more fares."

"You can keep the meter running, sir."

He smiled again at the title. "My name's Gabriel. OK, I'll wait."

"Thank you." Riley paused, her hand on the door. "Gabriel, if I'm not back in twenty minutes can you call the Black Hawk County Sheriff's Office? Say there's a Code Two at my address."

"Code Two," he said, nodding earnestly.

Leaving the cab, Riley made her way down the path toward her house, keeping to the shade of the sycamore trees. She halted, seeing the black SUV—a Chevrolet Suburban—parked in the middle of the drive. Again, she cursed herself bitterly for the oversight, which she'd realized the moment she got Maddie's call. She had canceled her credit cards on the way back from Des Moines, more as a matter of course rather than thinking the men who'd taken her purse would bother with them. But she'd forgotten all about the driver's license in her wallet.

On the way home in the cab, keeping her niece on the line as long as she dared, she'd learned there were at least two men inside the house. She'd told Maddie to hide. She had considered calling for backup, but her instincts told her to be cautious. If these were Hamilton's men, they were professionals. She thought it unlikely they would harm Maddie without reason, but she didn't know how a standoff with local law enforcement might play out, and she didn't want to risk the lives of any more colleagues.

The sunlit morning was humid, the only sounds the buzzing of insects and the distant thrum of traffic on the interstate. Riley stepped up to the SUV, sweat beading her skin. The vehicle was empty.

She turned her attention to the house—their old Victorian dame—for the first time aware just how many windows there were. She had no choice but to cross the open ground in full view. She did so quickly, boots soft on the grass. Maddie's bike was lying by the porch steps. Riley ran to the shed and slipped inside. An image of the rattlesnake winding its thick body beneath the rotten doors flashed in her mind. She knew what the bite of a rattler could do—had heard of people vomiting blood and bleeding from the bowels within minutes. Letting her eyes grow accustomed to the gloom, she ignored the thrill of fear and headed deeper in.

Her Winchester was hanging on one of the walls. It came down in a cloud of dust. Working quickly, she unzipped the bag and pulled out the shotgun. She hadn't used it for a long time. She checked it, just in case, but she'd always been careful, and the chamber was empty. Still, the intruders wouldn't know that. She kept the shells in the safe. She just needed to get to them.

The gun in her hands, she raced across to the house and up the porch steps, pressing herself against the wall with a grateful prayer that Scrounger was at Rose and Lori's. She risked a look through the screen door. The kitchen was empty. Maddie's backpack was on the counter, but there was no sign of life.

She entered, anticipating the point where the door creaked, then easing through. Sunlight dappled the kitchen walls. Drawers had been pulled out, the contents rummaged through. The hallway was in gloom. She raised the shotgun, stock snug against her shoulder. Her exhaustion was gone, blasted away by adrenaline, but she could feel her body protesting at all this movement. She paused in the doorway, hearing the squeak of floorboards upstairs. It was eerie how a place so familiar could feel so alien—the shadows ominous, full of threat. Closer, there were sounds coming from the dining room.

Riley stepped into the hallway, sweat trickling down her cheeks. A figure emerged from the dining room—a powerfully built man in cargo pants and a T-shirt. A black ski mask was pulled down over his face.

"Freeze!"

The man spun at her shout. He went for his weapon but halted, eyes on the shotgun. There were more sounds upstairs—pounding footsteps, a muffled cry.

Riley kept her attention on the man before her. "Turn around. Put your hands on your head."

The man was turning, hands reaching up, when two figures appeared on the stairs. Riley's eyes fixed in horror on a second masked man, who had hold of Maddie. One arm was across the girl's chest, pinning her to him, his gloved hand clamped over her mouth. In the other, he held a gun. The barrel was pressed against Maddie's temple.

"Put down your weapon." The man's voice was faintly familiar. When Riley hesitated, he tightened his hold on Maddie, causing the girl to whimper through his fingers. "Now!"

"OK!" Riley held up the shotgun. Slowly, she crouched, setting it on the floor.

"Against the wall."

As Riley flattened herself against the wall, she realized where she knew the man's voice from. It was his hands that had searched her while she was trapped in the overturned Dodge.

His comrade came forward to pick up the weapon. He went to empty the chamber, then gave a short laugh. "Thing's not even loaded." He put it down and drew his own gun, which he pointed at Riley as the other man descended the stairs, keeping tight hold of Maddie.

"Senator Cook gave you some files. I want them."

Riley wanted to tell him she had no idea what he was talking about. But she wouldn't risk it—not with that barrel pressed against Maddie's skull. "It's in the safe."

"Where?"

Riley pointed under the stairs.

"Open it."

The other man kept his gun trained on her as she crossed to the safe. She bent down, typed in the code. When Logan had left, she'd stuffed her laptop inside. It still had the flash drive sticking out of it. She went to remove it, cursing herself for not copying the files when she'd had the chance, but the man stopped her.

"Leave it on the floor and move back to the wall."

The man went to the laptop and opened the lid. Riley had left the document files open. He scanned the pages with a nod. "It's here."

"Have you sent these files anywhere? Shared them with anyone?"

"No."

Maddie let out a cry as the man increased his hold on her, pressing the gun into her skin. "Check her emails," he told his comrade.

The man tapped at the keys. "Last email was sent two days ago. Nothing attached."

"I'm telling you the truth."

The man holding Maddie studied Riley a moment more. "Stay where you are." He crossed the hallway, keeping the girl close. His comrade picked up the laptop and followed. When they reached the kitchen door, the man let go of Maddie, shoving her toward Riley. As the girl stumbled forward, the two men disappeared through the door.

Riley caught hold of Maddie as the screen door slammed shut. She pulled the girl to her. Her niece was shaking. "It's all right. You're safe."

A harsh cry outside made them both flinch.

Riley stiffened. "Wait here."

"Riley, no!"

Pulling herself from Maddie's grip, Riley approached the kitchen. Through the screen door, she saw one of the men collapsed on the ground, halfway between the shed and the creek. The laptop was in the grass beside him.

His comrade was running back toward him. He staggered to a halt. "What the fuck?"

Riley caught movement in the grass beside the downed man. A gleam of gold and black winding through the grass toward the creek.

The man was clutching his calf. "It bit me, Larson! A fucking snake! It *bit* me!"

His comrade grabbed the fallen laptop and hauled him to his feet. The wounded man limped with him toward the Chevrolet.

Riley was already dialing the sheriff's office as the SUV sped backward. She returned to the hallway, nodding Maddie toward the safe. "There's a box of shells in there, sweetheart. Get them for me, OK?" Dispatch answered after what seemed an age. "Sergeant Riley Fisher, requesting immediate assistance. Two armed men leaving my property. Suspects are in a black Chevrolet—"

"Sergeant?" It was Joan, the oldest of their four female dispatchers. "You're not en route to the scene?"

"Scene?"

"Charles Moore has been sighted." Joan's usual calm was frayed. "He's at Cedar Falls High School."

Riley realized she could hear sirens in the distance.

Shit.

After giving Joan the vehicle details, she finished the call, then grabbed the Winchester. Maddie was in the kitchen, hugging her backpack. The box of ammo was on the counter. As Riley crossed to it, she stepped on something. It was a fork, turfed from one of the drawers in the men's search. There were other bits of cutlery strewn around. Her eyes caught on something glittering gold among them. It was her necklace. Crouching, she picked it up. She went to put it in the drawer, then stuffed it in the pocket of her jeans instead.

"OK," she said, loading the shotgun. "Let's go."

"Riley. I have to tell you something."

"Not here, sweetheart. We need to leave." Riley didn't expect the men would return, but she wasn't going to take any chances. "Stay behind me."

"But—"

"We've got to go. Now."

Riley led the way out onto the porch, shotgun raised, Maddie close behind. The SUV was gone. The sirens were louder, only blocks away. She kept her eyes peeled, scanning the grass. There was no sign of the snake. But something else caught her gaze—silver in the sunlight. She took a breath. It was the flash drive. She guessed it had been dislodged when the man dropped the laptop. As she bent to pick it up, her triumph turned to alarm. How long before they realized?

As she led the way down the track, Maddie running to keep up, sirens wailed their urgent song all over town. Relief flooded Riley as she saw the cab still parked under the trees. "Come on."

"Riley, stop!" Maddie grabbed her arm. "I've got to tell you something!"

54

The cab pulled away, and Riley ushered Maddie up to Rose and Lori's front door. Her niece was white-faced and shaken. Riley wanted to tell her everything would be OK, but comfort would have to wait. As she rang the doorbell, hearing Scrounger's bark, she drew the USB stick from her pocket, looked around, despite the fact she'd made damn sure they hadn't been followed. "Maddie, I need you to take this." She pressed the flash drive into the girl's palm. "Don't tell anyone about it. Not Rose or Lori or your father. Just hide it until I'm back. And don't go outside. I'm dead serious."

"When will you be back?" Maddie asked, fingers closing over the stick.

"Not long. Just hang tight."

The door opened and Lori appeared. Her aunt's partner was wearing a thick robe over her nightgown, despite the warmth of the morning. Her pupils were dilated, and she stared at them a little too long. Upstairs, baby Benjamin was crying. "Riley?"

"Is Rose here?"

"No, she's with Ethan." Lori focused, bemused, on Maddie. "Looking for Madison."

"I need you to call them. Tell them Maddie's here with you. And I need to borrow your car."

"My car?" Lori looked baffled, but she reached for where the keys hung on a hook.

Riley took them from her and pressed Maddie in through the door. "I'll be back as soon as I can."

"Riley?" called Lori. "What's happening? All those sirens?"

"I'll explain later," Riley said over her shoulder. "Just call Rose and Ethan. And stay inside."

Lori's car was parked on the side of the road. A blue Ford Focus with a baby seat strapped in the back. Riley propped the shotgun in the well of the passenger seat and climbed in. Hearing more sirens, she put her foot on the gas, speeding back toward Cedar Falls.

She was left in little doubt, after what Maddie had told her, that the three men her niece had seen in the woods were part of Zephyr Farms. The girl, although shaken and a little muddled, had been able to recount the names Hoyt and Jacob. The older man she described had sounded like their father, Frank Garret. Riley had the distinct impression, from what Maddie said, that they'd been dumping a body.

She knew of the old Bible camp. It wasn't far from the fields where Chloe had been found. Zephyr Farms' fields. Their corn seed. John Brown's email to Hamilton. The pieces were all gathered like a puzzle in front of her. One thing, however, was certain. With Hamilton's security here in Black Hawk and James Miller seemingly at the heart of all this, she had sent Logan straight into danger.

Logan's car was parked outside Miller's house. Riley drew up beside it, her tension ebbing slightly. Maybe her fears—mounting when he'd not answered her calls—were unfounded. There was no sign of Miller's car. But his neighbor was kneeling on his front lawn, deadheading flowers. He paused to watch her run up the path.

Riley glanced down as her boots crunched on something on the porch. Her relief faded when she saw a window broken and the door open. She called into the gloom of the hallway. "Mr. Miller? Black Hawk County Sheriff's Office." When there was no reply, she entered warily. "Logan?"

She headed to the kitchen. There was no one there, but the back door was hanging open. On the deck a table lay overturned. Riley headed out. There were spatters of dark liquid on the boards. Crouching, she touched her finger to one. Blood. There were more droplets leading around the porch to the front. She followed them, but they stopped in the driveway.

"Excuse me, sir," she called, jogging to the neighbor, kneeling among his flowers. "Sergeant Riley Fisher. Black Hawk County Sheriff's Office." She reached for her badge, then remembered it wasn't there. She brazened it out, hoping he wouldn't ask to see it. "Have you seen Mr. Miller?"

The man rose, stubby white legs poking from beneath his shorts. His glasses were steamy in the heat. "Not since yesterday, ma'am. I tried him earlier, but there was no answer."

Riley recalled James saying that none of his neighbors had visited him since Chloe's death. "You called around?"

"There was a bit of a hullabaloo, ma'am. Woke me and my wife up."

"You're saying there was some kind of disturbance, Mr.—?"

"Erickson, ma'am. Wally Erickson. Sure sounded like it. Things breaking. People shouting."

"You didn't think to call the police?" She was pretty sure Wally Erickson was the type to be hanging on the phone at the slightest disruption in his street.

"Well, ma'am, to be honest, I thought it *was* the police."

"What made you think that?"

"One of them was your colleague, who I've seen you here with. It appeared there had been some sort of altercation. Your colleague looked wounded. His face was bloody."

Her stomach flipped over.

"The other four I've not seen before."

"Four?" Riley said sharply.

"Yes, they came out carrying boxes and a computer that they put into a vehicle out front. I rather thought they'd come to arrest Mr. Miller, but I didn't see him when they drove off."

"What time was this?"

"As I said, it was early." He glanced at his watch. "Just over an hour ago."

"What vehicle did they leave in?"

"A black Chevrolet Suburban. I've not seen it here before."

Same as the one that had pursued her from Des Moines. Same as the one outside her house. "I don't suppose you caught the plate?"

Wally Erickson blushed. "Well, I took a photograph, ma'am." He reached into the pocket of his shorts and pulled out his cell. He showed her the picture.

Riley cursed. The license plate was different from the vehicle the two men had left her house in. So there were six men in Black Hawk, at least. Two who had come to her house. Four here at Miller's. She zoomed in on the picture with her fingers. The Chevrolet's windows were tinted, but she could just make out figures inside. They had Logan.

Returning to her car, she called dispatch again with an urgent APB. Joan answered, sounding even more harried.

"Joan, I need another vehicle tracked. Same make and model. Different plates. I believe Deputy Wood has been taken in this vehicle against his will."

Joan's tone sobered further. "I'll patch the details through right away."

Riley turned the key in the ignition, but she paused there as the engine rumbled, her hands on the wheel. The fact they'd taken Logan and not just dealt with him on the spot left room for hope, but there was no telling what they planned to do with him. There was a sense of a cleanup going on here: the two who'd come for the file Thorne had given her, these men taking things from James Miller's house, Frank Garret and his sons sinking something in the creek. Her colleagues would react swiftly to a threat against one of their own, but all eyes, now, were on Charles Moore. It was her fault Logan was in trouble. It was her responsibility to get him out of it.

James Miller. Bill Hamilton. Zephyr Farms.

And Chloe—dead in the cornfields.

She glanced up at the house her friend had lived in, then dug her hand into her pocket and pulled out the necklace. As she held the gold star up by its broken chain, she remembered her grandfather handing her the little red box on her birthday, opening it to his crinkled smile. The rush of pride she'd felt as she lifted it out. It wasn't just a pretty trinket. Even then, at fourteen, she'd known she wanted to follow in his footsteps. With it, she had known that Joe Fisher—gold-starred sheriff of Black

Hawk County—had seen that, too. To her, the necklace had been the gift of his trust in her.

She imagined Chloe kneeling in the soil beneath those trees, hands in the dirt. Imagined her friend finding the necklace, bringing it back, and keeping it safe. That lost piece of her. That gift that had been taken from her. Tears stung her eyes as she thought of Chloe running in terror through those fields. Falling to curl around her pain, hands digging once again in dry summer soil. It didn't matter that she'd lost her badge. This wasn't about the job anymore.

Putting her foot down, Riley sped out of the manicured neighborhood and along the strip mall, the wail of sirens fading behind as her colleagues converged on Charles Moore. Crossing the Cedar by the railroad tracks, past the factories and the dark threads of creeks, she headed out on the back roads into the rolling expanse of cornfields, ripening to gold, the water tower rising in the distance, shotgun loaded beside her.

55

Charles Moore stood on the school field, the sun rising in his eyes. His skin shrank from it. He was shivering despite the heat. His arms prickled. It felt as though insects were burrowing in his flesh. All around him were the screams of sirens. Lights flashed, red and blue. He staggered in a circle, trying to understand.

He remembered men hauling him up out of his cellar. Fierce daylight, then a van swallowing him whole. Taking him away. The men had locked him in the echoing blackness of an empty grain silo. Beyond the steel walls, he'd heard their voices. Later, the rumble of an approaching vehicle. Shouting. The violent crack of gunfire. Growl of an engine receding.

In the hours of silence that followed he'd struggled free of the rope they'd tied his hands with, climbed his way out of the silo by its ladder. Out in the darkness of the world, he'd stumbled through miles of cornfields, lost and confused. He had meant to return to the twilit cocoon of his farm. But as dawn began to break, showing him the rooftops of the town beyond the corn, his feet had walked him here—to the high school football field.

It was the last place he remembered being happy since he lost his job. Thirty years he'd been a butcher. He didn't know how to be anything else. First came the drink and the brawls, then the drugs. Then—Sarah Foster.

Yes he had courted her at first because of her job, persuading her to bring him things from the pharmacy. A packet of this or that. No big deal. Just enough to make their Saturday nights more mellow. But somewhere in those pill-soothed days, he'd fallen for her. Sarah had made him feel like a man. Her protector. Him and her and Gracie. All together. The messed-up makings of a family.

As the sun cast its gold across the empty bleachers, Charles Moore could hear the cheers in his mind. Could see himself sitting up there between Sarah and Gracie. Handing out those hot dogs at halftime.

Hot dogs. Sweet meat. The smell. The taste. The crazy itch he couldn't scratch, no matter what he ate. Patties and raw steaks. Liver and blood sausage. The terrible, all-consuming hunger that could not be satisfied. The craving that gnawed at his mind.

Gracie, knocking on his door out of nowhere, eyes red, telling him she'd had an argument with her mom, asking him for money, saying she was going to stay with friends. Her fear building, seeing the squalor of his home—his descent into madness. She'd been backing out even as he begged her to stay.

He remembered the rest in brutal flashes. Her hands scratching at his face. Screaming. So much screaming. He'd grabbed the pillow to stifle the awful sounds, pressing down to smother them. She'd bucked like a lamb beneath him. Then, at last, she had stilled, gone limp and lifeless. When it was over, he had staggered back against the cellar wall. Had stayed there, crouched against the damp stone for hours.

In the end, his butcher's brain whispering of the dangers of spoiling flesh, he had forced himself to undress the girl, carving what he needed from her body before laying her gently in one of the freezers and crawling up the stairs to choke down as many pills as he could. But he hadn't been able to keep her. Her face—frozen in that final expression of strangled horror—haunted him.

Days later, her body stiff in his arms, he had staggered from his pickup to the dark of the creek—one of the many that dotted Black Hawk County, fed by the waters of the Cedar River. Rain on his face, pattering onto the plastic he'd wrapped her in. The weights he'd brought slippery with mud as he tied them to her arms and legs with rope, down among the reeds. The splash and swirl of water taking her down.

Back at the farm, mud drying black on his hands, he'd retched on the barrel of his gun but hadn't been able to pull the trigger. Only the drugs had helped, little white nurses that fizzed on his tongue and brought him peace. Until the hunger began to stir again. Tick, tick inside. And he had texted Sarah, telling her to come. Telling her he knew where Gracie was.

God, help me.

"Charles Moore!" The voice boomed through a megaphone, echoing across the field. "Put your hands above your head!"

He turned to see men hunkered down, facing him over the hoods and doors of cars. Could they help? Could they make this stop? He took a step toward them. Opened his mouth.

Special Agent Elijah Klein hastened across the parking lot. Sirens screamed as more cruisers joined those parked on the field of Cedar Falls High, blue lights flashing, doors flinging wide. Deputies and officers crouched down, dozens of guns pointing at the figure standing in the grass near the bleachers.

Klein headed for Sheriff Reed's vehicle, emblazoned with its gold star. There was no sign of Riley Fisher. Reed had left a message earlier, telling him she'd been sent home and he was taking over the investigation.

The sheriff was addressing the distant figure through his car's PA system. "Charles Moore! Put your hands up!"

"Sheriff."

Reed glanced around as Klein moved up alongside him, shielded by the open door of the vehicle, then returned his gaze to the figure on the field. "Charles Moore, we have you surrounded!"

Moore turned in a shambling circle. He barely looked like the man in the wanted posters. Gaunt and filthy, with a beard grown thick and grizzled, he looked like he'd wandered out of the wilderness. Klein saw strange lesions covering his arms and neck—scabs that looked almost scale-like. He'd not seen anything like them before.

Klein looked up, his gaze caught by several dark-clad men ducking across the roof of the school. The SWAT team moving into place. His jaw tightened as he scanned the dozens of squad cars with their various insignias and mottos—Black Hawk County and Waterloo, State Patrol and Cedar Falls. Everyone had come to bring down the man believed to have killed one of their own. A man who had brutally murdered four women in their county. A monster who had terrorized their towns. Eyes narrowed through sights, taking aim. Fingers itched on triggers. Klein knew how this ended.

"Sheriff Reed," he tried again, shouting over the approaching sirens. "Moore is unstable. This level of threat will only make him more so. If you let me talk to him, I might be able to calm things down. Bring him in safely."

Reed shook his head. "You've done your job, Agent. Let me do mine." He spoke into the PA system again. "Let me see your hands, Moore! Now!"

Moore took a step forward and called out.

Klein's yell was lost in the thunder of guns.

Amy Fox sat at her desk, eyes on the box of donuts on Cam Schmidt's desk. The detective had eaten two of them. The others had grown stale and hard. Cam's jacket was still on the back of his chair. How could it be here when he wasn't?

She felt exhausted yet wide-awake. She'd gone home after dropping Riley at the farm but hadn't even got undressed before the call came in that Charles Moore had been spotted. By the time she got to the office all the cruisers were gone and she'd come up here to wait.

Her computer pinged a message. She looked at it, hopeful of an update. It was an email from the doctor's office she'd contacted about Lizbeth Garret. She clicked on it to find Lizbeth's medical records attached. It looked like a pretty standard record—a fractured wrist two years ago, a stomach bug, biopsy of a suspect mole. Lizbeth suffered with epilepsy and took drugs to control it.

Fox's tired eyes drifted over the next entry, then flicked back.

Six months ago, Lizbeth had been prescribed a new drug for her epilepsy. Fox put her finger to the screen, traced the doctor's note to its conclusion:

Fenozen.

56

Leaving Lori's car on the side of the road, Riley took her cell and the shotgun and ducked through a hole in the chain-link fence, following Maddie's directions. She made her way into the undergrowth, the whine of bugs loud beneath the canopy. There was a low hum as a crop duster passed overhead.

It wasn't long before she reached the old cabins, scattered among the woods. Her eyes moved over crushed beer cans and spent firecrackers, a blackened fire pit. Maddie hadn't said who she'd been out here with, but there would need to be a conversation when all this was done. A lot of conversations.

Away—through the trees—the glint of water. Riley headed down to the creek, where a broken jetty jutted from the bank. There were footprints in the mud near the water's edge. Careful to avoid stepping on any, she took some pictures. Her cell had no service out here. The surface of the creek was soupy with algae. They would have to send in divers to find whatever—whoever—had been sunk in its depths.

Leaving the water, Riley moved north, in the direction Maddie said Frank Garret and his sons had appeared from. There were more footprints, buttonbush flowers and water sedge crushed by boots. She felt as though she was back hunting with her grandfather: the weight of the Winchester in her hands, the hushed tracking of their prey. But the sensation was very different when the quarry most likely had guns of its own.

After a short distance, she came to the perimeter fence again. She walked alongside it until she found a gap and squeezed through, gritting her teeth against the pain in her neck. The trees opened onto a dirt road. It was overgrown, poison ivy snaking across the path, but the ground was churned by recent activity. Lots of it, judging by the tire treads. Sticking to the cover of the trees, Riley made her way along.

Ahead, she caught sight of buildings—a ramshackle farmhouse, the windows boarded up, an Aermotor windmill with rusted blades towering over a dilapidated red barn. She paused, feeling an odd sense of recognition. She had seen this place before. After a moment, she realized where—it was the photograph in James Miller's house. The one he'd snatched from her. Those sagging steps outside the farmhouse were where James and his family had posed for the picture. The barn was where he'd said his father had put his gun in his mouth and pulled the trigger. Beyond, rusted grain bins and two enormous sheds made of corrugated metal disappeared in the shade of the trees.

To her left, the woods thinned out, offering glimpses of cornfields stretching into shimmering heat-haze. In the distance was the water tower, close to the billboard plastered with Zephyr Farms' logo. *From the banks of the Cedar to the county line,* John Brown had said when she'd asked him how much of this land belonged to the cooperative. James Miller's old family farm, she realized, stood at the heart of Zephyr's lands. Not far from where Chloe was found.

Riley flitted between the trees, making her way toward the buildings. She couldn't see any signs of life, but where the dirt road ended was a vehicle. She halted in the shade, hands curling tight around her shotgun. It was a white Ford cargo van.

Charles Moore lay on the field, riddled with bullets. The air was hazy with gun smoke. Reed was shouting orders through the PA, commanding the officers to stand down. Several deputies had gone forward, guns trained on Moore's sprawled body. Beyond the school field, squad car lights flashed at the cordons, keeping news crews and residents back.

Agent Klein watched as Reed gestured to the paramedics. They jogged onto the field, carrying a stretcher.

"Jesus."

Klein, his ears still ringing from the guns, turned to see Gooch.

The agent was sweating in the heat, eyes flitting around the chaos, taking it all in. "Who gave the order to shoot?"

When Klein shook his head, Gooch cursed. "Damn cowboys."

They watched as one of the paramedics rose, gloves stained with Moore's blood. He sought Reed in the crowd. Shook his head.

"I heard Moore shouted something before they shot him?" Gooch said.

"He said, 'Help me.'"

Gooch grunted and took out his notebook. "Interesting." He exhaled. "We should have had the chance to interview him."

As his cell rang, Klein took it out. He knew the number. "Quantico," he told Gooch, turning away to answer, hand clamped over his ear against the noise.

The call lasted only a few minutes.

"That was the lab," Klein murmured, looking back at Gooch, who was writing in his notebook. "They have DNA results on Chloe Miller and Nicole King."

"Guess we needn't have chivied them along after all." Gooch glanced up when Klein didn't respond. "What is it?"

"It's not Charles Moore's DNA."

"What do you mean? I thought Moore was in the system? Those priors of his?"

"Yes. But it's not Moore's DNA on Miller and King. It's George Anderson's."

"Seriously?" Gooch's brow furrowed. "Could they have been killing together? Moore and Anderson?"

"There's more. The lab found DNA from *two* separate sources on Chloe Miller—Anderson and another that doesn't match anyone in the system."

"Goddamn."

Klein nodded, his gaze shifting back to Moore's bloody body. "Lab says we're looking at multiple killers."

57

Riley moved from point to point, ducking down behind the oil drums to check that the coast was clear, then moving up alongside the white van. *Echo, November.* It was the vehicle that had sped from the Moore farm after Cam had been shot. The vehicle she guessed Tom and the war boys had heard rumors of, vanishing people. She couldn't understand what it was doing out here. Had Charles Moore abandoned it? Or had someone else driven it from his farm? Someone else who'd shot Cam? She drew out her cell. Still no signal.

The undergrowth was dense—weeds sprouting around the grain bins, ivy strangling the farmhouse. She recalled James Miller telling her his father farmed hogs and soybeans. She guessed the two massive corrugated sheds had been built for the animals.

As she approached the red barn, under the shadow of the Aermotor, more of the site became visible. She bobbed down behind a stack of tractor tires, catching sight of a black vehicle parked outside one of the pig sheds. As she read the Chevrolet's license plate, her heart thumped with anticipation.

The trunk of the SUV was open, and she could see boxes stacked inside. She was creeping toward the barn when two men came out of the shed. She dashed the last few yards and slipped into the barn. Both men were dressed in black, guns holstered at their hips. She watched them load more boxes into the vehicle.

Riley started at a noise behind her. She jerked around, raising the shotgun. The noise came again. It was just a pigeon flying across the broken rafters. Deep in the shadows of the barn she saw a car. The make, the model, the plate—all were familiar from her case files. It was Chloe's car. Her heart was racing now.

Riley looked outside. The two men had vanished, but she could hear sounds coming from the pig sheds. Bracing herself, she emerged and covered the open ground, making her way toward the rusting structures. Outside the sheds were a large generator and a propane tank. Wires and pipes snaked from them into the sheds. They looked new, out of place among the derelict buildings.

Riley slipped between the sheds where the undergrowth offered good cover. Sunlight dazzled off the metal. There were patches where the rust had eaten through, offering glimpses inside. She hunkered in the grass, putting her face to a hole. It took a moment for her eyes to become accustomed to the gloom within. Dust swirled in arrows of light, shooting through the roof and sides of the shed to strike the cracked concrete floor. Riley's gaze fixed first on the thing in the center of the hangar-sized space.

A large glass box, as big as a room, stood alone. It was lit by floodlights, illuminating the desks and steel tables within. It looked like some kind of rudimentary lab. There were computers and fridges, microscopes, trays of test tubes and petri dishes stacked up on metal shelving. On another shelf was a large, spider-legged drone. Inside the structure, another armed man was stacking petri dishes filled with something into a container. There was no sign of Logan or James Miller.

Beyond the lab, at the far end of the shed, Riley saw scores of plants in various stages of growth, spread out in trays beneath dormant heat lamps and a rigged-up sprinkler system. Cannabis, she thought, until she saw the yellow ears, hanging heavy. The plants were corn. She thought about those sheets of figures and equations in the Red Lance file and Jess Cook's speculation that they had something to do with corn.

Hearing a vehicle approaching, Riley stole back to the front of the sheds, keeping low. A second Chevrolet appeared. It was the one that had been at her house. The two men she'd seen carrying boxes emerged to meet it. With them was a third figure. He was bald and muscular with a brutish face. It was the man who'd trained a gun on her through the window of the car in the storm.

The driver's door opened, and the man who'd threatened Maddie climbed out. His ski mask was gone, his face troubled.

"Well?" said the bald man, crossing to him. "Did she have the files?"

"There was a flash drive." The man's jaw tightened. "But we lost it."

"What the hell, Larson?"

The man nodded to the car. "Jones got bit by a fucking snake. He must've dropped it. We went back to search, but there was nothing." He shook his head. "The cop was gone. It could've fallen anywhere. Or maybe she took it. We couldn't look forever."

The passenger door opened and another man struggled out. By his ash-white face, Riley knew he was the one who'd been bitten by the rattler.

After a tense pause, all eyes on him, the bald man started toward the shed. "We'll deal with this shit when we're done here."

"Walker?" called the one who'd been bitten.

The bald man turned. "What?"

The man winced as he took a step and gestured to his leg. "I need a doctor."

"When we're finished."

As they disappeared inside, Riley heard a rattling coming from the other shed, followed by a forlorn cry. The eerie sound sent a shiver through her. She scanned the corrugated sides, but there were no holes at a height she could reach. All six men were now inside the shed with the lab in it. Not allowing herself time for second-guessing, she darted to the front of the second structure. The doors were ajar.

The shed was the same size as the other, capable of housing a thousand or more pigs. Riley could imagine the sound, the stink. The interior was vast and gloomy. She made out the broken remnants of pigpens stacked up at the sides. There was a strong, musty odor. In the depths of the shed, a pale shape loomed in the darkness. Walking toward it, Riley saw it was some sort of large plastic tent.

Shotgun brandished, she approached the strange structure. Her foot landed on something thick. She jolted back, for one heart-stopping moment thinking she'd stepped on a snake. It was a wire—one of several—trailing from the tent. The wires crisscrossed as they disappeared through the side of the shed. Connected to the generator, perhaps. There was a zipped section at the front of the tent. A way in. She halted, hearing that moan again. It was coming from inside. Heart racing, she checked that the coast was clear, then eased down the zipper. The plastic flapped open, revealing the interior. Riley stood there for a long moment.

The tent was filled with two rows of beds, twelve in total. Six of the beds, which looked like the sort of basic metal cots found in a field hospital, were empty. Six had people in them. She could see their forms under the covers. Most were still, just the subtle rise and fall of breath to show they were alive, but there was movement from one bed halfway down, a slow shifting under the blankets. Another groan and a sound of metal rattling over metal.

She stepped in, sweat trickling down her face. The air was heavy with body odor and cleaning chemicals. Her heart had steadied to a hard thump, but her mind was racing, trying to make sense of what she was seeing. There were IV bags filled with fluids hanging by the occupied beds, tubes coiling under the blankets. Flies hummed in the gloom. The only light came from the sun slanting in through gaps in the rusting shed beyond, diffused by the plastic shell. There was a cart stacked with syringes, waste cans plastered with biohazard stickers, and a couple of fridges full of vials. Kristen Webb's words were in her mind.

Borosilicate glass. Found in medical or lab equipment.

That clanking sound again. She walked toward the shifting figure. As she approached, she scanned the shapes under the blankets. Her eyes alighted on a halo of blond curly hair in the bed opposite the stirring patient. It was a young woman. Her eyelids flickered as though she was trapped in a dream. Her fair hair was matted, and her face was glazed with perspiration. Riley knew that face. She'd seen this woman before. A face in a photograph, freckled and smiling. The shock of recognition struck her. The woman was Lizbeth Garret—daughter of Frank and Maryanne, sister of Hoyt, Ryan, and Jacob. Mother of those three kids.

Crossing to her, Riley saw one of Lizbeth's arms was lying outside the blanket. There was a drip held in place by a grubby Band-Aid, but it was her skin Riley was drawn to. Lizbeth's arm was mottled with weird red lesions that looked like burns or grazes, the skin peeling in places. There were more scaly patches just visible on Lizbeth's neck.

Sufferers can experience severe blistering and cracking of the dermis, particularly of parts exposed to the sun—arms, hands, the neck, and face.

Pellagra?

Riley leaned in to speak to Lizbeth, then halted in deepening shock. Lizbeth's hand was bound to the bars of the bed by a padded cuff. Straps and buckles protruding elsewhere told her the young woman was fully restrained. The sight of her pinned there—in this Godforsaken place where no human should be, let alone one so clearly suffering—made her desperate to wrench off the cuffs. But whether ill, drugged, or both, Lizbeth clearly wasn't in a fit state to move, and it was a long way back to the car.

Riley was reaching for her cell when a groan made her start. The patient who'd been stirring had partially emerged from the covers. It was a man with thin auburn hair and an unkempt beard. This man wasn't just tethered with padded restraints, he was also handcuffed. The chains were rattling against the bars of the bed. The man's mouth widened, and his tongue slid out to poke at the air. It was engorged and dark purple in color. A fly was twitching across his cheek. Riley watched in horror as the man's tongue roved toward it, the muscles in his neck straining. The fly took off, and the man tried to reach out his hand to snatch it. That hand ended in a knotted stump of flesh where two fingers should have been.

"Anderson."

George Anderson's head snapped up at her whisper. He struggled, the veins in his neck protruding. His eyes, wide and wild, were fixed on her. The chains binding him clanked against the bars. His lips pulled back to reveal rotting stubs of teeth, one of which was broken in half. Riley staggered back as he opened his mouth and screamed, spit stringing from his cracked lips. There were more sounds as the other captives began stirring, whimpers and cries echoing.

As she ran back through the tunnel, past the rows of beds, Anderson's shrieks followed her. Riley pushed her way out through the plastic as the doors at the far end of the shed opened. Sunlight and rough shouts spilled toward her. The bald man and the others were coming, guns raised.

M addie sat in the window, peering out through the curtains. Scrounger was next to her, paws on the windowsill. She stroked his head distractedly, eyes peeled for any sign of her father or Rose. It had been almost an hour. Why hadn't they come? She reached toward her pocket but remembered she didn't have her cell. She'd left it back at Riley's, where she'd hidden under her bed from the men before they found her. She didn't know her father's number by heart.

"Come get me," she murmured, tears threatening. She could still feel the cold of that gun barrel pressed against her temple. Still smell the man's hand clamped over her mouth and nose. She felt sick when she thought of it. Lori was in a weird mood, offering little in the way of comfort, locked upstairs with Benjamin, who hadn't stopped crying. Maddie could hear the footfalls in the nursery above as Lori paced, trying to quiet him.

A door opened and Lori's voice drifted down. "Maddie?"

She hopped off the sill and went to the foot of the stairs.

Lori was standing at the top, cradling Ben, his wails muffled against her shoulder. Her pallid face was pinched. "Maddie, I don't feel well. Could you get my pills?"

"Where are they?"

Lori frowned uncertainly. "I . . . I think they're in the kitchen. Rose always gets them for me. One of the cabinets?" She shook her head. "I don't know."

"I'll find them."

Maddie went into the kitchen, glad for something to take her mind off her thoughts. The phone was on the table by an address book. There was a pen and a pad of paper open, names and numbers scribbled down. Maddie had seen it earlier when she'd hidden the flash drive Riley had pressed into her palm inside a Tupperware box of homemade cookies. She'd felt terrible, seeing the names of her school friends, crossed off one by one.

She opened the cabinets, rifling through bags of cornmeal and tubs of muffins, a bottle of bourbon, nearly empty. No sign of any pills. She knew Lori had epilepsy. If she felt unwell, did that mean an attack would happen? This was too much.

Wait. Surely Rose would have her father's number? Turning, she went back to the address book and flicked through it. *Fisher, Ethan.*

She dialed quickly, her fingers shaky. "Dad?"

Ethan's voice came shocked down the line. "Maddie? Thank God! Where the hell are you?"

"Did . . . didn't Lori call you?"

"What? No! Where are you?"

"Have you found them, Maddie?"

Maddie looked around to see Lori in the doorway, ghost-like in her long robe. Benjamin was crying upstairs. On the other end of the line Maddie heard her father still shouting.

58

Where's the flash drive?" The bald man the others referred to as Walker asked the question, while the one called Larson dug through her pockets.

One of the others had her cell and shotgun. Riley could still hear George Anderson's desperate cries coming from inside the pig shed. "How would I know? Your men took it."

Walker looked as though he was going to say something further, but one of the others stepped in.

"We might not have long. If she knew to come here—?"

Walker's jaw pulsed. "Put her in with the others. Jones." He gestured to the man who'd been bitten by the snake. "Take over from Michaels. If any of them try anything, shoot them."

Riley winced as Larson seized her arm and marched her toward the old Miller farmhouse. Jones, sweating profusely, limped in their wake.

The steps of the porch bowed beneath her feet as she was propelled up and through the farmhouse door hanging off its hinges. Inside, it was dingy and smelled of mold. Bits of ceiling hung down. Fungus bubbled on peeling wallpaper.

A sixth armed man emerged from the remnants of a kitchen, eyes narrowing on Riley. "What the fuck's going on?"

"Walker needs you," said Larson.

The man headed out, leaving Jones to draw his gun while Larson compelled her into the kitchen. The remains of cupboards clung to the walls. Plaster crumbled under her boots.

Larson approached a door. "Stay back!" He slid across a bolt and opened it as Jones trained his gun inside. Larson shoved Riley in, then slammed the door shut, the bolt snapping in place.

Her fingers scrabbled over what felt like shelves. For a moment, all was breathless black, then, as her eyes sharpened, she realized there was some light still slanting through the keyhole and beneath the door. She was in some sort of pantry. Larson's footfalls receded. She put her eye to the hole, saw Jones leaning up against the crumbling kitchen wall, gun in his hands, his face pale as putty.

"Riley?"

The voice made her start. A figure loomed over her. "Logan? Thank God!" As he came closer, she saw dark stains on his shirt, a gash across his forehead. "You're hurt?"

He touched a finger to his head. "One of the sons of bitches pistol-whipped me." His eyes were bright in the dim. "How the hell did you know to come here?"

"Maddie, she—" Riley trailed off as another figure appeared behind Logan. It was James Miller.

"What are they doing?" Miller asked, his tone urgent. "Those men?"

"Cleaning up your mess, by the look of it," she said, her voice rising. "My God, those people?"

"Sarge—" Logan began.

"Have you seen them, Logan?" She turned to him. "Lizbeth Garret? George Anderson? He's got them chained in a Goddamn pig shed!"

"Riley, he's—"

"I've been trying to help them," James cut in.

As he stepped closer, Miller's face became visible in the faint light through the door. His lip was split, blood crusting the stubble on his jaw, and one eye was badly swollen. It gave Riley a new thrill of fear. If Walker and the others had done this to an associate of Hamilton's, it didn't bode well. That sense of a cleanup? Might it now include them?

"*Help* them?"

James slumped against the pantry's shelves. He was barely recognizable from the man she'd first interviewed only weeks earlier. In that short space of time, he'd unraveled like a ball of yarn.

"Please." She softened her tone with effort. "I need to understand. What's been happening here? That lab? This deal with Governor Hamilton?"

James's head jerked up.

"We know all about it." Riley nodded at his expression. "One hundred million dollars for a contract with China?"

"That wasn't my idea." James's voice rose. "That was never my plan!"

"Shut the fuck up in there!" The shout came from Jones, in the kitchen.

James continued, quieter now. "I never intended for this to happen. Any of it. My only crime was stealing the seed." He shoved his hands through his hair. "I wish to Christ I hadn't. God, if I could take it all back—?"

"The seed?" Riley prompted.

"Tell her," Logan said, eyes on James. "What you told me."

After a pause, James spoke. "Several years ago, I created a new hybrid strain of corn."

"In your work at GFT?" Riley asked, looking between him and Logan.

"Yes. It was a strain that grew faster and stronger than any I'd seen before. A super seed."

She recalled John Brown's words. *A new variety. We've been working on it for over three years.* "You gave it to Zephyr Farms?"

James nodded. "When I left university, I believed what I'd learned could be of real benefit to the world—giving countries that struggle to grow enough food the chance to modify crops to suit their environments. As the climate changes, we will all have to adapt. So will our crops. My work at GFT was never just a job. It meant something to me. You understand?"

Riley thought of Mia telling her James had wanted to be like Henry A. Wallace—the man with a plan to feed the world. She nodded.

"When I started there, GFT was an independent company, but within a few years they sold out to Agri-Co. After that they became just another cog in that vast machine. I saw, firsthand, how Big Ag worked. The devastation wrought by their practices. The desire to turn a profit at any cost. The backroom deals and bribes. It sickened me. I knew my seed's success would just be another way for Agri-Co to make a fortune at the expense of more farms and families. People like my father." James shrugged tightly. "Its creation had taken place in their lab, yes. But it was my work that brought it to fruition. So, I faked my research—wrote the seed off as inviable for GFT—and took it."

"Why give it to Zephyr?"

"After my father killed himself, we moved in with family in Waterloo, but we kept the land here. Ten years ago, I sold a portion of it to John Brown. He'd been a friend of my father's. The sale allowed him to expand, and he formed Zephyr Farms. I gave the seed to the cooperative knowing they would be able to test it for me. Having it sown here, on my family's land—?" James exhaled. "It felt like I was bringing my father back to life."

"Red Lance, Sarge," Logan chipped in. "It's the name of the corn."

James nodded. "Lance for my father's name. Red for the color of the seed."

"And Hamilton?" Riley glanced at the door but guessed Jones couldn't hear their low murmurs. "Where does he come in?"

"I had created the new strain of corn, but seed development takes time and money. I had Zephyr's lands on which to grow and test it. However, I needed funds for my own lab. I knew Hamilton through my work with GFT. Knew he had the capital and contacts to make Red Lance the success I believed it could be, given the opportunity. I approached the governor last year. I hoped to persuade him to use his influence to get the seed entered into the Iowa Food Prize. It's an award that can make a small company. Sponsorship deals, advertising, publicity. Zephyr and I envisioned our corn on shelves across America. Finally, the little guys would have a slice of the action. More and more people in this country *want* sustainable agriculture. They see how big industry is failing them, lowering wages and standards to maximize profit. They watch their towns sucked dry, livelihoods and jobs drying up."

"Did Hamilton know you'd stolen the seed from GFT?"

"Not at first."

"And Zephyr?" Riley thought of John Brown's hatred of Agri-Co. "Did they know?"

"Yes. But, by the second growing season, Red Lance really was *our* seed, genetically speaking. I had developed what I thought was a perfected genetic sequence, using parent seeds from the first harvest. We were on our way to a truly extraordinary product. Hamilton invested in us, and I was able to set up my own lab here. When the new corn was milled into cornmeal, Zephyr started selling it in the community, giving some of it away to charities, building their brand in Black Hawk. It proved popular. They'd been struggling to survive, and suddenly they were getting press and commendations from the mayor. Hamilton put Red Lance forward for the Iowa Food Prize, as we hoped. It was all working perfectly. But, then, the problems started." It was some moments before James continued. "After the second harvest of Red Lance, we began to notice what we thought were allergies affecting some people. It started in members of the cooperative, all of whom were eating the cornmeal themselves. A few became sensitive to sunlight and developed minor skin rashes, others complained of bowel issues. After the growing season ended, the conditions went away. But when they returned after the third harvest, I realized Red Lance could be the cause. The corn was faster growing, yes, but it was far less nutritious."

"Pellagra," Riley murmured. She thought of Lizbeth Garret strapped to the bed, her skin red with lesions. Thought of Dennis Packer, dying of the niacin deficiency in the derelict church. "Did you tell anyone? Recall the corn?"

"I didn't think it was a problem, initially. We'd milled all we had after the harvest, and I knew there wasn't enough in the local market to do any long-term damage to people's health. They used to call pellagra the spring sickness, because it followed the corn cycle. Symptoms came and went through the year, depending on how much corn people were eating.

I spent as much time as I could here at the lab, trying to modify the seed. I hoped to be able to iron out the kinks in its genetic sequence— make sure it was ready for the award."

Riley recalled something Webb had told her. "But, wait. Isn't niacin added to cereals to make sure pellagra doesn't happen?"

"It's normally added to white flour. Zephyr's cornmeal shouldn't have required any fortification. They use the whole dried kernel, which, when processed properly, should have all the niacin required. But that wasn't the case with Red Lance."

Riley thought of Mia suggesting James's claims of working late were cover for an affair. "You never told Chloe any of this, did you?"

James flinched. "No. I didn't want her getting into trouble."

Riley heard Jones coughing beyond the door, but kept her attention on James. "You said you didn't think it was a problem—initially?"

"After the third harvest, Frank Garret's daughter, Lizbeth, was one of those worst affected. She developed all the classic symptoms of pellagra. Her skin blistered when exposed to sunlight. She became aggressive, paranoid. At times delirious. Then, her condition deteriorated. Dramatically. That's when the cravings started. She began seeking out foods rich in niacin—red meat and liver. Her mother found her eating raw ground beef. After one of her brothers cut his hand, she—" James drew a breath. "Well, she bit the wound. Frank had to restrain her."

That puckered scar on Hoyt Garret's hand. "Oh my God."

"This isn't pellagra, Sergeant." James's tone was grave. "What Lizbeth and the others here have? Maybe it started as that, or at least caused the same symptoms, but in them it has transformed into something else. It's beyond anything I've encountered as a scientist. What they have—?" He shook his head. "It's something new. I don't know what the hell it is."

Riley thought of Maryanne Garret's agitation as she'd spoken of her daughter, telling her she was at a hospital. "Jesus, they know, don't they? The Garrets know Lizbeth is out here?" She stared at James in disbelief. "What are you doing with her? With all of them? Is this some big experiment for you?"

"No!" James lowered his voice with difficulty. "No. I spoke to Hamilton as soon as Lizbeth got sick. Told him something was terribly wrong with my hybrid. Asked him to withdraw it from the food prize. I was planning to scrap the whole thing, destroy my research. I didn't want to risk any more of my corn getting out into the world. But, by then, Hamilton had taken matters into his own hands. Without my knowledge, he'd been speaking to a major agricultural company in China. He'd secured a deal for Red Lance."

"One hundred million," murmured Riley.

"My corn, on the face of it, is ideal for the Chinese market, where they have less arable land and much tougher growing conditions."

"But you told Hamilton about the problems? About Lizbeth?"

"Yes. But he refused to back out. It wasn't just the money. The deal offered him access to major business opportunities and contacts in China. The kind of opportunities that can make a man's career. At the state fair, Hamilton plans to announce a massive program of Chinese investment in our state. All secured by this deal."

Riley nodded. The delegation Hamilton had been taking on a grand tour of Iowa. "He believes this will help win him the election in November?"

"Yes. Perhaps even get him a shot at the White House after his next term."

Riley thought of Walker and his men outside who'd shot at Thorne and run her off the road, held a gun to Maddie's head. "Hamilton is going to some extraordinary lengths to keep all this secret. It's not a crime to sell American products abroad."

"Yes, America sells its products—cornmeal, for instance, as livestock feed. But not its technology. The genetic sequencing of U.S. hybrid seeds—Red Lance included—is decades ahead of other countries. The data is worth billions. In recent years, Chinese spies have been caught stealing seeds from Iowa farms, taking them out of the ground, trying to unlock the genetic codes. The FBI considers the theft of agricultural technology one of the greatest threats to our country, second only to terrorism. Hamilton's deal—for the seed itself—is highly illegal."

"And he was still willing to sell it, despite what you'd discovered?"

Riley wondered how her father could have worked for the man. Had he known what Hamilton was capable of?

"He wanted me to try and solve the problem. He offered more funding. Whatever I needed."

"You accepted?"

"Not at first." James met her gaze. "The son of a bitch threatened me, OK? Said he would expose my theft of the seed from GFT. That he'd have everyone from Zephyr Farms thrown in jail for handling stolen goods. That he'd take everything. My family has been through poverty before. Bone-grinding poverty. I couldn't put them through that again. My mom?" He shook his head.

Riley thought of the family photograph—the skinny family in ill-fitting clothes, arrayed outside the crumbling farm. "Did the rest of Zephyr know what was going on?"

"Only the Garrets. I didn't want to risk bringing anyone else in. I worried Hamilton might be watching me. My phone? Emails? He certainly gave that impression. The Garrets agreed to keep Lizbeth at home. I was able to get drugs from my sister, Margaret, to keep her sedated."

His sister—the nurse at Waterloo Hospital. "They didn't take her to a doctor?"

"I told them what Hamilton had threatened. We were all scared." James paused for breath. "I returned to working on the seed, trying to correct it. Not long after, I heard about a rise in strange symptoms among the vagrant community from the charities Zephyr had been working with—skin conditions, mental disturbances. I began volunteering at soup kitchens to keep an eye out. At first, it seemed like isolated cases of pellagra. Minor ailments that would resolve when our cornmeal ran out, like we'd seen among the cooperative. But then . . ." He swallowed thickly. "I discovered there were others out there who were suffering like Lizbeth."

"George Anderson killed Nicole King, Sarge," Logan told her quietly.

"If I'd known?" James blew through his teeth. "I spoke to Frank Garret, got him to gather up and destroy as much of the cornmeal as possible. We didn't dare recall what was already out there in case Hamilton found out. Frank and his sons helped me track down those who were the worst afflicted."

Riley remembered the white van outside. "The vanishers," she murmured. "It was you abducting people?"

"I found them through my volunteering. The Garrets got them off the streets. Brought them here. I used the money Hamilton had given me to keep them as comfortable as possible until I could work on a cure, with Margaret's help."

"Wait?" said Logan, cutting in. "The Garrets? You mean—?" His voice was strained. "It was one of them who killed Cam?"

James looked confused, his gaze going from Logan to Riley. "Cam?"

"Have you seen the Garrets in the past twenty-four hours?" Riley asked him, her mind flashing with thoughts of Cam and her colleagues going after Charles Moore.

"No. When I arrived earlier, I saw their van, but they often leave it here. I was going to call Frank." James's eyes went to the door as Jones coughed again. "But then Walker came."

"Go on," Riley said when he lapsed into silence.

"While trying to treat Lizbeth, Margaret and I discovered a medication she was on had caused a sharp drop in her niacin levels, which became further depleted, dangerously so, when she was eating our corn. The drug was a barbiturate, prescribed for people suffering with anxiety or sleep disorders. Frank had a lead on a man we'd heard was selling this drug on the streets."

"Fenozen," said Riley.

"Yes. This drug seems to disrupt the body's ability to convert the essential amino acids found in meat, eggs, fish, and other foods into niacin. I believe Fenozen, combined with Red Lance, gave rise to this extreme condition. The consumption of Red Lance cornmeal, lacking the normal niacin levels needed for health, was causing pellagra symptoms in almost anyone who consumed it in high quantities, but those also on Fenozen? Well, they were turning into—"

"Cannibals," Riley finished for him, scarcely believing the word coming out of her mouth.

"As I said, I don't fully understand it. But it isn't the first time in history this has happened. High consumption of maize, particularly when improperly prepared, has been linked to aggression, suicide, and, yes—even cannibalism." He exhaled. "Obviously, we've taken them all off the drug, but it hasn't made any difference to their condition. Niacin treatment seemed to help a little, but we lost two to overdoses. I'm not a medical doctor, and this is way beyond my sister's expertise. All I can tell you is that it appears to start as a physical craving—the body desperate for the niacin it needs to survive. At first, this is relieved by certain foods. But, in the later stages, when the delirium sets in, the craving becomes—somewhere in the brain—a very specific desire for human flesh."

Riley saw them in her mind—Gracie, her skin carved away, Nicole King on the slaughter hall floor, Sarah Foster's severed head in Moore's freezer among the parts of her. And Chloe, curled among the roots.

"What happened to your wife, James?" She watched him hang his head.

"I lied when I said I thought Chloe was having an affair. I think she thought I was cheating, and that's why she came out here that night. She must have tracked my phone or followed me. She saw what you saw, Sergeant. You can imagine what she must have thought. I think she may have recognized George Anderson, perhaps from the thrift store? I don't know, but I guess that's why she removed his restraints. She managed to get him and one of the others out of their beds. Anderson had only been in there a few days. He was crazed. We could barely keep him sedated." James's voice was hoarse. "I was working in the lab when I heard the screams."

Riley felt her skin tighten. She thought of the wounds on Chloe's body.

A vicious attack. Tore right through the muscle.

"Frank Garret was here. He'd come to see Lizbeth. I was trying to get a needle into Anderson, sedate him." James's expression was pure anguish. "It took two of us to pull him off Chloe. She was wounded. She ran before I could get to her, fled into the cornfields." He spoke haltingly, his voice close to breaking. "I have a drone that I use to check the crops. I sent it up. Tried to find her. Frank took his pickup, drove after her."

"And John Brown and Ed Wilson saw the drone from the road," murmured Logan. "But it was Brown who found your wife's body? Didn't he know who she was?"

"They'd never met. Like I said, I didn't talk to Chloe about my work. Obviously, John found out when it was in the papers, but he had no reason to connect it to our corn. I think he's started to guess something's wrong, though. Frank said he's been asking questions."

Riley thought of what Maddie witnessed at the creek.

James's gaze was still on her. "I swear, I had no idea Chloe was out in the fields. I thought she'd run away. From what she'd seen. From me. I didn't know how badly hurt she was."

Riley was struck by the brutal irony—his wife dying in the corn he had created.

"I know I should have told someone. But I had no idea what Hamilton would do. You've seen the kind of men he's surrounded himself with."

"What do you think those men are doing here?"

"They showed up here with your partner," James said, glancing at Logan. "Assaulted me and threw us in here. My guess? Hamilton's tired of waiting for his seed. I think they've come to take it."

"Is everyone who's eating Red Lance in danger? How widespread could the problem be if your seed gets out there? The homeless can't be the only ones eating your cornmeal and taking Fenozen. Lizbeth was."

"Most people have varied enough diets and get the niacin they need from elsewhere. Margaret has access to county medical records. We checked all those who live locally who've been prescribed Fenozen. None had reported any severe symptoms. We think Lizbeth's condition may have worsened the effects somehow."

"Her condition?"

"The reason she was on the drug. As I said, it's prescribed for sleep disorders and anxiety, but it's sometimes used as an anticonvulsant. Lizbeth has epilepsy."

"My God."

Logan straightened. "Sarge? What is it?"

"Lori! My aunt's partner. She's epileptic."

"Is she on the same drug?"

"I don't know. But she hasn't been herself in months." Riley thought of the bags of Zephyr's cornmeal she'd seen in Rose's cupboards, thought of Lori's strangeness. She hammered on the door. "Hey! Let me out! Please! I need to talk to Walker!"

James was also on his feet. "What's her full name?"

"Lori Bell."

"There wasn't anyone of that name on the list Margaret had."

"There wouldn't be. She doesn't use her real name on official records." Riley shook her head. "Her ex-husband— It doesn't matter!" She banged on the door, harder now. "Goddamn it!"

Logan sniffed suddenly. "What's that smell?"

Riley put her eye to the keyhole. Jones had sunk down the wall. His chin was on his chest and blood had soaked the front of his T-shirt, spilling from his mouth. His gun was on the floor beside him.

James was sniffing now, too. He pushed Riley aside, put his face to the keyhole. He straightened quickly. "That's propane."

Logan stared at him. "You don't think? They wouldn't . . . ?" He looked at Riley. "Shit."

James's eyes went wide. "The heat lamps in the shed! They come on automatically. If there's a spark from them—" He didn't finish, but began pounding his fists on the door.

59

Lori Bell stood in the kitchen with no recollection of how she'd got there. Maddie was pressed against the sink, eyes shocked wide.

Lori went toward her, but the girl cringed. "Maddie?" She looked down as her slippered feet crunched on something. There were pills scattered over the linoleum. A white bottle was among them, still rolling. Had she dropped it? Thrown it? "Maddie, what's wrong?" Her voice came out croaky. "Did I shout? I'm sorry." Her hand wavered near her face. "I'm not feeling myself. I just need my medicine."

As she stepped closer, the girl dove around her and ran from the room. Lori heard the lounge door slam shut. Muffled sobs sounded beyond, punctuated by Scrounger's barks. Lori crossed to the sink, grabbed a glass from the draining board. She ran the faucet, then stooped to pick up one of the fallen pills. Leaving Maddie crying in the living room, she crept back upstairs, feeling bad but not sure why.

The morning sun filtered through the nursery curtains, shining on the mobile hanging over Benjamin's crib. Farm animals jigged around in the breeze coming through the window. She wanted to open it wider, let some real air in, but the sun hurt her eyes, so she stayed back, out of its glare.

Ben had stopped crying and was making gurgling sounds. She paused, looking down on him: her little miracle with pink cheeks and downy blond hair. The baby she hardly dared dream she'd have. The water glass sweated against her palm. Her smile dimmed. Why did she feel so uneasy, now she had what she'd always wanted? Why did Ben cry so much? She sometimes felt him twist away when she held him, like she was a stranger. Sometimes she barely felt connected to him at all. More than once she'd entertained the awful thought that something had gone wrong at the hospital—that, maybe, they'd presented her with the wrong child.

Lori turned from the crib and put the pill on her tongue. She swallowed with difficulty. The water tasted strange. As the liquid hit her stomach, she felt it cramp. She couldn't remember when she'd last eaten, but despite the pangs she couldn't think of what to have. Nothing satisfied, yet still the hunger gnawed.

She put the glass on a shelf and stared at herself in the mirror, pulling down the high neck of her nightgown. The rash was still there. She'd looked it up online as it had grown worse, but it seemed it could be a thousand things. She had wanted to show Rose, but with all that had been going on with Riley, she'd not wanted to bother her.

As Ben let out a shuddering cry, Lori returned to his crib and lifted him into her arms. He balled his fists, his face screwing up. "Hush, little man." She held him to her, despite his wails, feeling his tiny body wriggling against her. She could smell his oaty hair, his sweet warm skin, his milky breath.

Outside, a pickup truck juddered to a halt. There was a slam of a door, pounding footsteps on the path. She heard the front door open and Maddie's cry.

"Daddy!"

Lori closed her eyes, brushed her dry lips across Ben's soft cheek.

G age Walker had ordered his team to rupture the tank's pipeline, filling the pig shed that contained the lab with propane. Once at a safe distance, they planned to strap a flare to the drone they'd taken from Miller's lab. Fly it in. They had taken everything of use and anything incriminating. The rest of it? Well, there wouldn't be enough left to know what had been happening here, or who was to blame. Now, he just needed to force the cop to tell him where those files were. Then he would deal with the three of them. No loose ends.

As his men loaded the last of the Red Lance seeds into containers and stowed them with the boxes of Miller's research in the SUVs, Walker turned toward the farmhouse and racked back the slide on his gun.

He was halfway across the site when the heat lamps clicked on in the shed that contained the lab. It was the spark the propane-enriched air needed. The resulting explosion ripped through the metal structure, bursting it apart. Shards of steel and glass flew like shrapnel in all directions. The shock wave threw Walker to the ground, split open the side of the second shed, blew out the windows of the SUVs, demolished one side of the farmhouse, and sent a blinding ball of fire into the sky.

After the blast, everything was silent. Small fires had sprung up all over, kissed to life by the fireball. Leaves fell to earth as burning confetti. The flames danced through grass, tinder dry, to flick their way up the sides of the barn, where chunks of metal had embedded themselves.

Riley was lying on her back in dazzling sunlight. Things were eddying to earth around her—charred bits of wood turned to ash, smoldering blades of corn, scraps of burned clothing. Her ears were ringing. She tasted blood. Slowly, she turned over. The world swam in her vision. She pressed her palms into the crumbling soil, swayed up on her hands and knees. The farmhouse was in bits, its belly hanging open, rafters splintered like bones. For a second, she thought she'd been in a tornado. Then—she remembered. The smell of the gas. Their frantic shouts.

Logan.

She staggered to her feet. There were crumpled twists of metal everywhere. Flames bloomed. Smoke curled on the air. She caught sight of a tanned and muscled arm close by, outstretched beneath a section of plasterboard that still had wallpaper on it. She stumbled across the debris toward it. Logan was already stirring. She pulled the wreckage off him, gasping at the pain.

Logan sat up, shaking his hair, white with dust. He coughed and spat. The gash above his eye was bleeding down his cheek, but other than scrapes and cuts he seemed mostly unharmed. "Sarge?" he croaked, coughing again.

"I'm OK." Riley helped him to his feet. Her ears were ringing, and she felt she had to shout to make herself heard.

Logan wiped the blood from his eye, surveyed the devastation. "Where's Miller?"

"I don't know." Riley pointed to the second shed, split open in the center, a serrated hole yawning into dust-hazed darkness within. "Lizbeth. The others. We need to get them out."

The two of them teetered their way across the smoking ruins. The fires were spreading, licking around the base of the propane tank, which was still intact—only the gas inside the shed had been ignited. After a few more yards, they came to the first victim, partly visible beneath a layer of corrugated steel. It was Larson. A metal fragment was sticking out of his chest, blood oozing around it. His eyes were open, staring at the sky. Logan stooped down and pulled Larson's gun from his holster. Across the site, near the SUVs, another of Walker's men was crawling on hands and knees. Blood streamed from his scalp, where a flap of skin hung down. As they watched, he collapsed. There was no sign of James Miller.

Inside, the remaining shed was scattered with remnants of pigpens, shattered glass, and burned scraps of corn. Metal girders bowed from the roof, sheets of steel hanging precariously. The plastic tent had been partly vaporized by the blast; the rest of it hung in tatters. Within the charred cocoon, beds lay overturned. George Anderson was howling, trapped in his restraints.

Riley started toward the nearest bed when a figure loomed out of the haze. It was James Miller. He was clutching Lizbeth Garret. His neck had a piece of shrapnel sticking out of it and blood soaked his torn shirt. Lizbeth seemed unharmed, although she was heavily sedated and could barely walk.

"Take her!" he groaned.

Riley caught hold of the woman as Logan followed Miller back into the smoky depths. She pulled Lizbeth Garret's arm over her shoulder, gritting her teeth against the pain. For a moment, she had a shudder of thought, thinking of the ugly scar on Hoyt Garret's hand. Steeling herself, she dragged Lizbeth out into the sunlight. The barn was now alight, flames shooting above the trees. The fire around the propane tank had spread, and there was an ominous shrieking sound coming from the valves on the top.

Riley set Lizbeth down, out of the way of the fire. As she crumpled on the grass, Riley hastened back to the structure. There was a loud groan, and a metal sheet came loose from the roof. It fell with an almighty crash, dust billowing. Logan came choking out of the cloud, supporting two more figures—another woman and a man. Riley helped him haul them over to Lizbeth.

They were returning to the pig shed, coughing at the smoke, sweat stinging their eyes, when they saw Walker staggering across the wreckage toward them. As Walker raised his gun, Riley saw the flash and heard the crack. Something punched into her shoulder. She sprawled back, hitting the ground hard. As she tried to suck in a breath, pain like nothing she'd ever experienced surged through her. She couldn't even cry out. She lay there, blinking at the sky, feeling her T-shirt grow warm.

Logan was shouting, his voice rising above the shrieking of the gas tank valves. She sensed him duck down beside her, saw him draw Larson's gun and take aim. Shots cracked through the air. Riley heard the roar of an engine. Turning her head, she saw one of the SUVs speeding away through the ruins. She glimpsed two figures inside—Walker was driving.

Logan holstered his gun and tore off his T-shirt. He balled it up and pressed it against her shoulder. She cried out. "You need to hold it in place, Sarge! Hold it!"

Hands shaking, she did so, the world fading in and out. She gasped as he pulled her to her feet, gripping her around the waist.

James Miller was in sight, struggling to haul out another two men. His face was bone white between streaks of blood. "Get them in the car!" James yelled above the screaming valves. "The tank's going to blow!" He steered the two insensible men to the remaining SUV and maneuvered them inside. "I'm going back for Anderson."

As James ran back inside the shed, Logan half-carried Riley to the vehicle.

She grasped hold of the dashboard as they reached it, boots crunching on glass. "Go! I'm OK!"

As Logan went to Lizbeth and the others lolling on the grass, Riley pulled herself into the passenger seat. A cry tore from her throat. She could feel the bullet. It was lodged in her shoulder, grinding against bone.

Logan manhandled two of the others into the vehicle, then went back for Lizbeth Garret. He was carrying her across the rubble when there was a shuddering groan and the remaining shed collapsed in on itself in a roar of metal. Logan ducked through the cloud that gusted up and deposited Lizbeth in the trunk.

He jumped into the driver's seat and turned the key, still in the ignition. He looked at Riley as he started the engine. "There's no time."

She nodded, letting her head roll back against the seat.

They had made it onto the dirt track that led through the woods when the tank went up. The explosion was much bigger than the first. A huge red ball of fire that mushroomed into the sky over the cornfields. Riley closed her eyes, feeling blood soaking her clothes. She was slipping down in the seat, unable to keep herself upright. She felt Logan's hand pressing into the wound in her shoulder, his other still gripping the wheel.

"Stay with me, Riley. Stay with me, Goddamn it!"

60

The morning sun filtered through the venetian blinds, painting white ladders of light across the walls. Machines hummed. Outside in the corridor, nurses and orderlies came and went, clutching files, pushing wheelchairs. Phones trilled.

Riley shifted in the bed, grimacing at the pain. The meds had kept her comfortable these past few days since surgery, but the wound was only just healing. She'd been lucky, the surgeon said. The bullet had damaged the soft tissue, but with minimal injury to the nerves. With rest and physical therapy, she would make a full recovery. She would still be able to drive and use a gun. Still be able to do her job.

There was a knock on the door. Rose entered, carrying a bunch of peonies. Maddie followed.

"You could open a florist!" Rose smiled as she placed the flowers on the table beside the others.

One bunch was from Logan and his family, another from Kristen Webb, and there was a small bouquet from Sue Schmidt, which had left Riley weeping. There were balloons and a card from the department, signed by everyone, Sheriff Reed's "Get better soon" written in a frantic hand.

Reed had been one of the first to come see her after she was out of surgery. He'd seemed subdued, worn down by all that had happened: Schmidt's death and the shocking revelations about James Miller and Hamilton. "You were right to pursue Miller," he'd told her quietly. "I'm sorry I didn't listen. Whenever you're ready, your badge is waiting for you."

Rose kissed her forehead. "Ethan said he'd try and pop in later."

Maddie was hanging back in the doorway, shifting on her feet.

"Come here, sweetheart." Riley patted the bed. She studied the girl as she perched on the edge. "You OK?"

Maddie nodded, but hung her head, her hair slipping in a dark curtain over her face.

"I know we have a lot to talk about." Riley reached out with her good hand to hook her niece's hair behind her ear. "But I need you to know that you're safe now. Those men can't hurt you."

"You have a gift for Riley, don't you, honey?" pressed Rose.

Maddie's face brightened. She reached into the pocket of her jeans and pulled something out. It was a friendship bracelet. "I made you a new one."

"It's beautiful." Riley, held out her hand for her niece to tie it on beside her hospital wristband. It was black and gold, braided into neat little chevrons. It made her think of the rattlesnake, but she smiled the thought away. "Thank you. Hey, why don't you see if you can find me another vase for these flowers? The nurses might have one."

"Sure." Maddie hopped off the bed and headed out.

"How is she doing?" Riley asked Rose. "Really?"

"I think she'll be all right. We Fishers are pretty resilient." Rose smiled. "As you know."

"And how's Lori?"

Rose inhaled. "They tell me she's turned a corner. The treatment they have her on seems to be starting to work. The doctors say she's out of the woods, at least." Rose gave a brave nod. "God willing, we'll soon have her back."

"That's great."

When Logan had visited yesterday, he'd told her the men and women they'd rescued from the farm were starting to respond to treatment, albeit slowly. The hospital had had to bring in specialists from New York, who were astounded by what they found in these patients—their brain scans showing abnormalities they'd never encountered before. Lizbeth Garret was still in the ICU, but her condition was stable. Logan had filled her in on the ongoing investigation, only snippets of which had appeared on the news, still buzzing with Charles Moore's death-by-cop and his house of horrors, the headlines calling him the Butcher of Black Hawk County.

Agent Gooch had already been called away by the BAU on another serial killer case, but Klein had stayed behind to help with the cleanup. Two days ago, divers had gone into the creek and pulled out the body of John Brown. The investigation into Brown's death was ongoing, but Frank Garret had been charged with Schmidt's murder.

Cam would be laid to rest next week, in the same cemetery Riley's parents were buried in. It would be the first of many funerals in the coming weeks. The Miller farm had been cordoned off and specialists brought in to comb the ruins for evidence, where four of Walker's team, James Miller himself, and George Anderson had perished.

The door opened as Maddie returned, carrying a vase. A man appeared behind her. It was Agent Klein.

He nodded to Riley, then dipped his head to Rose. "Excuse me, ma'am. Can I have a word with Sergeant Fisher?"

Rose took Maddie's hand. "Let's go find some ice cream in the cafeteria."

Klein watched them go, then crossed to Riley. "How are you, Sergeant?"

"I'll be a whole lot better when I'm out of here." She struggled to sit up. "Is there any news? On Hamilton? The investigation?" The moment she'd come round from surgery, she had called Logan—had him get the flash drive from Lori and Rose's house. She had asked him to pass it to Klein, hoping it might prove vital when so much evidence had been destroyed in the blast, but she hadn't heard anything since.

"The vehicle Gage Walker escaped in was found last night, abandoned in Clayton County. There was a body in the passenger seat. Deputy Wood identified him as one of the men at the farm with Walker. He'd been shot. Execution style."

"Walker?"

"No sign of him. But from what you saw being loaded into the vehicle, it appears some of the containers have been taken."

"Miller's research?" she murmured. "The seeds? We can't let that corn get out there."

"Walker is on the bureau's most wanted. We'll find him."

"And Hamilton? Has he been arrested? Has the investigation started?"

"It has. Two of my colleagues who specialize in the theft of agricultural technology have taken over. They're here now, if you're up to some questions?"

"Of course."

"I'll call them in." Klein paused. "I'm sorry about Deputy Schmidt. I know how hard it is to lose any officer, especially one so dedicated." He crossed to the door, then turned and looked back at her. "Your team is a testament to you, Sergeant Fisher."

"Thank you, Agent."

61

The first snow had fallen last week. It hadn't settled, but winter was only just beginning. Jack-o'-lanterns sat rotting on doorsteps and piles of leaves shivered across driveways as Riley drove home to Cedar Falls in Cam's battered old Dodge. The first shift she'd driven it, she had found a picture of him and Sue taped inside the sunshade. They were standing on a mountain, pink-cheeked and windswept, bikes beside them. She had left it there.

Scrounger met her as she pulled into the yard, bounding around her as she got out. The shed had new doors on it, the cracks sealed so nothing could get in. Pest control hadn't found any sign of the rattlesnake, but they'd advised her to have the whole rotten structure pulled down to be safe. She hadn't heeded the advice. The place might have been falling down, but it still breathed with memories. Monument to her family's history.

The old pickup wasn't here yet, meaning Ethan was still on his shift at the Kum & Go. He'd said he would be home on time, with the cake. She wanted to trust him, but it was hard. Her brother had failed the last drug test, and his probation had been extended.

Riley ruffled Scrounger's ears as he followed her into the house. The kitchen was noisy with music and voices. Aunt Rose was at the counter, chatting with the mother of Maddie's friend Tanisha. Lori was stirring something on the stove. Riley smelled cornbread and brisket.

"Welcome home, sweetheart." Rose's cheeks were ruddy. She lifted the bottle of bourbon and shook it suggestively.

"I'll have a beer."

"Coming right up. Everything's almost ready."

Riley put her Glock in the safe. As she passed the lounge, she saw Maddie sitting with Tanisha on the couch. She was jiggling baby Benjamin on her lap. The little boy, who now had a full head of blond hair, was gurgling happily. There was a stack of gifts on the floor in the corner, waiting to be opened. Riley could hardly believe her niece was fifteen today. She still looked so young. Too young, really, for the boy sitting on the chair, making silly faces at Ben. Riley had tried to put a stop to the friendship between Maddie and Brandon, but in the end, she'd realized it was safer to keep them close. Besides, her niece seemed happier than she had in a long time.

Riley headed upstairs to her room and shrugged off her coat, wincing at the twinge in her shoulder. It was much better than it had been, although she'd been told the scar from the bullet would stay. As she pulled her hair free from its knot, her eyes fell on the copy of the *Des Moines Register* on the bedside table. Beneath the headline was a picture of Jess Cook, the new governor of Iowa, grinning and waving at the cameras, a host of supporters clustered around her in a storm of red, white, and blue confetti. The candidate put forward at the last minute to replace Bill Hamilton hadn't stood a chance.

Cook's win, however, had been overshadowed by the national scandal surrounding the former governor. Riley had glimpsed Hamilton in various news reports: being guided into the back of a car or led into government buildings, his smooth face unsmiling. While she'd learned that Cook's sister, Thorne, had been granted immunity from prosecution in light of the evidence she had uncovered, Riley knew little else about the investigation, which had been taken out of her hands from the moment the flash drive was handed to the FBI. She'd not been able to find out if Gage Walker had been found, or if the Red Lance seeds had been apprehended. She checked the news regularly, her focus on China, waiting to see if anything was out there.

She took her badge off and laid it on the vanity by the photograph of her grandfather in his sheriff's uniform. She kissed her finger, touched it to his cheek. She would go see him tomorrow. A nurse, last week, had told her quietly that it wouldn't be long now.

Beside her grandfather's photograph was a picture of her, Mia, and Chloe. Mia had given it to her at Chloe's funeral—the three of them cuddled up on the porch swing, arms around one another's shoulders. She and Mia had talked about having drinks, but she wasn't sure if they would.

The gold star necklace, though—that she had kept. She had taken it to a jeweler's soon after she'd come home from the hospital. The broken chain had been replaced, the star cleaned. It had hung around her neck ever since, a glittering line that cut across her old scar. A gift reclaimed. She had asked Bob Nolan to run that trace, using the photograph she'd taken from Chloe's album. But Nolan hadn't been able to find any record of Hunter since he'd left university. She hadn't taken it further. Not yet.

Downstairs, Riley took the beer Rose handed to her and headed outside. It had been a long week and she needed a bit of peace before she could enter into the spirit of the party. She walked down to the creek, breath fogging the air. The leaves had turned from gold to russet, scattering the grass. Already, it was growing dark.

This time of year always made her think of her parents. They were in her mind more these days, since she'd looked back over the reports of their deaths. It looked like the accident it had been ruled as, but a seed of doubt had been planted. Still, she refused to let it grow. The past was another country, and she wanted to move on.

There was a restlessness that had come with that feeling: a sort of fizz in her mind and body that had only grown since Chloe's funeral. She felt a need to travel, to get in her car and drive. But she had no idea where she might go.

"Hey."

Riley turned to see Logan crossing the grass. Beyond, through the screen door, she saw his sister, Carol, with Callie. His niece and Maddie had become friends, both now freshmen at Cedar Falls High. Last month, Logan had been officially promoted to Investigations. Amy Fox was continuing to help out, but they were recruiting for another permanent detective to replace Cam Schmidt. Jackson Cole was in line for the job.

Logan came to stand beside her. He clinked his beer against hers. "Lori's making a tofu stew."

"I wondered what that smell was."

He grinned. "I'll make a vegan of you yet."

Their smiles faded, both of them turning to look out over the creek, black in the last of the light.

"Come on, Sarge," said Logan after a while. He nodded to the house. "Before Rose and Carol have at the bourbon."

Riley laughed and followed him up. She was halfway there when her cell rang. She didn't recognize the number on the screen, but she knew the area code. Virginia.

Quantico.

Acknowledgments

Well, it takes a village, as they say.

Firstly, I want to thank my UK agent, Antony Topping at Greene & Heaton, for taking a chance on me and for believing in this book from the start—back when it all probably sounded just a bit weird. Antony, your support and guidance have been truly invaluable. Thank you for being so patient. I promise, one day, you will teach me to be more Zen. My thanks also to the rest of the fantastic team, especially Kate Rizzo and Imogen Morrell.

A huge thank-you to my U.S. agent, Dan Conaway at Writers House, New York. Dan, I very much appreciated those first encouraging thoughts over our lunch on how to move my mad idea forward, and all your excellent steers and prompts along the way. And thanks to the rest of your great team, in particular Lauren Carsley.

Thank you to Rupert Heath for his support on our incredible path to this point and for the kind handing over of the torch. And to Sylvie Rabineau at WME for championing the book so early on.

My gratitude to my editor Nick Sayers at Hodder & Stoughton. Nick, it's been a pleasure and a privilege working with you and I'm enormously grateful that you've taken another leap of faith in me. It's been quite a journey, made all the more enjoyable by your humor and generosity. Thank you, as ever, for your insightful comments.

My sincere appreciation to my editor Zachary Wagman at Flatiron. Zack, thank you so much for your enthusiasm and your incisive suggestions. I'm thrilled to have come out of this crazy year with such a dream team! Big shout-out to the rest of the Flatiron crew, especially Maxine Charles. I'm grateful to be working with you all.

There were several people who helped me with certain aspects of the novel, giving up their valuable time to do so. So, thank you to Michael Buckmaster, who pointed me in the direction of Jim Lanas. I'm so grateful to Jim for putting me in touch with Anthony Montiel, whose considerable help in answering questions about life as a detective in a U.S. sheriff's office I very much appreciated. (Any mistakes about police procedure are entirely my own!) A big thank-you, as well, to Andy Clark for his expert help on the technological side of things.

I want to thank the people of Iowa for their considerable Midwest charm. Some of the warmest, most generous people I've had the pleasure of meeting. From the helpful staff at the state capitol building in Des Moines and the instructor at the gun range for teaching me how to shoot a Glock (without shooting myself), to the cops who answered my questions at the state fair and the farmers we met there, to the team at the Black Hawk Hotel, Cedar Falls, and all the people in bars and restaurants, at ball games and gas stations from Waterloo to Okoboji, who gave me so much local color for this book. But a special shout-out goes to Karl at Strawberry Farm, Muscatine, who took me to a meeting with the mayor so I could hear about some of the real issues affecting Iowans and some of the challenges they face in their communities against big corporations.

A heartfelt hug to my friends and family for putting up with me banging on about this book for the past few years. With special thanks to David and Daniel at Goldsboro Books for debuting me in their short story anthology. To Anthony and Helen Riches for being such great sounding boards. To Alex von Tunzelmann and Imogen Robertson for reminding me—don't lead with the hamsters. And to Imogen and Laura Shepherd-Robinson for Novel Clinic (if only every writing day had good friends, wise words, and bubbles). And to the rest of you—you know who you are—I love you guys.

Lastly, my love and gratitude, as always, to Lee. Thank you for being my stalwart research companion and for driving me all over Iowa—through supercell storms and tornado warnings, to dive bars with Fireball and corn dogs. We didn't manage to try all those one hundred and twenty beers on tap, but we gave it our best shot.

About the Author

The Fields is **Erin Young**'s debut crime thriller featuring Sergeant Riley Fisher of Black Hawk County, in the first of a planned series. She lives and works in Brighton, England.

Made in United States
North Haven, CT
12 June 2024

53533017R00212